Wicked Work

Wicked Work

PAMELA KYLE

BLACK
lace

Black Lace novels are sexual fantasies.
In real life, make sure you practise safe sex.

First published in 1994 by
Black Lace
332 Ladbroke Grove
London
W10 5AH

Reprinted 1995

Copyright © Pamela Kyle 1994

Typeset by TW Typesetting, Plymouth, Devon
Printed and bound in Great Britain by
Cox & Wyman Ltd, Reading, Berks

ISBN 0 352 32958 0

Chapter One

'I really don't see what the hang-up is, Suzie. I mean, men have been paying women for it since the beginning of time; they don't call it the oldest profession in the world for nothing, you know? Wouldn't surprise me if old Adam didn't give Eve the occasional sweetener for letting him bonk her in the garden of Eden.'

Hilary Tonner chuckled her mannish chuckle, enjoying her own humour.

Suzie sipped wine to give herself time to think. What Hilary was suggesting was pretty radical, even by *her* standards. She regarded her friend over the rim of her glass.

Hilary was a short, plump woman who wore her mousey brown hair cropped close to her skull. She never wore make-up, and undisguised laughter lines drew sharp creases from the corners of her eyes that added a year or two to her actual age – which, the same as Suzie's, was twenty-eight. But she was not unattractive in her own way: green eyes would sparkle readily, and her lips were full and sensuous. Good even teeth would flash brilliantly whenever she laughed. And Hilary laughed a lot.

Suzie swallowed a mouthful of Chablis and set her glass down on the mahogany table in front of them.

At last, she shook her head, and said: 'But it's different, Hilary. Men paying women for it is one thing. But women – me – paying a man for sex? Well, that's something else.'

'Well I don't see why, love. Why is it different?'

Hilary and Suzie had been friends at school (unlikely friends, many had thought, even then), and had remained close despite their lives having led them along such very different paths.

From school Suzie had gone on to university, where she had obtained an honours degree in English before entering journalism, prepared for the climb to the top. A top she had all but reached when, at just twenty-six, she was appointed Publishing Editor of *Woman Now*, a prestige glossy monthly with a huge circulation. The magazine payed her an excellent salary, which afforded her many of the luxuries in life, including a sumptuous flat and a gleaming Saab Turbo. In anyone's book Suzie Carlton was a highly successful career woman; a high achiever indeed.

By contrast Hilary, predictably, had left school at the earliest opportunity; had worked in wine bars, in Woolworth's, and as a packer for a local factory. She had, for several years, aggressively supported a variety of left-wing causes, from CND to feminist issues, before giving it all up and finally settling down to a come-day go-day life of almost total hedonism, supplementing what she drew on the dole with occasional singing gigs around some of the seedier bars in town.

Suzie was a high-flying executive; Hilary practically a drop-out, a latter-day hippy. But though Suzie would, without a qualm, make momentous decisions daily on behalf of the magazine – decisions it would terrify many to make – when it came to her personal life, and ordinary everyday matters, Hilary had a simple pragmatism – a wisdom born of her cockney's slightly askance view of the world – that made her an invaluable confidante and confessor. Her down-to-earth, no-messing advice was usually just what Suzie needed.

But over this? Wasn't this just a little too pragmatic?

'I just can't see it, Hils,' she said. 'Something about it just doesn't sit right, you know?'

'Why ever the hell not?' Hilary leaned forward, almost challengingly. 'If it's all right for men, then why not for women?'

Suzie lit a More with a Cartier lighter and refused to look at her. 'I don't know,' she admitted through a cloud of exhaled smoke. 'Like I said, it just ... is ... different.'

'Nonsense,' Hilary retorted. 'Listen, we live in changing times, love. You should know that better than most, in your game.'

Suzie nodded. 'Of course.'

'Well, then, you go with the flow, don't you? Look, for one thing, you can afford it, right? Whereas years ago, virtually no woman could have. Changing times, see: these days women can. Long live the feminists, eh?'

Suzie threw Hilary a sidelong look: she didn't share her friend's extreme feminist views.

'All I'm saying,' said Hilary reasonably, 'is that these days what's good for the gander's good for the goose. And you can't deny that that's as it should be.'

'No, of course not,' Suzie conceded, letting it go. 'Anyway, just suppose – just for a minute, now – that I was prepared to pay for it. How? I mean, I don't see men soliciting women up along the Dock Road; wiggling their bums at kerb-crawling females.'

'Nah, but believe me, girl, men are out there to be had. Look, you're not on your own, Suzie, you know. These days there are lots of women like you; women who put their careers first. Who maybe don't have the time to get bogged down with relationships, yet who need the occasional screw. And, most important of all, who have the brass to afford it.

'There's a demand, see, and where there's a demand there's always someone out there supplying it, whatever it is.'

3

'The simple law of supply and demand? Applied to men?' Suzie sighed. 'I suppose you're right. As you say, where there's a demand there's always a supply, somewhere. Though I wouldn't have a clue how to find one.'

'Oh, God, in the evening paper, love,' said Hilary, turning her eyes to the ceiling as if astonished by her friend's naïvety. 'They advertise, for Christ's sake. Albeit under the guise of calling themselves Escort Agencies. Escorts, my fanny.'

'Are you serious, Hils? You're saying they're really a front for . . . for *that*?'

Hilary shook her head. 'Not all of them, no. But some of them are. There's one – the Benson Agency they call themselves – that I know for a fact is nothing more than a front. And they advertise every night in the *Standard*. So, they've got the men, you've got the cash. You put the two together, and bingo; everyone's happy.'

'Huh, you make it sound so easy, but.'

'Look,' Hilary interjected, 'you say you need an occasional man, right?'

Suzie inclined her head, yes. She sometimes wondered if it wasn't Hilary who had got it right with her lifestyle. She had no money, no position in life or status. But what good was all that without fun? And fun was something Hilary had in abundance. Not that *men* constituted fun for Hilary. But they did for her, Suzie, and she hadn't had a man in over three months, ever since her break-up with Geoff.

Geoff was a boyfriend with whom she had shared a long-standing, if not always perfect relationship. The final straw had come when she had caught him with a mouthful of a redhead's pussy in an upstairs room at a party, romping amongst the coats. And it was then she'd decided, to hell with relationships. She would throw herself even more deeply into her work and get the sex she needed on a casual basis. But she was finding that surprisingly difficult, and was beginning to feel somewhat desperate.

'Well?' Hilary prompted when Suzie hadn't replied.

Suzie came back from her reverie, seeing Geoff's head,

4

for the hundredth time, snap up from between the red-head's thighs at the sound of her entering the room, his face as red as the woman's bush and slick with her sexual juices. She shook her head to dislodge the image, and brought Hilary back into focus.

'What? Oh, yes; an occasional man. At least once in a while, yes. Of course I do.'

'Or, let's be more accurate: you need the occasional cock.'

'Hilary!' Suzie exclaimed. 'You don't have to put it so crudely.' Though after a moment she smiled sheepishly and added, 'But, well yes, I suppose.'

'Right. Now how else are you going to get one?'

'Well, the usual ways,' Suzie said. Said lamely, knowing at once that she had been cornered. This was how the subject had come up in the first place.

Hilary snorted derisively. 'What usual ways? The usual ways aren't working for you, are they? This is where we came in, remember?'

It was. The conversation had begun when Suzie had mentioned her frustrations of the previous night. She had worked late – the issue was running a little behind and she had needed to catch up – and, finished at last, she had gone straight from the office to a wine bar to wind down. And she would not have objected – to put it mildly – to a little male company. During the evening several men had come in, but though she had smiled encouragingly at the better looking of them (towards the end of the night, even the not so good looking), not a single one had come over; finding company elsewhere in the bar or finishing their drinks and leaving alone. And, as seemed to have become the norm these days, she had once again gone home, frustrated, with only her vibrator for company in bed.

'You see,' Hilary was saying, 'there are certain types of women who men simply do not approach in bars. And you and I, for our different reasons, both fit into that category. Me, because I suppose I wear my sexual persuasion a bit like a uniform: one look, and men know they'd be wasting their time . . .'

Suzie glanced askance at her. 'And because you practically growl at any man who so much as looks in your
direction,' she said, letting herself grin.

'Well, yes, there is that,' Hilary chuckled. 'Like I say,
they know they've got no chance. But don't you see?
That's just what they think when they look at you, too.'

Suzie was genuinely shocked. 'What? I don't growl at
men who look at me, Hils. And I don't think I exactly
look gay, either . . . Do I?' she added as a discomfitting
afterthought.

Hilary shook her shorn head. 'No, of course not. But
it's what you do look, love, that's the problem. You look
exactly what you are: a high-powered woman executive.
A lady boss; power-dressed up to the nines and with
your yuppie motor parked outside, complete with car-
phone. See, a lot of men feel intimidated by that. For one
thing, afraid you earn more money than they do – and
let's face it, love, you probably do – and men don't like
that one bit. Ain't good for their silly macho egos, is it?'

'No, I'm aware of that. But not all men have a hang-up
about money.'

'No, but they're pretty well all insecure. And in that
regard, Suzie, you have another problem, too – you're
too good-looking by far.'

Suzie's brow buckled in puzzlement, and Hilary explained: 'Look, the average man takes one look at you:
tall and slim, a cracking figure, beautiful – sickeningly
beautiful, bitch! – with your swathes of blonde hair and
your gorgeous blue eyes. Money *and* good looks, see:
he's going to figure you've got a string of toy-boys on a
leash you can have whenever you want.'

'I wish,' muttered Suzie ruefully.

'Yes, but that's what he's going to think. He's going
to reckon you've got as much man as ever you'd want
just waiting on your beck and call. And no chance for
him; he might just as well try to chat up me.'

Suzie was quiet for a moment, drawing on the cigarette and considering, seeing some sense in what Hilary
was saying. She let a plume of smoke drift lazily away,

6

then said: 'But I don't understand, Hils; I mean, I never used to have a problem finding men. Before Geoff they used to chat me up all the time. More than enough. And I don't think I've really changed. Not just recently anyway.' She sighed deeply. 'Maybe I'm just out of practice, is all.'

Hilary smiled at her gently, and shook her head. 'No, you haven't changed, love: men have.'

Suzie looked at her quizzically. 'How so?'

'They've learned, love. Don't forget, Suzie, women like you are a relatively new breed – I mean the high-powered executive female; independent woman; women who have toy-boys. Never existed, years ago, did they? Changing times . . .' Hilary took Suzie's cigarette, drew on it and handed it back; let smoke go with her words. 'See, it isn't long ago that a man could walk into a bar cock-sure – if you'll pardon the pun – that his chat-up lines would work on ninety per cent of the women in there. Certainly they'd be worth a try. That's what women went into bars for, looking for men.

'But then your sort began to appear: the self-assured Woman of Today. Not in the bar to meet male company, as a man could once have assumed, but just there for a quiet drink after a busy day at the office. So, the guy makes his approach, and gets blown away with a flea in his ear. And an articulate flea at that; not the sort of blow-out he'd get from just any Tom, Dick or uppity Mary. Well, it doesn't take too much of that before he realises, hey, these are the type you stay well away from. Not worth the hassle when there's plenty of other fish in the sea. Don't you see, Suzie, since you were last on the loose, men have learned to regard your sort as a no-no. They find you intimidating. Forbidding, even.'

'I'm not forbidding, for God's sake,' Suzie protested, suddenly angry. 'And anyway, what makes you such an expert on how men think all of a sudden?'

'Ah, because I see it from a man's perspective, don't I? Look, if I'm prowling a bar I'm looking for the same thing a man is, right? A new bit of skirt. And I'm telling

7

you straight. I've learned to give your sort a wide berth. You can only take so much rejection, and then you think: "To hell with this. Stick to the girls who look like they're common-or-garden secretaries, and leave the career sorts well alone." '

'So what are you saying, then?' Suzie demanded. 'That I should dress down? Make myself less attractive? What?'

Hilary shook her head. 'Your looks you've got, love. No disguising them, whatever you did. And as for dressing down, it'd do no good: women like you wear success like a permanent cloak, whatever you've got on beneath it. Believe me, you can spot a lady boss a mile off; you'd be sussed in a flash.'

Suzie threw up her hands. 'But this is ridiculous! You keep talking about my sort, women like me. But if some career women are intimidating or forbidding, as you say, then they're not my sort. They're not my sort at all. Yet you're tarring me with the same bloody brush.'

Hilary smiled at her wryly. 'Not me who's doing the tarring, is it, love? And besides, you can't cry foul, Suzie, because in one respect, at least, you fit their view of the type to a T, don't you?'

'What do you mean?' said Suzie defensively.

'Well, you're not looking for a steady relationship, are you?'

'No, you know I'm not. After Geoff, well ... If I'm honest, I'd have to say I was partly to blame for the problems we had. For what he did at that party, even. I mean, the magazine takes up so much of my time, and if I wasn't there for him, well, who can blame him for sniffing elsewhere? No, forget relationships. A man now and again would do me just fine.'

'There, you see?' Hilary slapped her thigh triumphantly. 'Career girl all over: no time for a regular man in your life. But men, more and more these days, are looking to form lasting relationships; less and less for one night stands. The AIDS risk, see: fewer partners equals less risk. Men are not so stupid as I sometimes

8

like to make out – they've managed to work that one out.'

'Changing bloody times,' Suzie mumbled unhappily.

'Exactly, love. Men take one look at you and, at very best, they see ONE-NIGHT STAND with capital letters written all over you; a girl too into her career to be interested in anything else. And nowadays, it's just not what a lot of them want.'

'So what am I supposed to do?'

'I've told you what you should do. You asked my advice and I've given it to you: pay for it. Forget disappointment and frustration: when you want sex, just buy it; no-nonsense, no-tie, no-uncertainty sex. Simple. Though personally . . .' Hilary reached out and plucked the cigarette from Suzie's fingers, took a long drag from it and stuffed the butt in an ashtray, 'I can't for the life of me see what you'd want with a man anyway.'

Her hand had been resting on Suzie's knee, and slowly, ever so slowly, it began to creep higher. Reached Suzie's skirt and slipped beneath it. Moved higher still, along her nylon-clad inner thigh, until her fingertips found the naked softness above the top of her stocking. She stroked there for a moment, and Suzie closed her eyes, locked in mental battle with herself; fighting the feeling of slight shame it always gave her to make love with another woman.

A sense of unease, this time, which won, and made her want Hilary to stop. (It didn't always!)

She laid her hand over Hilary's hand, gently restraining, preventing its moving higher.

'Actually, Hils,' she said softly, 'I'd rather not. Not tonight. Would you mind?'

Hilary pouted. 'Oh, you and your bloody hang-ups!'

'No, it's not that, Hils,' Suzie protested. (Though it mostly was.) 'It's just that right now I'm kind of fixated on men, you know? I've got men on the brain, and I just wouldn't enjoy it with . . . You know?'

Hilary withdrew her hand.

'Hmmf, men!' she snorted. 'What man, I'd like to

know, has ever excited you the way I can, on the rare occasions you let me?'

Suzie chuckled. 'Not all men are rotten lovers you know.'

'Oh no? So Geoff was a superstud, was he?'

'I didn't say Geoff, now did I?'

'OK, then who?'

'Well' – it didn't take much thinking about – 'there was Victor, for one.'

'Christ, Suzie, talk about digging deep – you must be going back all of five years there.'

And she was too, Suzie suddenly realised. She mentally rolled back the years – God, was it really so many? – to a time before Geoff. Victor was a one-night-stand she had met in a pub.

At fortysomething, Victor Delaney was a man much older than the men she usually dated. He was greying at the temples, his hairline slightly receding, and lines of experience were deeply etched into a face that was craggy and lean. But he clearly kept himself fit – even a cursory glance was enough to see he had a hard, well-muscled body beneath the stylish cut of his clothes – and something about his very maturity Suzie found highly attractive.

Even so, when he invited her back to his place at the end of the evening, she wasn't at all sure she was going for anything more than the promised coffee; she was probably naïve to have gone. And when, within minutes of them getting there, he suggested they go into the bedroom, she politely declined and stood up to leave.

But Victor would have none of it. Standing in front of her, his tall frame blocking her egress, he took her shoulders in powerful hands, pulled her towards him and, unbidden, clamped his lips onto hers in a hard, crushing kiss, silencing her protests. At first she resisted, at least as best she could in his powerful grip. But then, as if under the command of some unseen, unknown force, she was aware of her lips slowly parting to allow his tongue to enter her mouth, to entwine with hers.

Through the authority of his kiss, he seemed to exert a strange sexual power over her. She was unable to resist and could do nothing to help herself as the kiss went on and, almost against her conscious will, she began to return it, melting into his arms.

A hand moved from her shoulder, then, down to the small of her back, pulling her into him. When she felt his manhood stirring against her belly, hard and insistent, it was the final straw: her resolve dissolved in the flood of liquid heat that suddenly surged through her loins. She suddenly wanted him. Wanted him desperately.

Her knees weak, she allowed herself to be lifted in his muscular arms; he carried her through to the bedroom and laid her on the bed, where she stretched on her back in languid surrender.

She was wearing a light summer dress which buttoned up the front, and, deftly, he popped the buttons undone, slid his hands inside and ran his fingertips lightly over her skin, their touch soft and feather-like as they caressed the sides of her breasts. They moved slowly down to her waist, her hips, opening her dress as they went; then down further, down the outsides of her thighs. Kneeling at her feet, he caressed her calves, her ankles, her toes, before his hands began to move upwards again. And she moaned softly as they traced an exciting path on her skin; up, along the insides of her thighs now, until his fingertips reached the moist patch of silk at her crotch, where he ran a fingernail lightly along her hidden furrow, gently probing.

She moaned again: allowed her thighs to part to accommodate his experienced fingers, and felt waves of desire flow through her as those fingers eased aside the silk of her panties and began to probe in earnest; finding that tiny nub of erectile tissue that, at his expert touch, caused a sudden electric shock to spark through her belly.

She gasped, and Victor said, 'God, you're wet. You must be feeling as horny as hell,' his voice drifting to her from far, far away.

11

She felt herself blush. *God, what a slut he must think her.* He had hardly yet touched her, and already her juices were flowing in torrents ...

But she didn't care; was too enthralled by the exciting feelings he was arousing within her to let herself worry. 'I am,' she heard her own husky voice whisper back.

She let her eyes close, the better to float on a sea of erotic sensation; her being undulating on waves of pure pleasure as Victor's skilful caresses went on.

And then his fingers withdrew. And she felt them at the waist of her panties, drawing them from her in a whisper of silk against nylon. She lifted her hips to help him, and was aware of the movement of cool air against the moist heat of her sex; her lips, she knew, pouting open in need, exposed between thighs slightly parted. Thighs that were trembling now in excited anticipation as they awaited Victor's touch.

But a second went by. And two, then three. And still he hadn't resumed his yearned-for caress.

She opened her eyes. Victor was sitting there almost trance-like, his eyes glazed and distant. A tendril of horror squirmed in her belly – he had her panties pressed to his face and was taking deep breaths through their crotch.

He seemed to become aware of her watching him, yet it made no difference. He merely breathed ever deeper, and said in a throaty voice: 'Jesus, you smell sexy.'

Her cheeks burned. 'Oh, don't,' she whispered imploringly, desperately embarrassed by his intimacy with her underwear. *Deliciously excited by it.* His commenting on it making it worse. *Better!*

(Actually, it was just the sort of thing Hilary would do; deliberately embarrassing her in bed ... Hilary knew her so well.)

Watching Victor breathe through her panties, worms wriggled in the pit of her stomach. She wished he would stop. *Hoped he'd go on, while it continued to perversely excite her.* But, at last, he let the panties come away from his face, and she sighed a sigh of relief.

12

Though relief was but momentary.

Victor's eyes moved, from her eyes, to now gaze overtly at her aroused and naked sex. She squirmed.

'Oh, don't look at me there,' she begged. (Another of Hilary's tricks.) 'It . . . it's embarrassing.'

Victor's eyes twinkled knowingly; wickedly. 'Yes, I know,' he said. But he didn't look away. Instead, he reached for the crook of her knee, bent her leg gently and pressed it aside, forcing her thighs to part widely. And kneeling between them to keep them apart, his eyes remained riveted on all that was so blatantly exposed. 'Embarrassing, and a helluva turn-on, eh?'

Suzie's face flushed scarlet. For it was true. Though she did find it embarrassing – was, at that moment, finding it acutely embarrassing – that in itself seemed somehow to turn her on further. She didn't know how or why, she only knew that it did. And even now she made no move to cover herself; no attempt to close her widespread thighs, to hide herself from Victor's deliberate gaze. She couldn't; her excitement was building with each passing second, was beginning to dizzy her, and she had neither the wish nor the will to lessen it. She could have averted her eyes, or shut them, to allow herself mentally to block out what Victor was doing. But she didn't: she kept her eyes fixed on Victor's eyes, watching him looking at her wide open sex.

It was embarrassing in the extreme – mildly humiliating, even – but so damned exciting. She felt herself flood with her juices as she imagined what Victor could see; could not prevent the involuntary spasm that gave him yet more to look at as it squeezed her juices from inside to out, making them trickle.

Victor laughed, only just getting started. He reached out a pointed middle finger, and made her jump when he touched its nail to that sensitive spot between the two orifices. Scratched there lightly for a moment before tracing an upward path, up along the opened slit. Reached her clitoris and teased it for a moment with little circular movements, before sliding back down

13

again between the slippery inner lips. Never taking his eyes away for a moment: the path of his finger calculated, she knew, to heighten her awareness of all he could see. As if that were for one moment necessary.

Finally she could stand it no longer. 'Oh please, Victor, fuck me,' she cried, decorum thrown to the wind. 'I want you. I want you now!'

Victor shook his head. 'Oh, no,' he said. 'Not yet. A minute ago you were wanting to leave, and now you want me to fuck you. You obviously don't know your own mind, so I'll decide what we do. And I'll decide when we do it ... This comes first.' He flicked his tongue suggestively between his parted lips. 'Now, put your arms above your head, out of the way.'

And as she obeyed his command – for she could do no other in the grip of the strange sexual power this Victor seemed to have over her – he lowered his face to her groin.

He teased her for what seemed like an age; his fingers and tongue driving her wild, until her thighs were quivering with need, her taut belly shaking. Until her mind was a whirl, a-flood with erotic sensation. And until she felt she'd explode if he didn't mount her – or let her come some other way – soon.

But, at last, the teasing finally stopped; Victor's lips leaving her aching pussy to caress her higher and higher as he began snaking his way up her body. Somewhere among it all he had managed to shed his clothes – quite how or when, she wasn't sure, too engrossed in the sensations that wracked her to be aware of anything else – and at last, to her great relief, he lay himself, naked, atop her. His thighs pressed between hers, and she tensed in anticipation.

Yet still he surprised her. She had expected him, then, to enter her; as other lovers had done, to reach a hand down between them to guide himself into her. (Had only hoped he wouldn't fumble: she hated that.) But no, he used both his hands to pin her arms to the pillow high above her, while his knees spread her thighs im-

possibly wide. It made her feel helpless, deliciously vulnerable in a way she had never before known with a
man. And it excited her all the more, as she felt the head
of his penis position itself between the forced open lips
of her sex. To know she couldn't have stopped him now
if she'd tried (if she had wanted to); that her vagina was
an open receptacle for him, defencelessly awaiting his
thrust.

He held her there for a while, trapped and immobile
beneath him, letting her desire for him build as his swollen knob nudged tantalisingly at the hungry, dew-filled
mouth at his mercy. Suzie tensing again, holding her
breath, ready. More than ready.

And when, finally, he drove himself into her, cleaving
her with a single mighty thrust of his weapon, filling her
entirely as he buried himself to the hilt, so excited was
she that she climaxed instantly. An orgasm that went on
and on. That became two. Or three, she couldn't tell, as
sensation merged with sensation into a single fusion of
mind-shattering pleasure. Before he, too, tensed, then
exploded in the throes of his own urgent climax.

The two lay still for a while in the aftermath, their
bodies gradually uncoiling from the wound-up springs
they had been, as they slowly came down from the
heady summit of orgasm. But Victor's power of recov-
ery was amazing, and almost before Suzie's breathing
had calmed, he was hard and ready again. They made
love a second time then, and a third after that, and it all
added up to one of the most exciting nights of sex Suzie
had ever known.

Yet it was to remain just that: a single night. Despite
Victor's skill as a lover – or because of it – she never saw
him again. At twenty-three, she was frightened of the
intensity of feeling he had managed to arouse within
her; Victor was a man under whose spell it would have
been easy to fall, and she just wasn't ready to tie herself
down (and certainly not to a man twice her age). And
so, afraid of herself, she avowed never to see him again.

It was a decision she from time to time rued, for there

followed a series of unmemorable experiences, with even less memorable men. And then along had come Geoff, and a sex-life which, whilst reasonably satisfying, was at best mundane. But at least, with Geoff, she was always in control of herself and of her feelings.

That brought her to the present, to where she only wished she could as easily control her frustrations.

Hilary was staring into her wineglass, her lower lip pushed out while she hummed to herself softly. It was the closest Hilary ever came to a sulk, and, in the wake of Suzie's rejection, she was clearly frustrated herself.

Suzie patted her ample thigh with sympathy. 'Come on, Hils,' she said. 'It's not the end of the world, is it? What say we crack open another bottle: drink ourselves stupid while we talk about anything other than sex?'

'Your plonk, love,' said Hilary. And then she suddenly grinned, the sulk forgotten. 'Though I can't promise we won't get back onto sex. I mean, girl, what else is there?'

Hilary stayed until the early hours. And when she had gone, Suzie missed her terribly: alone in her bed, she felt frustrated and empty, and she almost regretted not having let the plump lesbian make love to her. Thoughts of Victor had left her aroused, more frustrated than ever, and Hilary would certainly have helped ease the nagging ache in her loins – as gay love-making went, Hilary's was great.

She began to think back through some of the passionate times they had shared, and grew still further aroused. And deciding it was useless to fight it, she squeezed her thighs together and began moving her hips in a sensual, circular motion, enjoying the feel of satin sheets on her skin; beginning, now, to enjoy the heat in her loins. She resisted for as long as she could, but knowing she would succumb in the end she finally put a hand to herself.

She was hot and wet and her fingers were soon drenched with her juices, sliding lubriciously over sex-swollen lips and setting nerve-ends alight as they went.

Her thoughts left Hilary and turned to men, in search of a suitable fantasy. Her fantasies were almost always of men. As good as gay love-making was with Hilary on the infrequent occasions they did it, as far as Suzie was concerned it wasn't a substitute for the real thing. Suzie was no lesbian. She didn't think she was even bisexual really. Sex with women was fine; when she could banish her inhibitions sufficiently to be able to let herself go, she enjoyed it well enough – but men were really what sex was about!

Enough to . . . The sudden thought trapped in on itself, as if afraid of its own expression. But then it formed fully – with Hilary's advice still nudging at the back of her mind, the thought was: *Enough to pay for one?*

Suddenly, her fantasy took her to Ancient Rome. She was the daughter of a wealthy merchant, and her husband had been recently killed in the wars. *Against the Gauls? Why not?* And she had come to the city to purchase a slave to keep her bed warm at night.

'I have twenty fine men to show you, my lady,' the slavemaster promises. 'Fine, strong bucks all. But first you must drink wine, and eat.'

With that he slaps his hands and two beautiful dusky maidens appear as if from nowhere, bearing trays. They are naked save only for loincloths, and as they stand before the slavemaster, their shoulders pulled back as they have been trained to stand, their pert breasts jut forward invitingly, darker brown nipples small but erect.

Suzie was teasing herself, building the fantasy up slowly: sexy, near-naked women first, the men would come later.

The slavemaster takes a gourd of wine from one of the trays, grapes from the other, and invites her to recline on a *chaise-longue* where he serves them to her. She sips wine from a silver goblet and watches the slavemaster fondle each of the girls' breasts in turn, as if simply to show that he may, before he dismisses them.

He shows yellowed teeth through a lascivious grin as

17

he watches them leave. Then turns to her. 'Slaves from the Africas are always so yielding,' he observes, nodding after the girls. 'Perhaps you will consider buying a handmaiden one day? They are compliant in every regard, my lady ... If you take my meaning?'

'Maybe I shall,' she replies, plucking a grape from the bunch and rolling it between finger and thumb reflectively. 'And yes, I do take your meaning.'

The slavemaster leers, no doubt imagining her locked in passionate embrace with one of his dusky maidens. Or both.

Suzie imagined it too for a while. By now, she was extremely aroused; rubbing herself more and more urgently the wetter she grew, her fingers the compliant tongues of dusky women. But it was time to stop teasing herself: *time to bring on the men.*

The slavemaster claps his hands and the slaves begin to arrive. Naked, they come through in batches of five. There are black men, white men, men with skin the colour of olives. But all are tall and handsome; well muscled, and with small, taut buttocks. And all have throbbing erections.

How? Because a young woman – a slave herself? OK – is employed to fellate them before they enter, so that as they stand before their prospective buyer, each is shown off to his best advantage, his member hard and glistening. Yes, that works ...

She sprawls on the *chaise-longue* in decadent comfort, casting greedy but critical eyes over the first batch of men and nonchalantly sucking grapes. Gradually the men's erections begin to subside. *No, wait. They had been led in by one of the two dusky maidens, who remains present, and the moment one of them begins to soften he is instantly taken in hand and restored to his former condition. Oh, yes, much better ...* Their cocks kept hard, the men are ordered to display themselves; to flex their muscles, to turn slowly around, to show their tongues and their teeth.

'You may of course inspect them more closely if you

wish, my lady,' the slavemaster offers. 'More, ah, intimately perhaps?'

But she declines: none of the men is quite what she's looking for.

The batch is led out and the next brought in, their penises glistening from recent fellation.

But it is in the third batch that she espies the man she wants. (She couldn't wait for the fourth and final batch: her orgasm was beginning to gather, and she was eager to get her hands on a man. Wanted the fantasy to come to a climax just as she herself did, for fantasy and physical reality to come together at the critical point of release.) In the third batch there is a tall blond Viking type, with a strong, handsome face and an enormous penis swaying in front of him.

'Him,' she tells the slavemaster. 'The one in the middle.'

'Oh, a fine choice, my lady,' the slavemaster fawns. 'Strong and healthy; a work-horse who will serve you well. And I'm sure you will not be disappointed by his, ah, stamina.'

'I'm sure I shall not,' she says with a secret smile, the innuendo of the slavemaster's words not lost on her. 'You say I may examine him more closely?'

'Oh, but of course.'

The slavemaster orders the slave to *No. She herself does. Yes, that's far better ...* She gestures to the man, who steps closer, until he is standing directly before her. His eyes are looking straight to the front, above her head, and his hands are clasped behind him, just as he has been ordered to stand for inspection. His chest is broad, his torso lean, narrowing to masculine hips. But her eyes travel on, to his groin, from where springs his magnificent erection. And a *frisson* of excitement tingles her spine.

She reaches a hand to him, and the Viking sucks in a breath as her fingers furl around him, gently squeezing his iron shaft. She uses his penis to draw him still closer, right up to her face, and begins to move it about. From side to side and up and down; not masturbating him – indeed, careful not to – but closely examining it from every angle. She licks her lips, her breathing shallow as she studies him with a lascivious eye: bluish veins stand out in relief against the tightly-stretched skin of the shaft, and its head is large and bulbous. It's like a hot iron bar in her hand, and she imagines that huge hard organ entering her; its full length sliding in and out of her as he rides her with long deliberate strokes.

But, not just yet . . .

'Turn around,' she orders, suddenly releasing his cock. It springs up to slap against his muscular belly and she watches it quiver with relish. 'Hands by your sides and your legs apart,' she says.

The slave obeys and she regards his buttocks now, with an equally lascivious eye. They are small and hard, the muscles well-defined beneath tanned, unblemished skin. Just as she likes. And they are clamped together as tightly as his wide-apart legs will allow.

A small but knowing smile touches her lips.

'Bend forward and down,' she commands. 'As far as you can go.'

Again the slave does her bidding, bending from the waist in reach of his toes. It brings his balls, large and pendulous, into view between his spread thighs and she resists the urge to fondle them, to reach between his legs and weigh them in her palm. Instead she looks back to his buttocks, which she sees are still straining to remain tightly clamped.

'The cheeks,' she says, allowing him no mercy. 'Spread them apart.'

This time there is a moment's hesitation, and she senses the slavemaster holding his breath, no doubt concerned that any recalcitrance on the part of the slave might cost him his sale. But the hesitation is fleeting and the slavemaster's sigh is a rattle in his throat as the slave at last complies; reaches behind him and spreads open the cheeks of his bottom with strong, well-manicured fingers. Holds them apart for all to see.

20

'As you can see, my lady, scrupulously clean,' says the slavemaster, the relief in his voice almost tangible.

'Indeed I can,' she says. She extends a fingertip to the balls that are dangling even more visibly now between the slave's legs; pauses for a moment before sliding her finger from there up into the held-open crevice. The slave flinches at her intimate touch and she scratches a fingernail, even more intimately, right across the puckered ring of his anus. 'See ... And feel, too,' she says.

God, how humiliating it must be for the poor devil, she thinks. All of it, of course, but not least this. To have a woman, a total stranger, look upon, toy with as she will, his most secret of all places. And to be able to do nothing about it, save suffer it. What a wretched life is that of a slave!

But she doesn't desist. After all, such inspection is but a necessary step in the choosing of one's slave. She continues to invade the private crevice, amused that the puckered ring twitches in involuntary spasm each time her fingernail is drawn lightly across it. But finally she tires of the game, and ceases her finger's teasing movement. Though she deliberately brings it to rest directly against the rosebud opening, prodding gently. The slave's thighs begin to tremble, and she senses his dread trepidation. And she smiles a cruel and capricious smile.

Suzie slowed the hand at her crotch, deliberately disrupting her rhythm. Too close to coming. She was engrossed in her fantasy and avid to see where it went; it was already in uncharted waters.

She took several deep breaths, found a new, more gentle rhythm, and returned to Ancient Rome ...

'Stand up,' she says abruptly, withdrawing the threat of her finger. 'And turn to face me again.'

The slave stands and turns and there is relief – *and gratitude? Yes, that too* – in his striking blue eyes. His erection has partly subsided, she sees – in fear, perhaps? – but the dusky maiden is no longer there. She has led the other slaves from the room, and her hand is no longer available to perform its salacious duty.

No matter.

Indeed, better . . .

'Masturbate,' she tells the slave in a husky voice, thrilling to her power. 'I want to see you hard and yearning.'

The Viking swallows in a dry throat, blushes crimson down to his neck. But he hesitates for only a moment, then slowly his hand moves to his softening shaft, takes hold of it and begins to perform the debasing act she has ordered. While his tormentress watches, amused by his shame.

'Yes, wank,' she tells him. 'Wank yourself while your mistress looks on. And' – *oh yes, good* – 'And look at me while you do it.'

God, thought Suzie, *where is this going? And who the hell cared; this was exciting.* Her hand had begun to move rapidly again – she had been unable to stop it – and she knew that orgasm was close. But she mustn't come yet. Not yet, the fantasy wasn't yet over . . .

She watches the slave's eyes come slowly, reluctantly, down to meet hers, reads in them his humiliation and shame. And the same cruel smile plays on her lips as she returns her eyes to his groin, knowing his shame will be all the greater now he can see her looking at him. Now that he must see the amusement in her eyes as he continues to masturbate, to debase himself before her.

She settles herself back to watch. His hand is sliding back and forth along his magnificent member. The shaft is responding, swelling and thickening, and soon his great cock is once again a hard and throbbing tool, its bulbous head purpled with need. His hand pauses there at the top of its stroke, just for a moment, then makes the long journey back down to the root from where his balls hang heavy and full. Then up again, to where the crook of his finger brushes the sensitive web of skin that makes his cock leap and twitch. Up and down, again and again in a steady mesmeric rhythm.

She looks back to his eyes, still on hers and now imploring her to allow him to stop. Or to allow him to

22

come, she doesn't know which. His breathing has grown ragged, she sees, and his thighs have begun to tremble. His balls have tightened in their wrinkled sac and his shaft is clearly straining; the overstretched skin is almost translucent, and blue veins stand hard and knotted beneath it. He must be close. Very close.

Yes, she decides, that was it. He was begging her permission to let himself come; his aching need destroying his last vestige of dignity and not caring now what spectacle he makes. His eyes reflect his agony, the cruel self-torture he is obliged to endure: while he must continue to stimulate his aching cock it only increases his suffering. His eyes beg her for relief from his plight.

But she permits him none; forbids him to do either – to come or to stop – with eyes narrowed in warning, and has him continue for her viewing pleasure no matter what his frustration or torment.

Just once, the slave's eyes flick fleetingly to those of the slavemaster, imploringly; begging the compassion of a fellow man. But though the slavemaster winces in sympathy, he turns away – it is not his place to interfere with a purchaser's whims.

And still she has him go on. After all, a slave must have self-control when amusing his mistress.

Self-control? thought Suzie wryly. *Who was she to talk? Her orgasm was fast approaching, and she could do nothing to stop it.* Her hand had a life of its own and refused to be moved from her crotch, or even to slow down. Of its own volition, it was rubbing her clitoris frantically and she knew she could do nothing, now, to delay the inevitable. It was time to stop all the games: she needed the Viking, and she needed him now.

Then, quite suddenly, she is alone with him. The setting is still Ancient Rome. But the slavemaster is gone. There is just her and her Viking. She is naked now; the toga she had been wearing has vanished. Her thighs are spread wide and the Viking is kneeling between them. He is looking at her ... there. For a long, long time it seems. She tingles with familiar embarrassment. Then

23

with anticipatory excitement as the Viking at last dips his face to her lap.

She almost cries out at the first velvet touch of his tongue, so intense is the thrill of it. And her excitement builds rapidly as his lips and tongue do their work, lapping greedily from her feminine font.

And then she can bear it no longer. She pushes the Viking's face from her crotch and makes him kneel upright. The faint but exciting scent of his musk assails her nostrils as his movement swirls the air, wafting it up from his groin. It makes her senses swim giddyingly; it is the final unendurable stimulus, and she loses control. His enormous penis is hard and ready, arcing up from his loins like a great scimitar of prurient flesh, and she screams: 'Fuck me! Fuck me, fuck me, *fuck me!*'

He positions himself to her, his bulbous, shining knob dipping into her juices, lubricating itself ready to penetrate. Pauses. Then pushes gently but firmly forward . . .

And she came.

A great shuddering climax that left her gasping for breath and slick between the satin sheets of her bed. Her own bed now, not a *chaise-longue*. Her own bedroom, not the slavemaster's quarters. And no Viking. Just her. Alone.

'Bloody hell,' she said aloud when she finally found sufficient breath to give voice to the words. 'What a come. What a fantasy.'

Parts of it had surprised her. Why had it turned her on to think of humiliating the Viking so? To treat him so cruelly and be amused by his suffering? She supposed it was because she could, triggered by the thought of buying a man; that she had no need to consider his pleasures, only her own, and that, bought and paid for, she could do with him whatever she wished. It was, in itself, an exciting concept. An exciting fantasy.

And then it struck her: *why did it have to be only a fantasy?* As Hilary had said, why not do it? Not the humiliation bit, maybe. But the rest, why not? Go for it; make it reality.

24

Of course, a male escort service would hardly operate like a slave market in Ancient Rome. No gorgeous naked hunks paraded before her to choose from, to inspect, as she'd inspected the Viking. More was the pity! But nevertheless, the principle was all but the same: women did buy bed-slaves in those days; were, in so doing, paying money for men to have sex with them. It was no new idea after all. *Changing times? Ha!* She laughed out loud. In changing, they'd come around the full circle. What goes around comes around, she thought, bringing to mind the slogan of one of their advertisers.

So, why the hell not? You need a man, pay for a man. Simple. And the decision was made.

She jumped out of bed and padded naked downstairs. Found the evening paper and began rummaging through its pages in search of the Classifieds. Came to them, and ran her finger down the page, and, just as Hilary had promised, there: Benson Escort Agency. Handsome escorts for all occasions. Discreet service. A telephone number.

She used a red biro to mark the advertisement and tucked the newspaper into her handbag. She'd ring the number as soon as she could find the time. *No, dammit, she would make the time.*

Beyond the windows, the sky was beginning to pale with the approach of dawn, mackerel cloud gradually emerging as the sun came slowly awake. It was almost morning and Suzie had a difficult day ahead of her: her secretary, Sally, who did much of the pre-reading, was off sick – a case of terminal period pain, knowing Sally – and the slush-pile on Suzie's desk, unsifted, would be huge. Nevertheless, as she crawled back into bed she felt more content than she'd done in an age – for the first time in a long time she knew without doubt she would soon be having a man.

Her head hit the pillow and she fell instantly into a deep and dreamless sleep.

Chapter Two

Suzie regarded herself in the bathroom mirror. She hadn't yet made up her face and two dark smudges that hung heavily under her eyes were the product of the late night she had had. But they would disappear with foundation, she knew, and otherwise what she was looking at was holding up well she thought; her twenty-eight years hadn't treated her badly at all. Her freshly washed-and-brushed hair, perhaps her most stunning feature, was in peak condition, and formed a golden aureole around a still-smooth, almost pixie-like face, before tumbling to her shoulders in a carefully organised chaos. Swathes, Hilary had said in describing her hair, and it described it well. Though God only knew where *she* had picked up so elegant a word.

Her eyes were a deep, sapphire blue (if their whites were slightly reddened that morning by lack of sleep and a glass too much wine), and her mouth was full and sensual, her lips seeming to form a naturally sexy pout. Her teeth were even and white.

She let her eyes move lower, down a slender neck to her breasts.

They were not large breasts, but they were large

enough; round and full. And still firm. Impudent nipples jutted from dark areolae and were slightly upturned. They brought the word pert to mind.

She reached up her hands to cup them proudly, flicked her nipples with her thumbs to make them erect. They obeyed instantly, forming two hard buds which begged cheekily for more. Not a bad pair of boobs, she decided; not bad at all.

She half turned to bring her bottom into the mirror. Her buttocks, too, were nicely rounded, and again showed no sign of sag; twin half-moons of firm flesh that any man, surely, would be pleased to grip as he drove himself into her in the final throes of orgasm.

If only any man were to get that far.

It was a rankling thought, but she refused to allow it to sour her mood. She pushed it away and turned again to stand full face in the mirror. Her hands left her breasts to move lower, sliding sensuously down her sides to come to rest on her hips.

'Yes, all in all, you'll do,' she told her reflection, not displeased.

Her hands were moving inwards, then, across a taut, flat belly to the V of flaxen hair she kept neatly trimmed. And then went further, burying into her bush. She watched her fingertips disappear as they slid between her legs, burrowed into moist softness and began to tease her clitoris with little circular movements. And as the moistness warmed and her tension gathered she thought about her vibrator; saw herself sprawled on her bed while her little toy first heightened then soothed away her growing excitement.

But the sound of the alarm going off in the bedroom made her start; it was the third of three reminders her bedside clock was programmed to give, and it told her she was already late. *Damn*, she cursed, pushing sexy notions aside as her hands left her pussy and flew for her make-up.

The office was hustle and bustle.

Sod's law: in the absence of her secretary, the slush-pile – the reams of unsolicited manuscripts that poured in daily from hopeful freelances – was even higher than usual. And with the deadline less than three days away, people in the outer offices were milling about like ants on an ant-hill; it was only a matter of time before someone was pestering her for something, further distracting her.

But for now she was alone at her desk, staring forlornly at the mountain of paper and doing a good enough job of distracting herself. She knew she should have been making better progress; it was already eleven o'clock and she had barely scratched the pile's surface. It seemed to stare at her with a malevolent eye, taunting her.

But she was finding it difficult to concentrate. For one thing lack of sleep had taken more of a toll on her than she had at first thought: she felt gummy-eyed and groggy, and even a continuous river of strong black coffee had failed to wake her fully. For another, images of Vikings kept flashing into her brain.

Annoyed with herself, she pushed back from her desk in need of fresh air. Crossed to the window and threw it open, and looked down five storeys to the square below. In the concrete heart of the city cars jammed, people meandered, and pigeons defiled the Cenotaph with no respect for the dead.

A Viking it had turned her on to humiliate.

The fumey air above the busy city was hardly fresh, and didn't help. And her brain was now flooded with sexual imagery. Images so sharp and clear that the Viking might have been there in front of her, bending over even now at her command while she made him flinch with a probing finger, a lightly scratching nail. Saw the puckered ring twitch in involuntary spasm as her fingertip made him acutely aware of all she could see and threatened his most dreaded intrusion. Or him standing before her having to masturbate, debasing himself for her viewing pleasure, his face flushed with humiliation and shame. His eyes at first begging her to allow him to

28

stop. Then to allow him to let himself come, dignity thrown to the wind as his balls ached and his need robbed him of what little he'd had to begin with; an agony that begged for relief. She permitting him neither, but watching his torment with cruel delight.

A Viking – a man – she had bought and paid for.

The thought drew her eyes back to her desk, where a newspaper poked from the top of her bag, beckoning. She went over and re-read the ad she had circled: Benson Escort Agency. Handsome escorts for all occasions. Discreet service.

One phone call was all it would take.

With a persistent, nagging ache in her loins, she studied the number, picked up the telephone beside the huge pile of work that was not being done ... and hesitated.

Last night, in a warm bed and the comfortable afterglow of post-orgasmic contentment, in the wake of exciting fantasy, it had seemed such a good idea. Now, in the cold light of day, she wasn't so sure.

Not sure? She threw down the phone as if it were something a dog had done on the pavement. She was damned sure. Her, Suzie Carlton, pay for a man? Never. Never in a million years!

It was almost five o'clock when she made the call.

Chapter Three

*T*he offices of the Benson Escort Agency were not
what she had expected. Indeed, she had not expected an office at all: she had envisaged the arrange-
ments being made by phone. To be asked for a time and
a place – and her credit card number – and to be told
that her escort would meet her there; that she would
recognise him by the carnation in his buttonhole. No,
surely not something as corny as a carnation. But something like that.

Instead, she was asked if she had used the agency
before, and, upon admitting she hadn't, was asked if she
would like to make an appointment to visit their office.
It wasn't compulsory, the woman had said, but they did
like to provide a personal service wherever possible. *A
personal service?* Suzie had mused wryly. *Well, that's what
I'm after all right.* She had made the appointment, and
had been given a city-centre address.

Still expecting a sleazy backroom somewhere, she had
been surprised to find herself in a sumptuous office
complex in the heart of the city's business quarter,
where the door bearing the discreet plaque – The Benson
Agency – was across the corridor from a merchant bank

and the city's oldest and most respected firm of solicitors. She had entered and given her name to a pleasant young receptionist who had asked her to please take a seat, and she was now sitting on a mahogany-bound Chesterfield in a tastefully furnished corner. The carpet was Axminster, the reading up-market – *Country Life, House and Home, Vogue*. No *Woman Now*, she noted with a spark of dismay. Pity, it would have sat well with the others. A Chinese-lacquered cigarette box held pride of place on a coffee-table and offered Black Russians, next to an expensive onyx table-lighter with matching ashtray. And what could have been a genuine Picasso hung on the wall.

'Some set-up,' Suzie muttered to herself. *They must be making a bomb.*

She suddenly imagined naked men being paraded across the Axminster before an audience of rich and powerful women, there to haggle over the best-looking of them with purses bulging with cash. The image caused an unwanted stirring between her legs, and she picked up a copy of *Vogue* with which to distract herself; browsing through it out of professional interest, though hardly absorbed.

Presently, the door to an inner office opened and a smartly dressed middle-aged woman came through it, said what might have been a slightly breathless goodbye over her shoulder, and left. A moment later a buzzer sounded on the receptionist's desk. The girl looked up.

'If you'd like to go through, Miss Carlton,' she said, indicating the door from which the breathless woman had emerged. 'Miss Cummings will see you now.'

Suzie smiled politely and stood up, smoothing her skirt. 'Thank you.'

In an inner sanctum that was furnished even more richly than the reception area had been, Suzie found an angular-faced woman with piercing blue eyes and a deliberate smile. She could have been forty but was probably much older: even at first glance she had that air of wealth about her which tends to belie its owner's age.

'Ah, Miss Carlton,' the woman said, her voice cut-crystal. 'Grace Cummings. Please, call me Grace.'

She was standing behind a leather-topped desk, over which she extended a heavily bejewelled hand.

Suzie took it. 'Grace. Pleased to meet you.'

'The pleasure is mine, Miss Carlton. Please, take a seat.'

'Nice offices you have,' Suzie observed as she sank into a comfortable chair. Crossed one leg demurely over the other in a soft rustle of nylon.

'Well thank you. Yes, we find our clients appreciate it. Our clientele is made up largely of ladies who are accustomed to a little luxury.'

I'll bet, thought Suzie.

'Of course,' she said.

'Would you like some coffee?'

'No, thank you. I'm fine.'

Grace Cummings steepled beringed fingers, dutiful pleasantries done with and ready to get down to business. 'So, this is the first time you have considered using the Benson Agency.'

It was a statement not a question, and Suzie nodded, yes.

'Well I'm sure you will find that we offer an excellent service, Miss Carlton. We do our best to please, and I assure you our gentlemen are all, indeed, gentlemen . . .'

Gentlemen? thought Suzie. *I don't want a gentleman: I want a raving satyr hung like a donkey who can screw all night.*

She smiled sweetly as Grace Cummings went on: 'Our standard fee for an evening is seventy-five pounds. That's usually from eight p.m. until one in the morning, but we do try to be as accommodating as we can . . . May I ask, is this a formal occasion?'

'I'm sorry?' The question had caught Suzie off guard.

'A presentation dinner? A premier? Anything of that sort?'

Suzie was beginning to wonder if she had come to the wrong place; if she had hold of the wrong end of what could be a very embarrassing stick. It all seemed so legitimate; Grace Cummings so straight-laced. Too straight-laced, surely, to be involved in what amounted to male prostitution. What amounted to it? What was male prostitution for God's sake!

'Oh, er, no,' Suzie stammered. 'I . . . er, no, I was just thinking of drinks. Dinner, perhaps. You know, like that.' She was beginning to feel distinctly uncomfortable.

'Ah. I see.' Grace Cummings unsteepled her fingers and laid her hands palms down on her desk. 'No, it's just that I do like to ask. Those formal functions do have an irritating habit of running on late, you see. I usually suggest we add a little to the fee just in case, refundable of course in the event it isn't required. Saves embarrassment, you know?' She suddenly laughed lightly. 'I mean, one doesn't want one's escort having to run off in the middle of one's dinner, now does one?'

No, one certainly doesn't, Suzie thought sourly. *God, this was a legitimate set-up; an escort agency full stop – wasn't it? How could she find out for sure?* She would certainly have to before getting in deeper. Trial and error was out: the last thing she needed was to pay for an escort for an evening only to discover that's all he was; to have him leave her high and dry – or worse, high and *wet* – at the end of the night. That would be frustrating beyond her endurance.

She cleared her throat with a little cough. 'Erm, exactly what does your fee include, Grace?'

'Oh, it's all-inclusive,' Grace Cummings said expansively. 'Your escort will collect you from your home, if required, of course; some of our clients prefer to be met at their evening's venue. He'll provide his company for the agreed time, and he'll see you home at the end of the night, again if required. Taxi fares and tips are included.'

'I see.' Suzie began to squirm in her seat, more sure than ever that the agency was no more than it purported to be. But she had come this far; she might as well find out for certain before giving up, make her excuses and leave. 'And, erm, when you say provide his company, would that be just, er' – *how could she put it?* – 'er, talking company. Or, er . . .'

She stopped in mid-sentence, halted by Grace Cummings's look.

'Miss Carlton,' she said, her voice brittle, 'the Benson Agency is strictly an *escort* service. Our fee is for the provision of *bona fide* escorts for the purpose of licit companionship. Only.'

'Of course,' mumbled Suzie, wishing the ground would open up and swallow her. She'd murder Hilary, with her 'Escorts, my fanny': she'd got it all wrong. She had never felt such a fool in her life.

That was until Grace Cummings's angular face cracked into a huge grin and her blue eyes practically chuckled. 'Of course,' she laughed, 'whatever business our gentlemen transact with our clients beyond their contract with us is entirely their own affair.'

The penny took a moment to drop, and then the knots that had gathered in Suzie's neck began to unwind. 'Oh, I see,' she said, thinking she saw. Hoping she saw.

Grace Cummings suddenly leaned forward and said in a low, guttural voice: 'Frankly, love, they're all meat on the hoof. It's how they make their brass.'

The straight-laced Miss Cummings had vanished; she might suddenly have been an ex-tart in charge of a brothel, or a fishwife in a dockside pub. And Suzie grinned, sighing a secret sigh of relief: Hilary had been right after all.

Grace Cummings became Grace Cummings again, the respectable escort agency boss, and said: 'And now, Miss Carlton, why don't we choose your escort?'

She produced a hide-bound album from the drawer of her desk and laid it in front of Suzie. Patted it lovingly and stood up. 'Please, take your time, Miss Carlton,' she said. 'I'm sure you'll find a suitable gentleman in here. I'll leave you alone so you may browse at your leisure.' And with that she left.

Suzie lifted the album onto her knee and turned over the front cover. A handsome face smiled up at her. It's owner was pictured wearing grey slacks and a polo neck pullover, and looked relaxed and at ease.

She studied the photo for a while, thinking: *mmm, not bad, not bad at all.* Then let her eyes move on down the page. Here was printed the man's christian name, Stephen, his height and weight, and a short paragraph briefly detailing his hobbies and interests. This latter ending with: 'And yours'.

Suzie flicked on through the album. There was page after page of the same. *So this was why they had suggested she visit their office,* she realised; *what they meant by providing a personal service.* And was probably, too, the cause of their previous client's breathlessness – certainly some of the men depicted were hunky enough to steal away anyone's breath. It wasn't quite naked slaves being paraded before her, but it was surely the next best thing.

One of the men, Jason, particularly caught her eye, and she found herself drawn to his photograph again and again. He was dressed in evening wear, but she mentally stripped his clothing away to envisage him naked. The large bulge that was showing in the front of his trousers helped, and she soon had a clear and exciting image in her mind's eye. Exciting enough, anyway, to cause a familiar stirring within her, and she squeezed her thighs together the better to savour it; couldn't help but wriggle into her seat and had to resist the urge to touch herself. She imagined she and Jason locked in a passionate embrace, and she began to perspire. Her capacity for eidetic imagery was partly what made her such an outstanding journalist, but it had its other advantages too. She could all but feel Jason's cock inside her, driving her wild, and her thighs began to tremble.

Just then she heard the door open behind her, and she jumped, feeling absurdly like a little girl caught playing with herself in the bath.

'Now, Miss Carlton, how are we coming along?'

Was there the hint of a knowing chuckle in Grace Cummings's voice? Suzie wondered. Or had she only imagined it?

The escort agency boss looked over her shoulder. 'Ah, yes, Jason,' she cooed. 'Excellent choice, dear. Excellent.' (It was reminiscent of the slavemaster complimenting her on her choice of the Viking.) Then the voice grew guttural. 'Got a cock like a rock, love,' the other Grace Cummings whispered into her ear.

Suzie laughed, deciding she liked the woman. Both of them.

'Now, Miss Carlton, when were you wanting him for? Friday evening, wasn't it?'

'Yes, that's right.'

The magazine's deadline was Thursday. It would be bedlam until then. But the first few days of the new month were always her quietest, when she rarely needed to work after hours; her evenings her own.

Grace Cummings had moved back behind her desk and was flicking through cards in a file.

'Ah, here we are,' she finally announced. 'Yes. Jason is free on Friday. Shall I pencil you in?'

Suzie could hardly say, 'Yes please,' quickly enough, her belly a-flutter with nervous excitement.

'Then, he's all yours ... Now, how will you be wanting to pay?'

Chapter Four

'*D*o you have the copy on that computer fraud story, Sooz?'

It was Terry, the scruffy little gofer attached to the magazine's Business section. No amount of telling, it seemed, could persuade the youth to address her as Miss Carlton, as she would have really preferred from an office boy, though she would at a pinch have settled for Susan (as Suzie was generally known at the office). But he would insist on calling her Sooz.

She was sick to the back teeth of chiding him for it.

Today, however, she couldn't be bothered. 'In the Current and Topical file, Terry,' she said long-sufferingly. 'Just where you would expect it to be. Why you have to ask me I have no idea. See Sally, she'll get it for you.'

'She ain't here. Norma says she's been stuck in the bog for the last couple of hours. Belly ache, or something.'

Oh, no. Don't say she's been struck down by one of her doses of menstrual malaise. Not today, deadline day.

Suzie turned her eyes to the ceiling in silent prayer.

'Well?' prompted the pimply youth.

'Well, you'll have to help yourself then, won't you,' said Suzie shortly.

'Ta, Sooz.'

Little shit.

Terry scuttled away to the row of cabinets in the outer office where all the most recent news items were filed, and she was about to resume the editorial she was writing when Keith Blundell put his head round her door.

'Any chance of me re-working my piece on the Collins interview, Susan?'

'What? We've got two hours to go before press, Keith, and you ask me that!'

'I know, but I was just thinking –'

'Well think with your brains, Keith, instead of whatever it is you're using right now. There'd be no time to get it re-cleared by our legal people. And you know her, of all people – put one foot wrong and she'd sue the pants off us.'

'Thought you didn't wear any.'

'Cheeky! Anyway, like I said, no way.'

Blundell went away, muttering under his breath.

Idiots all, though Suzie shaking her head in astonishment. It was the same every month. With the deadline looming, and her up to her eyes in it – putting final touches to the paste-ups (the vital final layouts that would go to the printer), and making last minute decisions on the content of the editorial (the magazine prided itself on its topicality, and new storylines, which might demand an entirely new slant on the issue, could break at any time), not to mention her actually writing the damn thing – and there'd be inane questions, idiotic requests; constant, unnecessary, interruptions.

It was almost as if the fools were unaware of how vital it was that the deadline was made. Miss it, and the printers might have moved on to other work; they couldn't wait for ever, even for so valued a customer. And for a deadline missed by an hour, it might be a week before they could be fitted in again. And late issues inevitably meant cancellations, lost future orders, irate advertisers refusing to pay or demanding back money they had paid. Which, on the budget they ran to, all added up to catastrophe: it could be fatal to a magazine like *Woman Now*. They certainly wouldn't be the first to go under due to a missed deadline. And ensuring it was hit was her responsibility. It was not an overstatement to say that all their jobs depended on her, and her making that deadline, yet still they pestered her. *Idiots all!*

Usually she coped with it better. Fine, even. But today it was getting her down. Today, all she wanted was for the day to be over. And then there would be an easy, first day of the month tomorrow . . . and then it would be tomorrow night. Sex, sex, and more sex. As much as she cared to pay for!

Erotic images flooded her mind, and she found herself becoming aroused. On another day it might have been her cue to discreetly take her vibrator off to the loo. But never on deadline day; too much to do. Reluctantly, she made the images go away, picked up her pen and tried to concentrate on the editorial she was about a quarter of the way through.

But no sooner had she begun than there was yet another interruption.

Bob Adams stepped into her room.

'Got a minute, Susan, love?'

Suzie put down her pen without throwing it, looked up and made herself smile. 'Of course.'

Bob Adams was Features Editor. Ostensibly Suzie and he shared equal status and power on the magazine, with matching salaries and identical perks. But Bob Adams was a lifelong friend of the Taunton family, the magazine's owners, which, in real terms, shifted the balance very much in his favour. Certainly he was a man who Suzie thought it unwise to rankle unnecessarily.

Which was a pity, since the man was a moron.

'I was just wondering if you were going to Maggie's party tomorrow night.'

Party! They were less than two hours to press, and he was on about parties. The man was a fool as well as a moron. *Keep calm, Suzie,* she told herself. *Keep calm.*

'Er, no. No I'm not, Bob. I've got a prior engagement.'
Flickering images suddenly came back: tantalising, teasing.

Bob clicked his tongue against the roof of his mouth.
'Oh, you're seeing a bloke, are you?'

'As it happens, Bob, yes.' More images, stronger now.
Heating and moistening. Suzie pressed her thighs together and winced as she felt herself blush. Could only pray that Bob wouldn't notice.

He evidently didn't; as usual, too wrapped up in himself.

'I've told you before, Susan, there's only one man for you.' He jerked a thumb back at his chest, and didn't even have the modesty to smile as he said it: 'Me.'

Suzie groaned inwardly. Bob Adams had fancied her since the day she'd arrived on the magazine's staff, and though she had never encouraged him he seemed never to tire of trying it on. He was constantly asking her out – to dinner, the theatre, to parties (presumably he had come now to invite her to Maggie's). A couple of times he had gone further than polite, if unwanted, invitations. Once, when they were working late alone in her office, he had come right out with it and said, 'How about we fuck right here on your desk? I'll show you what a real man can do.' She had simply laughed that one off. But another time he had had the audacity to put a hand on her breast, and that had earned him a slap in the face. (Friend of the Tauntons he might be, but she wasn't standing for that.)

It wasn't that he was particularly unfanciable – indeed, he was really quite attractive, physically at least – but one-night stands could be embarrassing when you had to work with the person the next day. And an affair between colleagues could prove a working disaster. Oh no, as far as Suzie was concerned, office shenanigans were off the agenda full stop.

'I really don't know why you bother with other blokes,' Adams was saying, 'when you could be having me. When you haven't even given me the chance to show you what I can do ...'

40

Suzie might have thought, *egotistical sod*, if her head were not filled with other, more interesting thoughts. She was in a hotel bedroom with Jason. And what they were doing.

'You know, Susan, you should seriously consider going out with me.' Adams was heading for her office door, thankfully on his way out. 'I could do you a lot of good with the Tauntons, you know.' And then he was gone.

If Suzie were not feeling so horny, she would have been furious. *Who the hell did he think he was?* For what he had just made was not a promise, she knew, but a veiled threat. He had not meant at all that he could do her some good with the magazine's owners, but: come across or I could do you harm. And that was well out of order. That man needed pulling down a few pegs.

As it was, she was too busy fighting an almost overwhelming need to run off to the loo with her vibrator to very much care. Until a new fantasy suddenly sprung into her mind. A fantasy that, if it could have been a reality, would have killed a whole flock of birds with one stone.

She looks up from her desk, and Bob Adams is back in her room.

'OK, Bob,' she says. 'Let's give it a shot. You reckon you're man enough to satisfy me, right?'

'Are you kidding?' Adams is clearly surprised, but quickly recovers. 'You're damn right I am.'

'With your tongue?'

'What?'

'You heard me, I said, with your tongue. Right here and now.'

Adams is taken aback. 'B-but, I don't understand,' he stammers.

She laughs. She has actually shocked Bob Adams. 'Well, it really couldn't be simpler, Bob,' she explains. 'I'm feeling extremely horny. But with the deadline less than two hours away, I can't leave my desk. But if you come and kneel under here, you can lick me to climax while I carry on working. Problem solved.'

Adams puffs his cheeks, seemingly horrified. 'Kneel under your . . . your desk?' He seems almost to choke on the words.

'Yes.'

'While you carry on working? And I . . . I . . .'

'Yes.'

'B-but . . . But that'd be bloody demeaning.'

'Yes, I know. Wouldn't it? But that's the deal. Take it or leave it: your big chance – and if you leave it, your last chance – to show me what a great lover you are. Or what a great licker, anyway.'

Adams seems lost for words, opening and closing his mouth like a pop-eyed goldfish. Finally, he manages to speak. 'I'll . . . I'll t-take it,' he stutters.

'Yes. I rather thought you would,' she purrs with a smile. 'Come on then, over here.'

She stands and pushes back her chair to open up the well of her desk.

'Go on then, what are you waiting for? Crawl in there.'

Adams hesitates, just for a moment, then does as she's said. And watching him crawl, she thinks with great satisfaction: that's him taken down by one or two pegs.

She reaches under her skirt and slips off her panties, notes with some amusement how damp they are at the crotch before dropping them into her bag. *Bob Adams was about to be drowned in her juices.* And, leaving her skirt rucked up to her waist, she perches on the edge of her chair and pulls herself forward.

She taps on the top of her desk. 'You may begin,' she tells the kneeling Adams, spreading her thighs.

She feels his face come to her, his breath warm on her thighs. Senses him hesitate. Savouring her sexy scent? Or is her aroma so strong, her having felt so horny for so long, that it's giving him second thoughts? But then she feels his tongue on her skin, licking aside damp hair to reach her, begin to lick along the pouting lips of her sex. She moans softly and reaches for her pen. Knows that, despite her level of arousal, the distraction of work

42

will keep her from coming for a long while yet. And she smiles to herself. *More than one peg or two*, she decides.

Several minutes go by – for her, several long, wonderfully exciting minutes – when she becomes aware of someone's presence in the outer office. She looks up and sees it's Keith Blundell, busying himself with the Xerox.

She grins wickedly, and calls out to him: 'Oh, Keith. Do you have a minute, please?'

She feels Adams's face jerk away from her.

'Don't stop!' she snaps down to him, keeping her voice low. 'I haven't come yet.'

She senses him balk, then feels his face come to her again. Feels his tongue in her bush just as Keith Blundell enters the room.

She has to put a hand to her mouth, feigning an itch, to hide her look of amusement.

'You want me, Susan?'

'Ah, Keith, yes. The Collins interview,' she says, finally managing to wipe the grin from her face. 'I've just re-read it and it seems fine to me. Why did you want to re-work it?'

It is, of course, just an excuse to bring Blundell into the room. It's giving her a delicious thrill to have him standing just feet away while Adams – his boss – is servicing her under her desk, his tongue in her pussy. A thrill so delicious, in fact, that it almost triggers her climax, and she has to bite on her lower lip to prevent herself coming.

'I mean,' she manages to somehow continue, 'there are no inaccuracies in it, are there?'

'Oh, no,' Blundell says quickly. 'I just thought I could do better, is all.'

'I see, just the perfectionist in you, eh?' She smiles kindly, outwardly calm. Or as calm as she can be. But inside, she is trembling with excitement, finding it strangely but intensely erotic to be holding so normal a conversation with her naked thighs splayed wide and the feel of Adams's face in her lap, his lips and tongue caressing her pussy while she and Blundell talk.

Just then there is a tiny sucking sound as Adams's lips fail to hold onto the slippery nub of her clitoris, and she senses him freeze, no doubt terrified that he has given the game away; that he will be caught by his subordinate in his debasing predicament.

There is also the faint tang of sex in the air, rising from under her desk. But if Blundell has noticed either he makes no outward sign of it.

'I try to do a good job, yeah,' he says.

'Of course.'

She jerks her hips forward, pushing her pussy into Adams's face as an order for him to resume. And he does, sucking her clitoris back into his mouth (more carefully now) and flicking it with his tongue. Sparks of desire shoot from her loins to her brain, and she realises she is again on the verge of coming.

'OK then, Keith. Thanks,' she says by way of dismissal.

Blundell turns to go, but stops at the door. He turns back. 'Are you all right, Susan?'

She looks him dead in the eye. 'Yes, of course. Is there some reason I shouldn't be?'

'Well, no, it's just . . . Oh, nothing.'

He shrugs his shoulders and wanders away, looking puzzled. And she can hardly suppress her laughter. *If only he knew.*

But it has all proved just too exciting, and she can prolong it no more: she needs to come. She closes her eyes, no longer trying to suppress it, and let's Adams's tongue take her on a final ascent, taking her closer and closer to climax. Building her tension higher and higher. Until finally she comes.

Suzie snapped out of her reverie to realise that she had, indeed, just come. In reality as well as in fantasy: she was still trembling from it, and beads of sweat stood out on her forehead. Not with a little horror did she realise she had been fingering herself throughout. There, at her desk.

'Good God,' she said.

And then she glanced at her watch. 'Good *God!*'

There was less than an hour to the deadline, and she was way behind schedule.

Her hand still trembling, she grabbed for her pen and began scribbling furiously.

Chapter Five

*S*he had missed the deadline.

Had been, in the end, half an hour late in producing the final paste-ups for the printers. Only by pure chance had they still been able to take it (by a stroke of luck, their next job had been cancelled and the presses had been able to wait), and in the event no real harm had been done. But it was an aberration, she regretted, that had not escaped the notice of Bob Adams; grist to his rotten mill should he ever decide to pursue his lightly-veiled blackmailing threats. That the delay had, in essence, been entirely his fault, Suzie was unable to tell him, of course.

It was a worrying thought. But one she pushed to the back of her mind. That was last night. Tonight was another night. Friday night, and one she was going to enjoy.

It had been a predictably easy day, and she had spent much of it in the photographic studio down on the third floor, where they'd been taking glamour shots for their sister magazine, *Man International*. 'Shouldn't it more rightly be called a brother magazine?' Sally had once asked with innocent logic.

Suzie had sat at the back of the cinema-like studio and watched a parade of gorgeous, lissom models reveal all – or almost all – for the cameras. It was an interesting way of passing the time.

On getting home she had lain for an hour in a hot tub, doing slow justice to a large Martini while her mind had bathed in a swirling sea of sexual imagery. Occasionally drifting back to the beautiful black girl with the large, firm breasts she had watched pose in only a thin leather thong, a curled bullwhip in her hand, and who, among all the models, had particularly caught her eye – her skin had shone like polished ebony, and her dominant poses had given her the look of a hunting panther: feral, and powerfully sexual. But though the vision of the sexy model had kept coming back to her, stirring Sapphic longings, her thoughts had never been far from the evening's main event – the *man*-sex she would have after dinner.

She imagined lying on the hotel bed, Jason beside her; his muscles taut and rippling, his penis erect and inviting. Imagined taking him into her mouth, driving him wild with sensual movements of lips and tongue, building his need. Finally, when he could endure it no longer, he would ease her onto her back, slide atop her, would penetrate her and begin to ride her with even, masculine strokes, filling her with his maleness. She imagined whispering, 'God, that's good. Yes. *Yes*,' into his ear as he took her to a crest of desire. They would climax together in a hot frenzy of mutual need, and, after it, she saw them lying in each other's arms, warm and relaxed, satisfied – until she would feel him stir once more, hardening against her thigh.

She pre-lived it all. Again and again. God, it was going to be good.

In the warm cocoon of her bath, it was hard to resist the urgent demands of her burgeoning nipples, erecting as she soaped them, the gnawing expectancy of her clitoris as the bathwater swirled there. But resist them she did. Satisfying them would be Jason's job.

Later.

When she had towelled and talc'd herself dry, she dressed in a tasteful, though, she hoped, alluring outfit, and drove to the Moorview Hotel, where dinner had been booked, and where she had taken a room for the night. Now she was waiting at a small round table in a quiet corner of the hotel's bar, surprised that she was not feeling nervous.

She supposed it was because there was no doubt as to what was to happen, no anticipatory would they or wouldn't they at the end of the night. It was all a foregone conclusion: what was there to feel nervous about? And though this certainty detracted a little from the thrill of a more normal date, it was only a little. Not enough to bother her as the exciting thought recurred: she needed a man, and tonight she was going to be having one.

To pass the time she looked casually around the room, taking the scene in.

On barstools up at the bar a young couple canoodled. The girl was attractive, if in a sluttish sort of a way, and was probably still in her teens. She wore a low-cut tank top, and a skirt so short that an expanse of milky white thigh showed above the tops of her stockings. The lad with her could barely keep his hands off her, and his eager fingers kept plucking at her suspenders; as close to her crotch as decency and her firmly crossed legs would permit. An elderly gentleman sitting at a nearby table stared at them with goggle-eyes and a red face that had nothing to do with the sherry he was guzzling.

Other than they, and the red-jacketed, dour-faced waiter tending to his ice-bucket, the bar was empty. Suzie glanced at her watch: it was almost five to eight.

The girl on the barstool seemed suddenly to become aware of the old man's interest, and – quite deliberately Suzie was sure – uncrossed her legs and shifted position to give him a quick look up her skirt. The lad seemed not to notice, but the girl definitely smirked at the look of shock that registered on the elderly man's face. The

48

flash of brown pubic hair she had given him, and Suzie too, had shown she was wearing no knickers.

The words 'dirty bitch' crossed Suzie's mind, before she remembered: *neither was she*. Knickers, that night, had seemed an unnecessary encumbrance and she had deliberately not put any on. And she couldn't deny that – though she was hardly flaunting herself like that slut at the bar – the unaccustomed freedom afforded by her lack of underwear was, indeed, erotic. Just knowing she was naked beneath her skirt, the feel of the cool night air circulating freely about her sex a constant reminder of the fact, was a turn-on all by itself.

The girl at the bar re-crossed her legs, the show over, and the old man gulped sherry with a trembling hand. And Suzie glanced at her watch: two minutes to eight.

She parted her thighs very slightly, to encourage the air, and wriggled into her seat, her excitement growing; nervous tension at last beginning to affect her. If he was on time he would be there any minute.

And he was. At eight o'clock precisely, Jason arrived. Tall and slim, he was every bit as handsome as she re-membered him from his photo in Grace Cummings's album. He was dressed in grey slacks and wore a dark blazer over an open-necked skirt (smart but casual, Suzie had requested upon being asked), and he had a self-assured, confident air as his eyes scanned the bar – every inch (many of them, Suzie hoped) a man. And a tingling *frisson* teased her loins. A thrill that suddenly sharpened as his eyes found hers and he started towards her.

His slacks were tight, and, just as it had done on his photograph, an encouraging bulge showed in the front of them. For a moment, Suzie was aware of nothing else, mesmerized. It was like watching an immense phallus striding towards her, two enormous balls above which his torso was a huge penis that rose from between them.

He reached her table and she reluctantly forced her eyes away to look up, trying not to blush.

'Miss Carlton?' he said.

'Susan, yes. And you're Jason.' She stood to shake his proffered hand, and disguised her embarrassment well. 'Hello.'

'I see you don't have a drink. Can I order one for you?'

'Martini would be nice. Thank you.'

She took her seat again as he went up to the bar, spoke to the dour-faced waiter. When he returned he sat down beside her; offered her a cigarette from a slim silver case.

She declined. 'Not just now, thank you.'

'Do you mind if I do?'

'Not at all. Go ahead.'

Jason lit up a Stuyvesant and smoke plumed in a lazy curl.

'Nice place,' he observed, looking around.

'Nice enough,' said Suzie, studying his bulge.

The waiter arrived to set glasses down on the table; Suzie's Martini, a gin and tonic for Jason. The waiter hovered, but Jason made no move to pay.

'Oh, er, yes,' said Suzie as the penny dropped. 'Please, put them on my bill.'

The dinner was pleasant enough. Jason was polite and courteous, and a reasonably good conversationalist. Though not that Suzie was paying a great deal of attention: she kept seeing him naked, in her room later, lying beside her on the bed while she enjoyed – no, positively revelled in – the feel of his maleness. Three months was a long time. Though she was vaguely wondering, too, just how it was to come about: *What was the protocol? Was she meant to raise it with him? Or would he bring it up?* As the meal wore on, it began to rankle her slightly.

But as coffee was served, the question was answered . . .

'Will I be seeing you home tonight, Susan?' Jason asked.

'No, I have a room booked here in the hotel,' Suzie told him.

'I see. Then might I suggest we have our coffee sent up there, while we discuss any, ah, extras you might wish for?'

Extras? thought Suzie. *Oh yes, she wished for some extras, all right.* She felt herself suddenly flood with her juices, reminding her she was wearing no panties. She imagined a damp stain spreading on the inside of her skirt – hoped it wouldn't show through.

She smiled. 'I think that's an excellent idea, Jason.'

Jason called over the waitress and arranged it, being careful to say *our* room to make it appear they were staying in the hotel as a couple. *He's done this before*, thought Suzie, impressed by his practised discretion.

In her room, Jason sat down on the bed and wasted no time. 'It's thirty-five pounds for straight sex,' he announced promptly, and suddenly very businesslike.

'My goodness,' said Suzie, 'you don't beat around any bushes, do you?'

Jason smiled at her crookedly. 'Only the one that matters,' he said. 'But, no. Why? Would you rather I did?'

Suzie thought about it for a moment, then shrugged her shoulders. 'No, I suppose not.'

'If you want oral,' Jason went on as if there had been no interruption, 'it's an extra ten pounds. But I do guarantee you an orgasm that way. With intercourse – well, one has to be realistic – you can't always be sure: there's nothing wrong with my staying power but I can't last for ever. Anything else you might be into – fantasies, spanking, whatever's your thing – I do the lot, but it's extra again.'

God, this is awful, thought Suzie suddenly. Oh, not that they were discussing money *per se*; that, she was quite prepared for. But it was the way it was being discussed – it all seemed so . . . so clinical. Why couldn't they simply have sex, with whatever that naturally entailed? Go with whatever their bodies were telling them? This was like being asked to choose from a menu. And how did she know, beforehand, just what she'd want as her passions rose? She imagined herself having to direct him in mid-flow. Her: 'Would you lick me just there, please, Jason?' Jason: 'Ah, licking of the left labia wasn't included; let's see, that'll be an extra two pounds.' 'Fine.' 'OK, then.'

Ludicrous.

'Look,' she said finally, deciding on a better solution, 'here's fifty pounds.' She took some notes from her purse and laid them on the bedside table. 'Just make love to me, eh?'

Jason angled his head and stood up. 'Sure, Susan,' he said, pocketing the money. 'Whatever you say.'

He came to her and stood before her, the scent of his aftershave reaching her nostrils. She breathed it in, savouring it, the masculine smell tangible proof of a man's closeness to her at last. Then her breathing shallowed in anticipation as he reached out a hand to her; gently brushed the backs of his fingers across her nipples, bringing a tiny gasp to her lips. He found the buttons of her blouse and slowly undid them, and freeing her breasts he lowered his head to suck a nipple into his mouth.

And this, at least – at last – was a promising start.

She sensed her nipple immediately respond, erecting between suckling lips, and moaned a small moan of pleasure as he rasped the tender bud with his tongue.

Still nuzzling her swelling breast he slipped her jacket off her shoulders and let it drop to the floor. Leaving on her unbuttoned blouse, his hands travelled downwards; palms moving sensuously over her arms, then down her sides and over her hips, back again to her waist. Reaching under her blouse his hands slid behind her then, and down over her buttocks. And sliding beneath the tensing nates, he cupped them in strong palms, kneading them with gentle squeezes which made ripples of want flow through her.

But then she had a distracting thought. The skirt she had on was of a sheer material and he must have felt she was wearing no panties; yet if he noticed at all he didn't react. That surprised her – many men, she knew, found it a turn on for a woman to be without panties. It was one of the reasons she had chosen to leave them off. And it was then she realised that he was locked into a kind of routine; undressing her almost by rote. His mind else-where he was switched onto a sort of automatic pilot: going through motions; doing a job.

For a moment it fazed her. But for only a moment, and then she thought: *well, what the hell. So he was doing a job, so what? As long as he continued to do it as well as he was doing it so far, why should she care where his mind was?* And, reconciled, she pushed conscious thoughts from her mind, the better to enjoy the sensations that were beginning to course through her body.

Jason's hands had left her buttocks, now, and she felt them searching for the zip of her skirt. Felt the zipper descend, then her skirt sigh down to her ankles. Apart from suspender-belt, stockings and shoes, she now stood naked from the waist down, with only her opened blouse on top. It felt strangely yet intensely erotic to be all but naked while he was fully clothed; it made her feel somehow vulnerable, in a way that excited her.

Butterflies began to dance in the pit of her stomach, and seemed to weaken her knees as she stepped out of her skirt and kicked it aside.

And then Jason's mouth left her nipple with a small plop, and he led her gently towards the bed. Laid her upon it, where the shakiness of her legs didn't matter, and with a few deft movements as economical as those of a cat, he too was naked.

She looked him over, her sexual tension mounting.

He had a well-muscled body, she saw, with a light down of hair on his chest, which thickened and darkened as it ran down his belly to where his penis was already a thickening tool. She eyed it libidinously, and when he came to the bed and knelt beside her she im-mediately reached for it, keen to stir it fully awake; to feel its hotness throbbing into her palm, to curl her fin-gers around it and grip its pulsing shaft. It was a long time since she had last had that pleasure, save for in fantasy.

But as she reached out to him he caught her wrist, gently but firmly restraining; easing her hand away.

And from that point on, the promising start he had made was sadly just that: a promising start that petered out to very ordinary sex.

Chapter Six

'So, I can't say it was the best sex I've had in my life, Hils, no.'

It was the Monday following her encounter with Jason. Suzie and Hilary had met up for lunch, and while they had eaten Suzie had recounted the whole story.

Hilary had been listening with amusement throughout, but Suzie's summing up appeared now to have niggled her:

'Well what did you expect, love?' she said, suddenly curt. 'Surely not hearts and roses? Or your ideal bedmate, your perfect knight in shining armour dumping his white charger to transport you to Heaven? Be real, love.'

Suzie put down her coffee-cup. 'No, of course not. But he was a bit mechanical, Hils. Like he was running through a hoary old routine, you know? Two minutes down on the muff – not a minute and a half or a minute and three-quarters; two minutes precisely. Then time to screw: in, out, in, out – give her thirty strokes to the minute until she comes. Not quite as bad as that, but not far off.' She paused to light up a cigarette, then went on: 'I suppose ... I suppose I was expecting a bit of, oh, I don't know . . . passion. And certainly I was expecting a mutual romp.'

'How do you mean?'

'Well, it was all one way, wasn't it? Like I said, he didn't want me to touch him.'

Hilary wrinkled her nose. 'Gawd only knows why you'd want to. Yech!'

Suzie chuckled smoke. 'Don't knock what you've never tried, Hils. Until you've had a hard cock throbbing hot in your hand, felt one swelling against your tongue until it fills up your mouth like a great hot lolly, you've never lived. God, I feel horny just thinking about it.'

Hilary's nose stayed wrinkled. 'Like I said, yech!'

A waitress came to a nearby table gathering plates, and Suzie lowered her voice. 'Anyway, no, he obviously didn't want me to touch him. And I think if I'd tried to go down on him he'd have thrown an absolute wobbly.'

Hilary shrugged. 'He's a professional, love; I guess he was just being careful. I mean, if he lets a client get him over-excited, well . . . Premature ejaculation earns him the paper hat, right? Don't suppose it'd get him many a repeat booking.'

Suzie giggled. 'I suppose not.' She stared off into space for a moment, remembering. Then came back. 'And the rest of it, it was almost as if, well, as if I wasn't there – or certainly I could've been anyone – while he ran through his act. A sort of "Satisfy The Anonymous Woman" routine. And over-excited he wasn't. You know, I don't even think he came. Well, when he took off the condom he stuck it into his jacket pocket. Didn't even bother to knot it, and they usually do, don't they?'

'No good asking me, love.' Hilary gave a sudden involuntary shudder. 'Uggh! Horrid things.'

'What? Condoms?'

'Men.'

Suzie laughed. 'Anyway, you're right, I suppose it was better than if he'd come too soon – he gave me a good enough orgasm, I'd have to say that for him. It was just . . . oh, I don't know. Grace Cummings's phrase probably sums it up best – "meat on the hoof". That's exactly what it was like. He turned up, did the business, and went.'

'So at least he went if he didn't come,' Hilary chuckled, liking that. She sipped coffee, and said: 'So, you won't be using the agency again, then?'

Suzie suddenly grinned broadly and winked. 'Now I didn't say that, now did I? Even having a robot was better than having no man at all. No, as ever, your advice was sound, Hils. I can put up with meat on the hoof.' She glanced at her watch. 'Crikey, is that the time? Listen, I'd better run.'

She swallowed the last of her coffee, stubbed out her cigarette and stood up.

'D'you fancy a movie tonight, Hils? We've just done a review on that new Kevin Costner film; it sounds terrific.'

Hilary shook her cropped head. 'No, can't love, I'm afraid. I've had my eye on this little blonde waif down at the gym –'

'You? At a gym?' Suzie's eyebrows rose in surprise. 'Since when did you start going to gyms?'

'Ever since I discovered all those sweaty near-naked bodies in those tight, skimpy leotards. Jesus, they're horny. And the showers are a voyeur's paradise!'

Suzie laughed. 'You are incorrigible, Hils, do you know that?'

'Yeah,' said Hilary. 'At least, I'll take your word for it. Anyway, like I was saying, there's this little blonde piece who goes in there, who I've had my eye on for ages. Well, I've finally persuaded her to come out with me for a drink tonight, and I think I've got every chance of getting into her knickers.'

'You devil,' laughed Suzie, slowly shaking her head. 'But good luck to you anyway. And I'll see you when I see you, eh?'

An elderly woman sitting at a nearby table must have heard Hilary's remark and let her see her look of disgust. Hilary gave her a middle-finger salute but otherwise ignored her. Said: 'Yeah, take care, love,' to Suzie's back as she left.

Back in her office, Suzie toyed with the slush-pile stacked high on her desk: short stories, articles, other bits and pieces that couldn't accurately be described as either. Sally had already weeded out the worst of the rubbish (actually, a lot of it not so much rubbish as material simply unsuited to *Woman Now*'s style). But still, if she found one usable piece in the pile she would consider herself lucky.

She was supposed to be working her way through it, but once again she was finding it difficult to concentrate; she had other things on her mind. (A couple of issues back, the magazine had featured a survey which claimed that the average man thinks about sex two hundred times in a day. There were no statistics for women, but Suzie would have certainly topped that.) Just then, she was thinking about Jason, about the Benson Agency in general and about all the other hunks she had seen pictured in Grace Cummings's album.

Finally, she reached for the phone. Punched out the number and listened to the ringing tone purr in her ear. At last there was a click, and a voice said: 'The Benson Agency. Good afternoon.'

'Good afternoon,' said Suzie. 'May I speak to Grace Cummings please.'

'Certainly. If you'd like to hold for a moment.'

There was a second or two of dead static, then a cut-crystal voice came to the line. 'Grace Cummings,' it said.

'Grace. It's Susan Carlton here.'

'Miss Carlton! How nice. What can I do for you?'

'You can send me some meat on the hoof,' said Suzie, grinning.

Grace Cummings chuckled. 'But of course. And when is this for?'

'Friday night again.'

'Fine, no problem. And will it be Jason again?'

58

'Er, no. Not Jason.'

'Oh?' The agency boss sounded concerned. 'I do hope he wasn't a disappointment to you, dear?'

'No, it's really not that, Grace. He was . . . satisfactory. No, I'd just like it to be someone different, that's all.'

'Fresh meat, eh, love?' said the other Grace Cummings.

Suzie laughed. 'Yes, something like that. Listen, I'll tell you what . . .' She suddenly recalled Stephen, the man on the first page of the album, and had an idea. Now she knew what the score was – knew not to expect anything more than non-emotional, if physically satisfying sex – then, for that, one man's body would do just as well as the next's. She decided she would work her way through the book. And she might as well start at the beginning. 'Is Stephen free Friday?'

'One moment, I'll see . . . Yes, he is.'

'Then he'll be fine. Would you have him meet me at the Moorview?'

'But of course, Miss Carlton. Is it to be dinner again?'

'I, er, think we'll dispense with the dinner, Grace.'

Grace chuckled. 'I see.'

Suzie put down the phone and pictured Stephen in her mind's eye. Not so much his face, more the body she hadn't yet seen. The body that would supply her with the maleness she needed, even if the sex wouldn't necessarily be great.

The mental image made her suddenly horny, and she wondered if there was a glamour session going on in the studio. She was getting nothing done in her office anyway; she might just as well bunk off for a while. And she quite fancied ogling some sexy, half-naked bodies. She decided to go down and see, making a mental note that *Woman Now* should start up a beefcake page.

She was in luck. Just as she arrived at the third floor studio, a blonde nymph, who couldn't have been more than eighteen, was just stripping off. She had small breasts with tiny pink nipples, slim, boyish hips, and pubic hair the colour of Chablis. She was lovely.

When she was naked, Gerry, the Irish photographer, tossed her a bottle of baby oil and told her to oil herself up. The back-drop was made up to resemble a desert island, and Gerry explained in his soft Dublin accent that she was to look like a castaway, hot and steamy: the oil would do the job grand, so it would.

The girl did as instructed, smothering herself in the oil, then sprawled on a hammock suspended between palm trees; the only concession to her modesty a strip of chiffon that floated on air from a fan, which barely kept her crotch covered – even that, not always.

Flashes began to pop, bouncing sudden volleys of brilliant light from huge white umbrellas, and Suzie took her favourite seat at the back of the studio to watch. Apart from the set-lighting, the studio was quite dark, and she risked putting a hand to herself; moving aside the leg of her panties to reach the slippery heat of her sex. She began to finger herself dreamily while the girl was directed from one sexy pose to the next.

But she had watched the session for less than five minutes when the girl was suddenly gone. Instead it was her, Suzie, there on the set. Naked and oiled, and with not even the chiffon scarf to afford her small comfort. She can feel the heat of the lamps on her skin, the warm air from the fan playing over her body and gently teasing her hair. She can hear the click of the camera, the brief whirr of its motor as it winds itself on, the pop of the flashlights. And she is aware – oh, so aware – of Gerry's male eyes upon her as he brings the lens into focus.

And what's that he's saying? His soft Irish brogue drifts to her, as if carried on the breeze from the fan.

'. . . Magazine's doing some real naughty stuff this month, Suzie, so we've got quite a session to do. But we'll do the tit shots first, so we will, and be after getting them out of the way before we get to the others. Come on now, let's see those nipples erect.'

Slowly, conscious of Gerry's eyes, she raises her hands to her oiled breasts. She has watched models spray hairspray onto their nipples to persuade them to erect for the camera. But she has no need of such tricks. The moment her palms slide over them they grow hard and demanding. She takes the sensitive buds between finger and thumb, gently squeezing.

'That's my sexy wee moth,' says Gerry. 'Just like that, so. Yes, just like that.'

And the camera clicks and whirrs, clicks and whirrs.

It goes on for what seems a very long time; her breasts swelling with growing arousal until they feel heavy and full, her nipples tender as she continues to pinch them. An aching need tugs ever more urgently at the pit of her stomach as Gerry clicks on. But then he stops and looks up, peers at her over the top of his camera.

'Right, Suzie, time for the open-crotch shots.'

What? She feels her stomach instantly lurch. *Open crotch shots?* Oh, no. Does she have to? Does she really have to spread her legs for the camera?

Yes.

Oh, but she couldn't. She can't. Not that. Not that of all things. The very thought . . .

But Gerry is adamant.

'Sit right on the edge of the hammock, Suzie,' he tells her. 'That's right, directly facing the camera. Then spread your legs wide for me.'

There is no point in arguing; he is insistent, she must do as he says.

Slowly, very slowly, she edges forward, until just her buttocks are touching the seat. Her knees are pressed firmly together, and she is trembling at the prospect of having to part them. But knows that she must.

Inch by inch she lets them come open, her breathing ragged, her pulse thudding, her heart pounding as her thighs slowly part. She stops. Hoping – praying – that it's enough.

It isn't!

'All the way apart now, Suzie,' she hears Gerry say. 'As wide as you possibly can.'

God, the embarrassment.

She takes a deep breath, hesitates, then in one rapid movement she spreads her legs wide, wide, wide; so wide that her thighs ache. So wide that the indentations either side of her pubic mound are deep pits, which seem to thrust her sex forward in wanton abandon. So wide that she knows nothing – nothing – is kept secret from Gerry's eyes; from the eye of the clicking camera.

She squeezes her own eyes tightly shut to blot out the shame of it. But it doesn't work: the warm air from the fan is playing directly onto her wide-open sex, caressing her and heightening her consciousness agonisingly of all the camera can see. Knows that her pussy is pouting open, lips glistening in the glaring light, and that Gerry is looking at her *there*. That the lens is focusing in on her as the camera clicks, and that soon the whole world will be seeing her *there*.

God, the embarrassment of it.

That dizzying, exquisite, desperately erotic embarrassment, that even now is driving her wild.

Her crotch aflame with urgent desire, she finally can stand it no longer. No longer caring of spectacle, unheeding of dignity, she throws a hand to her splayed sex and begins rubbing herself in a frenzy of desperate need.

'Yes, Suzie,' she hears Gerry say; his voice coming to her from a long way away, yet somehow achingly close. 'Go for it. Finish yourself off. Let me capture your climax on film. That moment when you lose control and your body racks in the throes of it. That moment when your pussy clenches and unclenches in wanton, shameless abandon. Let me capture it all.'

She feels the lens bore into her, penetrate her, ravish her. But she doesn't stop and she doesn't care, driven on by the one compelling need that fills her world entirely: the desperate need to come.

Her swollen breasts jiggling, her belly shaking, her hand continues to fly at her crotch as her tension mounts, orgasm beginning to gather.

And then, with a long, low guttural moan that comes from somewhere deep in her being, expelled from her throat in a rush of air by abdominal muscles that suddenly spasm in climax, she is coming. Again and again and again. In a multiple orgasm that goes on and on.

The orgasm brought Suzie back with a start, and she stared at the set in a sudden panic. *Had she made all that noise in reality, or just in her fantasy?* Gerry was still directing, and the girl was still striking poses. Neither was looking her way, with shock or knowing grins on their faces. They gave no indication they even knew she was there. She let out relief on a juddering breath and withdrew her sopping fingers; adjusted her panties and smoothed her skirt.

And pushing herself up onto still-trembling legs, she headed back to her office.

There, she found a memo awaiting her. She picked it up. It read: Told Clive Taunton that the missed deadline last week couldn't be helped; late material held up in traffic.

It was signed B.A. – Bob Adams.

There was a P.S. How about dinner this evening?

Chapter Seven

*F*riday evening came at last.

For Suzie, it had seemed an almost interminable wait, but finally it had come and she was sitting in the bar at the Moorview Hotel, freshly bathed and erotically charged, awaiting the arrival of Stephen. Notwithstanding the warm glow of anticipatory excitement that teased her loins, she felt relaxed, sipping Martini and taking occasional puffs from a More. She only regretted that there wasn't the floor show of the previous week to entertain her while she waited. The same po-faced barman polished glasses behind his bar, but otherwise the place was empty.

At precisely eight o'clock, Stephen arrived. The Benson Agency escorts were nothing if not punctual, she thought. Greeting Suzie with a polite smile, he crossed to her table and introduced himself; offered to order them drinks before sitting down.

Suzie declined. 'No, thank you. I'm fine. By all means have a drink yourself if you need one, but to be frank I'd just as soon we go on up to my room.' *There were several things she had decided to do differently this time around.*

Stephen, she could tell, was taken slightly aback by her forwardness. But he quickly recovered to say with a smile: 'Certainly, Susan, whatever you say.' He inclined his head at her half-full glass. 'Would you like me to take up your drink?'

Suzie picked up the glass and drained it in one. Set it back down on the table. 'That won't be necessary,' she said. She stood up and shouldered her bag. 'Shall we go?'

She led the way, and Stephen made polite small-talk as they went; in the lift, along the corridor, up to the door of her room. But once inside it was straight down to business:

'Well,' he said with a small shrug of his big shoulders, 'it's thirty-five pounds for straight sex. If you want –'

'Excuse me,' Suzie cut in. She regarded him squarely, her eyes not leaving his as she sat down on a chair beside the obligatory hotel writing desk; crossed one leg demurely over the other. 'You can save the monologue, Stephen. Or should I say, the catalogue. Let me tell you what I want. Then you can give me a price, and if I agree it we'll have a deal, OK?'

This clearly had Stephen fazed; taken aback for a second time. He was evidently a man unused to having the initiative taken away, and this time he didn't regain his composure quite so quickly.

'Er . . . er, yes,' he stammered. 'Er, yes, if you like.'

'I do like,' Suzie told him, faintly amused that she had managed to throw him. He was, after all, a professional at this, and she was just a beginner. A fast-learning beginner . . . 'So, first of all, I want a full hour of your time. That is not forty-five minutes, or even *fifty*-five minutes, but a full hour. Understood?' She inclined her head at him and waited for his nod before going on. 'I want you to strip first, and then to undress me. And then I want oral. Plenty of oral. But I also want to fuck.'

Stephen's face had slowly changed from registering mild shock and was now split in a wry, almost admiring grin. 'Well, you're certainly a lady who knows what she wants,' he said.

'Oh, yes. I know what I want all right.'

As the evening had approached, she had spent every spare moment thinking about just what she wanted. It might have been clinical, mapping it out as she had. But the nature of the animal made it clinical anyway – she had learned that – and at least this way she could turn that to her advantage and be fairly assured of a session she would enjoy. Besides, it had been a heck of a turn-on doing the mapping.

'And,' she added, 'I haven't finished yet.'

'Oh?'

'No. I also want to touch you.'

'Ah.'

'Is there a problem?'

'Well, it's just that we don't usually, er . . . that's not usually part of the, er, scene.'

Suzie's look demanded an explanation.

'Well, you have to understand,' he began, looking slightly embarrassed, 'some women – er, ladies – can get a bit carried away. Some of them don't read the signs very well, I suppose, and, er, well, the guy has, er, an accident shall we say. And then the lady gets miffed when he can't perform. Starts shouting for her money back, like that. It's really not good for business.'

So, once again, Hilary had got it spot on. Didn't she always?

'Well you needn't worry about me, Stephen,' said Suzie. 'I'm not exactly inexperienced, and I certainly know what the signs are; there'll be no accidents, I can assure you.'

Stephen was still looking doubtful. 'W-e-e-e-ll, I don't know . . .'

'Well that's the deal,' Suzie said crisply. 'Now do I get a price or not?'

There was a pause while Stephen considered. Then: 'How about seventy-five?'

'Fine.' It was more than she had anticipated, but she wasn't about to haggle. *What the hell, it was only money.* She reached for her purse and took out three notes, holding them out to him.

Stephen came to her and took the money, folded it into his jacket pocket.

He crouched down in front of her, putting a hand on her crossed-over knee. 'I suppose you'd like me to start earning it right away?' he said, his voice deep and gravelly.

Without waiting for Suzie's reply his hand slid upwards, under her skirt, where it reached bare thigh before she stopped him.

'Ah-ah,' she said. 'You undress first, remember?'

'Ah, yes. Of course.'

He stood up again, backing away and shedding his jacket.

She enjoyed watching him strip. There was a certain grace in the way he moved that excited her, as his fingers plucked at shirt buttons to reveal a hairy rug of a chest. She wasn't especially into hairy men as a rule, but on him it seemed sort of right – added to his masculine charm – and she imagined running her fingers through it as she watched him continue. He discarded the shirt and tugged at the belt of his trousers; and had the elegance to remove his shoes and socks before letting his pants drop and kicking them from him. Something stirred inside his shorts, and an expectant smile grew on her lips.

And when he slipped off the final garment and stood before her as God had made him, she sat entranced. His body was beautiful; lean and hard, with a broad chest and narrow hips. And his genitals were a sculpture Michelangelo might have been proud of. (Except he would never have fashioned a cock already beginning to erect, as was Stephen's.)

Stephen was not at all self-concious, and stood for her to admire him. And it might have excited her more if she didn't feel suddenly deprived; robbed of that exquisite sense of vulnerability she had experienced the previous week with Jason, when it was she who'd been naked while he was still fully clothed. She made a mental note for the following week, and let the thought go away. After all, this wasn't bad compensation.

Her eyes still riveted on Stephen's stirring member, she swallowed in a dry throat. 'Come closer,' she whispered, her voice a rasp of shortened breath.

Stephen stepped in closer and she reached out a hand to him, tickled under his balls for a moment then let her fingers come up to close on the thickening shaft of his cock. He was about half-way erect, she judged, and she was eager to see him fully aroused. She gave the shaft a gentle squeeze and it thickened further into her palm, encouragingly. He was hard enough now for her to stroke him in earnest, and she drew back his foreskin; rolled it back and forth in a gentle, teasing rhythm. She watched him respond in mute fascination until he was fully erect in her hand.

And wanted more.

Using her grip on him she drew him closer, parting her lips. She kissed the now bulbous and purpling head, running her tongue around it and making it glisten. It tasted faintly of lemons and soap. But mainly it tasted of man. Sparks of need tremored her thighs, and she continued to lick; worried the tiny opening at the weapon's tip with little jabs of her tongue; laved around and around the swollen knob. Stephen gave a small gasp of delight when at last she took him fully into her outh. And she, too, let out a soft, muffled moan – *it had been so long since she had last tasted man*.

Stephen's erection was strong, was a hot throb of promising flesh that flooded her loins with desire as she ran her lips up and down him, sucking greedily, and he seemed to swell ever further against her ministering tongue. She nibbled with careful teeth before letting him slip from her mouth, eager to see it.

The bulbous head now shone, and the shaft strained as she glided her hand along it, its passage oiled by warm saliva, sliding lubriciously over tightly-stretched skin. Stephen's moans became a constant hum as she wanked him. She continued for a while, revelling in the feel of him. But then his shaft began to pulse, and a glistening dewdrop grew from the moist slit at its tip.

She knew that, for now, it was time to stop. She released him and watched the swollen organ twitch and buck of its own volition, as if straining in vain to come.

A surge of erotic energy spread out from her loins, and she pushed herself up onto legs that were rubbery. Took Stephen's hands in hers and placed them onto her breasts.

'My turn,' she breathed, raggedly.

Suzie lay on the hotel bed, reflecting on an exciting hour.

As a lover, Stephen had not been at all bad – on a scale of one to ten, certainly a six or a seven. It perhaps wasn't great sex, still, but he'd definitely been better than Jason who had barely rated a four.

When he had stripped her (which he'd done slowly and erotically, taking his time) he had laid her on the bed, where he had knelt beside her and driven her wild with gentle, teasing caresses; stroking her breasts, her nipples, then down her belly to her waiting bush. But still he hadn't hurried. Easing her thighs apart he had stroked along them, his touch light and sensuous, barely brushing her skin as he'd teased either side of her eagerly proffered mound. And when his fingers finally found that part of her that yearned for his touch most of all, it was to find her quivering with need. The moment his fingers entered her, she came.

It was to be her first climax of many. He had been as competent with his mouth as he was with his hands, and his oral caresses had taken her time and again to that dizzying pinnacle from which climax is the only way down.

And, in between orgasms, she had enjoyed herself with him, using her own fingers and mouth to keep him fully aroused. Hard and yearning; enticing. Though always careful not to *over*-excite – she wanted no little accidents spoiling her fun. Revelling in the feel and the taste and the smell of him.

He had been true to his word, too, and had given her the full hour she had paid for. (Though not a minute longer.) They had finally screwed – she had been realistic enough not to have demanded it sooner, knowing it might easily have brought the session to a premature end. Not willing to risk it despite her longing for that wonderful hardness inside her. But as the hour had approached he had mounted her. Had driven his tool deep into her and began to ride her with strong, thrusting strokes that reached high into her body and touched parts of her that hadn't been touched for a very long time. And, on the dot of the hour, they had exploded in climax together; she uttering guttural obscenities into his ear, he shuddering hugely as he finally let himself come. No doubt glad, she supposed, to be relieved at last. Certainly, he had tied a knot in the condom.

Although she had paid for Stephen's agency time until one o'clock in the morning, she had let him go, then, as soon as he'd dressed. Keen to re-live it in peaceful solitude.

And yes, on the whole, it hadn't been bad. Not bad at all!

She ran her hands softly over her body; down over her breasts with their still-erect nipples, down her sides and over her hips, across her belly, still taut from rhythmic muscular contractions. Finally, to her crutch, still warm and wet and tempting. *Yes*, she thought, *definitely a seven out of ten*.

She resisted the urge to play with herself – after all, enough was enough – and instead stretched herself languidly. Through the hotel window she watched the silvery moon peek out at her from behind a dark cloud, wink at her as if to say, 'Hurrah for meat on the hoof!' and disappear from whence it had come.

And then she put all thoughts of Stephen out of her mind, and turned her attention to next Friday's man: now, how would she play it with him?

And wondering that, she fell into a deep and contented sleep.

Chapter Eight

The following Friday was a bitch of a day.

It was a series of little things but they all added up. She had snagged her tights on her way in to work, and had had to stop off to buy a new pair only to discover she had forgotten her purse. Having to return home for it had made her late, and when she did arrive it was to find Clive Taunton had been on the phone for her. Sod's law: the one day she was late to the office, there was a pointed, 'Please call me back, when you get in,' left on her answering machine. The pimply Terry had been sniffing around Sally in the outer office and had greeted her with a nerve-grating 'Hiya, Sooz,' when she'd looked out to ask Sally to call Taunton back. It was all adding up to a lousy start to the day.

And it hadn't improved. The slush-pile had comprised of even more rubbish than usual, it seemed, and had failed, yet again, to produce the short story she had been hoping it would; that she still had to find for the current issue. The month was already half through and they still didn't have a Romantic Interlude, one of the magazine's most popular features. She could always rake one up from the files, she supposed. But anything really worth running they'd have already used, and she hated the thought of going with second-rate material. But, unless something turned up, what could she do? Pressure, pressure, pressure.

And to cap it all Bob Adams had been in pestering her, wanting her to go out to dinner with him the following evening. He had left in a foul huff when she'd turned him down with shorter shrift than she'd meant. She could only hope she wouldn't come to regret it.

Altogether a stinker of a day. And on another day it might all have combined to depress her. But not today. Today was Friday ... and tonight she was seeing Paul.

Paul was the next on Grace Cummings's list, and, with him, she had decided on something excitingly different; something it had been ringing her sexual bells to have been thinking about all week.

The po-faced waiter regarded her with curious eyes when she ordered a Martini and went to sit at her table. For a moment, she thought he might smile. Or at least smirk at her knowingly. For it was obvious he knew what her game was: that at eight o'clock precisely a man would arrive, a different man, and she would take him up to her room. But he neither smiled nor smirked, and remained dour as he brought her drink to the table. She tried not to look at him when she signed the chit, embarrassed despite his sullen discretion.

In the event, Paul was five minutes late. Grace Cummings's description of him was accurate: he wasn't as handsome, or as tall as the others had been. Not by a lot, but such that she noticed. And not that she cared – what lurked behind the zip of his pants was all that really mattered. And according to Grace, that was plenty.

Her glass was already empty, so she pushed to her feet deciding to collect him and take him straight to her room. He could do without a drink: he owed her five minutes already.

Seeing Po-face's knowing look, she decided attack was preferable to nothing when she had no defence, and smiled at him sweetly – a 'fuck you' sort of smile – as she took Paul by the arm and led him out of the bar.

Up in the room, Paul turned to face her.

'I spoke to Steve,' he said. 'He clued me in; says you know the ropes.'

Word was evidently getting around.

Suzie smiled her sweet smile. 'Then you'll also know that I want a full hour. And that touching is something we do to each other.'

Paul nodded, a shock of mousey-brown hair falling over his eyes. He pushed it back. 'The same seventy-five quid?'

Suzie agreed. 'The same. But a slightly different scenario.'

'Oh?'

'Yes. I want you to undress me first. Make love to me for a while, while you're still fully clothed. Then you get undressed' – she had spent a delicious hour in a hot bath mapping out the details, trying hard not to play with herself – 'and we caress each other. I want oral. And I want orgasms – lots of them. Then later I want you to fuck me. But when you do, you're not to come.'

'Oh?' Paul looked suddenly wary.

'No. As you're orgasm mounts, I want you to stop, pull out. Take off the condom . . .' She watched a look of mild horror cross Paul's face, and he looked as if he were about to make his excuses and leave. Until she finished softly: 'I want you to come in my mouth.'

A sudden gleam shone in his eyes, then, horror gone, and he looked like a cat who's just found a bucket of cream. 'Really?'

By the agency's standards, Paul was unsophisticated; even a little uncouth. In the way he was dressed, in the way his lank hair fell over his brow in an unkempt sprawl. But he had bright, mischievous eyes, and cheeky dimples that deepened when he smiled as he just had. Well, more a salacious grin than a smile perhaps, but still. And anyway, what was wrong with a bit of rough

73

now and then? Especially – ideally – for the scene she envisaged.

'Really,' she said.

She took the money from her purse and laid it on the bedside table.

'Ready when you are.'

The hour sped by.

Paul's body was pleasing enough, as Grace Cummings had promised, and he certainly knew how to use it. What he might have lacked in finesse he more than made up for with raw, animal passion; a basic instinct for carnal pleasuring. And just as she'd ordered he had brought her to several orgasms, each more thrilling than the last as her sexual tension had mounted with thoughts of the finale to come.

And now they were screwing.

She watched his eyes; they were molten pools of lust. He was lying atop her and her hand was down between the two of them, encouraging his balls with gentle squeezes as he thrust into her, one moment filling her entirely, the next withdrawing until, it seemed, he was about to spring free. Long, long strokes.

And his rutting was growing perceptibly more urgent.

'Don't . . . forget,' she warned, her voice husky. Close to climax herself.

A crooked grin appeared on Paul's sex-ridden face. 'Are you kidding?' he muttered throatily.

He continued to thrust.

'And . . . it'll . . . be . . . soon,' he promised, his words grunted and timed to his stroke.

His eyes half closed and began to glaze.

And Suzie could wait no longer. 'Now,' she told him in an urgent whisper. 'Now!'

In the same fluid movement he slipped himself from her and lost the condom. Flowed up the bed until he was kneeling astride Suzie's chest. He slid a hand beneath her neck and lifted her head, and with the other he guided his swollen organ between her parted lips.

74

He began to thrust with controlled jerks of his hips, using her mouth as he would have used a vagina, and Suzie sucked and watched his eyes for the moment of no return. Thrilling at the lust she saw in them and aching in expectancy of the saline gift she was about to receive. *It had been so long.*

And then his body went suddenly rigid. His hand tightened its grip in her hair. His back arched, driving him deeply into her mouth and his eyes lost focus, smouldering pits of agony–ecstasy. A long, guttural groan vibrated his belly, and then he was coming, pumping his hot seed into the back of her throat; jet after jet of it as he jerked his hips in erratic spasms, fucking her mouth with urgent need.

Suzie took all that he gave her, swallowing greedily, and, when he had finished, when there was no more to suck from him, she finally let him slip from her mouth; continued to gently lick, savouring his taste, until he grew soft against her industrious tongue. The throes of her own orgasm gradually subsiding.

Re-lived it later, still tasting his come. And the day had finished a great deal better than the way it had started.

Chapter Nine

As the weeks went by, Suzie's Friday night trysts became an integral part of her life. Indeed, she couldn't imagine living without them: with every spare moment – many moments that weren't, or at least shouldn't have been so spare – she thought about them, re-living the last or planning the next in advance.

And, with those Friday nights, mostly gone were her sexual frustrations of recent months. Or, indeed, years – Geoff had never been the greatest of lovers, and, at their best, she had often felt there was something lacking in the sex between them. Frustration wasn't entirely gone, but it was certainly considerably eased, and she felt more content than she had in an age.

With her career in top gear, her personal life settled, and her sex-life in better shape than it had been in since the heady days of university, Suzie was doing all right. Though she would have been doing a lot better if it weren't for Bob Adams.

The man continued to pester her: to pursue her with relentless persistence, to harass her with his constant sexual innuendo – or with suggestions not so oblique.

Yet, ever mindful of his influence with the magazine's

owners, she continued to refuse his unwanted attentions as tactfully as her patience allowed. Bob Adams was better a friend than an enemy; the last thing she needed was him seeking revenge on her, baying for her blood with the Tauntons. It would be a hassle she could well do without. But, at the same time, she could well do without Bob Adams.

Or any office affair: her meat on the hoof did her fine . . .

Alan had been lovely, John a hunk. Peter had pleased her better than most, with his sensual grace and granite root. There had been handsome Stephen and rough-diamond Paul, both exciting in their different ways. And then there was James, dear exciting James, who had definitely merited an eight out of ten.

And Bob Adams could go to hell.

She never saw the same man twice – not even James – and her weekly phone calls to the Benson Agency had come to follow a familiar pattern: 'Grace, meat on the hoof for Friday, eh?' she would say.

'The next on the list, Miss Carlton?'

'Please.'

The other Grace Cummings: 'Got a dick like a brick, love.'

There was just one, slight something that stopped the whole arrangement a fraction short of perfection. A certain something that Suzie had not quite been able to identify, to quite put her finger on. When it had nagged at her for long enough, she finally discussed it with Hilary.

And Hilary knew right away what it was: 'It's because you've put yourself in the driving seat, love.'

'I don't follow.' Suzie puzzled at Hilary's remark. Surprised, yet not surprised, that she could have so easily come up with the answer. Apparently, anyway. 'How do you mean?'

They were in Suzie's flat sharing a bottle of wine, and whatever advice Hilary could give her would be

77

welcome advice indeed. But it had to be advice that
made some sense. *In the driving seat?* What did that
mean?

Hilary shrugged her shoulders. 'Well, the way you
work it, you have these guys dancing to your tune; practically following your orders, right?'

'Well yes,' Suzie agreed. 'I suppose that's just what
they're doing. I'm paying for the privilege, so why not?'

'Ah, but don't you see? You calling the shots like that
sits a dominant hat on your head.'

'So?'

'Well, you are essentially submissive.'

'Sub – *I am not!*' Suzie protested indignantly, shocked
at the very suggestion. 'Me? You must be joking. Listen,
I have a staff of thirty at work – and mostly men, at that
– and to run a ship as tight as I do with that many
people takes strong, dominant leadership. And I'm
pretty damned good at it too, though I say so myself.
Submissive, indeed.'

Hilary was unimpressed. 'Ah, but that's in the office,
love. In real life. But what we're talking about here is
sex, and sex isn't about real life; sex is all about fantasy.'

'Yes, OK, I'd accept that. But even in my fantasies, I
tend, if anything, to dominante. Christ, especially this
past few months ...' She told Hilary about her slave-
market fantasy and how it had turned her on to humiliate the Viking. And about having Bob Adams service
her under her desk while she ignored him and carried
on working. Finishing with: 'Does that sound submissive to you?'

'But you are, love,' Hilary persisted, still unmoved.
'Look, you're dominant in real life because you have to
be, to do your job. But in fantasy you can be what you
want. I read this thing once in a porn magazine –'

Suzie clicked her tongue against the roof of her
mouth. Yes, it would have been a porn magazine,
wouldn't it? It was about the extent of Hilary's reading.

Hilary narrowed her eyes. 'Well, do you want to hear
about it or not?'

78

'Go on,' said Suzie long-sufferingly. Awaiting what gem of wisdom might have been gleaned from such an authoritative source.

'Well, it was about men who visit dominant hookers; the Miss Whiplash types, you know? Turns out the vast majority of these guys have high-powered professional jobs. See, this psychologist reckoned it's because they have to be dominant in their normal lives, make all the decisions and so on, that when it comes to sex, and a fantasy world in which they've got nothing to prove, it comes as a welcome relief – an escape if you like – to be submissive in bed. Let someone else make the decisions for a change, see?

'And let's face it, love, that fits you to a T, doesn't it? Look how you love it when I get bossy in bed; tell you to do things. Especially things you pretend not to like.'

Suzie blushed; they had never discussed it in so many words, but yes, it was true.

'Yes, all right,' she conceded, taking a long swig of Chablis to give herself a moment to think. Went on at last: 'But I mean, that's nothing, is it? Look, you're right about having someone else make the decisions. I'll give you that; it is a welcome change. And I suppose that's why I like it, yes. But that doesn't make me submissive, for God's sake.'

'No?'

'No,' Suzie said firmly. She was feeling oddly discomfitted. She had always considered dominance, or assertiveness at least, a virtue. Not to mention one of her strengths. To be suddenly accused of being submissive had taken her somewhat aback.

'Look, Suzie,' Hilary said with patience, 'it's really OK, you know. So you have to be dominant at work, fine. But if you want to be submissive in fantasy – in sex – it's all right; it's allowed. In fantasy, anything is.'

'But I don't want,' Suzie inveighed, aggressively grabbing for the bottle of wine; slugging both their glasses full to the brim as if to prove her assertiveness. 'Why would I want to be submissive?'

'For one thing, because of your sexual hang-ups.'

Suzie glared. 'OK, so I've got a few hang-ups; I've never denied it, have I? You try being taught by nuns until the age of eleven. Taught that sex is for procreation only, and that for anything else it's a mortal sin. See if you don't end up with a hang-up or three.'

'Hey, I wasn't accusing, love. Just stating a fact, that was all.'

'Well.' Suzie was sullen for a moment. Then she suddenly grinned, her eyes flashing like a naughty schoolgirl; defiant. 'Doesn't stop me doing things though, does it?'

Hilary threw her a sidelong look.

'Well, all right,' she admitted. 'Sometimes, maybe.'

'Yes, and it always makes you feel guilty, right? And that's just my point.'

'*What's* your point?' Suzie snapped, suddenly impatient. 'Stop talking, will you, and say something.'

'Look, you enjoying being told what to do – it isn't just that it's a change from the everyday norm; that it's someone else who's making the decisions. It's that they then have the responsibility for those decisions.'

'The res – Look, Hils, you're really not making much sense.'

'I'm making perfect sense if you'll listen.' Hilary borrowed a drag of Suzie's cigarette, plumed smoke and said: 'See, when you're told what to do, you can do anything, no matter how kinky it is or whatever, and not feel guilty about it. What you're saying is: "Ain't my fault I'm doing this; this person is making me do it." Where it's not your fault there can be no guilt.'

Something rang true in the depths of Suzie's psyche. No culpability, no guilt? Yes, she could see that. But she still wasn't ready to accept the rest of it. 'But that still doesn't make me submissive, Hils. Not really.'

Hilary chuckled. 'Accept it, love. Look, I reckon there's a bit of the sadist or a bit of the masochist in us all. You just happen to be –'

'A masochist!' Suzie squawked. 'You're saying I'm a masochist now?'

'Masochism. Sexual submissiveness. Call it what you will . . .' Hilary shrugged her shoulders. 'Same diff.'

Suzie snorted derisively. 'Well now I know you've fallen out of your tree. God, Hils, I hate the thought of pain. If any man' – she glared at Hilary in warning – 'or woman came anywhere near me with a whip, I'd run a mile. And I certainly wouldn't find it a turn-on, for God's sake.'

Hilary laughed and sipped wine; pointed a finger round the stem of her glass. 'No, but there're levels and degrees in everything, Suzie. Levels and degrees of pain. Levels and degrees of masochism. And yes, you are, quite masochistic. I mean, look how you love it when I look at your pussy.'

'I don't love it. I hate it: it embarrasses the hell out of me.'

'And turns you the hell on.' Hilary fixed her with a challenging stare, as if defying her to deny it. 'Right?'

Suzie wriggled in her seat and felt herself blush. But she couldn't help the sheepish grin that spread itself on her face. 'You know it bloody does.'

'There, you see? It embarrasses you to be looked at *there*, as you put it – and that's another thing; you can't even bring yourself to say the word, can you? You've got a cunt, love. Or if that's too strong for you, a pussy, a fanny, a crack – you're the wordsmith, Suzie, you pick a word – but what you haven't got, for God's sake, is a *there*.

'But getting back to my point, it embarrasses you to be looked at there because you know your pussy's wet and glistening, your lips pouting open, showing you're excited and ready for sex; that you want it –'

'Hilary, stop!' Suzie was blushing furiously now.

But Hilary ignored her; pressed on undaunted. 'We're back to your hang-ups, see. That one a throw-back – whether you like it or not, Miss Lady Boss, Miss Modern Woman – to the old "nice girls don't" thing; only sluts want sex; only sluts have salacious desires; only sluts have wanton pussies. So it embarrasses you.

'Yet – and this is the point – that embarrassment excites you: you find it mildly humiliating, and are excited by that just as the hardened masochist is sexually excited by physical pain. Do you remember that time I made you hold yourself open for me? Made you hold your lips wide apart, glistening with your juices, while I just sat there and looked at you? You were squirming with embarrassment, but you came just like that, didn't you, without my even touching you?'

Things wriggled in Suzie's belly as her mind went back. But she couldn't deny it. It was turning her on now just to be thinking about it.

'There's probably another aspect of it too,' Hilary was saying. 'When I make you lie still and I look at your pussy, it makes you feel like you're proffering your most vulnerable part; almost like a dog will roll over and expose its belly to the pack as an act of submission . . . An act of submission, mind!'

'I heard you the first time,' Suzie said curtly, her head in a whirl as the concept challenged her to believe it.

And she was slowly beginning to. More and more of what Hilary was saying was beginning to make sense. Beginning to ring true.

'But how do you explain those fantasies, then?' It was ll very confusing. 'I mean, all right, so I've good enough reason for wanting to do something nasty to Bob Adams, the creep. But why the Viking? That was humiliation, pure and simple, for a sexual turn-on. It excited me to think of it. But wouldn't that make me a a sadist, rather than . . . you know?'

'Role substitution, love,' Hilary said confidently, sounding for all the world like a trained psychologist.

Suzie was astonished by her apparent knowledge of the subject – she hadn't got this from a porn magazine.

'Up until now,' Hilary went on, 'if what you're saying is right, you never thought of yourself as being submissive; it seems you've being repressing it. Though I'd never have known; to me, it's always been as plain as day where you're coming from sexually. But anyway, in your fantasy you put yourself in what you considered to be your natural role, the dominant role, and let the Viking act out the submissive part. Lived the experience of being humiliated through his eyes. A sort of subconcious role-reversal.'

'You mean . . .' Suzie hesitated, wondering if it could really be true. 'You mean, what I did to him was really what I'd like done to myself?'

'You tell me, love.'

Suzie continued to wonder. And yes, it was confusing all right. But more and more believable. More and more plausible.

The two were quiet for a while, Suzie thinking it through and just the clock ticking away on the mantel disturbing the silence. Hilary staring into space and leaving her to it.

Suzie sipped at her wine and thought herself back through all the best, most exciting sex she had had. Not that a great many experiences stood out (after Victor Delaney, who was there?) but only now did she realise that the common denominator among those that did was that the men involved, just as Victor had done, had taken control; been in command. They had intuitively known the things that she liked and had demanded them rather than tentatively suggesting. As, in retrospect, Geoff had tended always to do – deferring, no doubt, to her other, real-life dominant self. They had made her experiment by insisting she did, and to hell with her hang-ups. Just as Hilary did. It was why sex with Hilary was always so good, she realised, even though she, Suzie, wasn't really bisexual. Hilary knew, had obviously known all along, all the right buttons to press. Knew her better than she knew herself.

It was all suddenly so clear. Hilary was right – wasn't she always? – that was the problem with her Friday night sex; she was too much in control. She could see it now; she needed men to tell her what to do, not her to tell them. She needed men to dominate her.

She tested Hilary's theory and let herself reverse roles

with the Viking; imagined herself the slave and him the prospective purchaser, doing to her what she had done to him. Imagined bending over before him, as she had made him do, her buttocks splayed, while his fingertip threatened to . . .

Oh, God, this is all too much, she thought, her heart suddenly racing, a throb of libidinous desire screaming out from her loins. She forced the image away, almost terrified by the potency of it. But now she knew it for sure.

So, OK, she decided, *accept the fact that you're sexually submissive – a raving bloody masochist, if you like – what does it matter? The important question is . . .*

'So, what do I do then, Hils?' she said, finally breaking the silence. 'To improve my Friday nights romps? I mean, if I don't put myself in the driving seat, as you put it, if I don't tell these guys what I want' – she was thinking about the near-fiasco with Jason, the better times with the others – 'then I'm not going to get it.'

'And if you do, love, you won't get it either,' said Hilary, always the pragmatist. 'Not what you really want. Ever.'

'Oh, thanks, Hils. Thanks for the optimism; that's just what I need. You show me what's missing, point me in the direction of exciting, fulfilling sex – the kind of sex that I need – and then tell me I can't ever have it. Well that's just great.'

Hilary shrugged. 'All I'm saying, love, is that you can't ever have it your way; from the driving seat. The other way, who knows? There might be a few disappointments, sure, with guys who screw up. But you at least have a chance of coming across a man who instinctively knows what you need, and gives it to you. Like I do, I might pointedly add.' She flashed Suzie a suggestive wink. 'But you can't have your cake and eat it, love, no.'

'Well I don't see why not,' said Suzie defiantly, struck by a sudden idea. 'Why don't I just tell them I want to be, well, dominated? Make that the evening's instructions?'

'Oh, yeah, sure. And run the risk of giving them the wrong idea? What if some guy starts to get rough? Gets aggressive and starts to knock you about, thinking that's what you want; what you're into – as indeed some women are. Hurts, or really humiliates you, thinking he's turning you on and just earning his poppy?'

Suzie shivered at the disturbing image it conjured. Persisted anyway. 'No, well I'd tell them that's not what I meant, wouldn't I? I mean, I'd tell them I like ...'

'What? That you like having your pussy looked at?'

'Yes ... No! I mean ...' She became flustered: it did sound silly put like that. 'I don't know. But I could tell them I like to be told to do things, couldn't I?'

'And the moment you did, then who would be dominating whom? Even if you managed to get it across to them – and what we're talking about here is very subtle, you know, not easily put into words – they'd only be doing what you had told them to do. You'd still be wearing the wrong hat, love. Back to square one. No, I'm sorry, Suzie, but that just wouldn't work.'

'So what do I do?' Suzie implored.

'What can you do? You either stay out of the driving seat, and take a chance. Or you keep going the way you are, which' – Hilary chuckled – 'from what you've been telling me, is hardly bad.'

Suzie smiled whimsically, reflecting. 'True,' she sighed.

She lifted the bottle. 'Another glass, Hils?'

'No, thanks. Not for me.' Hilary laid a palm on top of her glass. 'I'd best be off, I've got a hectic day on tomorrow. Up at the crack of noon, as usual, then it's down to the gym to meet Cherry. She's the blonde waif I had my eye on for ages, remember?'

Suzie nodded.

'Yeah, well I finally cracked it. And what a little cracker she is, too. Comes across as being so sweet and innocent; like butter wouldn't melt, you know? Huh, don't you believe it. She's a depraved little minx, and no mistake. She's doing this course at the Uni in psycho-sexology.'

Ah, thought Suzie; so that's where Hilary had been getting it from.

'Talk about a sexually together young woman. She's terrific in bed; got a pussy that can take hold of your tongue and pull it out by the root.'

Suzie couldn't help but laugh at her friend's filthy humour. She really was incorrigible.

'Well, I'm glad for you,' she said, genuinely pleased that Hilary seemed to have found such a wonderful partner. If more than a little disappointed that, because of her, she was now about to leave – right then, she had urges that Hilary would have been welcome to satisfy. 'Still, it's a pity you have to be off though,' she muttered, thinking of what might have been. 'Though I suppose, anyway, you'll have eyes only for Cherry now, eh?'

'What? Do me a favour, girl,' Hilary snorted, her wicked eyes twinkling. 'You know me better than that. No, it's nothing to do with faithfulness that I'm wanting to shoot off – get real – it's just she's persuaded me to do some working-out with her tomorrow: exercise bikes, and like that.' She grimaced. 'Bad enough in itself, but on a hang-over, ugghh!'

Hilary lifted her plump frame from her seat and stood up, and Suzie chuckled at the thought of that ample body jiggling about on an exercise bike.

'So, I'd best be away, love. Think on what I've been saying, eh, and good luck. I'll see myself out.'

And with that she left.

Leaving Suzie alone with her thoughts. And a nagging ache in her loins.

You can't have your cake and eat it, love.

Over the following weeks, Suzie thought about Hilary's words often; they came almost to haunt her. And every week, as Friday approached, she would think: this time. This time there would be no preplan; no instructions at the start of the session. She would stay out of the driving seat, and trust to luck. Risk another Jason, but in so doing would chance finding a naturally

86

dominant man; a man who could explore and exploit her newly-realised sexual submissiveness to the full.

For Hilary was of course right. The moment she told the man what she wanted, whatever it was, it was she who would don that dominant cap. And with it, forgo any chance of the sex of her dreams.

But despite her resolve, when Friday night came, she just could not resist it.

'It's like knowing you're going to your favourite restaurant,' she had explained it to Hilary. 'As you anticipate it beforehand, you think of all the different dishes you're going to try out. But when you're actually there, and hungry, you won't take the chance on ordering a meal you might not like. You order the same dish every time, knowing you're going to enjoy it.'

And so, each time, at the' start of the session she would begin by mapping out what she wanted. She just couldn't help it.

Until, that was, the night she met Michael . . .

Chapter Ten

*T*he moment she saw him, she knew Michael was different.

There was something about his confident air as he strolled in the bar, his eyes casting casually about; there was an almost tangible aura about him that seemed physically to glow with his presence. All the Benson Agency men were self-assured and socially at ease – it would have been a prerequisite of the job, naturally. One of them anyway. But this man fairly oozed confidence, wore it like a comfortable suit. His charisma was phenomenal.

She recognised him at once, of course, from Grace Cummings's description, but Grace had not done him justice. Tall and slim without being rangey, he had a neat crop of curly black hair, and a face that was ruggedly good-looking rather than handsome. But it was a face she instantly fancied.

A young woman, not unattractive, was sitting at a nearby table, and Michael's eyes went to her. Suzie felt a momentary stab of what might have been jealousy, but which couldn't have been. Could it?

Michael nodded to the woman politely, but seemed to know she wasn't the one.

And then his eyes found Suzie.

Suzie's heart missed several beats and began suddenly to flutter as he smiled and started towards her. *Silly bitch*, she told herself, *what are you suddenly so nervous about? He's just a man, like the others. Your meat on the hoof for the night*. But she couldn't help it; she felt like a schoolgirl on her first date.

He reached her table. 'Miss Carlton,' he said. It was a statement, not a question. He was in no doubt.

'Er, yes,' Suzie squeaked. She cleared her throat, both surprised and abashed at the sound she had made, and managed to regain some composure. 'Suzie. And you're Michael.'

Michael inclined his head. 'At your service.'

'Would you, er . . . would you like a drink?' She could suddenly use another herself.

'Sure, but let me. What'll it be?'

'Martini. Thank you.'

Michael went to the bar. And her eyes followed him every step of the way, mesmerised. He moves with the grace of a cat, she thought. No, not a cat – a panther: yes, that was it. Powerful, yet light, supple. Though not at all like the black girl she had watched pose in the studio, who had also brought a panther to mind. Michael was as masculine as she had been feminine; like a prowling, male panther – a panther in search of a mate; feline and overtly sexual.

As he stood at the bar Suzie studied his buttocks: they were small and tight, deliciously delineated by the tailored cut of his slacks. (Suzie was definitely a bottom girl.) She imagined them naked, her hands on them, gripping those hard, muscular nates as she pulled him inside her. And she savoured the image with a lick of her lips; felt a familiar heat spread out from her groin to warm her all over.

He returned with their drinks; Suzie's Martini and a glass of white wine for himself – which he had paid for – and sat down beside her.

'A pleasant evening,' he said.

'What? Oh. Oh, yes, pleasant,' she muttered distractedly.

It was quite usual for her to be feeling nicely sexy by this time on a Friday evening, her thoughts of the night ahead readying her for what was to come. But this night her need was suddenly desperate: she couldn't wait to get this Michael up to her room.

She swigged at her Martini to steady her nerves, and said, 'Look, would you mind if we took our drinks upstairs?'

She had taken several of the others aback with her forthrightness, her keenness to get on with the action, but if Michael was fazed in the least he didn't show it. 'But of course,' he said smoothly, immediately standing and gathering their glasses. 'Why don't you lead the way?'

In her room, Michael set their glasses down on a table and turned to face her.

'Look, I'm sorry to bring up the subject of money,' he said. Without embarrassment, but with a look of genuine regret. And with none of the businesslike coldness there had been with the others, and that she had come to expect. 'But –'

Suzie stopped him with a shake of her head. 'No, really, it's all right.' She found her purse and took out the seventy-five pounds that seemed to have become the standard fee. 'I expect this will cover it, yes?'

Michael raised an eyebrow at the fanned-out notes. 'Oh, but that's really more than . . .'

'Please, take it,' Suzie insisted. 'Really.'

She had a feeling it would be worth every penny; she just knew it. She could feel it in her bones; in the surges of excitement that even now were tugging at the pit of her stomach. And that made her hand shake as she held out the notes.

Michael thanked her and accepted the money.

'But,' she added, 'I do expect . . . I mean, I would like a full hour for it.'

'I understand,' said Michael, sitting himself comfortably on the edge of the bed. 'Is there anything else?'

'Yes, I . . . er . . . no . . .'

Earlier, she had known exactly what she would say; what her list of instructions for that evening would be. Despite her resolve not to, she had spent a delicious hour in the bath mapping it out as usual. But now it was suddenly all gone; her mind a blank.

She shook her head dumbly.

'Then, come here.'

It was practically a command – it WAS a command – and the sound of it turned Suzie's belly to sudden jelly; sent an erotic shiver tingling along her spine. And on legs that were suddenly weak, she went to him; stood before him (as she instinctively knew he had meant she should do), and waited.

A moment passed. Another. And still she waited, standing passively before him and feeling his presence through every nerve in her body; expectant and tense. Then, at last, he reached up and cupped his hands to her breasts, squeezed with strong but gentle fingers. She gasped at the sudden assault, but remained still, her hands by her sides.

'You're wearing no bra,' he said.

'No,' she replied breathlessly. *It was almost a struggle not to add sir, or master.* 'I . . . I rarely do.'

Michael trapped her nipples between fingers and thumbs, and applied a firm pressure that again made her gasp.

'I see. And I'll bet you're not wearing knickers either.'

How did he know?

'Are you?' he pressed.

He was looking up into her face, his eyes locked on hers. They were striking, grey eyes, which seemed un-fathomable; as if they were hiding a million secrets. And there was something in them that made butterflies dance (or spiders crawl) in her belly. But she couldn't have looked away if she'd tried.

They were demanding an answer.

'No,' she admitted, blushing down to her neck.

'No. You are a dirty girl, aren't you?'

She swallowed thickly. 'Yes,' she muttered. It was a barely audible whisper.

As if in just punishment for her brazenness he gave her nipples a sharp tweak, and she sucked in a breath through teeth clenched in sudden pain. He watched the distress that appeared in her eyes and smiled. An enigmatic smile; a smile almost of sympathy, yet which seemed to conceal a deep understanding.

'A very dirty girl,' he said, tweaking again. Harder.

Suzie's blush deepened, and her nipples hurt. She wanted to twist away; to free the tender buds from his dreadful grip on them. But she didn't.

'Tell me, Suzie,' he said, his eyes still holding hers; his voice soft. 'Are you going to do everything I say this evening?'

The question was a shock, yet wasn't: it was as if she had known it would come.

'I . . . Yes,' she muttered weakly.

'Everything – anything – I tell you to do?'

Her senses swam dizzily. His grip on her nipples was tacitly threatening, daring her to refuse him. But there was much more than that: he seemed to exude a certain power, a sexual energy that demanded obedience and which she could not resist. What could she say?

'Yes,' she breathed on a rush of air, the thrill of total surrender preventing the word from properly forming.

'Good. Then open your legs.'

The simple command sent a shockwave through her. A shock she found difficult to construe. After all, she had opened her legs for other men; what was suddenly the big deal? But she had never before been ordered to, and that, somehow, was intensely erotic; thrilling in a way she had never experienced. However, there wasn't the time to consider it further.

Abruptly, Michael released her anguished nipples from his grip on them and they flared with sudden fire. She winced, but resisted the urge to rub them, to soothe the fire away, and instead kept her hands where they were; sensing she should. Sensing she must, as she set her feet a little apart just as he'd told her.

The backs of Michael's fingers stroked lightly for a moment across the now hardening buds, as if to explore the heat he had caused to burn within them, then he lowered a hand to the inside of her knee. Slowly, he ran his palm up her inner thigh, beneath her skirt, until his fingers reached the moist warmth at the top.

It was a fleeting caress, the briefest of touches; as though he had wished only to confirm that she had obeyed him, and had parted her thighs to allow it. Or, perhaps, to confirm for himself that she was not wearing panties. Whichever it was, his hand was there for but a tantalising moment and then was withdrawing again. Nevertheless, it was enough to leave Suzie's thighs quivering with need, her abdomen taut; excitement mounting in her lower belly as it gathered in search of release.

Michael reached back up, to the buttons of her blouse now. Deftly, he plucked the buttons undone; pushed the material aside to expose her breasts.

Then he sat back to regard them.

Suzie's legs turned to water and she started to tremble. 'Oh, please . . .' she whispered hoarsely.

'What?' Capricious eyes flicked up to meet hers, just for a moment, then deliberately returned to her breasts. 'You have nice breasts. I'm admiring them, that's all.'

'Em – Embarrassing,' she breathed.

'What's that you say?'

He made her repeat it. 'It . . . it's embarrassing.'

Michael smiled a knowing smile.

'Is it now? Then we'd better look at the rest of you, hadn't we?'

In a single fluid movement he sat forward again and pushed the blouse from her shoulders, laying them bare and now fully exposing the swell of her breasts. Then he reached for the clasp at the waist of her skirt. Unhooking it, he slipped the zipper and let the skirt drop down to her ankles.

Apart from her stockings and shoes, Suzie was now standing naked.

And when Michael sat back to look at her, she shuddered hugely and came.

Her thighs trembled and her belly shook. Her jaws were clenched in a struggle to keep herself silent. But she couldn't prevent the nasal grunt that sounded loud in her ears; that betrayed she was wracked in the shaming throes of orgasm. Her eyes were squeezed tightly shut, but she remained acutely conscious of Michael's gaze upon her, watching her. *Watching her come right there in front of him. God, what a wanton slut he must think her.* But she could do nothing to help it; only let herself finish.

And then, mercifully, her orgasm at last began to subside, through dying spasms of lesser intensity, to finally release her from its fervid grip. She wanted to open her eyes, but didn't dare. And then she couldn't help herself but, knowing the shame that awaited her, that would be reflected in Michael's eyes. And craving it.

Her eyes came slowly open to remind her poignantly that Michael was still fully clothed; sitting on the edge of the bed while she stood naked before him. Naked and vulnerable; her breasts rising and falling on the small juddering breaths she was still heaving; her thighs shaking; her blonde bush a scream of immodesty that begged to be covered. But cover it she dared not: he had not said that she could.

A small smile was playing on Michael's lips as his eyes drank in her nudity. It was a smile of amusement; amused, she knew, by the fact she had come so readily, with so little provocation. Right there, as she stood before him, the only stimulus that of his watching eyes. *What a wanton slut indeed.*

But seething tendrils of desire were already beginning to arouse her again, that very thought exciting her. An excitement that surged when Michael reached out a hand to her; slid a searching middle finger between her legs in quest of her hidden furrow; began to slide along it, teasing her lips apart to reach the pink inner sanctum.

94

His eyes came up to meet hers and commanded her to look into them while his finger continued to delve; bathing in the liquid, undeniable proof of her wantonness. And things squirmed in her belly as she read his knowing eyes, exciting her further.

'Was that a good come?' he asked.

His tone was teasing and her cheeks burned.

'Well?' he pressed when she didn't answer.

He was making her say it. 'Yes,' she whispered at last, the word catching on a ragged breath.

His finger continued to work.

'So I can feel. You're soaking down here.'

He withdrew his hand and held up his finger to where they both could see it.

'Look,' he told her, 'my finger's covered with your come.'

And so it was. It glistened with her juices and, seeing it, her cheeks burned hotter. Burned hotter still when he slipped his finger slowly into his mouth. She cringed with embarrassment and wished desperately to look away. But his eyes forbade it; held hers and insisted she watch.

'Mmmm ... You taste good,' he teased; his tone calculated, it seemed, to cause her the maximum embarrassment. It worked.

He gave his finger a final long lick, and then it was back in her pussy, probing deeply.

But not for long.

As soon as it had buried itself up to its hilt he withdrew it and raised it again, this time up to her face. It was fully re-charged with her juices, and she caught the faint tang of her feminine fragrance as she waited for what she knew, with dread certainty, was to come.

And come it did: 'Here, you taste.'

It was a command, not an invitation, and she slowly opened her mouth. He slipped his finger inside, rolling it on her tongue as her lips closed upon it.

The taste of a woman's sex was not of course new to her. Nor even her own; she had tasted it before on the lips of others, on Geoff's cock when she had fellated him hard again following intercourse. But this was in a different dimension: having to suck her own sexy juices from Michael's finger, at his command and while he watched, was acutely humiliating. And once again a part of her wished desperately she could look away; to avoid the look of almost mocking amusement she saw in the mysterious depths of Michael's grey eyes, on the small curl of his lips. Yet that other part of her, that darker part, thrilled to the shame of it, and she could not look away. Not even were those compelling eyes to allow it.

'Tastes good, doesn't it?' Michael said. 'Sexy.'

After a while he withdrew his finger, leaving only its lingering aftertaste on Suzie's tongue, and returned it to her now aching pussy – aching, ready to come again. All that was being done to her: the humiliations, her very submission to this man, the direct stimulus of his fingers, had re-aroused her once again to that peak of desire which refuses to be contained any longer – she was close, very close, to a second climax.

'Now, stand quite still,' Michael told her, as his clever finger slid back and forth, finding a rhythm. Teasing her slippery outer lips, tantalising the inner flesh with delicate, fluttering touches. Occasionally probing deeper but always, it seemed, maddeningly missing her clitoris; that very part of her which yearned for its touch most of all.

She tried to catch it, to rasp her frustrated nub against his moving knuckle; knew that just one touch would be all it would take. But she had been told to stand still and so dared allow herself no more than the most imperceptible shift of her hips, the barest squeeze of her thighs, and it wasn't enough. She failed, and only ached all the more for her efforts.

'You're not to come again yet,' Michael warned, as if reading her thoughts. And that explained it. He was purposely avoiding her clitoris, deliberately teasing her. 'There'll be time enough for that. But first I want to see all of you.'

He withdrew his hand.

'Turn around.'

Her heart was already a thing that pounded in her chest, but it suddenly leapt to her throat thudding harder. *See all of her? Just where did he mean?*

'T-turn around?' she muttered thickly.

The saliva in her mouth cloyed and was something she couldn't swallow, as visions of a Viking flashed to her brain.

Michael's face didn't change.

'I think you heard me, Suzie. Yes, turn around.'

Did he have any idea what he was doing to her? The torment, physical and mental, he was putting her through? Yes, of course he did; he knew exactly what he was doing.

But it seemed there was nothing she could refuse this man; he could do with her just as he pleased. And with that daunting–thrilling thought, her legs like jelly, she slowly obeyed his command.

Standing with her back to him, she fancied she could physically feel his eyes on her skin, travelling down her back, to her buttocks, settling there; eyeing the lush firmness of her rounded nates, the dark crevice between them.

That crevice which held secret her most inviolate place: the forbidden entrance that was the source of her most inhibiting hang-up of all. That place she had permitted no one – not Hilary, not Geoff; no one, ever – to openly view before. *Under this man's dominance, was that about to change?*

Long seconds took hours to pass. She was trembling all over now, her heart thudding adrenalin through her veins, yet it seeming to weaken rather than strengthen her. A thundering waterfall rushed past her ears as blood throbbed at her temples, and she felt light-headed; feared she would faint, as the tension mounted and she waited for something to happen.

And then it did.

She jumped and almost cried out at the sudden shock of it when it came: the sudden touch of Michael's hand on the underswell of her buttock. And then the hand was between her legs once again, sliding upwards, now, between her lightly-closed thighs towards her longing sex. Reaching there, gentle fingers stroked for a while, teasing her back up to the peak from which she had only slightly subsided. They were soon driving her wild, and she squeezed her thighs against them in an attempt to trigger her climax (the reason she had been ordered to turn around for the moment forgotten as her sexual tension rose to a heady summit and orgasm grew ever nearer).

But then, just as she felt she was almost there, firm pressure of fingertips against her inner thigh was a silent command, telling her to open her legs. She groaned in frustration, knowing this would deny her any hope of the self-help she had sought; that she had once again been thwarted. Aching with ungratified arousal, she obeyed the unspoken command; took a small step to the side, parting her thighs and regretting she could no longer use them to find additional friction against Michael's teasing fingers.

But those same fingers, pressed to her thigh, told her it wasn't enough and made her step out further, opening her legs wide.

And still, for Michael, this wasn't enough.

'Now bend your knees a little, Suzie,' he told her. 'Bear down slightly to open yourself wide for me.'

Her breathing shallow, her pulse racing, she did as he said.

The slight crouch opened her thighs obscenely, forcing her mound forward and her sex to gape, and Michael's fingers – the backs of them, she sensed – began gliding back and forth right inside the wide open slit, his knuckles grazing the delicate pink petals of her soft inner sex. She was aware, too, acutely aware, that it had opened that very crevice she had sought to keep closed.

It went on for a while, until the muscles of her thighs began to ache dully from the strain of holding the awkward posture. And until that ache became more acute, and her muscles burned in protest, her thighs beginning to tremble as the strain grew worse. But it was a pain she tried to ignore: she was so close to coming, and just a few more stokes of Michael's ministering fingers would be bound to take her over the brink, send her exploding to climax. With that in prospect she had no wish to move; the pain she would bear.

But then, as Michael's finger slid backwards, away from the nub it had all-too-fleetingly pleasured, she felt it go further, its nail scratching lightly at the delicate membrane beyond the join of the lips. And this time it didn't stop to return, but instead travelled on ... *Oh, God, no,* ... to draw right across the puckered ring of her anus. She groaned anew: Michael's hand sliding licentiously between the opened cheeks of her bottom a sudden and sharp reminder of why he had turned her around.

Oh, God. Oh, God. Oh, God, she thought, now seeing the Viking bending over, his buttocks widely splayed. Sweat sprang to her brow and she began to shake uncontrollably; her secret opening snatching tight on itself in guard against threatened intrusion. Even the frustration of Michael's hand leaving her pussy, denying her the orgasm that had been so maddeningly close, was of small consequence against that which she feared was to come. *He wanted to see all of her, he had said.*

Michael's hand withdrew.

And she waited with bated breath. Making her wait was something Michael liked doing, it seemed.

'You know, Suzie,' he said at last, 'just looking can be so incredibly erotic, can't it?' *Oh, God,* thought Suzie, her heart in her mouth; *here it comes.* 'Oh, touching of course. Touching, feeling; the scents, the tastes, even the sounds of sex can all be erotic. But none more so than just looking. Or being looked at, eh?

'And especially a body like yours, Suzie. A terrific body. A body I want to see every part of. And you'd let me, wouldn't you, Suzie? Let me see all of you?'

99

This was it; the brink from which there would be no return.

Suzie could barely speak. A part of her quailed. Yearned only for his resumed caress, a swift and natural path to much-needed climax. And why not? After all, she was paying the piper; she could have whatever she wanted. She could put a stop to this at any time: just the one word was all it would take. The one word: no.

She steeled herself. 'Yes,' she whispered.

The other, darker side of herself had answered the question: the part that yearned for the command to bend over.

But then his hands were on her hips, gently turning her round, and a surge of relief swept through her that almost – though not quite – compensated for perverse dismay!

But any dismay was instantly forgotten as Michael issued his next command: 'Keep your legs wide apart,' he ordered as he turned her to face him.

For somehow, even this – just being made to stand with her legs apart, submissively offering her sex – was humiliating enough. Enough to set delicious tendrils of erotic desire writhing within her, as she watched Michael's eyes on her bush.

Michael slid down from the bed, shuffled himself close on his knees. And reaching behind her he took her buttocks in his powerful hands; held on to them tightly while he leaned in with his face, his lips brushing damp hair aside in search of her throbbing sex.

Suzie moaned in agonised delight. His tongue probed into her, making white-hot spears stab at her loins. His lips found her clitoris, exposed in its need, and brushed against it. So did his tongue, making a single rapid swirl around its aching stem. Her belly juddered at the longed-for touch and her climax reared yet again; was again just a moment, just a touch away. Dizzy with tension she thrust out her hips, pressing her mound to Michael's face, her clitoris harder against his lips in urgent need of release. Of relief.

But just as she felt the melt-down begin – that reaction

100

in her sexual core that could not be reversed and would, inevitably, lead to explosion – he suddenly pulled away. Suzie cried out in shock, hardly believing it. He couldn't stop now; not now for God's sake!

Michael looked up at her. 'I thought I said you were not to come again yet. Not until I'd seen all of you.'

Suzie's knees almost buckled and her thighs shook. A groan erupted from deep in her throat, and the dull ache in the pit of her stomach was almost unbearable.

'Oh God, Michael. I don't think I can hold myself back any –'

Michael put a silencing fingertip up to his lips. 'Shhh,' he said gently. 'Of course you can. You must.' He pushed himself back and returned to the edge of the bed. 'Self-control is a virtue, Suzie; pleasure all the sweeter for having to wait ... But perhaps my tongue is a bit too testing; I'll let you off with that for now. So, now, I think it's time you should show me what I haven't yet seen.'

Suzie groaned inwardly. Knowing she must make herself wait. Knowing she must now display herself in some no doubt lewd and humiliating posture for this man; for this virtual stranger. For this wonderful, exciting, irresistible stranger. Knowing it would turn her on further, and that her desperate ache, the waiting, would be all the harder to bear.

'Now, Suzie, sit down on the floor,' Michael told her. 'Yes, there where you are, directly facing me. Now, bring your knees together and bring them up to your chest. Yes, that's right.'

Suzie was surprised to say the least: she would have thought that bringing her knees together would have been the last thing Michael would want. But she wasn't complaining; was glad to take a moment's comfort in the sense of modesty the position afforded – her legs had been apart for such a long time, it seemed, her sex open and available. And it came as some relief to now be sitting with her knees drawn up and together, that part of her which pouted sexily from between her thighs shielded from Michael's eyes by her shins. Even her breasts were covered, her nipples hiding coyly behind the tops of her knees. She still wore her shoes and their heels were now tight to her buttocks, and as she wrapped her arms around her legs for balance, it put her in the classic posture of modesty; that which any naked female will instinctively adopt in the presence of male eyes. It afforded her some respite from the excruciating tension that was quivering inside her.

But, as she might have known, it wasn't to last.

'Now, Suzie,' Michael told her. 'Lie back, your arms by your sides. Good. Now, keeping your heels together, let your knees drop apart.'

The sudden realisation of it hit Suzie like a thunderbolt: what a naïve innocent she had been not to have seen it coming! Not that it would have made any difference of course; she could refuse Michael nothing. Yet, still, she hesitated. For the position, she knew, would be staggeringly effective. Both for her and for him. For him, because it would give him a totally unimpeded view of her wide open sex – no position could have opened her wider. For her, because not even her fair bush would any longer provide her with even the meagrest refuge from his gaze. She could hardly conceive of a more humiliating position. Well, perhaps one.

But finally, knowing she could do no other, slowly, very slowly, she let her knees fall apart.

'Oh, wider than that, Suzie,' Michael chided her when she tried to hold back. 'Much wider than that.'

He was allowing her nothing; nothing short of total surrender. And, resigning herself to that fact, she suddenly let go; let her knees drop all the way open, until they were almost touching the floor either side.

Her groin screamed in protest at the sudden strain put on it. But physical discomfort was the least of her worries.

Never had she felt so utterly naked: her sex was obscenely, disgracefully displayed, and it was as if Michael's eyes bored into her, ravishing her, taking her.

102

The strain on her upper thighs forced the indentations on the insides of them into deep hollows, from which her pubic mound stood high and alone; as if proffering itself; abasing itself in its pride. Her sex-flesh pulsed in a wanton display of its hunger, her juices flowed freely, and things crawled in the pit of her stomach to know that Michael was watching it all.

'Good. Suzie, good,' Michael praised. 'Now, put your hands to your pussy; hold yourself wide for me. Let me look right inside you.'

God, was there no end to this? Was she to be allowed no dignity at all?

It seemed not. Swallowing hard, she tentatively slid her hands down her sides, then inwards, across her lower belly; pressed trembling fingertips either side of her prominent mound to spread herself wider still, aware that the pressure forced her clitoris free of its fleshy hood to beg with profligate boldness.

She almost cried out with the shame of it. It was no more, no less, than Hilary had once made her do. But with Michael it was a million times worse. *A million times better; a million times more thrilling.* For one thing, with Hilary, the humiliation of it had brought about the rapid onset of orgasm; the ordeal had lasted but seconds. But Michael had forbidden her from coming; this could go on for as long as he chose. And though a part of her cringed at the thought of him watching the inner core of her sex pulsing wantonly in the uncontrollable throes of climax – an embarrassment she was thus being spared – that other part of her thrilled to the notion, making resistance to it all the harder to bear. She was aching to come, was right on the verge, yet she was forced to contain it within her. Her sexual strings strung taut, almost to snapping, she was only glad of her earlier climax; but for that she doubted she could have borne it at all.

Michael slid himself down from the bed and came to kneel by her heels. Placed his palms on the floor by her hips and lowered his face to her groin. He flicked his tongue at her clitoris, making her jerk in sudden spasm and bringing a gasp from her throat. It was a single flick, and then he raised his head again, his eyes finding hers.

'Are you close to coming?' he asked.

'Oh, yesss!' she said, tension forcing the air from her lungs to make it a sibilant hiss.

He flicked her clitoris again. Again just the once, a single swirl of his tongue, then again found her eyes.

'How close?'

Her belly quivered then tautened at the flicking caress. 'Very,' she gasped.

He smiled then, and again dipped his head. His tongue lapped at her aching nub. Not once now, but twice. Then three times.

Was this it? Suzie thought desperately. *Was he finally about to relent and trigger her climax?* Tension clutched at the pit of her stomach, and she held her breath, her every muscle straining in expectancy of the final touch. But . . .

Was she allowed? Sudden horror snatched at her gut. He hadn't said she could come.

Yet surely he couldn't expect her to endure this and not. Surely he now meant her to let herself go, to avail herself of his tongue and erupt in the orgasm he had already denied her for so unbearably long. But she just didn't know; was impaled on the horns of a cruel dilemma. To come or not to come, that was the question: to surrender to orgasm or to continue, somehow, to hold herself back. Finally, in the split second it took for these thoughts to race through her mind, the decision was made. She would wait for the very next swirl of his tongue, and would allow it to burst the swollen dam; to snap her sexual tension and send her flooding in the relief of climax.

It was a long second before she realised that that next caress wasn't to come.

Michael had lifted his head again, was again searching her eyes.

A long groan issued from deep in her being, exhaled

on a rush of anguished breath; breath she had held in expectancy, but which now gushed from her in a long shudder of bitter frustration. 'Oh, God, n-o-o-o,' she cried, close to sobbing.

'You weren't about to let yourself come, were you?' Michael's voice was teasing.

'N-no,' she lied. Her belly heaved.

'Because you know you can't come yet, don't you?'

Her voice was barely audible. 'Yes.'

'And you do know why?'

Her mind raced. *Why?* She had said yes, but she couldn't think of the reason. Her mind was reeling and she couldn't muster her thoughts, couldn't think anything straight. *Why?*

Michael reminded her. 'Because I haven't seen all of you yet, have I?'

Suzie's heart almost stopped, then thudded all the more fiercely. When Michael had turned her to face him again, after she had stood with her back to him, she had dared to hope he had spared her that final ordeal; that final, utter, invasion of her privacy.

'You promised to let me see all of you before you came,' Michael went on. He chuckled softly. 'Why, you didn't think I'd forgotten, did you?'

Suzie could only roll her head slowly from side to side, not daring to trust her voice; knowing now, from his chuckle, that Michael had done it deliberately. Had deliberately allowed her to believe she'd escaped, only for the blow to be more cutting, now, when it came.

'So, then, how do you intend to show me that final place?'

Suzie gulped hard, seeing no way out. Saw herself kneeling on all fours while Michael spread the cheeks of her bottom – or made her do it herself, she couldn't think which would be worse – to expose her secret opening. Resigned, she slowly went to turn over.

But Michael stopped her.

'No, no,' he said. 'Before you move, I want you to tell me how you intend to show me.'

Suzie's tummy turned, squirming impossibly. 'I . . . I . . .' She could barely speak. Was she to be allowed not a single shred of dignity? Was it not humiliating enough that she would have to do it, without her having to describe the act in advance? It was mortifying, but finally she found a small voice. 'On . . . On all f–fours?' she ventured.

Michael smiled, but shook his head. 'No,' he told her. 'Interesting, but no; I've a better idea.'

He reached his hands under the crooks of her knees and raised them a little.

'Here,' he said. 'Hold your legs here. Hold them wide, then roll yourself back on your shoulders.'

Her shame was complete. As she rolled herself back as Michael had told her, holding her legs wide, she knew she could not have displayed her bottom more lewdly; more obscenely. It was utterly demeaning. Utterly degrading. *And utterly, utterly thrilling*: her worst nightmare, *her wildest dream* come true.

For how long Michael had her remain so, feasting his eyes on her most secret place, she had no idea; time lost all significance and no longer mattered, washed away on a tide of erotic sensation. If his eyes had ravished her before, they were buggering her now, and it was all she could do not to pass out with the thrilling shame of it.

But then, at last, he was telling her to sit up. And then to kneel.

'You can sit back on your haunches,' he told her as she hurriedly shifted position, not needing to be told twice. 'But you're to keep your legs wide apart. I want you available to me, to look at or to touch, at all times . . . And now, it's your turn to look.'

With that, he stood and quickly stripped naked; sat down again on the edge of the bed, his thighs apart.

'You can look,' he said. 'But not touch.'

Suzie stared at his crotch entranced. While she herself remained acutely aware of her wide open thighs – of the submissiveness of her position – Michael displayed himself without any shame; with pride, even. And a pride he had every reason to feel: he was superbly endowed, his penis long as it hung before his pendulous balls. And even as she watched, it began to erect. She had never seen a cock erect of its own volition before, with no direct stimulation. (At least, none other than that provided by his eyes, which were locked, she knew, on the V of her widespread thighs.) Yet as she watched, it thickened and swelled; began to stand upright and finally sculpted itself into a magnificent phallus. The shaft was thick and strong, its head large and bulbous, deeply clefted by the dewy eye at its tip.

And it was tempting, oh so tempting. She yearned to reach out to it; to grip it; to take it into her mouth and suck it until it throbbed. To straddle him, then, and force it deep inside her; ride it to the orgasm that was tugging unbearably at the pit of her stomach.

Even as she thought it she felt her climax, yet again, gather within her and she almost came. Fought for control and found just enough to contain herself. God, how she longed for climax.

'And now,' Michael said, as if prompted by her thought. 'I think it's time you came.'

Suzie breathed a sigh of relief. And Michael reached down and dipped a long middle finger into her splayed-open sex. Withdrew it, now glistening, and held it poised.

'There,' he said, 'use my finger to get yourself off.'

Suzie stared at the rigid finger for a moment, slightly puzzled. She had no need of such stimulus: now she had permission, she could come merely by allowing herself to; was aching to so badly she had only to allow herself over the brink, no longer in need of a physical trigger. And having watched her come earlier, Michael must know that. Yet he wasn't suggesting; he was, as usual, commanding. But, why? And then a little groan rose in her throat as the answer became patently obvious: at the position he was holding his finger, she would have to kneel up and thrust herself forward to reach it; put on a lewd and ignominious display as she strained for the offered stimulus – even in this, in finally allowing her the relief she craved, he sought to make it as humiliating for her as possible; an act of self-debasement.

Blushing scarlet, she kneeled up; pushed forward her widespread thighs and strained for Michael's finger. Found it, just, and began writhing her hips in an undignified display as she ground her aching nub against it.

Orgasm gathered, was about to trigger. Then suddenly, impossibly – *oh, God, no,* – it began to recede.

Suzie groaned aloud, suddenly seeing the wizened face of Sister Marianna leaning in towards her, her finger wagging.

'Sex is sinful,' the old nun was warning, the terrified child cowering before her. 'Wantonness will see you in the fires of Hell.'

It was a face that appeared to her all-too-often; always, when it did, just at the point of orgasm. It would instantly set up a mental block – try as she might she couldn't then come – leaving her frustrated and angry.

Oh but, God, not now. Please, not now.

But orgasm continued to recede; her bucking hips, her writhing sex, the friction of Michael's finger, the humiliating thrill of it all, none of it making the slightest difference. She was about to be left frustrated again.

But then, just as all seemed hopelessly lost, the mental block set firmly in place, Hilary's words came back to her.

Desperately, she clutched at the straw they offered: 'It isn't me,' she screamed at the black-swathed ghost in her mind, new hope rearing within her. 'This man's making me do it.'

No culpability, no guilt.

And the moment the words fully formed, the nun's image, miraculously, began to shimmer. Faded, then went altogether. And a sense of release swept over her the like of which she had never before felt.

And she knew, then, that thanks to Hilary and Michael, to the wonderful liberation of sexual submission, Sister Marianna was gone for good; would never trouble her again.

And it was then she came, shuddering to a massive second climax that was made all the sweeter for her victory over the Merciful Sisters; banished from her life for ever.

The session seemed to go on for a very long time, certainly for far longer than the promised hour, as Michael took her on a roller-coaster ride of erotic sensation: the headlong rush down of relief after climax, then the slow, inexorable build-up, the achingly long climb to the next. From where he could trigger her orgasm at will, or choose – as was his wont – to make her wait; to hold her there right on the edge, relief tantalisingly close, yet, until he chose to permit it, agonisingly unreachable. Controlling her sexual tension as if he had some secret, mystic dial he could turn at his whim. Controlling her, in his wonderfully masterful way – firmly but tenderly; demanding yet sensitive. Sometimes cruel but always kind as he thrilled her in ways she had imagined in only her wildest dreams. It was the most intensely exciting sex she had known in her life.

And then, at last, he had taken her; had pressed her onto her back, her legs round his waist, and had plunged himself into her. Again and again, his thrusting ever more urgent with the rise of his own burgeoning need; finally arching his back and driving into her one last time, making them come together as he let out a deep guttural growl and exploded in violent climax.

And now, in the aftermath, they were lying together. She with her head on his still-heaving chest listening to the sound of his breathing grow gradually more even.

With the other agency men, it would be now she would want them to get dressed and leave, so she could bathe alone in the warm afterglow of post-orgasmic content; reliving the evening minute by minute. But not Michael – he could have stayed for ever.

She looked down his belly, across rippled muscle, to where his penis, that just a few moments ago had been a turgid monster impaling her, now lay flaccid and dormant between his slightly spread thighs. She yearned to reach for him, to bring him to life once again. But she stopped herself: *she had already had more than she'd paid for, she shouldn't be expecting still more.*

But it was so tempting. His penis seemed almost to beckon her, to call out to her in silent command: 'Suck me,' it ordered. 'Suck me.'

It was about the one act, somehow, they had not got around to, and she wanted to badly. So very badly.

And finally she could resist it no longer. If there would be more to pay, then so be it. She didn't care.

Tentatively, she reached out a hand, cupped it gently over his crotch. He made no move to stop her as she had half-feared that he might, and she went on, encouraged. Felt the weight of his sleeping balls in her palm, heavy and slack. Then lightly stroked his dormant cock until it began to respond.

She kissed his chest, then traced her lips lower, lower, kissing all the while; reached those rippling muscles and flicked her tongue at his navel. Smelled his musk, his maleness, and tingled anew.

And then she felt his hand in her hair, gently restraining.

She turned her head to look up at him, her cheek on his belly, her eyes pleading. About to say: 'Whatever it costs, please let me; I must.'

But Michael spoke first. 'I, ah, haven't washed yet, you know, since . . .'

Her eyes followed his to the knotted condom by the side of the bed, and she understood what he meant. And couldn't have cared less. Only breathed with relief that he wasn't stopping her.

She again turned her head, her lips now brushing his hardening member. The scent of him pervaded her senses and her head swam in a dizzying sea of sensual pleasure. She parted her lips and took him into her mouth, tasted the slight salt of his seed on her tongue. Thrilled to it; his taste and his smell combining to send new waves of erotic desire through her loins.

She felt him twitch, stir with new life; filling her

110

mouth as he grew. Her lips and tongue worked to arouse him further, brought him fully erect once again.

Slowly, sensually, she slid her mouth down him, taking as much of the throbbing shaft as she could. Then, just as slowly, just as sensuously, she came up again; almost, but not quite, setting him free. She teased the sensitive frenum with little flicks of her tongue that made him groan and tensed his stomach, before sliding her lips back down him again, building his need with a steady rhythm.

With her free hand she toyed with his balls, felt them gradually tighten in her gentle grip. Felt the cock beginning to pulse in her mouth, sensed the tension grow in his body, and knew she had a decision to make – a decision she would have to make quickly: to carry on or to stop.

The urge to continue was strong; to suck him until that great knob was filling her throat with his sperm, to suck him dry and greedily swallow all he could give her. It was tempting. And surely, for all he had done for her, he deserved that pleasure.

But her loins were sending a different message up to her brain. They longed for the feel of him inside her once more; were demanding one last climax before this wonderful evening was over. And finally need won, vanquishing want, albeit narrowly.

She let him slip free of her lips. Kissed the bulbous and now glistening head a reluctant fairwell and crawled her way up the bed. Eyed the packet of condoms on the bedside table and wondered.

'Michael,' she said softly, 'do you always practise safe sex?'

His voice drifted to her, whispered on uneven breath. 'Yes, always.'

'Me too. Then I guess that makes both of us safe,' she said, ignoring the condoms.

Kneeling astride him she reached down and prized his iron erection away from his belly, positioned herself carefully above it, and sighed as she sank herself onto it. Ready to ride him to one last come.

Chapter Eleven

'Susan, did you read Keith's piece yet?'

'Wh-what?' Suzie came to with a start, and looked up to see Bob Adams's head round her door. She had been miles away, thinking about Michael.

She had spent the entire weekend thinking about Michael. She hadn't been able to get him out of her mind: her every waking thought had been centred on him. And, though she rarely remembered her dreams, she knew she must have dreamt of him too; for each morning, when she had woken, her thighs had been slick with her juices and there had been an empty longing in her loins demanding to be filled. Her vibrator had never been busier.

When that morning, Monday, had come, she had been relieved to come into work, to at last have something else to think about; to occupy her mind and so get it off sex for a while. But it had been no use: she had spent the whole morning lost in a daydream, seeing Michael's wonderful, naked body before her; his torso strong and lean, his chest broad and smooth, his cock . . . Christ, his cock was something else. Imagining herself in every conceivable sexual scenario with him; though she would have bet pounds to brass buttons that Michael could have thought up a few more.

'The piece Keith wrote,' Adams repeated. 'Have you read it yet?'

'Oh, er, yes,' Suzie lied. She supposed the piece was on her desk somewhere, among the mountain of papers that awaited her attention. But she hadn't got around to reading anything yet.

'Well, what did you think?'

Adams's demeanour suggested he obviously liked it, whatever it was, so she decided to go with his flow. 'Oh, excellent,' she enthused. 'Yes, very good.'

Adams came all the way in, and sat down, his expression ugly as he said: 'Yeah, stuff like that'll always sell mags, right? Juicy bit of scandal in high places, what? Can't go wrong.'

Suzie instantly regretted her feigned enthusiasm. It was probably some smutty piece; some sordid scandal raked up from the pits to bring misery into some poor soul's life. The sort of journalism Suzie despised – it might sell mags, but it would never sell her mag.

'I was thinking you could even use it for the cover story. What do you think?'

'Oh, er, I'm not sure, Bob. I'll have to see.'

'Could do a lot worse.'

'Yes, well, like I said, I'll have to see.'

'Well what would you use in its stead?' Adams persisted.

'Bob, I don't know,' Suzie was becoming irritated. Apart from anything else, it seemed ridiculous to be having a conversation about an article she had not even read. 'But whatever I decide, it's my decision to make, right?'

Adams held up his hands in surrender. 'OK, OK. Subject closed.' He suddenly leered. 'Let's talk about us instead.'

Suzie groaned inwardly. 'There is no us, Bob,' she said, making herself laugh so it would sound less harsh.

'Well there bloody well should be, is what I say. When are you going to finally give in, and come out with me?'

'You mean come to bed with you.'

Adams shrugged. 'I'd be happy to buy you dinner first.'

'I'm sure you would. But no. Bob, you know how I feel. I don't believe in office affairs.'

'So you're saying you would go out with me if you didn't work here?'

'Yes, probably. I think' – what could she say that wouldn't be a total lie? – 'I think you're a good-looking bloke.' That, at least, was true. But she suddenly caught herself; felt wary. *What was he getting at? Why had he said, if she didn't work there; why not if he didn't? Surely he couldn't be thinking to get her fired – or try to at least – thinking that then she'd go out with him. That was insane. Even Bob Adams wasn't that crazy.*

Was he?

She wasn't at all sure. To be on the safe side, she added: 'Though to be frank, Bob, you're not really my type, romantically speaking, you know?'

'Oh? And just how can you say that when you've never tried me romantically?'

God, didn't he ever give up? 'I just know, that's all.'

'You know nothing, Susan. What you're missing for a start: I'm telling you, I could do wonderful things for that body of yours.'

With that he grinned lecherously, and dropped his eyes to her breasts. Eyes that suddenly took on the appearance of slimy grey slugs, beneath heavy lids. Suzie could almost feel them upon her, stripping her clothing away. She might have been sitting there naked while those hideous grey slugs crawled all over her, leaving their slime-trails on her skin.

She shuddered.

And then his eyes came up again, and found hers as he pushed to his feet. 'Anyway, Susan, I'm going to have you one day, you see if I don't.' He wagged a finger in front of a lascivious grin. 'One way or another, I'm going to have you. You mark my words.'

Suzie seethed inwardly, but didn't respond. After all,

114

what was the point? What could she say or do that would ever put a dent in Adams's ridiculous ego? Though watching him leave her office the picture did flash back to her of him kneeling under her desk, servicing her while she worked, and that helped a little. The image stayed for a moment, but then was gone as a more exciting image returned.

The image of Michael!

She could see him as clearly as if he were sitting there with her. She could smell him. Taste him. So clearly, she ached for him. Finally she could resist it no longer: she reached for her phone and dialled the familiar number.

'Grace Cummings, please,' she said.

Grace Cummings had been more than a little surprised when she had asked to see Michael again; the same man twice.

'As good as that, eh, love?' the other Grace had said. 'And dinner, too, did you say? My, my ... Yes, of course; I'll tell him so he won't spoil his appetite by eating beforehand.'

And if some previous weeks Friday had seemed a long time in coming, this week the wait had been all but pure hell; she had thought it would never come. She had stayed at the office until ten every night; partly to catch up on work she had missed through her perpetual daydreaming, partly to avoid going home to a flat that had begun to feel somehow lonely; strangely empty, as if something – or someone – were missing. And, before leaving each night, she had scrubbed the day from the calendar on her wall, as if in so doing she was finally ridding herself of it; something nasty that had kept her from Michael. First there was that Monday lost in a daydream, then a Tuesday that had seemed to drag by for ever. Wednesday (a day she barely recalled), and an interminable Thursday. And then, at last, it was Friday.

And now, finally, it was Friday night.

She had changed her routine, and instead of first going home to bathe and change, she had driven from work directly to the Moorview and had bathed in her room. She had lain in the bath languidly soaking. Not planning, tonight, but dreaming of what Michael would do with her this time. Would it be exactly the same as the previous week? She wouldn't have minded. Or would he have other erotic tricks up his sleeve? Savouring her pleasures beforehand as she imagined what she could and tingled at the thought of what she could not – the surprises he might have in store for her.

She had dressed in a daze of dizzying expectation. And, for once on a Friday night, she had put on knickers. She had done so for exactly the reason she had changed other aspects of her usual routine: tonight, for the first time since she had started using the agency, she actually knew the man she was seeing. It was almost like a normal date. And she wanted to distance it from all the others in whatever ways she could.

Even now, she was sitting not in the bar but in the hotel lobby. She would meet Michael there, and he would escort her through for pre-dinner drinks. Even in such little ways, making it as different from the other times as she possibly could.

She glanced up at the clock by the check-in desk, and willed the hand to move more quickly towards the top of the hour. But it still hadn't reached it when Michael arrived, stepping in through the revolving doors with his usual confident air. He was almost five minutes early.

Suzie caught her breath when she saw him. *No, her mind had not played tricks on her, as she had half-feared that it had; he really was as gorgeous as she'd been picturing him all week.*

She stood up to greet him, and he smiled at her warmly; gave her a peck on her cheek. She thrilled when he did. *Just like a normal date.*

'I thought we'd have drinks,' she said. 'And have dinner about eight-thirty?'

She was asking, not telling.

* * *

In the bar, Suzie had her usual Martini, Michael a glass of white wine, and they sat with menus deciding what they would have, ordering when the waiter came. They laughed and chatted like old friends until the waiter returned to inform them that their table was ready.

Each had ordered pâté for starters, which turned out to be excellent, and as Michael dabbed at his lips with his serviette, the course finished, he suddenly looked up. His tone could not have been more casual when he asked from out of the blue: 'Are you wearing knickers, Suzie?'

Suzie was shocked. Not by the question itself, particularly – though it had taken her a little aback – but by the very fact he had asked it. The fact he seemed able to read her so well: last week he had guessed correctly that she was not wearing panties, now he seemed to know equally well that she was. *How did he know?*

She nodded. 'Yes, I am as it –'

'Then, take them off.'

'I'm sorry?' She wasn't quite sure she had heard him correctly.

'I said, take off your knickers.'

'What, now?'

'Now.'

The masterful tone of his voice sent instant butterflies down to her tummy, and caused a warm stirring elsewhere. She felt herself moisten with sudden arousal. He had said it so matter-of-factly, yet it carried all the thrilling authority of a command.

It was wonderful.

She inclined her head at him. 'All right,' she said with a little smile, as if she were accepting a dare.

She lifted her serviette from her knee and stood up. Took a step away from the table.

But Michael stopped her. 'Where are you going?'

Suzie looked at him with a puzzled expression. 'I'm going to the loo, to take off ... to do what you said.'

'*Ah-Ah.*' He shook his head, and wagged a finger signalling her to sit down again. 'Take them off here.'

The butterflies in Suzie's tummy danced wildly now, and she sank back in her seat feeling a little light-headed. *Take her knickers off there? Right in the middle of a busy restaurant?* But she knew he was serious. And knew just as surely that she had to obey.

She cast nervous eyes from table to table, to busy waiters and waitresses flitting from one to the other, to other diners. No one was watching; no one but Michael, who was watching her intently. With trembling fingers she lifted the side of her skirt; reached under it for the waist of her panties. Blushing furiously and praying no one was looking still, she wriggled them off as discreetly as she could and quickly smoothed out her skirt. With adrenalin still pumping through her veins, she went to secrete them into her bag.

But again Michael stopped her. He put out a hand, palm uppermost, over the table. 'Give them to me,' he told her.

Again her eyes darted, and embarrassment burned her cheeks as she stared back at his waiting hand; knew it would do no good to protest and at last reached over to give him her panties.

Michael held her eyes and smiled, almost slyly, as he took them from her.

Even tiny things like that, Suzie thought as his look sent a sudden *frisson* to tingle her crotch. Subtle nuances, inflections, the tiniest of things – he knew so exactly what turned her on!

He said. 'Thank you,' as his hand closed on the still-warm undergarment and brought it back to him.

And if Suzie had felt embarrassed at having to hand him her panties – across a restaurant table no less, with people all around – it was nothing compared with what was to come. She had expected him to discreetly dispose of them, but no. To her utter horror, he began to examine them. Right there at the table, in front of her. In front of anyone who cared to see, but in front of her was the worst.

She watched, her tummy crawling with spiders, as he

turned them over and over in his hands, inspecting them; turned them inside out in search, she knew, of their crotch. *The crotch she knew would be hot and damp, marked with telling stains.*

He found it; examined it closely.

She could almost have died with embarrassment, and squirmed in her seat as she watched him. Wanted to plead, *Oh, no, please don't,* but didn't; too entranced, even, to have thought about looking away. Felt intensely excited, and knew that Michael knew exactly what he was doing. Just what he was doing to her.

Finally, his eyes came up to meet hers. 'Well, we are feeling randy, aren't we?' he teased.

Doing it more. Deliberately, calculatingly, embarrassing her further; knowing it was turning her on.

'What a dirty girl you are, to have stained your knickers like this. You must be feeling as horny as hell.'

Suzie's eyes flashed. 'Yes, since you started doing that, you rat.'

'Rat? But I'm only observing what's here for all to see. Look, see for yourself.'

'Stop it, you . . . you bastard!'

She snapped her eyes away as he proffered the soiled crotch of her pants. But she had to grin, too, at the sound of his laugh; a laugh the sound of gravel beneath the wheels of a car. A laugh that said he knew full well she wasn't upset with him, despite her words or the vehemence with which she had spat them.

Her eyes were drawn inexorably back to him. And he slowly, very deliberately, raised her pants to his nose. And, ensuring she watched him, he inhaled deeply, drinking in her most intimate scents.

'God, you smell sexy,' he said, his eyes hooding with ecstasy.

A new wave of excruciating embarrassment swept through her. 'Bastard,' she repeated.

'Bastard, maybe. But it's turning you on . . . isn't it?'

'Bastard, bastard, bastard!'

'Yes, that's what I thought: turning you on like mad.'

Just then, the waiter arrived with their meals. Suzie's heart leapt to her throat, terrified he would catch sight of her panties. But to her relief Michael managed to slip them, unseen, into his jacket pocket. And for the moment the teasing was over; the sexual tension he had aroused within her allowed to ease. A little.

They chatted about trivia as they ate – Michael heartily, Suzie barely picking at the food on her plate (her stomach was knotted with sexual need and she wanted only for the meal to be over and to get Michael up to her room). But no sooner was his plate empty, than Michael began again.

'You know,' he said, washing down the last of his food with a mouthful of wine, 'just the thought of you sitting there with no knickers on is really turning me on.'

Suzie blushed, not needing reminding.

'Funny how the little things make such a difference.'

'The little things, the big things. Everything you do, Michael, turns me on.' She smiled at him, and despite the sexual tension that was aching within her she felt suddenly tender. She reached across the table and took his hand in hers. 'Everything.'

Michael returned her smile. 'I must admit, Suzie, you're a hell of a turn-on yourself.'

Suzie's heart skipped several beats, and a sudden warmth spread through her. 'Really, Michael?'

'Really.' Sincere.

He squeezed her hand and something special suddenly passed between them. Not just sexually special; something . . . deeper.

But it didn't make Suzie feel any the less horny. 'Let's not bother with dessert, Michael,' she said. 'Let's go up to my room.'

Michael grinned at her. 'No. I think we'll have coffee first.'

Making her wait. Deliberately, Suzie knew, making her wait.

* * *

120

They finally got to her room.

Michael had made her wait an agonisingly long time, while he sipped unhurriedly through two cups of coffee and she fidgeted, hardly knowing what to do with herself as the gnawing ache in her loins grew ever more urgent. But, at last, they were there.

They dealt with the money wordlessly, then Michael said: 'Go into the bathroom and get undressed. Come out wearing only your stockings.'

'Undress in the bathroom?' Suzie queried, puzzled.

'Why do you have a habit of repeating what I say?'

'No, it's just that . . .' She stopped herself. An order was an order. She shouldn't question it, only obey. 'Sorry,' she muttered, and went into the bathroom, nervous fingers already working at buttons.

When she emerged, it was to find Michael lying on the bed propped up on an elbow. He was naked, and already partially erect. He patted the bed, indicating she was to lie beside him. A welcome invitation indeed.

Quickly she went to him, and lay on her back, her thighs slightly apart (as she sensed was his wish), and Michael began to caress her; lightly stroking the tips of her breasts, erecting her nipples with gentle squeezes as he rolled them between finger and thumb. And then he was caressing the side of her breast, feeling its swell, stroking down and into her armpit. Gently moving her arm, he eased it above her head, brushing his fingertips along its inner surface all the way to her wrist, then back again. He moved to her other arm, raised it, too, above her head before rolling himself on top of her. He let his full weight bear down on her while his hands traced a sensuous path up along her arms, tingling her skin. He was crushing her slightly, but she didn't mind; her senses reeling with the thrill of his touch and too excited to care.

He nuzzled into her neck, nibbling with gentle teeth as his hands reached higher. Came to her wrists and gently gripped them; pressed upwards to stretch her arms ever higher. She could feel his manhood stirring between her thighs, distracting her, and she didn't understand why his hands left hers for a moment to reach beneath the pillows ... before it was already too late.

'Those are two I prepared earlier,' Michael announced, rolling himself from the bed. 'I can take my own time with the others.'

For a moment Suzie was puzzled; didn't understand what he meant, or why he had suddenly rolled off her. Then, to her horror, she realised there were cords round her wrists: two silken nooses that had been slipped over her hands, and which, she found, drew tighter the harder she pulled. The other ends of the cords were secured to the bedhead: he had tied her hands to the bed.

'Michael, untie me this instant,' she shouted in outrage. Knowing now why he'd had her undress in the bathroom: he had been setting his infernal trap. 'Or I'll scream.'

Michael was crossing the room, his back to the bed. She strained her neck to see what he was doing. His jacket was hanging on the back of a chair and he slipped a hand into one of its pockets, took something from it; she couldn't see what. Then he came back to the bed.

He reached down to her breast.

'I mean it, Michael, I'll scream.'

He took hold of a nipple and pinched it, suddenly and hard. Her lips came open in protest, forming a round zero of pain, and the instant they did something was pushed in her mouth. And sudden awareness of scent and taste told her what: it was her panties. She had been gagged with her knickers.

Michael held the panties in place with a thumb, pressing against her pushing tongue, and looked into her eyes.

'Look, I can always tie them in if you're going to be noisy,' he said. 'But promise you won't scream and I'll take them out. Trust me.' There was sincerity in his fathomless grey eyes. 'Trust me, and I'll give you an experience to remember, I promise.'

122

Trust him? thought Suzie. *How could she trust him when he'd just tied her hands to the bed.* But right then there wasn't a lot she could do about it. And whatever it was he had planned for her, she would rather endure it without her soiled knickers stuffed in her mouth.

At last she nodded her head, and Michael removed the panties.

'What –' Suzie began.

But Michael stopped her with a fingertip to his lips. 'You'll see,' he said.

He went back to his jacket and returned with two lengths of cord. Like the ones securing her wrists, each had one end tied in a noose, and these he slipped over her ankles. Then, pulling her down the bed towards him until her arms were stretched taut above her, he drew one of her legs out wide and tied her ankle to the corner of the bed. He drew her other ankle to the opposite corner, spreading her legs so wide that her groin ached, and similarly tied it, tightly spreadeagling her.

He stood up then, apparently satisfied, and Suzie pulled at the bonds to test them. They held unnervingly firm. And she knew she was now at Michael's mercy – utterly helpless. And being unable to close her legs made her feel especially so: the core of her womanhood felt achingly vulnerable, defenceless against whatever ravages might be in store.

Finally, Michael shoved a pillow under her hips, the bolster raising her buttocks and making her yet more accessible to him as he settled himself on the bed; brought his face to her lap and kissed the hollows either side of her helplessly proffered mound.

Suzie gasped.

His tongue and lips began playing along her inner thighs, kissing her bush, up along one side of her mound, down the other. So far avoiding her pussy, but always full of promise. And she wondered why on earth Michael had needed to tie her down for this – it was wonderful.

And then, at last, his mouth found her sex.

As excited as she already was, skilled lips and tongue took only moments to take her to the very pinnacle of erotic desire; to that point when just one more flick of the tongue, just one more brush of sensuous lips, would be all it would take to send her to heaven.

She held her breath, tensed her muscles, waited for it . . .

But it didn't come. There was no more than the feel of Michael's hot breath on her pussy. Enough to hold her there right on the edge, but not more.

She strained to come, but couldn't; was held on the desperate edge, pulling uselessly against the cords in frustration, her stretched body shaking. Until, gradually, the moment passed, and she let out a despairing groan on uneven breath as orgasm began to recede.

But no sooner had it done so than Michael began again; licking, kissing, caressing; taking her again right to the brink.

No further.

She slowly emerged from a timeless haze. Unaware of how long she had lain there. Concious that her legs were now free, were together, but with no recollection of Michael untying them.

It had quickly become obvious why he had wanted her tied up in the first place.

Again and again he had taken her to the very brink of climax. Never permitting her to go over, but always right to the edge, then holding her there. On that excruciating knife-edge between agony and ecstasy: between wanting it to go on and on and on, and the need, the ever more desperate need, for it to end. For release. For relief.

And still he had cruelly denied it. With a just-too-gentle caress of his lips, a teasing flick of his tongue enough to send hot tendrils of desire ripping through her loins but just-too-light-to-trigger, he had kept her at an agonising peak of arousal.

Until she had felt sex through every nerve in her

124

body. Until her senses had swum in an endless, bottom-less sea of sensation. Until she had bucked and writhed in total abandon, and had she been free she would have snatched a hand to her aching sex to rub herself to completion. No command could have stopped her. No thought of decorum or dignity; heedless of all save the all-consuming desperate need to come. Until her entire body had ached with that need. And still it had gone on, unremitting, unrelenting. Until every nerve-end grew raw and exquisite torment had become a torture she could no longer endure. And she had screamed for relief. And he had told her to beg, and she'd begged. Had begged pitiously: 'Yes, I beg you, I beg you, Michael. For God's sake let me come, please,' her voice someone else's, not hers, and a long way away.

And only then had he finally relented, taking her once more to that ultimate pinnacle but this time mercifully not stopping. This time the touch had come and she was sent exploding into a series of shuddering orgasms the power of which she had never before known, that went on for ever and ever and made lights flash and fireworks pop behind her closed lids. Until she'd been drained absolutely, and had lain exhausted and lifeless in a time-less oblivion.

She was not sure, even now, for how long she had lain there, only that it must have been for a while: the wracking throes of orgasm were a dim memory, and sweat was cool on her skin. She let her eyes come slowly open.

The haze cleared and Michael was sitting on the edge of the bed, smiling at her.

'Wakey, wakey,' he said.

Suzie narrowed her eyes. 'You really are too much, you know. I was aching to come even before we came up here. And you knew it, yet still you did that to me.'

'What? I only teased you for an hour.'

'An hour?' On one level it felt he had teased her for ever. Yet on another she could hardly believe it had gone on for so long. That she could have endured it for so long. *An hour! And she had already been desperate before he'd begun.*

'I let you come on the dot of it.'

The hour she had paid for. For a fleeting moment the thought disturbed her. But then the warm contentment that bathed her body soothed negative feelings away.

'Well you certainly earned your money, Michael, I'll say that for you. I've never come like that in my life.'

Michael grinned. 'Yes, I did manage to evoke a reaction, didn't I? When you came, I'm surprised the noise you made didn't bring the whole of the Moorview running.'

'Yes, well . . .' Suzie said, blushing. 'Anyway, come and untie my hands; let me give you a hug.'

'Oh, I don't think so. Not yet.'

'But the hour's up. I mean –'

'That didn't seem to bother you last week. Besides, it's time I had some fun. Time to fuck.'

'Oh, Michael,' Suzie said. Not sure. 'Let me give you a blow-job instead. I'm not sure my poor pussy can take any more.'

'Who said anything about your pussy?'

And with that he was sliding the noose from one of her ankles to up behind her knee. Bending her leg, he raised it, began pushing it upwards and back, over her head.

'Michael, what are you doing?' Suzie squealed in protest. A part of her knowing full well. *A part of her dreading it and a part of her yearning.*

'Be quiet,' Michael said. Masterful. 'Your knickers are still handy you know, if you'd prefer.'

'Er . . . no,' Suzie muttered. As Michael tied her knee to the bedhead close to her wrist.

He dealt with her other leg likewise, rolling her back on her shoulders to tie the cord to the bedhead. The position it left her in was not intrinsically uncomfortable, physically at least. But psychologically it was the most discomfitting position she could possibly imagine. Just as the previous week, her secret opening was dreadfully exposed. But now she was tied too.

And nor did it ease it for her that Michael had looked

126

there before: as his eyes played over her she was agonisingly conscious of them. That it was not the first time he had seen her there did nothing in the least to inure her from the intense humiliation it caused her. Nor from the staggering thrill of it.

She couldn't move, and she couldn't cover herself. Again she was utterly helpless. But now her knees were spread achingly wide above her head, and if she had felt sexually vulnerable before, it was multiplied a millionfold now; both her orifices, now, so blatantly exposed and available.

Michael touched a fingertip lightly to her clitoris, making her jump at its sudden touch, then traced a slow downward path along her slippery groove. It paused for a moment to prod gently at the sensitive membrane between the two holes, then moved on. As she had known it would.

His fingernail scratched lightly right across her anus, and she sensed it twitch in involuntary spasm just as the Viking's had done. She knew Michael's eyes were fastened there, that he had seen it, and her cheeks burned at the thought. The fingernail scratched again, then paused at the forbidden entrance.

Suzie held her breath and spiders squirmed in her belly.

Then the finger was teasing her open, easing itself inside . . .

She let out her breath in a sudden rush. 'No, Michael, don't!' she cried.

Michael immediately stopped. But didn't withdraw his fingertip; left it fractionally inside the delicate opening.

'Really?' he said.

Suzie's mind was whirling. She felt dizzy and nauseous. But desperately excited: she didn't know what she wanted.

'You don't really want me to stop, do you?' Michael pressed. 'You find it humiliating, yes. Degrading, even. But that's what you love, isn't it? Isn't it?'

Suzie heard herself whisper, 'Yes,' her cheeks aflame.

And then her senses were swimming in a giddying spin of excitement as Michael's finger pushed slowly inside her. Went in its full length, then partially withdrew. Drove forward again, and began moving in and out of her, twisting this way and that as it went.

Suzie moaned softly, beginning to enjoy the forbidden intrusion.

After a while Michael's finger withdrew, was replaced by a thumb (Suzie sensed) while the finger entered her pussy. He squeezed finger and thumb together, gently trapping the silken membrane between the two channels, working the soft flesh between them. And Suzie let out a groan from somewhere deep in her being as orgasm trembled her thighs.

Michael chuckled softly.

And then he was kneeling above her, positioning the bulbous head of his cock to where a moment before his thumb had been. Gripping the bedhead with his free hand he came up on his toes and pressed down. Suzie held her breath, tense and unsure. But too excited to stop it. There was a momentary flash of pain as the swollen knob passed her sphincter, but then it was gone and his pole of a shaft slid into her with surprisingly lubricious ease; went deeper and deeper, filling her virgin passage and thrilling her with unfamiliar sensation.

Suzie was amazed at herself. That part of her, which until only last week inhibition had caused her to keep her most guarded secret – secret from even the eyes of her lovers – was now being reamed by a cock. A week ago she would not have believed it. But that was before she had met Michael. And before, with Michael's help, she had banished for ever the ghosts of the Merciful Sisters.

As she watched Michael's cock plunge into her, withdraw and plunge again, she still felt the same humiliation – the shame, even – that both burned her cheeks and thrilled her. But no inhibition: not a trace of the old guilt. This was the new, the liberated Suzie. And it was wonderful.

She looked up into Michael's eyes, half closed in ecstasy as he slid in and out of her, and sensed his growing need. Didn't expect his sudden command.

'Open your mouth,' he told her. 'I'm coming.'

She didn't expect it, but was nevertheless quick to obey. She parted her lips, and waited.

There were three short, urgent pumps in her bottom, and then he was suddenly out of her, gripping his pulsing cock in his hand to guide its emission and spurting into her face. Jet after jet of it, thick and viscid. She swallowed what found her mouth, felt that which had missed its target running down her cheeks and the sides of her nose. And, her humiliation complete, she licked a gob of it from her upper lip and sighed in libidinous rapture.

Suzie lay in a warm womb of insouciant bliss, relaxed and content; her head, resting on Michael's chest, rising and falling with the rhythm of his gentle breathing.

Michael had at last untied her and they both had used the bathroom, showering together. And now they were lying in a cocoon of contentment, relaxed and satiated.

But as she came gradually down from her high, a question began to prod lazily at the back of Suzie's mind.

'Michael,' she said at last, still dreamy, 'would you mind if I asked you something?'

Michael's chest vibrated against her cheek as he spoke. Said: 'Not what's a nice boy like you doing in a job like this?'

Suzie jerked herself up on her elbow and looked at him, suddenly wide-eyed. 'How ever did you know?'

'It's been asked before,' he told her, shrugging.

He didn't go on, and Suzie prompted him. 'Well?'

'I'm an actor,' he said at last. Then grinned wryly to add: 'At least, that's what it says in my passport. Though from the amount of work I'm getting at the moment, I sometimes wonder. Hence this. I have to put a roof over my head somehow in between work.'

'While, what, you wait for your break?'

'Yeah, something like that. Oh, one day it'll come; I know it will. The right part will come along, that one will lead to other right parts, and my career will be up and running. But, until then, well . . .'

'Until then the Benson Agency pays a few bills, right?'

'Exactly. See, with acting, you never know when a job might come up. Or which part is going to turn out to be the part, the one that leads on to bigger and better things. The famous big break. So you can't afford to turn anything down, just in case. But with the commitment of a normal nine-to-five-type job, that mightn't always be possible. The Benson Agency, as you say, pays a few bills yet leaves me free to do acting work when I can.'

Suzie was quiet for a moment, reflecting. And suddenly disquieted. His answer had prompted another question, and she returned her cheek to Michael's chest, not wanting to look at him while she asked it. Not really wanting to ask it at all, but knowing she must. 'Acting,' she said finally. 'Is . . . is that what you're doing when you're with me, when you do the masterful bit? Is it all just an act?'

She waited with bated breath for Michael's reply.

'Yes and no, really. In one way it is, sure. After all, sex – unless it's very boring sex – is all about acting out fantasy.'

'I have a friend, Hilary, who says that.'

'Then your friend, Hilary, is very perceptive,' Michael said. He suddenly chuckled, making Suzie's head bob on his chest. 'I always say people who agree with me must be highly perceptive. My actor's ego, I guess.

'But no, she's quite right. See, when women come to someone like me for sex, they're looking to fulfil a fantasy – Oh, I'm sorry, that's rude of me: I'm presuming to tell you about yourself.'

'No, that's fine,' Suzie told him, eager to hear what he had to say. 'They're looking to fulfil a fantasy. Go on, I'm interested.'

'Well, I try and get inside their heads if I can; see what

130

sort of man the man of their fantasies is, then act the part for them. Make their fantasy live.'

'Be all things to all women, eh?' Suzie bit on her tongue. She hadn't meant it to sound sour, but her tone had been tainted by the sudden pang of jealousy she had just had at envisaging Michael with the other women he was talking about. Even if he was only acting a part with them.

She pushed it away, and was glad that Michael seemed not to have noticed.

'Well, I try,' he muttered drily.

There was a pause, then Suzie said: 'So what you're saying is, that when you're with me you're acting a part in my fantasy.'

'Of course. But –'

Suzie cut in. 'But how did you know what my fantasy was? How did you know what part I would want you to play?'

'Yes, well that's it: just what I was about to say. See, when I'm with you, Suzie, not only am I acting a part in your fantasy, but I'm also living my own.'

Suzie came back up on her elbow, looked into his eyes feeling oddly elated. 'So it isn't false acting, then, with me?'

Michael laughed. 'Well all acting is either false or it's real, depending on your viewpoint. But I know what you mean. And with you, no way. With you, I just enjoy myself; play the part I like to play best.'

Suzie tingled all over. So he really was the man she had thought he was. The man she had been dreaming of, all that week. The man she had had two fantastic sessions of fantastic sex with; her masterful, thrillingly dominant hero. For a minute she had thought that he wasn't, and somehow it mattered.

But that still didn't explain how he had known, right from the start, that she was sexually submissive; even, she had finally accepted, a tiny bit masochistic. She had only come to realise it herself just a few weeks ago, for God's sake.

131

She had to ask. 'But I never said anything, Michael. How did you know that I'm . . . well, what I like?'

'Ah, I found that out in no time,' Michael said with a grin.

'But, how?'

'Well, as I've told you, I like to try to get into a client's head; see if I can pick up some clues as to what her fantasies might be, what sort of a scene she's looking for, you know? Usually, of course, there's a meal first, or a few drinks at least – plenty of time to do a bit of gentle probing, ask a few of the right questions, that kind of thing.'

'Yes, but we didn't have a meal,' Suzie reminded him. 'Not last week, we didn't. And we took our drinks straight up to my room. You had no time at all to –'

Michael stopped her with a shake of his head. 'No, let me finish. Usually I can get a pretty good idea of what's wanted, and when I do I naturally go with that. After all, that's what they're paying me for. But when I haven't been able to: maybe the woman's been a bit shy about talking, whatever; or when she's in such a mad rush to get at it there's been no time to chat.' He winked cheekily at Suzie, who raised a hand as if to slap him. He laughed, and went on: 'Anyway, in the absence of any positive sign that I should play it some other way, I have a little trick I use to see if I can play it my own: the way that I'd really like. Do you remember I said, "Come here" – just like that – to you, when I was sitting on the edge of the bed?'

'Do I?' said Suzie, remembering it vividly. 'One of your masterful commands I've come to know and love so.'

'Ah, but actually it wasn't that strong: it sounded like a command to you only because you were receptive to being commanded. I was testing, you see; looking for your reaction.'

'I went all weak-kneed,' Suzie recalled, beginning to comprehend.

'Exactly. I knew it'd given you a buzz. See, another woman might have said, "No, you come here to me."

Or another might have come over and sat beside me on the bed, thinking I'd merely invited her to. Either way, I would've known that my kind of scene wasn't on: that that night, as is usually the case, I'd be performing solely for them, not me.

'But you, Suzie. You knew exactly what "Come here" really meant. And when you came over and stood compliantly before me I thought, "Wow! This girl's a real Sub. The perfect sexual counterpart to my Dom." I couldn't believe my luck.'

Suzie smiled shyly and blushed. Laid her head back down on Michael's chest to hide it. His perfect sexual counterpart? Yes, that said it well. No wonder, then, that sex between them was so incredibly good: they were opposite sides of the same sexual coin. And explained, too, how he knew so exactly what turned her on: if something excited him, then he would know it must also be a turn-on for her. It really couldn't be simpler.

'Do I take it then, Mister Counterpart,' she whispered into the hairs of Michael's chest, 'that you'll be free next Friday night?'

She felt his hand touch her hair, stroking gently. 'Not through the agency, no.'

Sudden panic fluttered her stomach; brought her back up on her elbow. 'Oh?'

'I can't keep on taking your money, love.'

'Wh-why not? What's wrong? What do you mean?'

'Exactly what I said, Suzie. I can't keep taking your money. Not for this. Haven't you heard a word I've been saying? Sex with you is the best sex I've had in my life.'

'Yes, me too. So, then, why can't we –'

'So then,' he butted in, 'so how can I carry on taking your money?'

'But I don't mind, Michael,' she protested anxiously. 'I really don't care! I –'

'But I do, Suzie. I care very much. It'd make me feel like a sponger, which I've never been. No, from now on there's to be no money involved. And that being the case, there's no point in you paying the agency's fee.'

133

'Oh,' said Suzie, feeling relief flow through her like a warm river. For an awful moment she'd thought he had meant he didn't wish to see her again. 'I see.'

'Before I leave tonight, I'll give you my number. Call me any time. If I'm not in, there's always my answering machine: leave a message on that and I'll get back to you.'

There followed an empty silence, while Suzie listened only to the sound of Michael's rhythmic breathing. That, and the voice in her head that was locked in fierce debate with itself: there was something she wanted to say – felt should be said – but she was afraid to say it, fearful of what Michael's reaction would be. The voice in her head argued it back and forth, struggling with the dilemma. But finally she couldn't resist it: she would have to say it and pray.

'Michael,' she said softly, 'I . . . I think I'm falling in love with you.'

She crossed mental fingers, her breath tight in her chest; prayed that in saying it she wouldn't drive him away.

Michael said nothing. But she sensed his head come forward and felt his lips brush her hair in a gentle kiss. Again the warm feel of relief flowed through her, and she smiled: it was all right; he appeared not to mind.

The silence gathered once more. A silence in which Suzie let herself dream, thought happily about all the exciting nights – the exciting sex – she would enjoy with her new-found love in the weeks and the months (who knew, even the years) ahead. All that wonderful, glorious, sex.

Michael was evidently thinking along similar lines, for after a while she saw him stir, begin to erect.

'You goat of a man,' she said, grinning, as she curled her fingers around him . . .

Chapter Twelve

I'm in love, Hils,' Suzie gushed. 'Madly, passionately, blissfully in love.'

Hilary had been away on holiday (with Cherry, who, of course, had paid for the trip), and it was almost a month since the two had last met. Suzie could hardly wait to bring her friend up to date. 'His name's Michael, and ...'

Almost without pausing for breath, she told the whole story, finishing with (for the third time): 'And what a lover, Hils. He knows just what makes me tick; just what buttons to press to pop my sexual cork.'

'Well, well, well,' said Hilary, popping the cork on the bottle of Chablis to which she had helped herself from Suzie's fridge. Suzie had been so engrossed in telling her all about Michael that Hilary had decided she had best do the honours. It was that or die of thirst.

She filled two glasses and passed one to Suzie. 'Real love, then, eh?'

'Oh, Hilary, I can't tell you. Smitten, I am.'

'And how does this Michael feel? Does he love you?'

Suzie's eyes dropped to her glass. 'I don't know,' she said reflectively. 'He hasn't actually said so; not in so many words anyway. But I do know he cares for me, and sees me whenever he can – three times last week, twice the week before. But in the future, who knows? Maybe he will come to love me, if he doesn't already and just hasn't said it, and we'll get it together.'

Hilary's eyes made sudden saucers. 'What? You don't mean wedding bells, marriage, like that?'

'That, or living together anyway.' Suzie shrugged. 'Same difference.'

'My God. And this from the committed career-girl. The girl who didn't have time for relationships; a regular man in her life.'

'Yes, I know.' Suzie's tone was almost rueful. 'And I'd be lying if I said it wasn't interfering with work a bit. God, I spend half my life in a love-sick daze thinking about him. But then I always was given to daydreaming.'

'Fantasising.'

Suzie grinned. 'All right. But anyway, Michael's different. He's worth getting involved with.'

'Getting involved with's one thing, love,' said Hilary, pointing a finger around the stem of her glass. 'But marriage? Living together? Gawd, now that's something else. I coundn't see me tying myself down to a single bit of crumpet for the rest of my life. Not even a darling like Cherry.'

'Well you're just a promiscuous cow, Hils,' Suzie laughed. 'Always were, always will be. Besides, I could do a lot worse. Like I said, Michael's an actor. And he's going to make it one day, I just know it; make it big. Who knows, maybe if we do get it together then five years from now I could be living in a Hollywood mansion. I'd've given up work altogether, and could be making babies that we'd give daft names to like all the filmstars do.'

Hilary shook her head in amazement. 'If someone had told me that Suzie Carlton would ever be talking like this – making babies: yech, what a thought – I'd have wanted a shot of whatever they must be on. Where ever did the ambitious, go-for-it-and-be-buggered lady boss go to?'

Suzie's grin was sheepish. She shrugged, and said: 'I don't know. It's Michael, he's . . . he's . . .'

'Different. Yeah, we know.'

'Yes.' Suzie feigned a pout. 'Well, he is.'

She fell quiet for a moment, sipping wine and reflecting. A life in Hollywood? Probably not. But having Michael's children? Oh, not this year, or next maybe. But somewhere out there in the future, who knew?

Suzie shook her head to bring herself back to the present. 'Anyway, that's all in the future.' she said. 'For now, I'm still a working woman; still the lady boss. Well, except for when I'm with Michael of course: I'm anything but the boss, then. And, for now, I'm just glad to be with him whenever I can. Whenever he's free.'

'And you say he's still working for the agency? Benson's?'

Suzie nodded. 'Yes, that's the trouble. Why I can't see him more often – he has bookings four or five nights a week.'

'And that's the only trouble with it, love?'

There was knowing accusation in Hilary's voice, and Suzie became defensive.

'What do you mean?'

'Well, it doesn't bother you? This bloke you're crazy in love with, smitten by, knowing he's with other women four or five nights a week?'

A dark cloud seemed to cross Suzie's face for a moment. And then was gone.

'I try not to think about it.'

There was a pause before she shook her head and said: 'Actually, that's not strictly true. Sometimes I do think about it; sometimes I actually find it a turn-on to think of him with other women.'

'See, I told you you were a masochist, love.' Laughing.

Suzie laughed too. 'No, it's not that. It's just . . . I don't know really. He's got some clients who are quite kookie; I suppose I'm a bit fascinated.'

137

'Kookie?' Hilary repeated, suddenly animated and wanting to know more. 'Kookie, how?'

'Well, for one, he's got this client – she's a middle-aged woman with blue-rinsed hair, apparently – who's not the least bit interested in having sex with him. Silly woman doesn't know what she's missing: God –'

'What a lover,' Hilary finished for her with an impatient cluck of her tongue. 'Yeah, you said. Go on, stick to the story.'

Suzie lit up a More and chuckled smoke. 'Yes, sorry about that. I suppose I'm a bit of a Michael bore at the moment. Anyway, so this woman, she lives all on her own in this big house up in Hitchfield. Michael says it's a bit like that one in *Psycho*: really creepy, you know? And he has to visit her there. Well, all she wants him to do when he gets there is to take off his clothes in this huge sitting room she has, and sprawl on a couch while she sits there and looks at him. Doesn't take off her own clothes, just sits there fully dressed and ogles his body. They don't even speak: she doesn't say a word, just sits there. Except she'll occasionally wave a hand at him, which is the signal, he says that she wants him to play with himself. He isn't to come, just to get himself hard, you know? And then she'll apparently get this little gleam in her eye, but mostly she shows no emotion at all.'

Suzie paused to sip at her wine, imagining the scene, then went on.

'Anyway, at the stroke of midnight – she has this big old clock that Michael says you can hear ticking half-way down her driveway, and that chimes incredibly loudly at the top of the hour – that's it; he can get dressed and go. And for that he gets thirty-five pounds, can you believe?'

'Takes all sorts, love,' Hilary said sagely. 'Though why anyone would want to sit and look at a rampant male organ, or even a flaccid one for that matter, is beyond my comprehension. For thirty-five quid or otherwise.' She slugged wine as if to rid herself of a nasty taste in her mouth. 'Yech!'

Suzie chortled. 'Yes, well, that's the one part I can

understand: he does have a terrific body. What I can't fathom is why she doesn't want him to do something with it. It seems such a waste.

'Course, in my fantasy about it, I'm there too. I go down on him, and I ride him, and all the while I'm sneering over my shoulder at the silly old bat because I'm getting what she isn't. In the fantasy she wants it, see; desperately, but can't have it.

'And come to think of it, Hils, as for my thoughts about Michael's clients being motivated by masochism, well, doesn't that rather belie the fact? I mean, my mocking this pathetic old woman, turning on to the fact that she's aching for what she can't have, is hardly masochistic of me, now is it? More the exact opposite, I'd say.'

She paused to consider that, vaguely wondering not for the first time if there might be a slightly sadistic side to her too. Finally she shrugged it away. 'Anyway, so that's her. And then he has this other kookie client. Another middle-aged woman. She likes him to screw her to Beethoven's Fifth – belting out so loud you can hardly think, he says – finally coming in time to the music, climaxing as it does.'

'Now that I could go for,' said Hilary. 'Not with a bloke of course, forget that. And I'd rather have Queen than Beethoven any day of the week. But, oh, yes; letting loud music transport the aesthetic part of –'

'Aesthetic, Hilary?' Suzie chipped in, amused. 'Who's been rooting in the brain drawer, then?'

'Shut up you. I might not have your vocabulary, clever clogs, but I do know some words, you know?'

'And vocabulary,' Suzie teased. 'Now that one's longer than marmalade, which I thought was the longest word you knew.'

'I know the word cunnilingus, don't I? And that one's even longer. Talking of which, as I was saying: yes, letting loud music transport the aesthetic part of the brain' – she fixed Suzie with a look, as if daring her to butt in again – 'to climax, while some sweet thing's busy little tongue takes care of the rest. Oh, yes. Now that I could go for.'

'You're incorrigible,' said Suzie, grinning. 'And that word's longer still.'

But Hilary wouldn't have heard her. Her eyes had glazed and she was evidently lost in the thought she had conjured.

At last she returned. Frowned, and said: 'But Michael actually tells you about these other women? Isn't that a bit off of him? Sort of rubbing it in, like?'

Suzie shook her head. 'I actually insist, Hils. I decided that if I have to come to terms with it, then the more I know the easier it'll be. There's nothing worse than not knowing, and imagining things to be worse than they actually are. I just try not to . . . to dwell on them, you know? Especially the younger, more attractive ones, the non-kooks, the ones who use his body as it should be used. And,' she added, as if it made all the difference; emotion beginning to rise in her voice, 'that's what they're doing, you know – just using his body. I should know: I've been there haven't I? Been there, done that, got the ruddy T-shirt. It's not like his mind's involved: not like he cares for them, like he does for me. He rents out his body for money, that's all. So what? So bloody what?'

Her lower lip had begun to quiver and her eyes suddenly brimmed. 'Oh, Hilary,' she sobbed, breaking down. 'I do wish he didn't.'

Hilary slid an arm round her shoulder, comforting; brought her cheek to her ample bosom and patted it gently. 'I know, love, I know,' she said softly. 'You get it out, girl. It's OK.'

For a while there was just the sound of Suzie's sobbing and the tick of the clock on the mantel. Smoke from her cigarette, burning down in an ashtray, rose in a lazy blue plume, then spiralled away to nothing.

As, eventually, did Suzie's sobbing.

Pulling herself together, she smudged tears away with her thumbs and reached for her drink. Swallowed wine noisily, and said: 'Sorry about that, Hils. Carrying on like a love-sick teenager.'

Hilary chuckled. 'It's all right, love. I can't say I've ever been there, the true-love thing I mean, but I do understand. And even lady bosses are allowed to cry sometimes.'

'And here I am,' Suzie went on with a sniff, 'gibbering on and on about Michael, and I haven't even asked you how your holiday went.'

'Oh, like a dream, love. I mean, what more could you want? Sun, sand, and a beachful of tanned tits to ogle. Sheer heaven. Bacardi and coke at a few pesetas a throw, and a companion who can't get enough of it. And I don't mean Bacardi! Gawd love us, but she's a randy one is that Cherry. D'you know, she even wanted it on the plane on the way over; said she couldn't wait till we got there.'

'You didn't, of course.'

'We did, of course. Joined the gay equivalent of the mile-high club somewhere over the Med. In the toilet; stark naked and taking it in turns to perch up on the wash-basin, our legs stuck over the other's shoulders and going at it hammer and tongues – if you'll pardon the pun. We got some funny looks when we came out, all right, and found a queue the length of the plane. But who the hell cares? Anyway, that set the tone for the holiday, and we were at it almost non-stop from then on.'

'Sounds like you had a whale of a time.'

'We did. One night I made Cherry pick up this black girl – an American she was – in a nightclub, and we ended up three in a bed. Oooh, what a night that was. Lovely. Those silky black thighs clamped to my cheeks giving me a face full of pussy, while Cherry's tongue was down there on me doing what Cherry's tongue does best. God, I thought I'd died and gone up to heaven.'

Suzie laughed. 'What makes you think that's where you're going, Hils, when you finally turn up your toes.'

'Yeah, well, they probably have more fun in the other place anyway. Talking of which, just thinking about that three-in-a-bed has gone and got me all hot and flustered. I'm feeling as hot and horny as that hell you reckon I'm bound for.'

Her arm was still on Suzie's shoulders, and she reached round further. Let her fingers find the neck of Suzie's blouse and slip inside. She cupped Suzie's breast in her palm and found the nipple between finger and thumb. Tweaked it lightly.

But Suzie put a hand over hers, stopping her. 'Hilary,' she said gently, 'would you mind very much if we didn't?'

'But why? You've just got through telling me your hang-ups are all in the past.'

'Yes, they are. And it's not that. It's just, well, now I have Michael, I . . .'

'I know,' said Hilary, reluctantly removing her hand, 'you want to stay faithful to him, right?'

'Something like that,' Suzie said, smiling gratefully. 'Thanks, Hils.'

Hilary refilled her wineglass, pouting.

'I don't know,' she mumbled with a shake of her head. 'I only hope I never catch a dose of this true-love stuff: takes all the fun out of life.'

And Suzie laughed.

Later, when Hilary had gone, Suzie sipped the last of the Chablis and thought.

She almost regretted, again, not having let Hilary make love to her. That was twice in a row she had turned her down; it was just as well Hilary was the friend that she was!

Besides, so much talk about Michael had left her missing him and wanting him badly, and feeling extremely randy.

It crossed her mind to ring him and see if he would come over. But she knew he'd been out that night – might still be out, and she hated the sound of his answering machine reminding her he was in the arms of some other woman – and she resisted the urge. She hated, anyway, the thought of him coming to her from another woman's bed, and knew that, yet again, her only lover that night would be her vibrator.

Wryly glad she had remembered to purchase new batteries, she drained her glass and headed for bed.

Chapter Thirteen

The room was full of beautiful women. There were blondes, brunettes, women with rich Titian hair, but all were astonishingly beautiful. They were all naked or near-naked, and all had gorgeous lissom bodies. She, alone, was fully clothed.

The women were standing or sitting in small groups, chatting and sipping what looked like champagne; there were vol-au-vents on silver trays here and there. And there was a large circular bed, upon which several female bodies lay entwined in sensual embrace. It was impossible to see how many bodies, as they writhed in a tangled mass of prurient flesh; fingers probing, tongues licking, hardly an orifice left unattended or idle. Faces locked between trembling thighs, lapping hungrily, others contorted in sexual ecstasy.

As she watches, two anonymous nylon-clad legs, shapely and lithe, emerge from the heaving mass. They slowly part, and as the thighs are spread wide she finds herself looking into the glistening pink core of their owner's sex; the lips swollen with unabated desire, pouting erotically at her from within the halo of a golden bush. It seems to invite her; to beckon her to it.

But she has no wish to go there. She is fully clothed; she isn't ready; she isn't a part of this – whatever this is. She doesn't know what she's doing there. She thinks, but can't recall how she got there.

She manages to force her eyes from that beckoning, gaping slit, and casts about, searching for clues ... And there, suddenly, is Michael, naked and magnificent, standing in the middle of the room.

'Michael,' she calls out to him; so pleased, so relieved, to see him. *He will know what she's doing here; how she came to be there.* She steps forward to go to him. But he, the women, the room and everything in it, recede by the same pace she has taken. Despite her step forward, she is not an inch closer to him.

'Michael, what's happening? What is this? Who are these women?'

Michael looks at her. Doesn't smile. 'These are my clients, Suzie,' he says.

'All these beautiful women?' She is stunned. 'But, but they can't be, Michael. I thought, I mean, you told me, most of your clients are middle-aged, unattractive women. Women who can't find men in conventional ways; that's why they come to you.'

'Ah, but these are my favourite clients, Suzie. I'm holding a party for my favourite lovers. The women who love me the most.' He smiles, but it is not a pleasant smile. A leer, as he looks around him. 'As you can see, they're, ah, fond of each other too.'

He makes a sweep of his arm, and as she follows its path round the room she sees that all the women, now, are locked in sapphic embrace.

She looks back to Michael. 'But, I don't understand.' She takes further steps forward, trying to go to him – *if only she can reach him, hold him, it will all be all right* – but again the room recedes. She begins to feel frightened. 'Michael, what's happening? Why can't I come to you?'

'Because you're not really here, Suzie. You weren't invited; you're not meant to be here.'

'Not meant? But you said it was a party for your favourite lovers.'

'Precisely.'

She feels a stab of sudden panic tear into her heart. Real fear now.

'But Michael, what are you saying? I'm your favourite lover of all. The best sex you've had in your life, you said. Your perfect sexual counterpart. Don't you remember?'

At that moment, one of the women – a tall, elegant woman, with gorgeous raven hair – goes to Michael and kneels before him.

'Oh, Master,' she says, 'may I pay homage to you?'

He looks down at her bowed head and smiles. A pleasant smile now. Almost avuncular. 'You may,' he tells her.

'Oh thank you, Master.'

The woman crawls forward, parting her lips. She reaches him and takes his penis into her mouth.

'You see, Suzie, I now have many such counterparts.' His arm sweeps the room once more. 'These are my worshippers; my acolytes.'

'You – your worshippers? But I worship you, Michael. More than anyone could.'

'But I no longer have need of your worship, Suzie: as you can see, I have more than enough.'

Fear claws at her stomach, clutches her innards with vicious unseen talons.

'No, Michael, this can't be true. Don't shut me out. Please, please, don't shut me out. I love you, Michael. I love you, I love you, I love you.'

Terror burgeoning.

Michael begins moving his hips in a steady, sensual rhythm; back and forth, back and forth. The woman kneeling before him closes her eyes in ecstasy; accepts her master's thrusting.

'I'm sorry, Suzie, but I no longer need you.'

'No!' She forces her tone to soften, to reason. 'Michael, no. Don't say that, please. I know I must share you with these other women, with even these beautiful other women. But that's all right. Really it is. I understand.' Desperate. 'P-l-e-a-s-e.'

'I'm sorry, but no.' Cold, unfeeling. Unloving. Uncaring.

'N-o-o-o-o!' The cry comes from deep within her; the long, low grown of utter despair.

Michael becomes a blur to her as her eyes flood with tears.

His hips are thrusting more urgently now, the mouth of the kneeling woman a passive receptacle for her master's straining sceptre. Then, abruptly, his hips stop moving, his thighs go rigid and tense, and begin slightly to tremble. And the raven-haired beauty shivers in rapture as she accepts her master's gift, a dribble of it spilling from the corner of her mouth as her master pumps in more.

Other women begin to move in, then, and are adoring Michael's body; licking his come from the woman's cheek, pressing their breasts to him, offering themselves for his pleasure.

A tear-blurred kaleidoscope which she watches in abject dismay.

She must go to him. Hold him in her arms. And then, she knew, it would all be all right. She begins to run forward. Faster and faster. As fast as she can, in a breakneck, headlong charge. But it is to no avail: the faster she runs, the faster the room backs away from her. She can make no progress. No progress at all. And finally, exhausted, unable to run a single step further, she stumbles to a halt.

Michael is now swathed in a cloak of wanton female flesh; naked women seeming to drip from him and no part of him free from the lascivious attention of sucking mouths, of licking tongues, of caressing or probing fingers.

She is forced to watch as he is bathed, by women other than she, in a molten pool of carnal pleasure. Hears his voice say, 'Goodbye, Suzie, goodbye,' as he is drowned, so lovingly, by his sea of naked worshippers.

147

Colours fade and grey. And the greys gradually merge into a single lustreless monochrome, which in turn grows darker, darker, darker. And the sound of Michael's voice, *goodybe, Suzie, goodbye,* fades too; grows fainter, fainter, fainter. Until she is staring into a silent black void. Screaming, 'Michael, Michael, Michael,' at the top of her lungs without a single sound coming from her, her lungs aching at the strain of it despite their abject failure to produce any noise.

Suzie awoke from the nightmare sweating. A cold sweat, that sent chilly shivers through her body and made her shake uncontrollably. She lay for what seemed like an age, staring up at the featureless white ceiling of her bedroom, lit only be the grey first light of dawn that scratched feebly through her uncurtained window, not daring to close her eyes lest she be cast directly back into the grip of her hideous dream.

Her vibrator still lay next to her thigh, where she had left it before falling asleep. Suddenly, inexplicably, it sprang to new life, startling her, but at least breaking her state of near-catatonia. Without wondering at the vagary of it, she grabbed the silver toy and strangled it silent. She flung it from her, then swung out of bed to head for the kitchen, deciding she needed coffee: hot, black, and strong. *How Mike Tyson likes his women,* she heard Hilary's voice say. But didn't smile.

'How's the issue coming along, Susan?' Clive Taunton asked her when he phoned later that morning.

Her immediate reaction was one of mild surprise, since he didn't usually bother. Usually, the only aspect of the magazine in which Clive Taunton showed the least bit of interest was the current circulation. But it was his magazine, or at least that of his family; he had every right to ask, she supposed.

She pressed the phone to her ear. 'Oh great, Mister Taunton –'

'Clive. You must call me Clive.'

His affability made Suzie wonder, not for the first time, if Clive Taunton might fancy her. Which, if true, could prove a nuisance. Not that she was in principle against sleeping her way up the corporate ladder – and Editor in Chief of the Taunton publishing empire was a tempting thought – but with Clive Taunton there simply weren't the Brownie points to be had. It was the old man, Humphrey Taunton – the Colonel as he was known – who wielded the real power. And she couldn't imagine sleeping with him. Clive's interest in her, if it existed, would be only a hassle.

But she pushed the thought away: maybe she was just imagining it; maybe he was just being pleasant, that was all.

'Clive,' she said. 'Yes, though I say so myself, it's brilliant. I'd say it's our best issue yet.'

'Good. Pleased to hear it. And we're, ah, going with the exposé that Bob's man came up with, are we?'

Ah, so that was why he had rung. Bob the Bastard had been working away in the background, going over her head.

She had managed to avoid including the awful gutter piece in the previous issue. Fortunately, an excellent story had broken concerning the young royals, which always made for good copy, and it had slanted the entire edition; leaving no room for the smutty details of the love-life of the unfortunate Lord Lingthrop, as even Adams had been forced to concede. But though the news was now old hat – the tabloids had had a field day with it, as usual, and had done it to death – Adams had been stubbornly pestering her to run it.

And now he had gone over her head.

'Er, no, Clive,' she said, her chest suddenly tight. 'We won't. In fact, we won't be running that story at all.'

'Oh? But Bob said it was an excellently written piece. Well researched, and that his man had found an angle for it that had slipped right by the dailies.'

Yes, an angle that was even more filthy, that would have been an even greater embarrassment to the poor Lingthrop family than that they had suffered already.

149

But careful, Suzie, she told herself: *back off.*

'Oh, yes, it is well written,' she agreed. 'And there's nothing wrong with the research: Keith Blundell is a talented young journalist.' *Just steered the wrong way, by Adams,* she wanted to add but didn't. 'And Bob's right, yes, the angle is a bit different.'

'Well, then. In my view Bob has excellent judgement; I think you should reconsider.'

Back off, Suzie, maybe, but don't back DOWN. Never, for the sake of expediency, back down. She took a deep breath.

'Mr Taunton, when you appointed me Publishing Editor of this magazine, it was my judgement you were backing with regard to editorial policy. And I believe the circulation figures show that my judgement, so far, has been largely sound?'

'Oh, of course, Susan. Indeed. But I just feel –'

'And if I am to continue as Publishing Editor, I have to be allowed to make the decisions as to which stories we run and which we don't. And this one I say we do not.'

There was a long pause before Taunton said slowly: 'I see. Well, yes, as you say, it is your decision. Er, and I suppose we are rather close to the deadline to be making non-essential changes at this late stage.'

Suzie glanced at her watch. The deadline was at four o'clock the following day: if Taunton needed an excuse to take back to Adams, he certainly had one.

'Less than thirty hours to press,' she confirmed. 'And the paste-ups are all but finished.'

'Yes. Quite. I'll, ah, tell Bob there was simply no time then, eh? So, Susan, keep up the good work, what? I'll look forward to reading the issue.'

The line went dead and Suzie put down the phone. Feeling virtuous to have remained true to her principles despite pressure from above; pleased to have made Clive Taunton back down, yet more than a little disquieted too. *Bob Adams was becoming more than a bloody nuisance.* She might have won this time, but what of the future? Now it had begun: now Adams had started to

150

interfere with her job, the decisions she made, was this only the first of battles to come? She feared probably yes.

The thought turned her mood sour, and with that came unbidden memory of the dreadful dream she had woken to. Bob Adams went away, but the pit of her stomach felt suddenly heavy as the nightmare came back to torment her. She again saw Michael, coldly and unfeelingly, turn her away in favour of his worshipping acolytes.

How could you do it to me, Michael? How could you hurt me so?

And though she knew it was irrational of her to blame Michael for what she had dreamt, an image nevertheless formed in her mind of her punishing him for it: he was tied down naked and helpless, and she was whipping him mercilessly . . . with a glowing heat in her loins and a sadistic gleam in her eye, enjoying what she was doing.

Christ, she thought, I'm going mad. Do-lally-bloody-tap! What ever the hell is wrong with me?

She shook her head to dislodge the image and it eventually shimmered and went. But it left her feeling strange and disoriented. And, to her utter surprise, not a little aroused.

She pushed up from her desk deciding she would go for a stroll, a walk round the building in an attempt to clear her head; knowing she would make for the third floor.

The month's issue, already cut-and-pasted and in almost its final form, sat on her desk where she had been attending to last minute detail. She slipped the pages into their folder, then the folder into her drawer where she carefully locked it. Things had a habit of going missing from her office whilst she was out – pens, ashtrays, staplers, anything that wasn't nailed down. But the thought of the paste-ups going missing, so close to the deadline and too late to put another together in time, was enough to fill her with horror. It didn't bear thinking about.

She tucked the key in her pocket and started for her door.

Decided she wouldn't, after all, go anywhere near the third floor: watching naked female flesh would be far too vivid a reminder of a nightmare she would rather forget.

Chapter Fourteen

As the weeks rolled by into months, her love for Michael deepened. She came almost to live for the nights he could see her; which, depending on his escorting assignments, continued to be two or three evenings a week. Except for once, when an acting job took him for a fortnight's filming in Edinburgh; the longest two weeks of her life. Her own busy schedule she worked around him: if Michael was free, then she was free, whatever it took.

And sex between them continued to be great: Michael, whose imagination seemed to be boundless, for ever coming up with new ways to excite her.

Like the time he decided they would go for a drink, but allowed her to wear only a coat, insisting she remain naked beneath it.

It was deliciously erotic: as they walked into the small country pub he had chosen, she felt as if all eyes were upon her; as if those people knew she hadn't a stitch on under her coat. It was as if they could see right through it anyway. She might just as well have been totally naked for all the concealment it seemed to afford her.

Michael bought them drinks and they sat at a table in

a quiet corner. But quiet corner or not, they were still in public, and she remained acutely conscious of her secret nudity, blushing whenever an eye strayed her way. Her hand trembled as she sipped from her glass.

Michael came close and slid an arm round her shoulder. 'How do you fell, Suzie? Sexy?'

'Horny as hell,' she admitted, blushing pink.

Michael grinned. 'Yes, I rather thought you would. But I want to feel for myself.'

'Michael! But you can't; not here.'

'Who can't?' His eyebrows lifted in what appeared to be genuine surprise as, without further ado, he slipped a hand inside her coat. 'With you, Suzie, I can do whatever I like.'

Suzie's eyes shot round the room, praying no one was watching. Doubting that Michael would have very much cared if they were.

As it was, no one appeared to be looking their way, but it did little to assuage her nervous excitement.

Slipping a finger between her thighs, Michael said: 'While we're here, I want you to sit with your legs slightly apart, so you'll be available to me throughout the evening. I'll want to feel you from time to time, to check on your, ah, progress. Test your little sexometer here.'

His finger was inside her now, moving lubriciously; turning her on further. She moaned softly. 'Mmmm, we are wet, aren't we?' he teased. 'Who is a sexy girl then, tonight?'

'I am,' she gasped.

Michael spanked her clitoris with the tip of his finger, making her gasp again, then withdrew his hand with a chuckle. Letting Suzie grab for her drink; needing it.

But there was no relaxing of her sexual tension: even just having to sit as he had directed, with her thighs slightly apart, was erotic. The slight draught in the room seemed to seek her out and caress her, a constant reminder to her of her clandestine nakedness – as if she had needed reminding – and she was soon aching with sexual need.

154

But it was to get even worse. *Better.*

Finishing his drink, Michael reached over and undid the bottom two buttons of her coat, exposing her upper thighs. The table at which they were sitting was broad, and pulled up close to them as it was it provided adequate cover; unless someone were to purposely look beneath it they could not actually have seen. But it was enough that she knew her bush was exposed.

She squeaked in protest. 'Michael, please . . .'

But Michael ignored her. Pressed on: 'Now lift your bottom off the seat,' he told her.

She new at once what was coming. But knew equally that it was useless to argue. Slowly, she leaned forward onto the table, lifting her weight from her buttocks.

Michael pulled the coat from beneath her, making it ruck up behind her and baring her from the hips down.

'There,' he said, 'now you can sit.'

'You're a sod, Michael, do you know that?'

Michael grinned wickedly as he watched her sit down again, knowing the leather of the seat would be cool to her naked buttocks. It was, and the sudden feel of it caused an intense sexual thrill to stab at her loins: little could have done more to heighten her consciousness of her predicament.

'I know,' he said. 'And a worse sod than you think, too.'

And with that he pushed her thighs apart. Wide, wide apart.

'Now, stay exactly like that,' he told her, 'while I go and get us some drinks.'

He pushed to his feet collecting their empty glasses, and headed for the bar leaving her just as she was.

Sitting there, alone at the table, her thighs spread brazenly apart beneath it, the moist lips of her womanhood pouting open with hungry desire, never had she felt so conscious of herself, so utterly exposed; the cool draught in the room now a thing that tormented her as it brushed the heat of her sex.

She thought about closing her legs – at least until Michael returned – but didn't. She had to be true to her new-found self: submissive and totally compliant. Obeying Michael's command even though he wasn't there to enforce it. Especially as he wasn't there to enforce it.

So, she remained as she was, quivering with sexual tension; the strings of her sexual bow drawn taut. The risk, slight that it was, of her being discovered serving only to tighten them further, making them sing with tension.

At last Michael returned, a foxy smile on his face as he made his way back with their drinks. It was a smile that said he knew exactly what he was doing to her, exactly what she was feeling – he knew her so well – and she blushed a bright scarlet to know that he knew.

He sat down and immediately put a hand to her under the table, cupping her sex; knowing she would have complied, but checking anyway.

Finding she had, his grin broadened. 'Hell of a turn-on, Suzie,' he said, 'knowing you were sitting like this while I was up at the bar.'

'God, Michael, that's as maybe' – there seemed little point in her saying that it was a hell of a turn-on for her, too; that, he could feel for himself – 'but please can I close my legs now?' she implored.

'No, of course not,' Michael told her. *As she had secretly hoped that he would. She'd asked, just for the thrill of hearing him say it.* 'I want your legs apart for me the whole time we're here. What, don't you want that I should be able to do this, whenever I please?'

With that his fingertip nudged her clitoris and she almost squealed out loud; managed, somehow, to contain it within her.

'But Michael,' she gasped, her breathing ragged, 'in public . . .'

'Shhh! Who's to see?' he said.

And his fingers teased on. They were working their usual magic, and she was soon quivering as her orgasm gathered: both fearing and praying he would make her come.

He didn't.

He kept her in a state of aching arousal throughout the entire evening. Always on the edge of climax but, as was his wont, never quite allowing it. Always, always making her wait.

Bastard.

Until, at the end of the night, as she was driving them back to her flat, her loins aflame with unsated desire, Michael leaned over and unbuttoned her coat. Pushing it aside, he told her to spread her legs wide. (The Saab was automatic, so she was able to crook her redundant left knee to comply.) And, with the passing streetlights strobing their sodium glow across her naked widespread thighs, his skilled fingers went to work on her yet again.

And, this time, they didn't hold back at the critical moment.

'I don't suppose this is exactly practising safe sex,' Michael quipped as she began to shake with the onset of climax.

It was an understatement: the car veered drunkenly and she was fortunate not to have crashed when she came.

Another time, they had been making love in her flat when Michael suddenly stopped; withdrew.

'We're going to your office,' he announced from nowhere.

'What? Why?'

She had been close, very close, to orgasm, and the sudden interruption, his sudden withdrawal, was irksomely frustrating.

But he insisted. 'I want to have you across your desk,' he told her simply.

They drove there. It was close to midnight, and the building was deserted. They went up to her office. And, there, for once she wasn't the boss.

Michael made her strip naked, then had her kneel

before him to fellate him erect. There was still the taste of her juices on his penis from their love-making earlier, and the scent of it combined with his musk soon had her dizzy with need. Fortunately he, too, was easily excited and his cock was quickly a turgid pole in her mouth that throbbed with desire as she sucked him.

It was all strangely exciting: *what if someone – Bob Adams, even – should stop by to pick up some forgotten work, or to refer to the files for some piece they were writing?* It was not very likely, but it had been known. And the possibility of it, the risk of their being caught there by one of her staff – she naked and submissive, kneeling before Michael with his cock in her mouth – kept her on a nervous edge that added a thrilling new dimension to it all. And which more than made up for her earlier frustration.

At last, Michael was ready. He lifted her onto her desk, perching her buttocks on the edge of it and lying her back. And while she wrapped her legs around his waist, he slipped himself into her; began to ride her with long penetrating strokes that hit her G-spot with every inward thrust, and which, together with the perversity of being taken across her desk, soon had her shuddering in climax. And she couldn't have denied taking a certain perverse pleasure, too, in doing with Michael exactly what Bastard Bob Adams had once suggested she do with him.

With Michael there was always something different. Something to surprise her, to keep her slightly off-balance, and so keep the sex between them vibrant and fresh. He always had some new trick up his sleeve to take her to unknown heights of erotic pleasure, and she never quite knew what to expect. Only that, whatever it was, it would be fantastic.

And all the while she revelled in the freedom of her newly-discovered sexual submissiveness. A submissiveness that liberated her, that allowed her to enjoy it all to the full, with none of the feelings of sexual guilt that had gnawed in little corners of her mind ever since she could remember.

It all added up to a wonderfully heady time, and Suzie was happier than ever she had been in her life.

Only one dark cloud hung on her otherwise azure horizon: the four or five nights a week when Michael wasn't with her. That, and knowing where he was on those four or five nights; knowing what he was doing.

This latter had become more of a problem for her following the nightmare she'd had of those beautiful acolytes worshipping him, as irrational as that was. But after the dream she had found it increasingly difficult to pretend to herself that he was with middle-aged, blue-rinsed ladies those nights he wasn't with her; women who represented little or no threat to her. She increasingly envisaged him with gorgeous, sexy young women who might well be a threat, and who made her insanely jealous.

'It's driving me crazy,' she confided to Hilary one day. 'At first I could cope – well, almost anyway. But now . . .' She let her voice peter out with a sigh.

Hilary's brow was crumpled with sympathy. 'It was bound to get to this sooner or later you know, love,' she said gently. 'I'm only surprised you stuck it so long. How long is it now, since you and Michael met?'

'Four months, two weeks, and a day.'

Hilary nodded wisely. 'Exactly. Long enough to have fallen properly in love, see? Not just those first heady throes of it, when you're so head over heels you can't see anything but roses and light; when you're prepared to put up with anything just so long as you get to get something. This is proper love, now, and that's not enough any more; now you want Michael all to yourself.'

'No, it's not th –' Suzie stopped herself. *Yes, it was exactly that.*

She was surprised Hilary understood it so well. Hilary, who had never been in love in her life; who was promiscuous by nature, and who shared her lovers with no more qualm than a child will share sweets. But then, Hilary often surprised her.

'Well, Suzie, it seems you have only two choices. Either you get Michael to quit the agency, or you quit him, now, before it gets any worse and it really does drive you nuts.'

'Oh, but I couldn't, Hils; there's no way I could stop seeing Michael.' The very thought of it filled Suzie with horror. 'I mean, don't get me wrong, I'm not exactly miserable you know: Michael has made me happier than I've ever been in my life. I shouldn't be whining at all, really. It's just me; me and this insane jealousy of mine.'

'Then, what about the first option?'

'Get him to quit the agency? But how? He can't do a normal job because he has to be free for acting work. So how do I get him to quit?'

Hilary threw up her hands in surrender. 'Hey, you're the one with the brains, love; you work it out. I'm only giving you the options, that's all; the details are down to you.'

Suzie disappeared into thought. Get Michael to quit the agency? But how? There didn't seem any way.

Nevertheless, with Hilary's help as always, a seed had been sown in her mind.

By the following week that seed had germinated, had grown and blossomed into a full-blown idea. But even so, Suzie was horribly unsure of her ground.

It came to a head on the Monday night.

She and Michael had dined out that evening, and though the meal had been excellent she had barely tasted a thing; worrying and wondering throughout. What would Michael's reaction be to what she had in mind? Should she or shouldn't she broach it with him? Did she or didn't she dare?

They were sitting in a comfortable ante-room taking coffee and After Eight mints, when she finally decided: yes, she would have to.

She crossed mental fingers so hard that her head

ached, and took a deep breath, ready to take the bull by its horns.

'Michael,' she began, 'can we talk seriously for a while?'

Michael turned to look at her. Didn't smile when he said: 'Meaning we talk rubbish most of the time?'

'No, you know that's not what I mean. I mean –'

'I know,' Michael said, cutting her off; his voice tight with controlled impatience. 'And yes, I think it would be a good idea if we were to talk seriously for a while. Whatever it is you're thinking to say, Suzie, I think it's best for us both that you get it said – it's been on your mind the whole evening.'

Suzie looked down at her coffee-cup. 'I'm sorry. I didn't realise I'd made it that obvious.' Michael had been his usual wicked self that evening, turning her on in all sorts of subtle ways throughout dinner, managing to, despite her distraction. But even so it must have been obvious that her mind was elsewhere.

'It isn't a problem,' Michael said with a shrug. 'But something is a problem, right?'

Maybe now wasn't the time, Suzie thought. Michael was clearly uptight, annoyed by her unwitting lack of attention. But she had begun now. It was too late not to go on.

'I . . . I want to see more of you, Michael,' she said, her breathing shallow. 'Just two or three nights a week, well, it just isn't enough. Not any more.'

Michael took her chin between finger and thumb; gently lifted her face and turned it towards him. 'Suzie,' he said softly, 'I'd like to see more of you, too. But you know it just isn't possible. Not at the moment.'

'Would you, Michael?' There was honest pleading in Suzie's voice. 'Really? Is that the truth; you'd really like to see more of me?'

'You know I would. But what can I do?'

'You . . . you could give up working for the agency.'
There, it was out.

Michael released her chin and threw up his hands.

161

'Yes, I thought this was coming. Knew it would sooner or later. But how can I? Be fair, Suzie, you know how it is. We've talked about it: the agency is the only way I can earn a half-decent income while at the same time keeping my options open. If – when – I get my break, well then it'll be different. Then, the income I earn will be decent in both respects. But for now –'

'Yes, for now you screw for money,' Suzie cut in, instantly regretting the bitterness of her tone. But she *was* bitter: this was the man she loved, for God's sake. She had every right to feel bitter. 'I'm sorry, Michael, I didn't mean it to come out like that. But it's true, isn't it? And I just can't stand it any more, thinking of you with those other women. Alone in my flat, thinking about what you're doing. It's driving me crazy.'

Michael's voice softened with sympathy. 'No, I know it can't be easy for you, love. But like I said, what can I do?'

Suzie's chest tightened, her heart thudding within it as the idea she had had took form in her mind. As she steeled herself to say it. Then: 'You could move in with me,' she suddenly blurted.

And now it was all out

It seemed, to Suzie, the perfect solution. But would Michael agree? He was such a proud man, and if he thought for one moment that what she was offering was some sort of charity, then he'd turn her down flat.

'I earn enough for us both,' she said, ploughing on regardless. 'And you'd be free to do whatever acting jobs come your way while you wait for the big one. Well, what do you say?'

She stared at her coffee-cup, not daring to look at him as the silence gathered and lengthened.

And as the silence continued to lengthen she felt the beginnings of panic. *He was going to say 'no', she just knew it*. And what then? What had she done? Her mind suddenly flooded with negative thoughts and she wished she had never spoken. Let it go on as before. After all, how bad had it been? She could have lived with it – just.

But now? Now, she had told him she couldn't live with it; had put him under pressure. And what did Michael need with that kind of hassle? It would probably drive him away; he would probably want never to see her again. She had blown it all.

And still the silence went on.

And then she felt his hand brush her cheek, move into her hair gently stroking. Heard his voice, ever so softly say, 'Suzie, I love you.'

Her heart almost stopped; flooded with joy. He had never said it before. Her eyes shot up to meet his, already brimming with tears.

'Then, the answer's yes?' She could hardly believe it.

Michael nodded, and she threw her arms around him, hugging him to her as happiness filled her being. 'Oh, I love you, I love you, I love you,' was all she could say.

Finally, Michael eased her away. Held her eyes with a sincere look.

'But I won't sponge,' he said. 'I'll earn my keep. I'll keep house for you.'

'Ah, er, no,' Suzie said. The thought of him cleaning house was too far from her image of him; the image she loved and admired. Though the idea of him washing her undies had a certain embarrassing appeal. But she pushed that away. 'No, you can't really do that, Michael. I have a lady who comes in and does: Mrs Fletcher. She's a dear: you'll love her, and I wouldn't want to put her out of a job.'

And then she had an idea. 'Listen, didn't you once say you can cook?'

'Is the Pope Catholic? Can Laurence Olivier act? Are you hot and horny right now?'

Suzie grinned and blushed at the same time. 'You know very well I am. But stick to the subject, will you? Listen, so that's the deal then: I pay the bills and you have a meal on the table for us for when I get home from the office. Then we can eat before we ...'

'Only every night,' Michael laughed, finishing her sentence.

Suzie gripped his hand in hers. 'Oh, Michael, I'm so happy. I just can't tell you how happy I am. When will you move in?'

Michael thought for a while. Then: 'Well, I have a booking for the night after next . . . Oh, don't worry,' he added quickly, seeing Suzie's frown, 'it's just a straight escorting job. No extras. Some old harridan, apparently, who wants an escort to some function or other. Now I have the booking, I ought really to do it. And then I have an audition at three the following day. I could move my stuff in straight after that, if that suits you?'

'Couldn't be better,' said Suzie. 'That'd be Thursday, my deadline day. I can get away from the office early, just as soon as the paste-ups have gone to the printers at four, and be home for when you get there. Though, just in case I'm not . . .'

She wrestled her spare key from her keyring and gave it to him, her heart something that swelled in her chest.

And for a while they sat in a comfortable silence, lost in their thoughts and sipping coffee.

And then the gnawing ache in Suzie's loins which Michael had so cleverly caused there earlier could be ignored no longer.

'Michael,' she said. 'Will you take me home and relieve me of this desperate need I have for your body?'

'Of course.'

Michael grinned at her slyly, his eyes flashing. 'Eventually.'

Chapter Fifteen

*T*he two were lying on Suzie's bed, relaxed and content; the only sound that of their breathing gradually slowing in post-orgasmic calm.

There had been no domination that night; no prolonged session of sexual athletics; no kinks. That night Michael had declared his love for her, and in celebration of that they both had felt the need, for once, for only tender, loving love-making. And joined in gentle coitus they had risen together on a warm tide of sensual pleasure to a tranquil plateau of mutual fulfilment.

But, even as their bodies cooled in the comfortable aftermath, Suzie's thoughts had again turned kinky: *she was thinking about Vikings.*

'Michael,' she said at last, 'do you ever feel submissive? Sexually, I mean?'

Michael rolled himself up on an elbow; looked into Suzie's eyes.

'That's a strange question.'

'No, it's just ... I sometimes wonder about me: I mean, I know I like to be submissive in bed, but I sometimes wonder if there might be a slightly sadistic side to me too.'

She told Michael all about her slave-market fantasy –
it was beginning to sound repetitive – finishing with:
'Hilary reckons I was just playing psychological games
with myself: reversing roles to live out what I enjoy
through the Viking's eyes because I hadn't yet come to
terms with being submissive.'

'It's an interesting concept,' Michael ventured.

'Yes, but I'm not sure it's right. The thing is I enjoyed
what I was doing in that fantasy. For me, not for what
the Viking, or for what anyone else might be feeling, but
solely for me. And there've been other times, too, when
I've felt sadistically inclined. Do you think it's possible
to be both submissive and dominant?'

'Ah, hence the question.'

Suzie hesitated for a give-away moment. Then: 'Well,
yes and no.'

She let her words hang, and waited for puzzlement to
dawn into comprehension on Michael's rugged face. She
blushed, then, and said: 'I mean, if I don't find out I'll
never know, will I?'

'And you want to find out on me, you mean? To
dominate me?'

'I'm not sure.' It was something of a quandary. She
both loved and respected Michael. Deeply. And on the
one hand the idea of subjugating him, of subjecting him
to sexual humiliation, was anathema to her. Yet on the
other . . . On the other, she was keen to explore the un-
explored; to discover, insofar as it existed at all, the opposite side of her sexuality.

'I think so. Just to see,' she said at last. Added quickly:
'But only if you think you'd enjoy it, Michael.'

Michael shrugged, appeared to consider it. 'I don't
know, I've never tried it . . . But, yes, I've often fantasised about it all right. And I can't deny, the idea of
being dominated by a beautiful, sex-hungry woman,
being her sex-slave as it were, does have a certain appeal. Even suffering some degree of physical pain –'

'Pain?' Something exciting tingled between Suzie's
legs. 'You mean, you could actually stand pain?'

'Not blood and guts, no,' said Michael honestly. He went on with a chuckle: 'But, hey, to a macho-man like me? What's a bit of pain? Anyway, in all seriousness, the dividing line between pain and pleasure, between agony and ecstasy, can sometimes be extremely fine. The two can easily cross over.'

Suzie reflected on the agony and the ecstasy of being held on the edge of orgasm, not permitted, quite, to go over that edge and into the relief of climax. Bitter-sweet frustration. Pleasure-pain. Yes, she knew all about that.

She studied Michael's eyes. Eyes she had often seen hooded in ecstasy at the critical moments before release, ecstasy that was itself a sweet sort of agony, and she wondered what it would be like to see in them real pain. A tendril of desire wormed in her loins; she may be soon to find out.

'Then, are you saying we can try it?' she said eagerly.

Michael shrugged. 'I don't see why not. I'm not one for knocking what I've never tried. And if being a sex-slave to a beautiful woman is half as exciting in reality as it is in fantasy, then I'd say I'd enjoy it very much. Besides, if your friend's role-reversal theory bears any substance, then what you do in dominating me might give me a few pointers on what to do with you.'

Suzie chuckled dirtily. 'I doubt I could give *you* any ideas on what turns me on; you're already the bloody expert.'

Nevertheless, it made her wonder: *maybe there would be an interesting spin-off to their reversing of roles. She would have to think carefully about what to include.*

'Though in any case,' she said, 'not everything I might do to you would be an automatic signal I'd enjoy it my-self, you know. For a start, some things would be ana-tomically impossible. And anything resembling real pain, ugghh!'

Michael grinned. 'Don't worry, love, I've got a pretty good idea where your limits lie; I might take you right to them, but never beyond. So, when do you want to give this a go then?'

There was no hesitation. 'Tomorrow night?'

'Blimey, Suzie, talk about the eager beaver, eh? But, well yes, why not?'

'Be here at eight o'clock sharp, then. And that's an order!'

'Yes, Mistress,' Michael chuckled. 'But, for now, just come here and love me, eh?'

Suzie cuddled up to him happily and loved him with all her heart. Felt him beginning to stir against her thigh and reached down a hand to him; furled her fingers around his thickening member, and had an exciting thought.

'I'm going to enjoy controlling this,' she said, giving his shaft a gentle squeeze.

'Controlling Percy? Oh, no chance of that, love: he's always well and truly in my command.'

'Is he now? We'll have to see about that, won't we?'

'Well, you little minx,' said Michael. 'I can see I'm going to have to teach you a lesson in self-control. Hands behind your head and open your legs,' he ordered. 'Now!'

Suzie obeyed, her loins suddenly tingling.

She looked forward to the following night, but knew that this night was far from over.

Chapter Sixteen

'*B* ollocks,' said Hilary, her usual primary self.

Suzie and she had met up for lunch, and Suzie had been bringing her up to date with the exciting developments of the previous evening: that Michael had promised to quit the agency after one last job, and that he was moving in with her the day after next. This had raised an eyebrow. And how that night – of less importance, but in its own way just as exciting – they were going to reverse their sexual roles; that she was to dominate him. Which Suzie had thought would raise an eyebrow but which hadn't: it seemed to be only what Hilary expected.

But she had gone on to explain that, though the thought of dominating Michael was a real turn-on, she did have some reservations.

'It's just that I respect him so much,' she had said. 'And I like that; it's important to me and I don't want anything to spoil it. Yet if I dominate him, and all that that entails – humiliate him, have him do demeaning things, see him degraded – won't that change how I feel about him? Destroy that respect I have for him?'

And that was when Hilary had said, 'Bollocks.'

'Look, love, you're talking about play-acting a fantasy here,' she expanded, somewhat impatiently. 'What the hell's that got to do with how you feel about anything in real life? Fantasy is as far from real life as you want it to be. And like I've told you before, in fantasy anything's OK, everything is.'

'Ah yes, but Hils,' Suzie argued, 'tonight I'll be living this fantasy, won't I? Actually doing it. Making Michael –'

'No,' Hilary cut in. 'Not making Michael anything, if that's not what you want. Tonight he needn't be Michael. He can be whoever you want him to be: your slave, that flippin' Viking you're always on about, whoever, but only as much Michael as you want him to be.

'You want my advice? Enjoy it, love. Do whatever you want with him. And afterwards, when the fantasy's over and you're back in the real world, Michael will be Michael again and you'll feel about him just as you do now.'

'Mmm,' Suzie muttered, not entirely convinced.

Hilary threw a long-suffering glance at the ceiling, but persisted stoically. 'Look, you say you respect him, right? Well, does it work the other way? Does he respect you?'

'He loves me, Hils. He told me last night, oh God, for the first time, he told me last night: it still makes me feel all gooey inside. And yes, of course he respects me; he always has.'

'Right. Yet he dominates you, doesn't he? Makes you do things that are humiliating? Things that, in any other context, would be degrading or demeaning? But what he does to you in bed, love – in sex, in fantasy – doesn't change how he feels about you, the real-life Suzie Carlton, does it? Whatever he does to you in bed, or out of it he still respects you, right?'

Suzie stared at her coffee and took a moment to allow this to sink in: she'd never thought about it in such terms before. But yes, it was true: no matter what Michael did to her sexually, non-sexually – in real life –

he treated her with all the respect in the world; she couldn't imagine a more caring, considerate man. And no matter what he had made her do, had seen her do in bed, afterwards he certainly didn't look at her with disdain or derision. As Hilary had said, the two – fantasy and real life – were entirely separate.

And Hilary had been right in the other regard too. Hadn't Michael said it himself? He would be her sex-slave, he had said. Tonight he wouldn't be Michael, but her sex-slave; a different persona. And she, Suzie, needn't be Suzie, but, who? Mistress Suzie, yes.

A sexual *frisson* tingled her loins, and she looked up feeling suddenly much brighter.

'You know, Hils,' she said, as ever grateful for her friend's practical wisdom, 'thank God I've got you. Because you're right, of course. Just as you always are.'

Hilary pointed a finger. 'Then let me give you another piece of advice too, then, seeing as I'm on a roll. What he does to you in bed, he does because he knows you enjoy it, that you'd be disappointed if he didn't. And tonight he'll be on the receiving end, looking forward to some of the same. My advice: go for it. Don't hold back or you'll only disappoint and frustrate him.'

Suzie grinned a wicked grin, her mind flooding with erotic imagery. 'No, I won't hold back, Hils. Not now you've set me straight I won't. Frustrate? Oh, I'll frustrate him all right: it'll be my turn to make him wait for a change. But no, I can assure you, disappointed he won't be.'

' 'At's my girl,' grinned Hilary. 'Another coffee?'

Suzie shook her head. 'No, I'd better be getting back. We're putting the paste-ups together early this month because I won't be able to work late tomorrow night, as I would usually the night before the deadline.'

'Oh? Got something on?'

'Yeah, it's the magazine's fiftieth edition this month – the half-century, you know; a big deal – so the Tauntons are throwing a party up at the mansion to celebrate. Not only that, but it's bound to go on until two or three in the morning. After that I'm not going to feel a lot like rushing around the following day, so the more I can get done beforehand the better.'

Hilary shook her head slowly. 'You know, love, I just don't know how you do it. All that pressure every month. Working to a deadline that's as good as life or death. It'd drive me crazy.'

Suzie shrugged. 'It's my job. And besides, it does have its compensations sometimes. If it gets really hairy, it gives me a sexual buzz.'

'You're kidding.'

'No, really. Actually it's not so strange, it would seem. We ran this piece, once, on the psychology of soldiers at war. Evidently a lot of them get a storming erection just as they go into battle, as the adrenalin pumps in response to the danger. I suppose my own reaction to the sheer dread of missing the deadline is something akin.'

'Jesus, love, if you can turn on to that you can turn on to anything, you randy cow.'

Suzie laughed, drank the last of her coffee and stood up.

'They've never made a law against being randy.'

'I'm only surprised the bastards've never tried to tax it.'

'If they did, you and I'd both be broke in a week.' Suzie chuckled dirtily. 'Anyway, like I said, I'd best run.'

Hilary smiled. 'Good luck tonight then, love.'

'Oh crikey, yeah.'

The day was warm and sunny, and Suzie was in jubilant mood as she made her way back to the office.

She began planning the evening ahead, turning herself on with thoughts of Michael and all she would do with him as her slave.

Memories of the previous night were never far from her mind: teach her a lesson of self-control, Michael had said. And so he had.

He had made her lie on her back, her arms above her

172

head and her legs spread wide, and had caressed her until she was a quivering wreck; her every nerve-end alive and expectant. He had quickly become aroused himself, his cock huge and inviting, and she had yearned to grab it, to impale herself on it and urgently ride him to much-needed climax. But he hadn't let her; had made her lie perfectly still while he had tormented her with it. He had rubbed it over her breasts, its velvet warmth tingling her skin; had run its swollen glans around her nipples, leaving them glistening with the viscid dew that leaked from its tip; had lain between her outspread thighs and had brushed it against her clitoris, up and down her liquid groove. But no more.

Even though she had ached for him, and even though he had known it, he had continued to tease her. Building her tension yet further; stretching her like a steel wire drawn almost to snapping, singing taut. Making her shake with sexual need as thrill after thrill stabbed through her, wracking her body with tiny shudders that came one after the other; the one beginning even before the last had quite died away.

He had made her get up then, and stand by the foot of the bed while he had lain back, his cock so erect it was flat to his belly. Her eyes had been unable to leave it, wanting it. Wanting it so badly she could barely stand, so weak were her knees with desire. Michael had known it all right, but it had made no difference: a lesson in self-control he had said. And he had certainly meant to provide it.

Making her stand and watch, he had caressed himself for a while, and had then held his penis – that magnificent, achingly tempting penis – at right-angles to his body, pointing straight up. It was as if to say: Here it is, hard and ready for you. But you can't have it yet. Knowing how much she longed for it, but cruelly denying it. Making her wait. The bastard.

And then, at last – at long, long last – he had told her to go to him.

With a great shudder of relief she had scrambled onto

the bed, straddling his thighs. He was still holding his cock directly upright, inviting, and she had positioned herself over its bulging head; felt hot, hard flesh part the aching lips of her sex. Had tensed herself to accept it . . . And then he had stopped her. Right at the very last moment, just as her belly had tightened in anticipation of his hardness entering her. Just as she'd thought her torment was over, he had stopped her.

'Suck me first,' he had told her.

Making her wait. Bastard, bastard, bastard. He had let her come so close, so very close – quite deliberately, she knew – only to thwart her at the very last moment.

With tears of frustration stinging her eyes she had shifted position to suck him: had taken him into her mouth; had felt his shaft throb and suddenly feared he would come, spend himself there in her mouth and so deny her the use of that turgid phallus where she desperately yearned for it, deep inside her. But she hadn't stopped: he had told her to suck him and suck him she must. She had sucked on, all the while knowing that at any moment he could be filling her mouth with his seed; the fluid of his masculine need that kept him hard and erect, the tool she so badly needed. Sucked on, suffering the cruel torment of knowing that her own mouth was to be the instrument that would ultimately deny her that which she craved.

But then, just as she'd thought there was no hope of reprieve, and she had steeled herself ready for the first hot jet of his sperm in her throat, he had suddenly eased himself from her, had told her to mount him.

She had scrambled back up the bed and had again straddled his thighs, again positioned herself over the head of his magnificent organ. Again she had felt it ease open the sodden lips of her sex. Her breath held lest he should once again stop her at this, the very last moment; she had begun slowly to sink herself down. And this time there had been no forbidding command. With a sighed groan of relief that had juddered her belly she had hungrily swallowed his shaft; down and down until she had engulfed him entirely ... And had climaxed almost instantly.

It had been a terrific, explosive orgasm. But oh, for how long had he made her wait for it, made her ache for it.

Well, now it would be her turn.

Tonight.

Up in her office, Suzie shook her head to clear it of sexy thoughts and unlocked the drawer of her desk. Removed the buff folder containing the paste-ups that were well ahead of schedule, and flicked it open.

The cover page looked up at her. It was a beauty this month too, she thought: the model they'd used was a stunning redhead with sexy, pouting lips and eyes that seemed to smoulder right through the page. The titles were letrasetted over her photo and the page was complete. With nothing more to be done on it, she turned it over.

Page one was also nearly complete; most of the artwork was done – again, good stuff too – and most of the text was pasted in place. A blank space ran down the left-hand side of the page where it awaited her editorial. But that she would delay writing for as long as possible in case a last-minute story should break that required comment. The editorial was normally the last blank of all to be filled.

She continued to flip through the pages, admiring the work that had so far been done on them, until she came to page eight. There, too many blanks screamed up at her. She picked up the telephone and punched out an internal number. Waited.

Presently there was a click as Bob Adams answered.

'Bob, I need the feature we're running on page eight.

'No, not tomorrow, Bob. I could do with it now. I want this issue done and dusted well head of time.'

This was one month there would be no sexual buzz of last-minute pressure.

'No, later's no good; I have to be away at five.

'Yes, I know I said I was going to work late tonight. But something's come up.

'What? Yes, a date.

'Of course a man.

'You pretentious old rogue, you . . .' Making herself laugh.

'Yeah, soon as you can. See you then.'

Prat.

She put down the phone and looked up from her desk, watched Sally do nothing in the outer office, and wondered. Wondered at Bob Adams's laid-back attitude to work; at Hilary's life of hedonism; wondered what she, Suzie, was doing working herself dizzy while the rest of the world took it easy. And when all she wanted anyway was Michael.

A blister of yearning popped in her loins and she longed for the night ahead.

Chapter Seventeen

M ichael swallowed in a dry throat, feeling tense as he waited for the traffic lights to change in his favour.

But his tenseness had nothing to do with the traffic, or with the slowness of the lights to change: he had never been dominated by a woman before, as he was about to be that night, and it was somewhat disquieting in prospect. How would it feel not to be in control for once? But in fantasy he had lived it often enough and had always found it a turn-on, very much so, and despite his nervousness he was looking forward to the experience with enormous excitement. But that was another problem: could Suzie carry it off?

She was, after all, a natural submissive: could she wield the necessary authority to make a convincing dominatrix; she of his fantasies? Or would it just be a farce? A disappointing, frustrating farce at that. For his thoughts of it throughout the day had been turning him on and he was feeling exceptionally horny; if the whole thing were to flop now it would be as frustrating as hell.

A car-horn blared to tell him the lights were on green,

and he pulled away putting up two fingers out of the window, returning his thoughts to where they had been.

If it wasn't working he could, he supposed, always switch roles in mid-session. So in that regard the night couldn't flop completely and end up a total disaster. But he had tuned himself in to feeling submissive now. A change of roles would need a psychological shift, and that would be irksome. It would be like thinking oneself into an acting part only for the effort to be wasted when the part was given to somebody else. And the feeling of that he knew only too well.

A cyclist wobbled in front of him and he swerved to avoid her. Yelled 'Idiot' out of the window, and drove on.

But, who knew? Maybe she would pull it off after all.

He rubbed the aching bulge in the front of his pants and hoped so. He signalled left and pulled into Suzie's road, swallowing hard.

Suzie cast her eyes about the lounge, checking it over.

Earlier, she had spent an exciting half hour collecting together a few bits and pieces from around the flat which she thought might come in useful, her imagination running wild as she saw sexual applications for all sorts of commonplace household items. And these were now in her writing desk, out of sight. Along with a little 'toy' she had cobbled together out of velcro and some pop-rivets she had salvaged from an ancient leathercraft kit. Cords tied to the legs of her heavy sofa were also out of sight, tucked discreetly under the seat, and her old riding crop that hadn't seen the light since her gymkhana days was waiting out in the hallway.

An opened bottle of Chablis stood on the coffee table, beside two full glasses, and everything seemed in order as the doorbell chimed to herald Michael's arrival. *No, the arrival of her slave for the night.* That was an exciting thought.

She smiled, and went to let him in.

* * *

178

Michael's eyes made sudden saucers as Suzie opened the door to him. She didn't look like Suzie at all. She looked so . . . dominant.

Her make-up was untypically heavy, with dark flashes of colour over her eyes that lent her a vaguely feline look; blood-red lipstick glistened on her sensuous lips. Her hair was scraped back from her face and hung in a golden ponytail, when normally she wore it loose. And her clothing was untypical, too: she was wearing a sheer, calf-length dress in black satin that showed a great deal of cleavage and that clung to her figure like a second shiny-black skin, excitingly delineating secret mounds and crevices where it clung. Her outfit was completed by high stiletto heels on patent leather pumps, and she could have been Mistress of the Month in one of the bondage mags he kept in his underwear drawer.

Christ, he thought in the second it took to drink it all in, *she certainly looks the part anyway*.

Suzie didn't smile.

'Go through to the lounge and strip,' she said, making it a curt command. 'Naked. Then stand with your hands on your head and your legs apart, and wait.'

And sounds it, too, thought Michael, feeling his cock stiffening uncomfortably in the tight confines of his pants.

Suzie didn't step aside and he had to brush past her on his way in, the heady scent of a subtle perfume lingering in his nostrils as he made his way through to the lounge. Thinking: *Jesus, I'm in for one hell of a night*.

He felt naked. He was naked, of course, but he felt especially so to be standing there on Suzie's command, awaiting her, and for once not in control. His hands were clasped behind his neck, his elbows pulled back, and his legs were apart; the classic stance of submission that he so often had Suzie adopt for his pleasure. His genitals felt exposed and vulnerable – precisely the point of the posture – and his cock was a thing with a life of its own; was already partially erect when Suzie at last came into the room ... A riding crop held in her hand.

At the sight of the whip a tendril of sudden fear tightened his scrotum, and he almost regretted his macho bravado of the previous night. *What's a bit of pain?* he had scoffed. Now, seeing the leather crop, he suddenly didn't feel nearly so brave.

But fear was irrational, he reasoned. After all, if things were to get out of hand – if she were to try to lay into him too hard with that whip – he could easily enough stop her; take it from her and call it a night. And anyway, it was unlikely to come to that: Suzie loved him didn't she; would never wish to cause him any serious pain.

No, maybe Suzie wouldn't, the thought occurred, *but was this Suzie?* By her look, her manner, everything about her, this was no Suzie he knew. This was a woman with a sadistic gleam in her eye, and who looked serious about what she was doing.

The thoughts took but a moment to flash through his brain, and despite his rationale that he could end it at any time, a trace of fear remained. A fear, he realised – if only of the unknown – that seemed to further excite him, and he was aware of his penis reacting to it, hardening fully.

Suzie saw it too.

She took a step closer and reached out with the whip; touched its tip to the tip of his penis.

'What's this doing hard?' she demanded. 'Did I give it permission to get hard?'

Her tone was convincingly stern. But Michael was flinching at the feel of the crop and didn't immediately answer.

'Well?' she pressed.

'Er, no,' he muttered distractedly. It was all he could say. For no, he couldn't deny it; she hadn't given him permission or otherwise. He rallied, then, and put a casual shrug in his voice, smiling sheepishly. 'I, er, don't suppose you did, did you?'

It was a nonchalance that he instantly regretted, and

180

that suddenly went, when the next moment Suzie flicked out with the crop. Not viciously hard, but enough to make him suck in a breath through teeth clenched in sudden pain as its leather tip snapped against the swollen head of his cock. His hips jerked back, his genitals shy of the whip, but otherwise he managed to hold still.

Suzie stepped in close. 'I control this tonight,' she said, curling her fingers around his erection. She looked into his eyes while her hand worked on him, sliding the length of his iron shaft and gradually soothing away pain. 'It gets hard when I want it hard, and it stays soft when I don't. Is that understood?'

Michael mumbled a yes (wondering if that would be actually possible, though not about to argue the point), and Suzie's feline eyes narrowed as she let go of his penis and took a step back.

'Yes *what*?' she snapped. 'What happened to *Mistress*? Let me hear you say it.'

Michael swallowed hard. Even play-acting it felt oddly demeaning to have to address her as such; to have to address any woman in that subservient way. But it was, he supposed, all a part of the game he had agreed to play, and he finally forced out the words. 'Yes, Mistress,' he muttered thickly.

'Better. And don't forget again.'

Suzie's eyes bored into him and she appeared to be waiting. And he suddenly winced, newly aware of the crop and realising he was meant to respond. 'Oh, no Mistress, I won't,' he said quickly. The whip was between his legs, now, tacitly threatening his testicles.

'Good,' Suzie whispered. And she smiled, then.

Though it wasn't a pleasant smile, a smile of innocent pleasure. It was more a smirk, a smug self-satisfied grin, and seeing it made a worm of humiliation wriggle in Michael's gut. But he didn't have time to dwell on it; he soon had more to think about.

The crop came to the inside of his thigh, its pressure there telling him to step out further, to spread his legs wider apart. And with a trepidation that blotted out his lesser concerns he obeyed the unspoken command; flinched as the crop came slowly up to his testicles, weighing them on its tip.

Suzie's smile went. 'Because this is what you'll get if you forget again,' she said.

And the whip suddenly dropped and snapped back up again twice in rapid succession on the tender parts of his inner thighs.

'Ouch!' he howled, as searing heat flashed in his groin. And any doubts he had harboured of Suzie's ability to 'carry the part' were gone altogether as pain flowed in white-hot waves from his groin up to his brain. She could do better than merely carry the part; she could damn well play it for real. She was an absolute bitch.

But a damned sexy one. And as pain gradually ebbed, it transmuted to erotic sensation – an exciting pleasure-pain that was deeply arousing, and that had him thrilling at the thought of what was to come.

'That should've been "Ouch, *Mistress*",' Suzie chuckled. 'But we'll let that one go. Now, seeing as your cock seems to have lost interest a little, you can get it hard again and amuse me with it for a while.' She stepped back and sank herself comfortably into an armchair. 'Masturbate, slave,' she said.

Watching Michael doing her bidding, Suzie felt incredibly horny.

Even though they were only play-acting – living out a fantasy – dominating Michael was giving her an exciting feeling of power. A power that in itself was a turn-on, and which confirmed for her beyond any doubt that there was indeed a sadistic side to her nature. A part of her that thrilled to sexually humiliate just as it excited her to be humiliated herself. And seeing the pain she had caused to appear in Michael's eyes when she had punished him had given her a perverse thrill of such intensity that it had almost buckled her knees.

And now she was watching him masturbate. Was mesmerized by his frisking hand; the rigid arc of his shaft as his hand rode up it, the glistening eye at its tip that seemed to wink at her as the skin was stretched back with each downward stroke. It was exciting to watch. Even more exciting to see the look on Michael's face as he did it, the humiliation that showed in his eyes. She had been moist between her legs to begin with – had been for most of the day – but now, delighting in Michael's abasement, her juices flowed freely and her loins were aflame with erotic desire. She would have to have him lick that away for her soon.

But, not just yet; first she would savour it awhile. And pressing her fingertips to her pubic mound she applied a gentle, rhythmic pressure there, massaging herself close to the brink, the better to relish the lewd display she was having Michael put on for her.

'Don't come, slave,' she warned, thrilling anew to the sensation of power that it gave her. 'Get yourself close, I want to see that look of need in your eyes, but don't dare come. If you do' – her eyes locked onto his – 'you'll lick it up.'

This had an immediate and gratifying effect, and she enjoyed the shudder it evoked from him, the grimace of revulsion that crossed his face. And her mind raced with ideas.

Earlier she had wondered if, without the liberation afforded her of being submissive, her old hang-ups might re-emerge to inhibit her; prevent her from fully enjoying herself. From doing, especially, some of the more bizarre things her imagination had been conjuring for that evening. But the moment she had put on her make-up she had known. No, it would not be a problem. For looking in the mirror she had seen not her, Suzie, but Mistress Suzie, an entirely different persona. And how could she feel guilty for what someone else were to do?

And now, as her mind raced with myriad kinky ideas, she wondered only one thing: just how far would Michael allow her to go?

And the test of that would come soon.

* * *

Michael's cheeks burned at the subtle smirk on Suzie's face as she continued to watch him masturbate. He wasn't sure quite why, really, it should discomfit him so. After all, it wasn't as if it were the first time Suzie had seen him with his cock in his hand. She had seen it before many times, the times he had wanked himself over her face, into her mouth. But this, somehow, was different. Was very different: here, he was doing it on a woman's command. While she watched. *Watched, with that bloody smirk on her face.* He supposed it was that which made it humiliating. But, whatever the reason, humiliating it most definitely was; his belly crawled with it.

Not only that, but by now his enforced masturbation had given him another, even more difficult problem with which to contend: the combination of the humiliation of it, and the direct physical stimulus of his hand, had aroused him until he was literally aching to come. (Enough, even, that he would have borne the ignominy of making himself spurt on the carpet at Suzie's feet.) Yet, he couldn't: Suzie had specifically forbidden it. *Not that she would really make him lick it up if he did. Would she?* He could guess already the answer to that, and knew he had better not.

So, he couldn't stop and he mustn't come; could only continue to stimulate his sensitised cock, making himself ache all the more. It was wickedly clever of her: with almost no effort from her, she was tormenting him cruelly; making him torture himself.

And, by the look on her face, she knew it too!

Suzie kept him at the abasing, and increasingly unbearable task for some time, narrowing her eyes in warning whenever he dared slow his hand in an attempt to lessen his self-stimulation – to let himself down for a moment from the excruciating knife-edge right on the brink of orgasm. But, at last, she seemed to tire of the sport.

'Stop now, slave,' she told him. 'Come and relax for a while. Kneel over here by the table and have a drink while you calm yourself down. Though keep your legs wide apart; I want nothing hidden from my view.'

It was just the sort of command he so often gave her. Nevertheless, Michael sighed with relief as he released his aching organ. Relieved, anyway, to be allowed to stop tormenting himself, if further than ever from the relief he needed the most. His cock was throbbing almost painfully as it swayed before him and his balls felt uncomfortably full. But at least he wasn't having to worsen it further, and his agonising need would at last be allowed to subside.

Suzie pushed one of the two full wineglasses across the table towards him. 'Your wine, slave,' she said.

She seemed to be watching him with undue intent, Michael thought, as he went to kneel where she'd told him. There was an odd tension in her manner and it puzzled him slightly. He picked up his glass, wondering vaguely what the reason for it could be. Raised the glass to his lips and sipped – and instantly knew.

It wasn't Chablis.

It wasn't wine!

He dropped the glass back down on the table and pushed it away with a scowl of disgust, grimacing at the faintly salt taste in his mouth; whatever it was it was foul. And only then did he notice that the liquid in Suzie's glass was a slightly paler yellow than the liquid in his; only then knowing for sure what it was he had drunk.

The bitch.

His eyes flashed up to Suzie's eyes. There was the hint of cruel amusement in them, confirming what he had guessed. And there was the touch of a smile on her lips as she shook her head and said: 'Oh no, slave, don't put it down. That's your wine for this evening. Each time I sip, you are to sip; we'll finish our glasses together.'

Then, very deliberately, her eyes locked on his, she raised her glass and took a long swallow.

Michael's stomach crawled in horror at what she meant him to do.

185

The bitch. The depraved, perverted bitch. But he was aware of his penis twitching between his widespread thighs, betraying an excitement he couldn't deny as the very perverseness of it translated to erotic suborn. The depraved, perverted, wonderfully kinky bitch.

Suzie held up her glass, signalling him to do likewise; waiting insistently for him to comply. And, at last, he reached for his 'wine'. Her eyes were still on his, as if daring him to do anything less than to match her swallow. And slowly, very slowly, he brought the glass to his lips. And, taking a deep breath to steel himself to it, he sipped.

An intense thrill shot through Suzie's loins as she watched Michael hesitate, then finally drink her golden champagne.

It had been an inspired idea, she thought, to have arranged so kinky a test early on in the evening; a test to see how far Michael would allow her to go. If he would submit to that, she had reasoned, then he would submit to just about anything. And she knew now there were virtually no limits; that for the rest of the evening she could do with Michael just as she pleased. It was a thought that dizzied her with excitement.

She raised her glass and sipped. Watched Michael do likewise and grimace, and delighted in the utter depravity of it.

It seemed to excite Michael too, she noticed, for as he swallowed, albeit with a slight shudder, his cock gave a little tell-tale jump. She smiled, and reached out to it with her foot; ran the sole of her shoe lightly along its length.

'What a lovely cock this is, slave,' she purred, 'hard and throbbing like this. But for now I want it to go soft. So, slave, calm yourself down.'

'Jesus, I can try,' Michael muttered, squirming to the feel of her foot. 'But Christ, you don't make it easy, you know.'

Suzie chuckled. 'Maybe not. But, still, you'll do as I say slave, or else: I have a reason for wanting it soft.'

'Oh?' Michael looked wary. 'Like what?'

'Oh, you'll see soon enough. But I'm going to tie you up first, then you'll find out. And talking of which, it's high time I did. So, come on, enough relaxation; I want to get on.'

And with that she drank the last three-quarters of her glass down in one.

Michael was tied to the sofa. His legs were secured to the sofa's legs and drawn widely apart, leaving his genitals obscenely displayed, and feeling terrifyingly vulnerable. His hands were roped together above his head and were secured to somewhere behind, pulling his elbows high and back. And he was, he knew, utterly helpless. So much for his being able to put a stop to it if anything went too far, he thought; he was now completely at Suzie's mercy.

After checking the knots for a final time to see they were tight, Suzie stood up and crossed to her writing desk, took something from it – he couldn't see what – and returned. She knelt on the floor between his widespread legs, and laid a gentle hand on his crotch.

It had taken her several minutes to tie him up, and in that time his erection had largely subsided. He wasn't completely flaccid, but nor was he fully hard. Though beneath Suzie's hand he could feel himself stirring anew.

'You remember I told you,' she said, giving his shaft a gentle squeeze, 'that I was to control this tonight? Well now I'm going to show you just how in control of it I really am. This little toy I've made is going to help me demonstrate.'

With that she produced what appeared to be a square of black velcro. But when she turned it over Michael could see it was actually two pieces stuck together, and from one side were protruding a dozen or so small metal studs, their bases trapped between the two halves to secure them. Suzie rolled the affair into a tube about six inches long, studs innermost, and held it for Michael to see.

'This is going around your cock,' she explained.

Michael groaned inwardly. Explanation hadn't been necessary: its purpose he had already guessed. The studs didn't look especially sharp, not sharp enough surely to actually break skin, but he could imagine they'd be pretty painful nevertheless. His eyes were drawn to his defenceless genitals and he groaned again.

Lifting his semi-erect penis, Suzie wrapped the studded velcro snugly around its shaft, the velcro knitting together to complete the tube and holding it firmly in place. It sheathed the entire length of his cock, all the way from its root to just below its bulbous head; the glans protruding from its top like a ripe, purple plum. Satisfied, Suzie stood up.

'Not too uncomfortable right now, is it?' she said. 'But let yourself get any harder, and, well . . .'

She didn't need to finish: Michael could well imagine.

And he groaned a third time when Suzie stepped back from him and began moving her body in time to some exotic, unheard music, and he knew instinctively she was about to perform a sexy strip in front of him. To his chagrin his cock began to stiffen at even the thought of it, and he clenched his teeth as the studs began to bite.

He quickly shut his eyes and fought for control of his recalcitrant member. Forced himself to think of anything and everything except what Suzie was doing, and sighed with relief as he slowly began to succeed; felt his cock beginning to soften and the pressure of the studs ease. And he had just begun to relax when a sharp retort across his thighs put a swift end to his comfort.

His eyes snapped open in shock and pain to see that Suzie was standing over him with a plastic ruler bowed in her hands; it was bent almost double and poised, like a cobra, to spring open for a second strike.

'Makes an effective little punishment device, doesn't it?' she said, her eyes glinting as she flexed the twelve-inch length of plastic.

Michael flinched, steeling himself for the sudden pain

that would result if she let the ruler's end slip from her restraining finger, unleashing its energy.

'Now, are you going to watch me? Or do I have to use it again?'

'No!' he said quickly, wary eyes riveted on the menacing ruler. 'I'll watch.' And decided he had better add: 'Mistress.'

To his relief, Suzie dropped the ruler onto the seat of the sofa and stepped back. She resumed her sexy writhings, and Michael was only glad that the pain had for now shrunk his penis inside the vicious sheath; the studs no longer digging quite so uncomfortably into the tender skin of its shaft. For now.

Suzie looked into Michael's eyes as she slid slowly out of her dress, reading in them his growing arousal as she performed her sexy strip. Discarding her dress, and almost naked now, she began running her hands sensuously over her body; stroking her breasts until her nipples erected, then moving on, moving lower, down over her belly to the silk of her panties. Let her fingers caress still lower until her fingertip nestled in the patch of warm, damp silk at her crotch. She began to gyrate her hips, then, in simulated intercouse while she rubbed herself there, letting her eyes move from Michael's eyes down to his exposed groin.

A minute ago she had watched his penis instantly shrink when she had punished him with the ruler. But now, forced to watch her sexy gyrations, he had quickly begun to swell again, stiffening into the sheath. She slipped aside the leg of her panties to arouse him further with a seductive glimpse of her glistening sex. Ran a fingertip along the lips to separate them, and was gratified to see him flinch as his body couldn't help but respond to the sight of her pink inner-flesh.

She immediately looked back to his eyes. There was discomfort in them again, she saw, but not yet real pain. So far he was holding out well she thought, impressed by his self-control. Though she supposed the metal studs were helping a bit.

Still, it meant a more direct approach was called for. She went to kneel on the floor between his outspread legs. Gently fondled his balls for a moment, then bore down on them to stand his cock upright away from his belly. And leaning forward, she parted her lips.

Michael groaned at the first touch of her mouth on his sensitised glans, protruding defencelessly from the top of the sheath. Continued to groan as she suckled the swollen bulb; sliding her tongue around and beneath it in the attempt to bring him fully erect. Wanting to see that pain in his eyes.

She sensed him harden a little, begin to writhe as the studs bit in a little more deeply, a little more painfully. But, still, it wasn't enough: despite her oral skills, he hardened no further. She let him slip from her mouth to look.

He was almost erect. But still not fully; not hard and throbbing, when the studs would really bite in and hurt. He was still managing, just, to keep himself enough in control. She ran her fingertip absently over the shiny purple plum, slippery with her saliva and the dewy emission that seeped from its tip, considering. There was only one thing for it, she decided: it was time to play her ace.

Standing, she slipped off her panties.

'Fond of my knickers, aren't you, slave?' she said impishly.

She thrilled at the look of horror that instantly crossed Michael's face.

Suzie knew that to many men a woman's sexy smell could be a powerful stimulant. But to Michael, it seemed it was especially so: to him, the scent of a woman's sex was the most potent aphrodisiac in the world. And with just this in mind, she had not changed her panties all day and knew that the scent of them now would be a force he'd be helpless to resist.

'And these I've had on since this morning,' she told him, 'preparing them especially for you. Look.' She dangled the flimsy garment from a fingertip, close to his face. Not, it surprised her to realise, feeling the least bit embarrassed herself. Things felt altogether different from a dominant perspective. Their crotch was damp, their fragrance strong. 'Oh dear, look,' she went on slyly, 'I've been feeling so horny all day, looking forward to tonight, that I'm afraid I've rather moistened them, haven't I?'

Michael stared at them with horror-filled eyes.

'Oh, God, Suz – Er, I mean Mistress . . . you wouldn't.'

'Wouldn't I?'

And in one deft movement she slipped the panties over his head, carefully arranging their soiled crotch directly over his nose.

'Now, close your mouth,' she ordered. 'Or else.'

She picked up the ruler and flexed it above his balls.

And Michael's groans became grunts of agony as he closed his mouth, and when with his very next intake of breath, his cock reared, instantly swelling to full and painful erection.

Suzie chuckled, delighted. Total control.

Michael writhed in agony, begging Suzie to remove the cruel sheath.

The moment she had produced her panties he had known the battle was lost; knew the effect their scent would have on him, and that he'd be powerless to resist it. Even at the thought of it, as he'd watched them dangle from her fingertip, he had felt himself losing control; his cock swelling into the biting studs.

And when she had put them over his face, ordering him to close his mouth so forcing him to breathe through his nose, her sexy aroma had pervaded his senses, causing his cock instantly to fully erect; become a thing that screamed in agony as the cruel spikes dug deeply into its shaft.

But worse had come. With his every breath turning him on further, his penis had begun to throb. And now, with every pulse of it, a new wave of excruciating agony stabbed through his groin.

An agony, finally, he could bear no longer.

'Please. God, please,' he implored. 'The sheath or your knickers, I don't care which. But, please, take off one or the other.'

Suzie looked into his eyes, hers aglow with sadistic pleasure as she watched the pain in his; clearly enjoying it.

She let it go on for a few seconds longer, ignoring his pleas, then finally sighed; reached forward and tore open the velcro, freeing his tortured member.

Michael grunted with merciful relief, and Suzie smiled at him.

It was a smile of triumph. 'So, Percy's always well and truly in your command, is he?' she said, throwing his words of the previous night back at him. 'Ha! Admit it, slave: I, and I alone, have control of your cock. Total control: I can make it go hard, as you've just seen, even when it's the last thing it wants, or I can make it go soft at will.' She flexed the ruler close to his balls. 'Or do I need to demonstrate?'

'Er, no Mistress,' Michael said quickly, his buttocks squirming into the seat of the sofa as his genitals cringed from the threat of the ruler. 'There's, er, really no need. I concede; yes, you have control.'

The admission was strangely emasculating, he realised, as the truth of it sank in. He was not in control of even his dick, his proud manhood, his beloved Percy. He stared down at it forlornly, it's straining shaft a rash of tiny red dots, the imprints left by the studs, and wondered what further cruel and emasculating delights Suzie might have in store for him that night. Felt agony diffuse into sexual ecstasy and thrilled at that thought.

Suzie was close to coming. Michael's screams and pleas for mercy, the look of pain in his eyes, had almost, alone, been enough to trigger her climax. But hadn't quite, and had instead left her right on the edge, aching with need. She couldn't wait any longer: it was time to put Michael's tongue to good use.

She climbed up on the sofa, and pulling her panties from Michael's face she replaced them with her pussy; clamping her thighs to his cheeks and thrusting her sex-lips onto his mouth. Tied up as he was he could do nothing about it. Not that he would necessarily have wanted to, perhaps – Michael was as fond of giving oral as he was of receiving it – but, still, the thought gave her an additional thrill. He was hers to use as she pleased.

'Lick,' she said, the single word enough.

Michael's tongue went obediently to work, making her thighs shake as her orgasm almost instantly gathered. The tongue found her clitoris, and the next moment she shuddered and came, drenching Michael's face with her juices.

'Damn!' she cursed.

Not that she was at all discontent with the intensity of her orgasm, or in any sense with its quality, it was just that she had come so maddeningly quickly. She loved the feel of Michael's tongue on her body and it had not been made to delight her for nearly long enough. She wanted more of it. Yet she sensed that if she were merely to have him start over, she would climax again just as quickly. Fine in one way, maybe, but in another not at all satisfactory. And then she had an idea.

Turning around, she bent forward at the waist and backed herself up, easing her bottom, now, into Michael's face.

'Now lick me there,' she said.

She had no idea if she could come that way. But knew if she could it was unlikely to be readily, and that Michael's tongue would thus be kept busy for some while; humiliatingly busy, with his face buried into her bottom the whole time. It was a thought that both amused and excited her.

The plastic ruler was on the seat of the sofa, and as she felt Michael's tongue extend between the cheeks of her bottom to begin its degrading task, its tip pushing into her slightly, she decided she could amuse herself in two ways at once. Reaching for the ruler, she gave his defenceless balls a sharp rap with the flat of it; felt him expel air against her buttocks in a grunt of sudden pain, his tongue momentarily withdrawing, and chuckled.

'If you're to make me come,' she laughed down at him, 'you're not going to have to keep stopping like that, you know? And you're going to have to get your tongue right inside me there, too. Or else!'

She gave his testicles another sharp rap to remind him, and settled herself for a pleasant interlude of enforced and prolonged analingus.

Suzie was over by her writing desk, rummaging again, and Michael wondered what the hell might be coming up next.

She had kept him licking her bottom for what had seemed like an age, her buttocks thrust in his face at times threatening to suffocate him. Eventually she had come, but not before his tongue had ached cruelly and had screamed at him for relief. Every so often – but at irregular intervals so he had never known when it was coming – she had smacked his balls with the ruler, and it had taken a monumental effort of will to keep his tongue to its task. But he'd known that he'd had to, or she would never have come. And he would have bet his last penny he would still be licking her now if she hadn't.

Even now his tongue ached and felt too big for his mouth, and he could still taste on it the slight nuttiness of Suzie's secret passage. His face was slick with sweat, both his and hers, which only now was beginning to cool. As too, mercifully, was the burning fire in his balls.

Though he wondered for how long that would pertain.

Suzie came back to the sofa, and dropped something onto the floor beyond his field of vision. He wondered what.

The pain of the ball-smacking had shrunk his erection, and she gave his slack penis a disdainful slap as she knelt down before him.

'This is no good to me, is it?' she said, making it flop

over with a second slap. 'What use to a woman is a soft cock? And I suppose you'll expect me to get it hard again, eh? Or, can you do it yourself? Yes, that's it: go on, get it up for me all by yourself.'

Michael tried to, desperately focussing his thoughts. But though his penis twitched in response, it failed to do more. Testicular pain had taken its toll, and in the absence of physical stimulation it refused to obey his command. He mentally cursed it. Suzie wanted him hard; get it up for her, she had said. Maybe, he dared hope, it was because she wanted to screw, and he would at last have the relief he so desperately craved as she rode him to mutual climax. Yet try as he might, even despite such tempting promise, his cock refused to erect.

Suzie smiled slyly, watching him struggle. Then finally sighed. 'Oh, well,' she said, 'I suppose if needs must . . .'

And with that she leaned forward to take the semi-flaccid organ into her mouth.

To Michael's relief it immediately began to respond, hardening against her tongue, and he moaned softly as pleasure surged in his groin. Her mouth was hot and sensual, and as it continued to work on him, hardening him fully, he felt the first stirrings of orgasm begin. He could sense it gathering deep in his balls; his seed collecting ready to spurt. And he was suddenly struck by an exciting thought: *maybe she meant to fellate him to climax*. He hardly dared believe it. But as orgasm grew ever closer and still she continued to suck him, his hopes burgeoned. *Yes, it must be what she intended; she was going to make him come in her mouth.* And as his climax mounted he tensed, held his breath, ready.

But at the last possible moment, the very last second before orgasm would have been certain, she abruptly let him slip from her lips, and the breath he'd been holding rushed out in a long groan of frustration as his cock was left unattended to twitch in mid air.

Suzie laughed, watching it bob and jerk in the frantic if futile attempt to finish by itself what she had begun.

'What?' she teased. 'You didn't think I was going to let you come, did you? Oh no, slave, you won't be coming for a long while yet. Your cock might be aching to spurt, but I want to play with it first.' She gripped the twitching shaft at its base, forcing it upright. 'Oh, and yes,' she crooned, 'now it's hard again, it's a much better toy. Though I think we can improve on it still.'

Reaching down to the floor she produced a thick rubber band; answering the question of what she had brought from her writing desk. And keeping her grip on his penis, she began winding it around its still-throbbing shaft; winding it before rolling it down to the root. A length of thinnish cord came next, and this she wound again around the base of his cock, then around each of his balls in turn, separating them into two individual – and to Michael, extremely fragile-feeling – orbs. A final loop encircled his cock and balls together, and she drew it tight enough to make him wince before tying it off.

'Yes,' she said, sitting back to admire her handiwork, 'and now it's the prefect toy. See, with such tight constriction around the base of your cock, entrapping the blood within it, you won't be able to lose your erection. And you'll also find it almost impossible to come. So, you can't come and you can't go soft. Like I said, the perfect toy: a permanent hard-on for me to amuse myself with. And I don't have to worry about going too far; about misjudging how close you are to coming and causing a little accident: I can tease it as much, and for as long as I want.'

Michael looked down at his trussed up genitals and swallowed hard, marvelling at her cruel ingenuity. Both loving and cursing her for it.

Suzie gave his penis a playful pat, making the distended organ sway from side to side in a huge, bobbing arc. 'Shame, isn't it?' she taunted. 'All that fun for me, no relief for you. No matter how much I play with it.'

And as if to prove the truth of her words, she set about cruelly teasing him, making him ache by alternately wanking and sucking him. He was soon writhing

196

in torment; could feel his molten seed gathered in his balls, aching to burst free, but trapped within them. He knew that no matter how close he might feel to coming he wouldn't be able to, and that he would remain frustrated, and could only suffer the agony and ecstasy of it as Suzie continued to tease him.

Suzie was enjoying her dominant role. It wasn't the role she would choose all the time, perhaps, but now and again – if Michael would let her – it would make an exciting change.

If Michael would let her? She felt sure he would. She was still teasing him mercilessly, now sliding his foreskin back and forth with a saliva-slick hand, but though his groans were now almost constant and his suffering obvious, there was, too, an unmistakable ecstasy deep in his eyes. Whatever his anguish, he was enduring it in rapture.

She paused to study his tormented cock. Veins were standing out in great knots on its shaft, its central ridge a solid cord, and its bulbous head was purple and shiny. The two delicate orbs below it, that would normally hang free in their wrinkled sac, were instead a pair of swollen captive grapes, the skin covering them stretched so tight as to be almost translucent, showing fine blue veins beneath it. The whole organ bucked and quivered as she played with it, straining to come, but in the half an hour she had been teasing him – continuously and without relent – only a tiny dewdrop of pre-seminal fluid had managed to squeeze itself to the glistening eye at its tip.

She now wiped this away with a fingertip and put it in Michael's mouth, thrilling at his involuntary shudder as she made him suck off the sticky dew.

Even though she had already teased him for as long as she had, she was tempted to carry on longer. She was finding his tormented writhings as he strained vainly for a climax he couldn't achieve an incredible turn-on. It was that erotic sensation of power again: knowing that Michael was aching to come, but, until she, Suzie, chose to allow it, there wasn't a thing he could do about it. It was wonderfully exciting. But there were so many other things she wanted to do to him too. And it was, she supposed, time to move on.

For what she had in mind for him next, first she would need to untie him, and almost reluctantly she released his beating cock to reach for the cords at his ankles.

Michael winced as the blood rushed back to his hands and feet, making them burn as his wrists and ankles were untied and the circulation was allowed to return to them. Vaguely wondered how his cock and balls would feel when they too were unbound, and winced again at the thought. But he wasn't yet to find out: to his dismay, Suzie left his genitals tethered and told him to stand up.

'Now kneel over there,' she said, allowing him no more than a moment to stretch life and new feeling back to his stiffened limbs. She was pointing at an upholstered tabouret standing in front of an armchair: 'There, in front of the stool,' she told him. 'Knees wide apart, then lean forward, lying your chest across it.'

Michael did as instructed. Or at least thought that he had, but it was seemingly not good enough for Suzie.

'Oh no, that's far too comfortable,' she said, reconsidering. 'We can't have that, now can we? Kneel up again.'

He did as she said, and crouching behind him Suzie reached between his legs and grasped his straining shaft; pulled it sharply downwards, making him gasp as his ramrod erection was bent painfully away from his body and pulled back between his legs.

Keeping her grip on it, she said: '*Now* lean over the stool.'

And now when he did, and she released his cock, it sprung only as far as the side of the tabouret; prevented from arcing up in its natural curve as it had before, and kept bent at an uncomfortable angle.

'Oh yes, that's much better,' said Suzie, feeling for

198

herself as she ran her fingertips over the down-pointed head of his cock. 'I should imagine that's really quite painful.'

She said this last with a gleeful chuckle, and Michael could only grunt in reply as he struggled to absorb the discomfort that her fondling fingers were doing nothing to lessen.

And then he sensed Suzie moving away, leaving him there.

Trying to ignore his genital discomfort, he strained his ears to listen, for some give-away sound of what it was she was up to. And hearing her rummaging again in her writing desk, he wondered what wickedness that box of tricks was about to produce now.

Suzie came back, and knelt down behind him.

'Reach back with your hands and spread the cheeks of your bottom,' she said.

He had expected this: after all, it was what she had done with her fantasised Viking. He remembered the gleam there had been in her eye when she had related that part of the fantasy to him, and it came as no surprise that she should wish to repeat it now in reality. No surprise, but still he blushed scarlet at the humiliation of it as he reached behind him to spread open the cheeks of his bottom; felt Suzie's fingernail scratch lightly over his anus, making him acutely aware of all she could see.

His cock surged in response to it, to press ever more painfully against the side of the tabouret, and once again cursed himself for his lack of self-control.

Suzie stared, entranced at the puckered opening so temptingly available to her, daring herself to go further.

But she knew that some men found even the thought of anal penetration to be utterly repugnant, and she had no wish to do anything to Michael that he really wouldn't like. Or, more accurately, that he wouldn't find sexually exciting; knowing from her own experience that the two were not necessarily the same.

So, like it or not, would he find it a turn-on? That was the question. She continued to tickle his puckered ring while she pondered it, her fingertip lightly toying with the delicate skin. Watched Michael's thighs begin to tremble in response to her inimate touch, and decided, probably, yes. Humiliating, of course, just as she did when Michael did it to her. But, like her, he would also find it a turn-on, she hoped.

And so, her breathing shallowed in case she was wrong, her fingertip at last pried open the forbidden entrance, then drove forward and in. Michael groaned as his virgin citadel was breached. A groan of mortification, of anguish even. But a groan, too, that was laden with rapture.

She had been right! And she smiled to herself, thrilling in the sense of Michael's shame as she began to explore his rectum in earnest, her finger twisting this way and that as it worked.

Michael's moans continued to be those of anguished pleasure as the digital buggering went on. *Though for how much longer?* Suzie wondered as she withdrew her finger at last and reached for the thick white candle she had brought from her desk.

Michael swallowed hard when Suzie's finger slid into him, his belly a mass of wriggling worms. Yet his cock twitched beyond his control, betraying his excitement as humiliation crimsoned his cheeks and the finger allowed him no dignity.

And then the finger withdrew. And something else was brought to his anus. Something thicker. Something that prodded at his anal ring and that momentarily caused a sharp flash of pain as it was pushed forward and in, breaching his sphincter. Then was mercifully more comfortable as it began to slide slowly inside him.

Something long, he realised with a twinge of sudden panic, as inch after inch of it continued to ease into him, seemingly without end. Until it was as if it filled him entirely, and caused a dull ache to begin deep in his bowels.

But to his relief it finally stopped: was not pushed in

any further. But nor was the object withdrawn: it was left high up inside him, filling him.

He sensed Suzie stand up, then. Heard her chuckle, then say in warning: 'Don't let it slip out, slave. Keep it right where it is.'

And he groaned. The thing felt huge in his rectum. It was as if he needed to move his bowels, and the urge to push was strong; to defecate the degrading intrusion. But instead, despite the protesting ache in his balls when he did, he clenched his sphincter to hold it within.

Suzie came round to the armchair in front of him, and sat down. Bringing her buttocks to the front of the seat, she lay back, parting her legs widely and opening her sex. She was close enough to him that he could perceive its intimate fragrance, and the combined sight and scent of her caused him to groan anew as the gnawing ache in his loins flared.

'Now,' she said, 'I think it's time I came again. And this time I want to come on your cock. Push the footstool out of the way, and come here and fuck me. Oh, and the candle is to stay in while you do, by the way.'

Ah, so that's what it was, a candle: *she had stuffed a candle up his behind*. But the ignominy of that was quickly dismissed, for he had far worse to consider: the thought of intercourse in his present condition, his genitals tightly bound and unable to spurt, so disallowing him the slightest relief, sheathed in Suzie's wonderful pussy and forced to make himself ache all the more. It was enough to water his eyes with frustration.

With an inward groan he pushed himself back from the footstool. The abrupt release of his cock made it spring up to slap at his belly before regaining its natural curve, and, as it did, at least his erection was considerably less painful than it had been the moment before. But what comfort it afforded him was immediately tempered as he felt the candle shift in his bottom. Knew that the feel of it there, shifting inside him, stimulating his prostate as he thrust into Suzie, would drive him crazy; make his ordeal all the more difficult to bear. And as he pushed the tabouret aside to crawl forward to begin, he could only pray that she would come quickly.

Knew she would delay it for as long as she could, merciless bitch that she was. The merciless – wonderfully merciless – bitch that she was.

Suzie lay back, gradually recovering from the throes of her orgasm. She had delayed her climax for as long as possible, but finally she had succumbed.

And what a terrific orgasm it had been, too, spurred by the look of pleasure-pain in Michael's eyes as he had thrust into her, frustration contorting his face. She knew it could not have been easy for him, forced to keep his bottom tightly clenched to hold the thick candle inside him, to have to thrust his aching cock into her again and again with no hope of release for himself, and she had thrilled all the more to his suffering. She had watched frustration deepen to anguish when she had come and he had not been able, her vaginal muscles clenching and unclenching in spasm around his swollen cock, the throes of her orgasm heightening his consciousness of what he himself was being denied.

But she knew that despite his anguish – because of it – he was loving it all. That he was loving her for doing it all to him. He had told her last night that he loved her. Tonight, when the fantasy had been lived and they were Michael and Suzie once more, he would tell again; would declare it all the more ardently in thanks for the thrilling night she had given him. Her heart warmed to think of it, and she shook her head to bring herself back to the present. For the fantasy was far from over.

Michael was still inside her: she hadn't yet let him withdraw, and he was still kneeling up between her widespread thighs, his own thighs beginning to shake with the strain.

She looked into his eyes. 'You can pull out of me now,' she told him. 'Sit back on your haunches, but keep your knees wide apart; I want to inspect your cock.'

202

She knew she had bound his genitals with some severity and she was anxious to see he was still all right.

She slid from the armchair to sit on the floor, and regarded his tortured member. The whole organ was now a deep, deep purple in colour, knotted veins knobbling its shaft; it looked almost impossibly swollen. She reached out and grasped it, and though it had just a moment ago left the heat of her sex it was cool to the touch.

She decided she had better unbind him. After all, she didn't want to do him any permanent harm, and especially not to Percy.

Telling Michael to kneel upright again, she reached between his legs and watched the relief on his face as she eased the candle out of his bottom. Then watched him wince as she carefully unbound his genitals.

She chuckled to see that despite his discomfort, and despite the removal of the tightly constricting bondage, he remained hugely erect. 'I'll bet you're ready to come, aren't you, slave?' she laughed.

There was sincere pleading in Michael's eyes. 'Oh, God, am I!' he groaned. Adding quickly: 'Mistress.'

'Then, I think I'll be merciful and let you.'

Michael seemed to swell with relief. Until she added slyly: 'Oh, I don't mean now, slave. Just, eventually.'

And she laughed again, thrilling to his groan as she dashed the hopes she had raised for precisely that purpose.

Chapter Eighteen

S uzie was sitting in her office trying to work.
     The paste-ups, all sixty-four pages of them, were on
her desk, and were all but ready for press. The deadline
was not until four the following day, but with the party that
night at the Tauntons' – and with prescience of the inevitable hang-overs there would be in the morning – she had
had the entire staff working flat out to produce the edition a
full twelve hours ahead of their usual schedule. If a new
story broke now, it would just be too bad. And what an
edition it was she thought, as she flipped through its pages:
the text was great, and the artwork superb; easily the best
she had seen. There was no doubt about it, they had done
themselves proud for the magazine's fiftieth issue.

And now, apart from the odd touch here and there,
there was just the editorial to write.

But, as seemed to have become increasingly the norm,
she was once again distracted, finding it difficult to concentrate. Between excited thoughts of Michael moving in
with her the following night, and thoughts no less exciting of their role-reversed sex of the previous night, there
was little room left for the vagaries of feminist politics
she was planning to slate.

She sighed and put down her pen. Let her mind, yet again, wander back.

She had done some deliciously kinky things as Mistress Suzie, she reflected. Some, no doubt, that Michael would pick up on when he was again in command, their roles reverted to normal. She hoped so anyway. She imagined herself having to tongue Michael's bottom just as he had been made to tongue hers, and an erotic shiver tingled her spine. Her depraved trick with the wine she was rather less sure about. She shuddered just at the thought of it, though she couldn't deny it had a certain kinky appeal. And the candle she would leave lying around, just in case Michael should need a hint. Though she doubted that. And, unlike the candle, lest he should mistake it for one, the riding crop would fast disappear.

She let her mind race on through the entire session, taking the submissive part in all she had done with her 'slave' – at least where that was anatomically possible – and thrilling to the imagined sensations of it all being done to her. But the finale was different: that she re-ran exactly as it had happened, with her in command. The imagery so perfect she might have been living it again.

Michael was lying on his back, his cock huge and swollen, after almost four hours of near-constant stimulation; never had she seen it so big. Following the severe bondage to which she had subjected it earlier, it had returned to a more natural colour, but, still, its sheer size and distension made it obvious he was desperate to come. And she had decided, finally, to let him. But even then, even in her mercy, she intended to be wickedly cruel.

She was standing above him, between his ankles, and she kicked them apart to spread them. Then, reaching down, she took hold of his legs, lifting and rolling him back until his weight was full on his shoulders, his parted knees falling either side of his head.

He could obviously guess her intent, or part of it anyway, and his dismay was clear in his eyes.

She laughed to see it, and delighted in confirming his

fears. 'Yes,' she said, 'you've come over my face often enough, haven't you? Well, now you're going to come in your own.'

With that, she reached between his legs and took hold of his penis, directing its tip at his face while she stroked it with light, brushing caresses.

'So, slave,' she teased, 'you want to come then, eh?'

'Oh God, y –' Michael stopped himself, warily eyeing the tip of his cock and patently aware of the humiliating consequence of climaxing now. But it was a brief hesitation: physical need evidently overwhelming his mental reluctance. He suddenly blurted: 'Oh God, yes. Yes, please,' his voice a hoarse, imploring croak, desperation obvious within it.

She smiled down at him. A deliberately cruel smile.

'Then, open your mouth,' she said.

Michael's eyes flew wide in sudden horror.

'Oh God, no, Suz –. Mis –. Suzie. Please, no.'

His plea sounded sincere, his confusion telling of the depth of his anguish, and she almost reprieved him. But the pulsing of his cock, yet again, betrayed him: whatever he might be saying, there was a part of him, too, that was thrilling to the perversity of what she was threatening. There would be no reprieve.

Instead, she took a firm grip on his balls and began to squeeze with steadily increasing strength. 'You'll open your mouth sooner or later, slave,' she said. 'I could simply carry on teasing you, keeping you right on the edge until you were forced to obey me out of sheer desperation. But' – she gave his balls a sudden sharp squeeze – 'this way is quicker. Like I said, you'll obey me sooner or later: why not save yourself unnecessary pain?'

It was enough: slowly, reluctantly, but with an air of defeated resignation, Michael's mouth came open.

'That's better,' she said.

And using her knees in the small of his back to fine-tune his position, manoeuvring him until the head of his cock was just inches from his opened mouth, pointing

206

directly at it, she began to masturbate him. She did so with deliberate slowness, and with the lightest of teasing caresses. She could guess his dilemma: he was desperate to come, yet, now, was at the same time dreading it; was almost as desperate not to. And she wanted to prolong his agony. To watch it in his eyes as he strained for climax even while struggling not to; as he stared at the tip of his own cock in utter dread of what it must finally deliver.

She managed to prolong it for some time, too, her soft, feather-light touch as her fingers brushed the length of his cock not sufficient, quite, to trigger an early release. But enough to drive him wild with a desire he both wanted and didn't; to take him closer and closer, to an agonising brink that contorted his face as the inevitable grew ever nearer. Until, at last, it began: his balls tightened in her palm and his bottom clenched, and she knew the volcano was about to erupt. And Michael groaned, unable to hold himself back any longer, a long shuddering groan that was part relief and part anguish as she tightened her grip on his scrotum and took careful aim with his cock.

Kept boiling within him for as long as it had, his come was thick and glutinous, and the first spurt of it left the tip of his cock in a long string. His face twisted in a grimace of revulsion as it splashed to the back of his throat. He looked as if he were about to close his mouth, perhaps to spit it out, and she tightened her grip on his balls to ensure he did neither.

'You have to take it all,' she warned, as the second string of it followed the first. 'And, of course, swallow it.'

It seemed to go on for a very long time, as spurt after spurt of Michael's long-held semen shot out directly towards his mouth. She continued to stroke his straining shaft, teasing out more of it and torn between watching the angst in his eyes and his pulsing, gushing cock; her grip on his scrotum making certain he swallowed while still it went on. And only when she had milked the last

207

drop of it from him, it dribbling onto his chin, did she finally relent.

It took Michael some while to recover, his breathing ragged as she let him down to the floor. His eyes were open, but glazed, and he seemed oblivious to her as she leaned over and licked the dribble of sperm from his chin; sat back to watch him slowly come round.

But, at last, his breathing calmed and his eyes cleared, and he finally propped himself up on an elbow.

His grin was sheepish, and he wagged a playful finger. 'I'm gonna get you at playtime,' he said.

'Ooooh, promises!' she chuckled.

And they both agreed that her domination of him had been a success; an exciting departure they would definitely have to repeat.

Suzie shook her head to bring herself out of her reverie. Glanced at her watch, and knew she had better get on; the afternoon was fast disappearing and she still had that editorial to write. And picking up her pen, she forced herself to begin: *These bra-burning bitches who would turn our society into an ochlocracy of harridans would do well to realise* . . .

And then the words ran out. Thinking about Michael had turned her on to distraction, far too horny to be able to think about feminists. She felt hot and dithery, and not for the first time that day she decided a trip to the loo was called for, her trusty vibrator for company.

She picked up her bag and pushed to her feet, just as Sally put her head round the door.

'Susan, I'm really not feeling very well. Would it be all right if I went off home?'

'Oh, yes, Sally. Do what you must,' she muttered distractedly. She had already begun to re-live yet again the experience of last night, had begun again at the beginning: Michael was standing naked in her lounge, his hands on his head and his legs apart, his magnificent cock swaying before him, and she was in no mood for Sally and her menstrual mitherings. All she could think about was getting to the loo and relieving the ache in her loins.

In a dreamy haze she wandered past Sally and out of her office, not looking back.

And not seeing the paste-ups she had inadvertently left on her desk.

Fifteen minutes later she was back, feeling content and relaxed and ready for work. She dropped her bag on the floor and sat at her desk, eager now to get on. She picked up her notepad and re-read the few words she had written.

'Right,' she said aloud, knowing exactly, now, how the piece was to go.

And only then, as she picked up her pen, did she begin to grow vaguely uneasy. As though something was wrong. She looked around her but everything seemed normal. Sally was missing from her desk in the outer office – yes, quite normal, she thought wryly – and everything seemed in its place. Finally, she shrugged to herself and looked back to her pad; scribbled a few words. But the feeling remained, grew stronger, and she was again forced to stop. Something was disturbing her. She couldn't think what it was, but she was sure now: something was definitely wrong. *What was it?*

And then it dawned.

The beginnings of horror prickled the hairs on the back of her neck, and she felt suddenly clammy; a knot tightened in the pit of her stomach. *The paste-ups. Where were the paste-ups?* They had been there on her desk but now they were gone.

She spread her palms over the leather top, as if they had merely become invisible and she would feel them there if only she tried hard enough. But no, they were definitely gone.

She grabbed for the top drawer of her desk, the one in which the paste-ups would normally be locked, and yanked it open. Slammed it shut again when she saw it was empty. Worked her way down the rest of the drawers. They weren't in any of them. Irrationally she even looked under the desk; hardly surprised not to find them there but in her panic willing to look anywhere.

Flinging herself out of her chair, she ran to her door. Scruffy Terry, the gofer, was there in the outer office rummaging through some files.

'Terry!' she screamed at him. 'Have you seen the paste-ups?'

The pimply youth looked up in alarm at the sudden sound of her voice. 'I 'aven't. Sooz, no. Should I 'ave done?'

She charged at him like a bull. Grabbed him by the shoulders and shook him, her face just inches from his as she yelled at him: 'How long have you been here at the files? Have you seen anyone go into my office? Anyone go anywhere near. Think, you idiot, think. Anyone ai all?'

'Hey, have a heart, Sooz. I haven't done nothing wrong. And I haven't seen nobody, neither.'

She shoved him away as if discarding something useless, and ran back into her office. Grabbed the phone on her desk and began ringing the Heads of Departments. Nobody should have needed the paste-ups once they had reached her desk; they were her responsibility; hers and hers alone. But someone had to have removed them from her desk. For some reason. Somebody had to have done.

But the phone calls proved fruitless: no one had seen anything of them. And ten minutes later she threw the phone down. Spent a further half hour frantically searching, but to no avail. And finally she gave up. Sat slumped in her chair with her head in her hands, close to tears.

What was she to do? There was nothing she could do. The paste-ups had vanished, and that was it – she would miss the deadline. For even if she were to forgo the party, work all night, persuaded the rest of the staff to do likewise, there was no chance – no chance at all – of putting new ones together in time. The text alone might have been manageable, just, since all the material written in-house would still be on disk; it could simply be run off again. And most of the freelance input could be replaced via fax. But it was the artwork: that was irreplaceable. The lay-out and design – all that made the magazine – would all take far longer to re-do than the time she had available. No, there was no question about it: without those missing paste-ups she would miss the deadline by a very long way.

It was her worst nightmare. Not only was she about to miss a deadline, itself unforgivable, she was about to miss the deadline of the magazine's fiftieth edition. Which they'd spent a fortune promoting; a fortune that would now be as good as lost. As lost as her job.

For that was another certainty: her head would definitely roll.

And with that thought came another, one that was even more chilling, and that made horror claw at her innards: *how could Michael move in with her if she couldn't support him? If she had no job, and with limited prospects of finding another? She was now, after all, an editor who missed deadlines: a journalistic pariah. Her daydreaming had finally caught up with her. Because of it, her life was suddenly in ruins. No job; her career in tatters and no Michael!*

And with that, the tears did at last come.

'Not quite the end of the world, is it?'

Suzie jumped, startled, and looked up to see the tear-blurred image of Bob Adams standing in front of her desk. She hadn't heard him come in, and she quickly scrubbed the tears from her eyes, feeling foolish and a little ashamed. Regretting that anyone, and Bob Adams especially, should have seen her cry.

She found a smile that didn't work, and said ruefully: 'Not quite, Bob, maybe. Though closer to it than you know.'

'Oh? Sounds intriguing. What, there's something more?'

Adams, of course, had been one of those she had

telephoned in her panic, and so was well aware that the paste-ups were missing; that her job, perhaps even all of their jobs, were thus on the line. But he knew nothing of the personal tragedy that, for her, would be the result.

And nor would he.

She shook her head. 'The fact the paste-ups are missing is serious enough, Bob, without my burdening you with the rest of my troubles?'

'Please yourself,' Adams muttered, inviting himself to sit down. 'So, there's still no sign of them then?'

Again her head shook, no. This time in silence.

'And if they don't turn up, then we'll miss the deadline by what' – he tutted – 'twelve hours? Twenty-four?'

'Twenty-four, and the rest,' said Suzie miserably.

Adams sucked in a breath through his teeth. 'That could be serious. I mean, seriously serious.'

'Don't you think I know that, Bob?' she said curtly, throwing him a withering look.

But Adams was undaunted; seemed determined to rub it in as deeply as it would go: 'I mean, you know how fussy the big distributors are. That sort of delay, and we could be looking at ninety per cent of the run left gathering dust in the warehouse. And with the money we've spent on promotion this month, we'd never survive that. It'd be enough to put us under.'

Suzie was too miserable to be further irked by his insensitivity. Felt too guilty and too ashamed to feel angry.

'I know, Bob, and I'm sorry,' she said, tears springing back to her eyes. Not caring now. 'I mean, I know I'm history now anyway, as regards *Woman Now*. But, well, if it goes under, the staff, Sally, you, all of you. You'll all be out on your ears . . . God, I'm so sorry.'

There was a pause, before Adams said quietly: 'Of course, it doesn't have to come to that, you know.'

Suzie stared at him, her brow wrinkled in puzzlement.

'I mean, the paste-ups.' Adams went on, 'it might just be that somebody has them – someone, who knows, not a million miles from this very office – and could be persuaded to spirit them back.'

Suzie continued to stare at him, as comprehension began slowly to dawn. And with it came astonishment, relief, finally anger.

'You!' she accused, knowing it. Though hardly believing he could have pulled such a sick prank, that anyone could. 'You have them, don't you?'

Adams showed her his palms. 'I didn't say that, now did I?'

'But you have. I know you have. Admit it, you bastard.'

'Oh, Susan, so coarse. You disappoint me for so articulate a lady.'

'Cut the crap. Talk to me. What is it, a joke? A sick joke?'

'Oh, it's no joke, Susan. Oh, no, that it isn't. Let's just say that I now have a certain, ah, bargaining power.'

'Bargaining power? To bargain for what, for Christ's sake?'

Adams smiled. A nasty, lecherous smile. He inclined his head at her. 'Susan,' he said, 'obtuse you are not.'

And nor was she. But still it took a moment for the penny to drop. Finally, it did. 'Oh, but you can't mean ... Bob, not even you would stoop so low.'

'You know how I've lusted after you, Susan. But you've never given me so much as a chance. Now, unless you want to see the magazine go under, you'll maybe think differently, eh?' He suddenly grinned, and his eyes were those slimy grey slugs again as he looked at her and said: 'I told you I'd have you one day. Remember?'

Suzie's stomach turned, even as her mind raced. He was trying to blackmail her into going to bed with him. But with what he was threatening, he surely couldn't be serious.

'You're bluffing,' she said at last. 'Because it's not only me, is it? If the magazine goes under, you'd be out too. You'd be doing yourself out of a job.'

Adams shrugged. 'There's always a job for me on *Man International*. Might even welcome the change.'

'What, after I've told the Tauntons what you had done? That their magazine had gone bust because you, Bob Adams, had stolen the paste-ups so as to blackmail me into bed? Come off it, Bob, who do you think you're kidding?'

'The Adamses and the Tauntons go back a long way,' Adams said easily. 'Did you know I was even at school with Clive? Oh yes, him and me are like *that*.' He held up crossed fingers in mime of their closeness. 'They'd never believe you. They'd think you were making it up; passing the buck to save your own neck. Oh no, I'd be all right.' He paused, his eyes glinting coldly, like dabs of wet slate.

Then he went on: 'You, on the other hand, Susan? Well, Publishing Editors who miss deadlines, who put their magazines out of business, are not exactly in popular demand.'

And Suzie knew that only too well. That in the circumstances, she would find it extremely difficult to find a new job; one with anything like a comparable salary anyway. And, until she did – if ever she did – Michael would have to stay on with the agency. *Would have to keep on selling his body for sex. With those other women, who would be having him while she couldn't; while she would be home, alone, her thoughts of it torturing her.*

Adams had her over the cruellest of proverbial barrels. And he knew it, if not just how far over it she actually was bent.

And then, suddenly, she saw the way out; a glimmer of hope.

'I'll have security shut down the building,' she said, reaching for the phone. 'Have your office searched; search the whole damned building until the paste-ups are found.'

But to her utter surprise Adams remained easy. 'I don't think you'll do that, Susan.' There was smug self-assurance in his voice. But there was more, too; it held the hint of warning. 'You don't know the paste-ups are still in the building. And once you'd gone as public as

214

bringing in security, well, I would then find it impossible to discreetly return them, wouldn't I? Under any circumstances. They would then have to stay lost for good, wouldn't they? And I wouldn't want that any more than you would: all those lost jobs . . .'

He let his words hang, shaking his head slowly and tutting.

The glimmer of hope flickered out. It seemed he had thought of everything.

For a while, Suzie said nothing. She could see no way around it: if she wanted to save the magazine, to keep her job, to have Michael move in with her as planned, if she wanted her life back in order then she would have to capitulate; there was no other choice. At last she slumped back in her chair.

'What exactly, is it you want?' she said, finally resigned.

'I've told you, your body,' Adams said simply. 'In fact tonight, at the party.'

'At the Tauntons!' Suzie exclaimed, incredulous. 'But why on earth there? And . . . and how? I mean, what, you're suggesting we sneak up to their bedrooms?'

'Er, no. Not exactly sneak, no. That's, ah, the other part of the deal. You see, Clive wants you too.'

'What?' This was becoming more absurd by the minute. 'What are you talking about?'

'Well you know he fancies you?'

'So maybe he does. But I don't see what . . . I mean . . .'

'Yes, he told me a while back. "A blonde cracker" he called you; said he'd love to get his leg over you. So I threw him a sickener: I told him I was.'

'You told him what?'

'Oh, just a bit of schoolchum bragging, you know? Anyway, I figured it wasn't a lie; that it was just the truth in advance.' He suddenly chuckled, evidently pleased with his wit.

'Well that's another reason, you see,' he went on, 'why they wouldn't believe your story that I had played dastardly tricks to get you into bed. Clive thinks I'm already bedding you, so why would I bother?' He chuckled again, this time reflectively. 'Funny how it's worked out, isn't it?'

'Oh, bloody hilarious,' Suzie muttered sourly.

'Course, when I told him I was knocking you off, he was as envious as hell. Exactly why I'd said it of course. Anyway, so I told him I'd see if I could use my influence with you to arrange it for him: get you to come across for him.'

'You told him what?' yelled Suzie, beginning to sound to herself like a stuck record. But furious now.

'Well, schoolchums or not, it never hurts to earn a few extra Brownie points with one's boss, does it? Even if he is only the baby boss. And I always figured that one day I'd find a way.'

'You smug, cocky bastard,' Suzie railed, giving vent to her fury.

Adams looked surprised, even hurt. 'What? I mean, well, I have haven't I? Where's cocky in that?'

Suzie was stunned speechless. But the barrel was still there, and she was still over it. What could she do?

There was a long pause, and then she said: 'So let me just get this clear. To get back the paste-ups, to save the magazine, I have to screw both you and Clive Taunton?'

'Got it in one, Susan. There, I knew you weren't obtuse. Course, I haven't said anything to Clive yet, so I don't know if we'll be taking you in turns or if we'll make it a threesome. But what's in a detail, eh?'

Again there was a long pause, and then Suzie nodded slowly. 'All right, you bastard. You win. Now get those paste-ups back on my desk right now.'

'Ah, now that would be foolish of me, wouldn't it?' Adams said with a wag of his finger. 'Wouldn't want you backing out of our little agreement, now. Or going ahead but like a dead fish, letting Clive know you'd been persuaded.'

'Blackmailed.'

'Words, Susan, just words. And blackmail is such an ugly one: I much prefer, let's see, yes, insurance. Yes,

216

that's a much better word. The thing is, I want you to make it good for us tonight, Susan, be the sexual tigress that I've told Clive you are. Basically, Susan, to fuck us ragged. The paste-ups are my insurance that you do, that's all.

'Anyway, from what I've seen they're all but ready. You won't be needing them today; tomorrow morning will be soon enough plenty.'

Suzie fixed him with a stare of resentment. 'You're an evil bastard, do you know that, Bob?'

Adams pushed himself up to his feet. 'D'you know why it's easier to be a bastard than a nice guy, Susan?' He didn't wait for an answer. 'Because it takes seventy-four muscles to smile, and just the one to fuck someone.'

And with that he was gone.

Leaving Suzie both numb and sick with what she'd agreed, alone with her thoughts.

Chapter Nineteen

The main reception room at the Taunton mansion was a magnificent affair. A spectacular chandelier captured its centre, cascading from a high ceiling in a spill of shimmering crystal, and cloned miniatures of it elsewhere, masquerading as wall-lights, were only marginally less impressive. An original Manet held pride of place above a splendid Edwardian fireplace that was marble and polished oak. And period furniture that an antiques' dealer would have given his eye-teeth for was almost carelessly scattered about. From the luxuriant pile of the Axminster to the beautifully corniced ceiling, the room reeked of money. The Tauntons had it in plenty.

A few latecomers were still arriving, but the party was well underway: dress was formal, and men in dinner-jackets and women draped in elegant evening gowns, their jewels a-glitter, stood chatting in groups, their voices a constant hum, while a squad of pretty girls dressed as French maids moved like silent wraiths between them offering champagne and morsels of food.

The Colonel was holding court by the fireplace, surrounded by a gaggle of toadying lackeys who hung on his every word; their group the hub of the party.

But it was a group Suzie had taken care to avoid – such sychophancy, common at Taunton gatherings, was something she loathed – and after the obligatory peck of greeting on the Colonel's cheek, she had quickly moved away. And had found herself, instead, in the company of Marjory Crichton of Crichton Books; a fortuity, it seemed, that was hardly much better than suffering the Colonel's fawning covey. Her mood had already been soured by the debasing experience of being winked at lasciviously by Clive Taunton, making it known to her that Bob Adams had tipped him the nod. She had forced a smile and winked back, and he had gone off grinning like a Cheshire cat. So she was in no mood for being further abased, talked down to by a literary snob like Marjory frigging Crichton.

'Of course, when one is publishing books, as opposed to magazines,' the obnoxious woman was maundering, managing to make the word magazine sound like something you wiped off your shoe, 'one has the question of its shelf-life to consider.'

Her voice grated, like fingernails drawn down a blackboard, and she was interminably boring as well as downright insulting. Suzie stopped listening, and drifted off into fantasy.

Marjory Crichton was wearing a toga. As, suddenly, is everyone else. Everyone, that is, except for the French maids: they are naked, carrying gourds of wine from group to group. Each group fondles them intimately as they serve, sliding hands between their legs, or else slap their rumps in passing, their pert bottoms spanked as pink as their blushing faces. And all around, an orgy is in full throe of which Bacchus himself would have been proud.

The Colonel's lackeys, all female now, are kneeling at his feet stroking his elderly penis, vainly attempting to tease it to life: acolytes hoping to win favour with the ageing Zeus. The one who can stir life into that tired old organ would be favourite indeed.

Suzie smiled at the thought, and let the fantasy return her to Marjory Crichton.

The woman is sprawled on a *chaise-longue*, now, and a man appears at her side: a tall black Moor. He lets his toga slip from his body to show he is massively erect, and the publisher's eyes widen with shock. And maybe a little fear too, for the man's organ is huge.

Wordlessly he straddles her chest, pinning her to the couch, and puts his bulging knob to her lips. It's obvious what he requires of her, but she quails and resists; shaking her head in refusal and keeping her lips tightly pursed. But the man will not be denied: he reaches down and pushes her toga aside, exposing a breast; smacks it sharply in punishment for her recalcitrance. And as her milky globe reddens with the angry marks of his fingers, he takes hold of a long fleshy nipple and begins to squeeze. His other hand is gripping her hair, keeping her head quite still as he presses his cock to her lips. And as he twists her nipple to enforce her obedience, she can do no other and quickly opens her mouth for him. His hips lunge forward, driving his ebony tumescence deeply into her throat, and she moans her discomfort as his massiveness stretches her jaws. He fills her mouth completely, and that's her shut up for a while!

Beyond the squirming, penis-gagged publisher, a naked slave is being led in by his master. He is hobbled and cuffed, and is being pulled along on a lead; this attached to a leather strap fastened tightly around his scrotum. He is clearly in abject misery, and in some physical pain, too, as the cruel leash is jerked, dragging him forward. But it's no more than Bob Adams deserves.

The master is known to her too, Suzie sees. He is the one from the slavemarket who sold her the Viking. He bares his familiar yellow teeth in a grin as he pushes his slave to a wall, chains him to metal rings set into the stone for the purpose, stretching his arms high above him, his legs wide apart. And to the delight of several watching women, he reaches to the helpless slave's groin and begins to handle his genitals.

Adams's cheeks blush crimson, clearly mortified at being handled thus by a man. Not to mention it being done in front of these women. But the slavemaster allows him no quarter, and as the audience of smirking women continues to watch, now joined – to Adams's evident dismay – by an appreciative young man, he begins actually to masturbate him. Adams writhes frantically, in the vain attempt to escape the humiliating fondling; to somehow shrink himself from it. But he cannot, and is forced to endure it. And as it goes on, to his visible horror, he begins to erect. He squirms, cringing to the slavemaster's masculine touch, but can do nothing to help himself: his penis continues to stiffen. And as it finally stands fully erect, to the jeers of those watching, he hangs his head in shame.

Suzie would have happily watched on for a while, enjoying Adams's disgrace, but the fantasy had materialised a man at her side, who needs her attention.

The man is tall and handsome, and a crown of laurel leaves adorns his majestic blond head: a god, no less. Yet, like the slavemaster's, his face is familiar to her: he is, or he was, her Viking.

With no attempt to seek her permission – he is now a god after all, who may do as he will – he slides a hand inside her toga and cups her breast in his palm, tenderly squeezing the swelling mound in his long, strong fingers. Finding her nipple, he rolls it gently between finger and thumb, instantly erecting the sensitive bud and bringing a moan to her lips. Thus encouraged, his other hand reaches lower, in search of a more secret prize. Lifting the hem of her toga his hand slides beneath it, and up along the inside of her thigh. Up and up, until it reaches the moist core of her womanhood, where his fingertips ease open the outer lips of her sex to signal their desire to go further. And as her thighs part to allow it, his finger penetrates her, delving deep within her and causing sparks of desire to course through her trembling belly.

221

Over by the fireplace, Zeus's tired old organ has finally managed to rise. It arcs up from his groin in a fragile, tentative curve, the skin sheathing it floppy and loose as though he can no longer fill it, the foreskin heavy and slack. His pendulous balls dangle beneath the pathetic tool in their long, wrinkled sac, jiggling grotesquely as his penis is worked ever faster. Several of his acolytes are attending to the task, but when the tip of his purple glans at last begins to moisten with pre-seminal dew, long-awaited climax finally nearing, none is prepared to be sullied by his jaded emission: it is one of the naked serving girls who is brought forward to receive the ageing god's seed. The young girl is pressed to her knees before him, her legs kicked wide to provide the old god with the sight of her opened sex; an additional and necessary stimulus to him while the hands strive to relieve him. The girl's small breasts rise and fall on her sobbing breaths, and her innocent cheeks blush pink as she is forced to maintain the shaming position, Zeus's leery eyes feasting on her maiden sex. And as the old god tenses, her young face is tilted backwards and up, held ready and waiting for his demeaning discharge.

Suzie looks away before it begins, having no wish to witness the innocent girl's degradation.

Bob Adams's, however, was another matter.

The fantasy returned her to where the slave Adams was chained to the wall, his genitals still being fondled by the slavemaster for the amusement of those watching. He is grossly erect now, and his cock is twitching and pulsing helplessly in the slavemaster's frotting fist: his face contorting with shame and despair as, despite all he can do to prevent it, he is reaching the verge of climax. A humiliating climax: brought to public orgasm in the hands of a man.

The watching women smirk knowingly as they see he is about to come, and the young man with them licks his lips in anticipation and stares transfixed, his own erection billowing his toga.

Finally, the slave Adams can hold it no longer. With

a long despairing groan that seems to come from deep in his being, his back arches, thrusting his genitals obscenely forward as his crisis begins. And though it clearly shames him to do it, it's as if he cannot resist the slavemaster's hand, and despite the indecency of it he pushes his cock into the calloused palm in desperate need of its friction. The women snicker to see it, deepening his shame still further.

But he cannot help himself, too close to coming to stop now. And all dignity gone his hips jerk on, lewdly fucking the slavemaster's fist. And then, with a mighty shudder, he is coming: his cock jerks in spasm as it spurts its first string in a long arc to splash on the floor at the feet of the laughing women; humbling tribute to the masturbatory skill of his male tormentor. The women cheer, giggling at Adams's shame. And the young man drops to his knees, lowering his tongue to the puddle of semen and greedily lapping it up.

Adams groans at this new ignominy. Yet his cock pumps on, though each spurt is a little less strong than the one before it, travelling a little less far, so leaving a trail of semen across the floor for the young man to follow, licking it up as he goes. Until finally the man is kneeling up to take Adams's still-twitching cock in his mouth, and Adams squirms, mortified, as male lips suck him dry.

The slavemaster shows his hand to the snickering women, where Adams's sperm has sullied his fingers. Then, as a final cruel kick to his slave's ruined ego, he lifts his hand to Adams's mouth.

Suzie thrills to see Adams's shame thus complete, and she looks away as the fantasy moves on: the god's fingers are still deep inside her, now sending wave after wave of delicious desire through her body. And she can feel his rampant hardness against her thigh, pressing insistently: he is clearly ready for more serious pleasures.

A sexy murmur tingles her spine: 'Are you ready, Susan?'

'Oh, yes,' she breathes. 'I'm ready. Take me. Take me now.'

'Susan, I said are you ready?'

But hasn't she just told him she is? Why is he asking again? And then she realises that the god's lips haven't moved; that it wasn't he who had spoken. It was a voice from behind her, whispering into her ear. A voice that she knew. Yet, it couldn't be: the owner of that voice was a slave chained to the wall, his head hung low in disgrace, and . . .

And suddenly, there wasn't a slave. No stone wall with rings and chains. No naked serving girls with their spanked-pink bottoms. No Zeus and no bacchanalian orgy. She was back at the party. Marjory Crichton was standing before her, once again fully clothed. And still whittering on like a shell-shocked budgie: the egotistical bat had not even noticed she had been away.

She remembered the voice, then, and turned to its source. And there was Bob Adams, looking excited and fidgety.

'We're all set, Susan,' he told her. 'Are you ready?'

Michael was sitting in decadent comfort on the back seat of a Rolls, beside an elegant but elderly lady.

'I loathe these functions,' the woman grumbled cantankerously, 'but one does have to attend. Family affairs, you see?'

'I see,' said Michael. Not really seeing at all. And caring less; what did it matter? He was there to do a job, was all. *His last.*

'But that does not mean one has to sit and be bored out of one's mind the whole evening. And I've always found you escort chaps to be quite passable company; decent conversationalists, and with minds capable of thinking along more than one track. Which is more than can be said for the majority of those sorts.'

Michael smiled politely. Vaguely wondering what those sorts were. Supposed he'd find out soon enough. 'Well, it's nice of you to say so, Mrs Dunwitty. We do try our best.'

'Oh, to the devil with Mrs Dunwitty, young man –

Michael, isn't it? – if we're to sit chatting all evening, you'd best call me Eleanor.'

'Then, Eleanor it is.'

'And don't overdo the charm. I'm an old woman, but I know when I'm being patronised.'

Michael smiled to himself. She might be an old grouch – a harridan as Grace had described her – but she had a certain straight-talking charm of her own, and he liked that.

'Course, there was a time,' Eleanor went on, her old eyes sparkling with memory, 'before Mr Dunwitty, you understand, when I'd have wanted a good-looking chap like you for more than just chat. I was a bit of a gel in my day. Isn't that right, George?'

The chauffeur nodded his capped head. 'So I believe, ma'am.'

Eleanor chuckled. 'I once had three Cambridge Blues in a punt up the river. All three together; didn't have an orifice I could call me own. All afternoon we went at it, and there was nothing coxless about those boys I'll tell you! But' – she sighed deeply – 'all long in the past, now. Now, all I'm good for is chat.'

Michael was grateful for that. Eleanor Dunwitty wasn't the oldest woman he'd had to make love to on behalf of the Agency. But she wasn't far off, and the idea was hardly appealing. But if all he had to do was chat, then how bad? She was certainly a character, and the evening ahead might not be so bad after all, he decided.

Just as the Rolls pulled into the extensive grounds of the Taunton mansion.

Suzie followed Adams from the reception room and into a spacious hallway, where Clive Taunton was waiting.

Taunton was a man of about thirty-five, she supposed. Of course, he would be; he was the same age as Bob, wasn't he. He was not quite as tall as she and a pound or two overweight. And she had always thought his chin a little too weak for her liking. But otherwise he was not unattractive.

He was grinning at her broadly and his eyes glittered in eager anticipation, like those of a small boy awaiting the start of his favourite bedtime story.

'Go on up, the two of you,' he said. 'My room's the second one on the left, just along the corridor. I'll be up in a jiff.'

So, it was to be a ménage à trois, *then,* thought Suzie. That, at least, was a plus. She had never experienced a threesome, but she had often enjoyed them in fantasy. And turned on as she was, anyway, from her fantasy of a minute before, not least in watching Bob Adams get a deserved and fitting comeuppance, she pushed aside niggling thoughts about unfaithfulness to Michael and decided: yes, to hell with it, she was damn well going to enjoy it. Even if she had been blackmailed into it.

She treated Taunton to a sexy smile. 'Don't keep me waiting now, will you?'

'Raring to go, eh? As you said, Bob old chap: a veritable tigress. But no, I'll keep you waiting no longer than it'll take me to grab a bottle of plonk and three glasses. Don't start without me, now.'

'As if we would,' said Suzie sweetly.

Taunton went off for the wine, and Suzie and Adams made their way up to his room.

'You're playing a blinder,' said Adams, sitting down on the large double bed.

'Only because I know you're rotten enough to let the paste-ups stay lost if I don't.' She wasn't going to give him the satisfaction of knowing she was now, in fact, playing it for real. That she was actually looking forward to it. He was still a bastard.

Adams grinned. 'Oh, you know me so well,' he said.

That killed the conversation and they sat in a heavy silence, Suzie re-conjuring the image of Adams's head hanging in shame, his macho ego in shreds as he succumbed to the slavemaster's hand. Only wishing she could have seen it for real. Until, a minute later, the door opened and Clive Taunton came into his bedroom. He

226

had the glasses and the promised bottle, and setting them down on a bedside table he filled the glasses and handed them round.

'Cheers,' he said. 'Here's to a good romp, what?'

And he drained his glass in one.

Suzie barely had time to sip at hers before he was taking it from her again, returning it to the bedside table. And then the two men's hands were upon her.

Michael beat the chauffeur to the door of the Rolls, and held it open while Eleanor Dunwitty stepped out.

'Aaah, my back,' she groaned as she straightened, her withered face showing her pain. 'I'm a martyr to my blessed back.'

Michael offered her his arm and she took it, glad of his strength to help support herself while the pain took a moment to ease.

'The trouble with getting old, Michael, is you begin to seize up like a rusty old bus. Right, I'm all right now. Come along.'

The house had a huge double front door set between fluted Gothic pillars, and a high step with which Eleanor needed some help, but they finally made it inside.

'They're all publishing types,' Eleanor said, showing Michael into the palatial reception room where the party was already buzzing. 'It's how the family made its money, so perhaps one shouldn't complain,' she went on. Then added in a voice that made no attempt at discretion: 'But they're all such crashing bores, dear, who talk about nothing else.'

They started across the room, Eleanor stopping to chat – very briefly – to one or two of the guests, naughtily introducing Michael as 'my bit of stuff for the night', as they made their way over to the least busy corner.

Reaching a polished hide couch, Eleanor sat down with a groan and dispatched Michael to find them champagne.

Michael quickly located one of the French maids, and returned with two glasses. Handed one to Eleanor and sat down beside her.

'I take it these people all work for your family?' he said, to make conversation.

'Mostly, yes,' Eleanor agreed. She nudged his arm. 'You see the old fart standing there by the fireplace?'

Michael followed her eyes, and nodded. *Not unhappy with her turn of phrase: this was going to be far from the boring evening he had originally envisaged. Eleanor Dunwitty was a character indeed.*

'My baby brother, Humphrey. He's the head of Taunton Publishing; the whole empire. These arseholes all call him the Colonel. Well, he was a colonel once, of course, out in India. But that's a long time ago now. This lot just pander to his military ego; toadying up to him because he is who he is. You see, most of the family's involved in the business, but Humphrey runs the show.'

'I see,' said Michael. 'And your role? Obviously an important one if you attend these dos when you hate them so much?'

Eleanor's eyes suddenly flashed. 'My role? I, dear, run Humphrey.'

Michael chuckled, believing it, and sipped his champagne. 'I must admit, I've never heard of Taunton Publishing. It's a large concern, from what you're saying?' *A brief question, then settle back for a hopefully lengthy answer: the key to successful professional escorting.*

Eleanor shrugged. 'Large enough,' she said. 'The people here tonight are mostly the heads of our subsidiary companies, which gives you some idea. Her over there' – she flicked her bird-like head towards a heavily bejewelled, sour-faced woman – 'she's Marjorie Crichton of Crichton Books; they produce upmarket, literary-type works – books that hardly anyone reads and so cost a fortune. Whereas Peter Brogan there' – another flick of the head – 'he runs Freedom Paperbacks, pumping out pulp fiction by the ton, but selling the stuff like hot cakes.'

Michael nodded. 'Yes, I know of Freedom.'

'Doesn't everyone, dear,' said Eleanor. 'But it takes all sorts, you see. And we have all sorts, covering the whole market spectrum. That's Taunton Publishing.'

228

Michael nodded again. Thinking about Suzie and wondering vaguely if she, in her line of work, would know of the firm. *He must remember to ask.*

Suzie was wallowing in rampant maleness.

The two men had sat either side of her on the large double bed, and had gradually stripped her, pausing to pay lascivious attention to each new part they exposed before moving on. And naked at last, she had stretched full length on her back and parted her thighs, and had revelled in the feel of four hands and two eager tongues exploring her, caressing every inch of her and delighting her with their touch. While she herself had fondled whatever had come to hand, kissed and sucked that which had been put to her mouth.

And for the past five minutes she had lain with her eyes closed, the better to savour the erotic sensation while the two men alternated, taking it in turns to screw her or enter her mouth; going from one to the other with their throbbing erections and keeping her guessing into which of those orifices they would finally spend their seed.

And then one of them – which one, she didn't know or care – suddenly did. The taste of it – *yes, she might have known it would be in her mouth* – was salt and slick on her tongue. She swallowed greedily, sucking him dry, until, with a groan, he slowly withdrew. And, her senses filled with his exciting musk she felt him softening against her cheek, for now spent.

While the other man continued to thrust.

Downstairs, Eleanor stretched herself painfully and put her hands to her sides. 'It's no good,' she groaned, 'my back is killing me. I can't sit on this blessed couch any longer.'

She had been chatting to a small fat man with a pencil moustache whose company she actually seemed to enjoy, and seeing she was happily occupied, Michael had spent the past few minutes passing the time with a daydream. Thinking back to the previous night.

Eleanor's complaints reached him through a flood of exciting memory, interrupting his thoughts and bringing him back to the present. She was rubbing her back and was clearly in a great deal of pain.

'Would a walk help?' he asked. A hand quickly shielded the bulge he was horrified to see had grown in the front of his trousers. 'A stroll?'

Eleanor shook her head. 'No. Though I thank you for the thought. No, I need my chair, that's all. I have one here; it's not actually orthopaedic, but it seems to do the trick. You'd think they'd have some regard for an old woman, wouldn't you, and have it out for me. But no, I always have to ask.' She looked over to where the Colonel held court, and beckoned to him. 'Humphrey, do you have a moment?'

'But of course, dear.'

He came instantly to her summons. A tall, dignified gentleman, with a head of grey hair and cheeks that had been mottled red over the years by too much good port. He looked every inch the colonel.

'Yes, dear?'

'It's my back, Humphrey. I have to have my chair.'

'Oh, but Eleanor dear, must we have that monstrosity in here? It's so blessed ugly.'

'Yes, Humphrey, we do.'

'But –'

'Humphrey!'

She fixed him with a look that would have curdled milk, and he sighed resignedly.

'Oh, all right, dear. It's up in Clive's room; I'll have it fetched down.'

'No, don't bother, Humphrey. Michael will fetch it for me, won't you dear?'

'Of course,' said Michael, standing. 'Happy to oblige.'

'It's up the stairs from the hallway.' Eleanor told him, 'then the second door on the left. You can't miss it. And you're looking for a green straight-backed chair.'

'Bright green,' muttered the Colonel with a little shudder of distaste.

Michael kept a grin to himself. 'I'll find it,' he said.

Suzie was lost in a sea of sexual sensation. She had been only vaguely aware, a few moments before, of the man who had spent himself leaving the bed, padding across to the *en suite* bathroom; the sound of a toilet flushing, running taps. She had been too enthralled to register it all on any conscious level; her climax fast approaching as the other man (*who was Michael*) continued to thrust into her, his rhythm growing ever more urgent as his own climax gathered.

And now she was coming. Gasping and moaning in the throes of it; her muscles in spasm and clutching the iron penis (*which was Michael's penis*) that continued to drive into her, transporting her to a plane of consciousness on which she was aware of nothing save for wave after wave of giddying sensation.

And not aware at all of the bedroom door that opened, was held open for a moment, and then softly closed, as her orgasm went on.

Michael wandered back into the party in a daze.

'Great Heavens, dear, you're as white as a sheet!' Eleanor exclaimed on seeing him, her brow wrinkled with concern. 'You're ashen. Are you all right?'

'N-no, er, not . . .'

At first, he hadn't realised who it was in the bedroom: just two naked bodies thrashing away on a bed. Clive – was that whose bedroom they had said this was? – humping one of the staff. And he'd grinned, intending to beat a hasty retreat; leave the two to their fun and explain to Eleanor as discreetly as possible that she would have to wait for her chair. But then he had stopped in his tracks.

Some women make a very distinctive sound when they come; some grunt, some squeal, some like to cry out obscenities or scream. Michael had heard them all. And he knew the sound of Suzie's orgasm as well as he knew his own name. It was that which had stopped him.

Even before he had seen her face. A face contorted with sexual ecstasy; her eyes squeezed shut in her rapture; her breasts jiggling as the man on top of her arched his back and plunged into her a final time, his buttocks taut. While her hands gripped his hips to hold him inside her, to savour the feel of him for a few seconds longer.

It had felt like a kick in the stomach. And he had let the door close to as he'd turned away unable to look, feeling sickened and numbed with shock.

A numbness he still felt as Eleanor's face looked up into his.

'I, er, not well . . . have to go. Sorry. Grace Cummings . . . refund your . . . I'm sure.'

And he turned and reeled away.

Chapter Twenty

S uzie marched into the building and made for the lift, an angry clip to her stride as she left the morning sunlight behind her for the fluorescent blue–white of the foyer. Reaching the lift she hit the button for the fourth floor, heading directly for Bob Adams's office, and waited impatiently while it took forever to rise.

She was in a foul mood: she had slept hardly a wink that night, kept tossing and turning by feelings of guilt; of remorse for what she had done. Not so much for the deed itself, particularly, though wasn't that bad enough? Letting herself be coerced into bedding two men. At least she had been coerced; blackmailed into it and left with hardly much choice. But it was the fact she had actually enjoyed it, that was the unforgivable part: she had not been coerced into having a good time. She had been unfaithful to Michael not only in body, but in mind and spirit too, and for that she had no one to blame but herself. And with him due to move in with her that very day. She couldn't believe the recreant bitch she had been.

But her enthusiastic performance at least would have earned her the return of the paste-ups: the deadline would be met, and the edition – not to mention the magazine itself – would be saved. Which was some consolation. And as long as it hadn't, too, given Clive Taunton any mistaken ideas, turning him into a pest she would now have the hassle of fending off, then she could put the whole sorry incident behind her not too much the worse for it. *Just bloody angry, that was all.*

The lift glided to a halt and the doors slid apart. And she stormed out, straight into Bob Adams's office.

Adams was sitting behind his desk, and as he looked up he fixed him with an irate glare. 'Right, now give me the paste-ups,' she demanded. 'Right now.'

Adams leaned back in his chair, casually steepling his fingers and clearly in no mood to be hurried.

A smug grin spread on his face. 'Well, we really are the tigress in bed, aren't we?' he said.

Suzie felt a flush of embarrassment drive some of the wind from her sails. She struggled to hold onto her anger, the better to cope with the other, less useful emotions churning inside her. 'It was an act for Clive, and you know it,' she snapped.

Adams was unmoved. 'Come off it, Susan,' he sneered. 'You were well into it, and *you* know it: you loved every minute of it. And you were good, too, I'll give you that. I always knew you would be, of course. But yes, you were good.'

'I don't get complaints,' Suzie said tartly. 'Now, can I please have those paste-ups?'

'And didn't I always say,' Adams persisted, 'that I could do wonderful things for your body? Come on now, be honest – how did I rate?'

'Five out of ten,' Suzie shrugged. 'Not great.'

Actually, guilt aside, the session had merited a positive nine. But she wasn't about to tell Adams that. And as for his individual rating, it suddenly occurred to her that she didn't know. She realised, somewht disconcertingly, that she wasn't sure which of the two men he had been: was he the one who had come in her mouth, or the one who had zapped her to climax? *She just didn't know.*

234

The thought flustered her, and she felt herself blush.

Adams saw it, and as she might have expected, mis-read it. 'There, you see!' he exclaimed with a triumphant laugh. 'What did I tell you? You can't fool me: fives out of ten don't warrant blushes. Go on, admit it; I was good, wasn't I?'

'Oh, shut up, Bob, you egotistical fool.' What little patience she had was fast running out. 'Now look, I kept my side of the bargain. Are you going to keep yours and give me those paste-ups, or are we going on with this inane conversation until we miss the deadline anyway?'

It was a few seconds before Adams replied. Then he said quietly: 'I haven't got them.'

'What? Well what have you done with them? Where are they?'

'I haven't the faintest idea. You see, I never had them.'

'What the hell are you talking about? Of course, you had them. Or else what was last night all about?'

'Last night, Susan, was all about fun. A bit of rumpo-pumpo. Oh yes, and great fun it was, too. But I never had the paste-ups. If you think about it, I never actually said that I did.'

'But, but . . .' Suzie was stunned, shocked speechless. *What was he saying? Of course he had the paste-ups. He had to have.*

Adams chuckled a little self-consciously. A little guilt-ily, even. 'I got the idea when you rang me to ask if I'd seen them,' he said. 'I saw an opportunity that was too good to miss, so I went for it. And it went like a dream, too: a hint here, a hint there, but I never actually said that I had them.'

Suzie felt her world begin to dissolve, disintegrate into tiny pieces and collapse around her as the truth of it slowly sank in. She had been duped. Conned into hav-ing sex with two men, into being unfaithful to Michael. On the eve of his becoming her live-in partner, loyal and faithful to her. But, worse – yes, worse even than that – there were still no paste-ups. With the deadline less than seven hours away, they still had no magazine.

She stared at Adams on the verge of tears, her eyes burning.

'Tell me you're kidding, Bob,' she implored despairingly. 'For God's sake tell me you're kidding.'

But she knew he wasn't. And as he shook his head, confirming it, her next words came slowly. Though were none the less vehement for that.

'You're an even bigger bastard than I thought,' she snarled. 'Bigger than I ever thought anyone could be.'

Adams shrugged his shoulders and kept his smug grin. 'They'll probably think the same at *Man International* I shouldn't wonder. Since it looks as if that's where I'll be from next month.'

'You ...' The words stuck in her throat. She could scarcely believe his callousness, the casualness of his attitude in the shadow of such calamity. Here they were on the brink of disaster – the magazine about to go under, all their jobs lost – and as long as he was all right with *Man International* he couldn't have cared less. 'You just don't give a damn, do you?' she spluttered at last.

Again Adams shrugged. 'I didn't lose the paste-ups, Susan. You did.'

Suzie choked, unable to deny it; unable to speak at all, and could only stare at Adams's mocking grin feeling wretched. Until, finally, she could bear it no longer, and she turned and ran from his office.

His laughter following her out.

Stinging with humiliation, Adams's laughter burning her ears, Suzie reached the lift and banged a fist at the call button. Decided she couldn't wait for the lift and ran for the stairs instead. Made it up the flight to the fifth floor in record time, and ran for her office, needing sanctuary.

And all the while hoping – praying – that by some miracle of fate the missing paste-ups would have come back. Would be, even now, there on her desk.

'Morning, Susan,' Sally said as she barrelled past.

Suzie ignored her and ran on to her room, crossing mental fingers so hard that her head ached.

But the paste-ups weren't there. She dragged open her top drawer. It was empty. And in final despair she sank slowly into her chair, energy draining from her like the current from a worthless battery.

Sally looked in, her brow creased with concern. 'Are you all right, Susan? Only you look a bit pale.'

Suzie didn't look up. She stared straight ahead, and said in a small, thin voice: 'We've lost the paste-ups.'

'The paste-ups?' Sally said brightly. 'No, they're fine.'

Suzie spun to stare at her incredulously. 'What?'

'They're in my cabinet.'

'*What?*'

'Yes, you left them out on your desk yesterday, when you went to the loo. So before I went home – you remember, I went off early only I wasn't feeling too well – I locked them in my cabinet.'

Suzie's immediate reaction was rage. 'Why the hell didn't you put them in my drawer, Sally?' she screamed.

Sally looked hurt. 'But I don't have a key to your drawer, Susan. And you always say that the paste-ups have to be kept under lock and key. Well, the only key I have is the one to my cabinet, so that's where I put them.'

Suzie could have both kissed her and slapped her. For she couldn't deny that what Sally was saying was true. It was the one golden rule: when left unattended, the paste-ups must be locked in a drawer. And the girl had simply followed instructions. *But what an imbecile not to have said.*

'But why the hell, then, didn't you at least leave a note?' Suzie shrieked at her. *Had she done so, then last night need never have happened.* 'Or told someone; at least let me know what you'd done?'

But her rage was already dissolving. Turning instead to a sensation of glorious relief.

After all, what was done was done; it couldn't be undone by raving at Sally. And it wasn't Sally who had left the paste-ups out in the first place. And what did it really matter anyway, in light of the relief – the utter relief – of knowing the paste-ups were safe?

Sally was looking contrite, and a little bewildered, too, as if she herself couldn't fathom why she had not left a note. Suzie softened her voice: 'I'm sorry, Sally, I shouldn't have shouted. You did what you thought best, I know, locking them away as you did. And the important thing is, we know where they are.'

Sally looked more comfortable, and smiled a forgiving smile. 'Oh, that's all right. I'm used to it: my mum and dad are always shouting at me for something or other. Shall I bring them to you?'

'What, your mum and dad?' Suzie teased, her heart suddenly so light she could have floated up to the ceiling.

Sally giggled. 'No, you know what I mean.'

'Of course I do. Sally. And yes, please, that would be wonderful.' *Wouldn't it just!*

Sally ducked away and returned a moment later with the large buff folder, which she laid on Suzie's desk.

Suzie fingered it for a moment, almost reverently, then opened the flap. And there they were, those wonderful paste-ups: all sixty-four pages of them. Pristine, and all but complete.

She was about to begin flicking through them when the telephone rang on her desk.

Sally answered it: 'Miss Carlton's office. Oh, er, yes. Yes, of course. One moment please, she's right here.' She covered the mouthpiece with her hand. 'It's Clive Taunton,' she whispered.

Suzie groaned inwardly. He could, she supposed, be ringing on magazine business. But she doubted it.

'Ah, fine, Sally,' she muttered, concealing her chagrin. 'Well, that'll be all for now. Would you pull my door to on your way out?'

While Sally left, Suzie quickly rehearsed what she had decided to say, then lifted the receiver to her ear.

'Clive, how are you?'

'Susan. Yes, I'm just ringing to say how very much I enjoyed the, ah, party last night. Quite, quite wonderful.'

'Yes, I enjoyed it too. Very lavish, as always.'

'Ah, but I mean, ah, you know . . .'

'Oh, you mean upstairs?' As if he could have meant anything other. 'Yes, it was fun wasn't it? Just what I wanted actually; a sort of final fling, as it were. You see, my boyfriend is moving in with me tonight, and I just fancied one last fling as a single girl before finally settling down. Go out with a bang, so to speak.'

'Ah, your boyfriend. Yes I see.' Taunton sounded deflated. 'So we won't be, ah, I mean . . .'

'Again? No, I'm afraid not, Clive. More's the pity, eh? But I do so believe in fidelity in a steady relationship, don't you?' she said sweetly. 'I always said I'd be totally faithful to anyone I lived with. I mean, only fair isn't it?'

'Oh yes, quite. I understand. As you say though, a pity, what?'

'Still, it'll live on in memory, won't it, Clive?'

'Quite so. Oh, well, I'll say cheerio then.'

'OK, Clive. Thanks for ringing.'

Suzie put down the receiver, and smiled to herself. Another problem solved, she thought, sighing warmly; both pleased and relieved that Clive Taunton had accepted her put-off with no animosity.

The world was an altogether happier place than it had been just a minute ago. Now, the paste-ups were safe; the magazine was safe; her job and career were safe. She had dealt with the problem of Clive Taunton becoming a potential sex-pest as she had feared that he might, and with no harm to her prospects apparently done. And just as she'd told him, her boyfriend was moving in with her later that day. Wasn't life just wonderful.

The one single blot to remain was Bob Adams. And, one day, she would find some way of paying him back for what he had done. For what he was. But that could wait; just at that moment she felt far too happy to be harbouring negative thoughts of revenge.

She pushed up from her chair and went to her door. Pulled it open and leaned through. 'Sally, would you bring me a coffee, please?'

And returning to her desk, she finished the editorial that yesterday had seemed such a task in under ten minutes flat; the paste-ups complete and ready to go.

At four-thirty that afternoon, with the precious buff folder safely in the hands of the printers, Suzie called it a day. The magazine put to bed, there was nothing more to be done for the month: she might just as well go home, and be there for when Michael arrived; help him in with his cases and things.

Outside, the autumn sun was shining brightly – as brightly as her life, it seemed – and as she drove she sang to herself, blissfully lost in her thoughts. She was thinking of the evening ahead. Of the night – for the first time the whole night – there would be with Michael. She suddenly thought about razors and aftershave in her bathroom, his toothbrush there in the morning, and a feeling of inner warmth spread through her.

And then she was thinking of future nights, of all the nights there would be. No more for her the frustration of those nights spent alone, of never knowing when next she'd see Michael. He would be there. And there would be sex; sex whenever she wanted. And not just sex, but that special kind of sex for which she had so recently discovered her need – sado-masochistic sex. No more the hang-ups that had once blemished her love-life; no more the Sisters of Mercy and no more the feelings of guilt. All would be things of the past as she revelled in the insouciance of sexual submission to Michael; sometimes donning the persona of Mistress Suzie, equally liberating, to occasionally dominate him. But always, that glorious feeling of sexual freedom. It was going to be wonderful.

Letting herself into her flat, she was still singing and tingling as she pottered about, tidying away the odd things old Mrs Fletcher had missed, making room in her bathroom cabinet for those wonderful man-things that would be there from now on, and thinking she had never felt happier.

But that was before she had discovered the note.

240

Chapter Twenty-One

S he stared at the letter in a cold, numb daze, horror sending myriad malignant spiders to crawl through her gut as she read it again and again, over and over.

She had discovered it propped up on the mantel next to the clock, left where it couldn't have been missed. And seeing Michael's key to her flat beside it, a sickening sense of foreboding had swept through her even before she had read the first word.

Michael's handwriting was strong and masculine – a perfect reflection of the man himself – and it almost spoke with his voice as she read through his letter for the hundredth time.

It said:

Dear Suzie,

You have broken my heart.

I may never have known the truth, but by an unhappy coincidence I was at the same house as yourself last night; the same party. Though for me, it would seem it was a very different *sort* of a party. You see, by an even unhappier coincidence I happened to look into a certain bedroom. A bedroom in which you were enjoying yourself – and very obviously so – in the arms of another man.

And that, my love, as much as I might wish to, is something I can neither forget nor forgive.

Do you recall, Suzie, that I never said the words I love you until the other night? I did, you know, so much that my heart ached. From the very first time we met, I think. And oh, how I longed to tell you. But I never did. You see, to me, those words mean something special. They mean: I want to share my life with you; with you and you alone. They offer one's body. But they also offer one's soul. And even though the women I was meeting through the agency meant nothing to me, I could not in all conscience have said those words to you while I was still seeing them. Only when I was to quit the agency and move in with you did I feel it proper and fair to offer you my soul.

I had assumed – perhaps that was wrong of me, but I did – that when you told me you loved me, the words meant the same to you as they do to me. I know now that they don't.

My love, I will never forget you. The memory of you will for ever burn in my heart. But I cannot live with you knowing that love to you means something different than it does to me. It would tear out my heart even to see you, knowing we had not exchanged souls as I'd thought. So, I'm going away, and you won't see me or hear from me again. I hope you will find happiness, my love, sincerely. I doubt that I will, ever, but better an empty void in my heart than a heart that is torn out and destroyed.

Please understand.

I love you, Michael.

Suzie's eyes flooded with tears and she could no longer see the words on the page. But it made no difference: they were engraved on the very fabric of her brain. *But I do love you, Michael*, her mind screamed as she heard

242

them over and over. *And in just the same way that you love me: you do have my soul, I promise.*

If only he had been there to hear.

Wait! The telephone.

Yes, he would hear her say it. Maybe he wouldn't believe her, but he would hear her say it.

She flung the letter from her and ran to the phone. Lifted the receiver and frantically dialled Michael's number. Waited with bated breath.

Three rings, then a click. His answering machine: 'Hello, this is Michael. I'm out of town right now. If I know you, I'll be in touch when I'm settled and have a new number. Thank you for calling.'

The sound of his voice sent a chill down her spine: *like hearing a voice from the dead.*

She broke the connection and immediately dialled a second familiar number; the only other she could think of that could possibly offer her hope.

The wait seemed interminable, but at last the telephone was answered.

Grace Cummings's cut-crystal voice said: 'The Benson Agency. How may we –'

'Grace, it's Suzie Carlton,' Suzie cut in.

'Ah, Miss Carlton. So long since we've heard from you. How –'

'Michael, Grace; have you heard from Michael?'

'Well, yes as it happens. He rang me earlier to, ah, perhaps I shouldn't mention this. But it was his last job, I suppose, so how can it matter? Anyway, to apologise for walking out on the date he had last night. Quite unforgivable, really, and –'

'Who was his date with?' Suzie cut in again.

'Oh, my dear, you know I can't tell you that. We offer our clients a totally confidential service, as well you know.'

'Yes, yes,' said Suzie impatiently. 'But can you at least tell me, was he escorting someone to a party?'

'Quite an up-market one, I understand. Formal dress, anyway.'

For a moment Suzie said nothing, staggered by the

243

cruelty with which fate had played its hand. *So that was how it had happened*. Of all the places in the world his final escorting job might have taken him, fate had led him to the very same party as she, where she was being unfaithful to him. For the first and only time; the only time she would ever have been. What a wicked player fate could be in the impossible game of life.

At last, she recovered sufficiently to ask: 'Do you know where he is, Grace? How I can get hold of him?'

'I'm sorry, Miss Carlton, but I don't, I'm afraid. In fact he mentioned he was going away.'

'Did he say where he was going? Leave an address? Anything at all?'

'I'm afraid not, dear. As I said, he was leaving us anyway. There was really no reason.'

'I see,' said Suzie, her voice a barely audible whisper, muted by the depths of defeat.

She let the receiver drop from her hand without thinking to say goodbye. And sank to her knees on the floor, despair finally robbing her of even the numbness of shock to help dull her pain. And she began to cry in great heaving sobs, her body shaking with grief.

Knowing Michael was gone for ever.

Chapter Twenty-Two

The lift in the squalid council block stank faintly of urine. There was damp litter on the floor, and there was barely an inch of the drab brown paint on the walls that didn't have filthy graffiti scratched into it, down to bare metal: everything from the telephone numbers of prostitutes who worked in the building, to lavatory-humour jokes and obscene schoolboy protrayals of unlikely genitalia. Suzie tried not to look at it all while the lift shuddered up through the floors.

She chewed on her lower lip to stop herself crying and waited, staring at the column of numbers that one by one lit up (those that were working anyway) then blinked out as the lift progressed.

It at last groaned to a halt on the fifteenth floor and the doors grated open with a metallic squeal. Suzie stepped out onto an austere concrete landing which at least was free of litter, and sucked in a breath of more breathable air. Two glass-fronted doors stood before her, and she rang the bell on the one on the right: number 153.

Presently the door opened. That the occupant was wearing a dressing gown didn't especially surprise her, even though it was well past noon. Hilary's eyes were wide with surprise.

'Suzie!' she cried. 'What are you doing here? I mean, how come you're not at work?'

'I rang in sick,' Suzie told her. 'I . . . couldn't face going in. Not today.'

Hilary frowned, and said: 'You've been crying, haven't you?'

She managed a thin smile. 'Only all night.'

'But what on earth's the matter, love? Here, come on in.'

Hilary slid an arm around Suzie's shoulder and gently led her inside, where, in contrast to the external squalor, her flat was tidy and clean. With its simple but functional furniture and cheap but adequate carpet, it was a far cry from the luxury of Suzie's sumptuous flat, but it still managed to be reasonably cosy.

Suzie sat down on a sofa, and handed Hilary Michael's letter to read. It was now badly smeared with her tears, some of the words obliterated entirely, but most of it was still just legible.

Hilary read it through in silence, then handed the letter back.

'Oh dear,' she said, cocking an eyebrow at Suzie. 'So you got caught playing around, eh? Caught in the very act no less, and now – surprise, surprise – he's walked out on you.'

'But I wasn't playing around, Hils,' Suzie protested, tears stinging her eyes. 'Not really. I mean, it wasn't like that: I was blackmailed into it.'

And she proceeded to tell Hilary the whole sorry tale. All but that she had actually enjoyed it. Too ashamed about that to admit it even to Hilary, who would have been the last to have condemned her for an act of infidelity.

'And I swear to God, Hils, that's exactly what happened,' she finished. 'And now he's gone and I don't know what to do. I so desperately want him back, I'd do anything. But I don't even know where he is. Oh God, Hils, what do I do?'

Hilary looked at her with sympathy in her eyes, but shook her head and said gently: 'Love, for once even my advice will do you no good. You said it yourself; you don't even know where he is. So what can I advise?

'No, the next move, if there is one, has to be his. You can do nothing more than to hope that he makes one. Though frankly, love, I wouldn't put your life on hold while you wait; that letter sounds pretty final to me. It sounds like you've cut him up pretty badly.'

'Oh God,' Suzie wailed, 'I know I have. And if I could only undo . . .' She stopped. Behind Hilary was a door which she knew led out to a landing. It was standing slightly ajar, and her eye had been caught by the glimpse of a figure crossing the gap. 'Oh! I didn't realise you had company, Hils.'

'What? Oh, yes. Crikey, I'd almost forgotten. Cherry.'

'Oh, I'm – Ah, so that's why the dressing gown.' She laughed sheepishly. 'I thought you were just slouching.'

Hilary made a pout of feigned hurt. 'As if,' she grinned.

'Oh, well look, I'm sorry; I didn't mean to interrupt, er, things. I'd best be getting –'

'Nonsense,' Hilary cut in. 'You haven't met Cherry, have you? Well, now's your chance. You'll love her; she's a dote.'

Ignoring Suzie's protests that she wasn't in much mood for socialising, she turned to the opened doorway and shouted. 'Cherry, love, come on in here; there's someone I'd like you to meet.'

There was the sound of a toilet flushing, and then the girl appeared.

She was wearing only a shirt, with just a single button fastened in front. And which wasn't quite long enough to conceal the fact that her blonde was natural. The lower corner of her flaxen triangle was clearly visible, but if she was the least bit self-conscious of it in front of Suzie she didn't show it.

She smiled sweetly. 'Hello.'

Hilary introduced them, and Cherry perched herself on the arm of Hilary's chair.

Suzie could see at once what Hilary saw in the girl; she was lovely. Young – about seventeen she'd have guessed; eighteen at most – and very attractive. Not an inch above five-foot-two, she still managed to look lithe and slender, her shapely legs long. Her breasts were not large, but the twin points that poked enticingly at the front of her shirt, darkening the material there, showed she had highly suckable nipples. Her golden hair was cut in a page-boy, the perfect frame for her fresh, pretty face, with its button of a nose and brown come-to-bed eyes.

'I've heard a lot about you, Cherry,' she said.

'She's heard a lot about your cherry, Cherry, is what she means,' Hilary amended with a dirty laugh.

Cherry tutted at her in mock disgust, then turned to face Suzie. 'I've heard a lot about you, too, Suzie. Hilary's always talking about you.'

'Oh?'

'Yes. She calls you the lady boss.'

'Yes, I know,' Suzie laughed.

'Oooh!' Cherry touched the tip of her tongue to her lips; a sexy gesture. 'And don't I just adore bossy ladies!'

Hilary slapped her rump.

'Ouch! That hurt.'

'Well don't you be cheeky, then, or you'll be getting another.'

Cherry grinned mischievously. 'Promises, promises.'

'And it didn't hurt, at all.'

'Well it surprised me,' Cherry said with a pout.

'So that's another one for fibbing, you imp. And one that will hurt. But I'll save that one for later.'

'Oooh, please,' said Cherry, wriggling her buttocks on the arm of the chair. She turned to Suzie and winked. 'She's a real tyrant, you know? Always bullying me, she is.'

'The minx needs keeping in hand,' Hilary said.

Suzie laughed. 'I can believe it.'

'Hey, who's side are you on?' Cherry complained.

That earned her another smack on the rump; another mock warning for cheek.

The slap caused Cherry to shift position, to put a foot to the floor to steady herself. Her thighs came apart as she did so and Suzie caught a fleeting glimpse of her sex, the outer lips nestled in their bed of golden fur. She felt she ought to avert her eyes, but couldn't; secretly hoping for another glimpse. And despite all, she felt the beginnings of heat stir between her legs; hoped her blush and her stare weren't obvious.

'If you don't watch out, young lady,' said Hilary, 'your bottom's going to be the colour of a ripe tomato by the time I'm finished with it.'

'You and your promises,' giggled Cherry.

The banter went on for a while, Suzie gradually relaxing. Slowly coming up from the depths of her misery. As well as the overtly sexual atmosphere, itself a welcome distraction – Cherry's pussy continued to wink at her at every opportunity, it seemed – the two were great company, and her laughter with them was giving her a much-needed lift. They were the perfect therapy, and as their banter went on she was soon feeling very much better; both surprised and relieved that she seemed to have escaped so readily if, as she knew, temporarily from the painful clutch of Michael's letter.

And then Cherry suggested she open a bottle of wine, which was chilling in Hilary's fridge. That received a welcome response, and Suzie was by then sufficiently up to enjoy watching the girl's buttocks jiggle deliciously below the cut of her shirt as she hurried off to the kitchen.

She turned to Hilary. 'A dote,' she agreed.

'Oh, the best. And in bed, wow. What a whore!'

They were quiet for a moment, and then Hilary said: 'You know, love, that could be just what you need: a good sexy romp to take your mind off things, off Michael for a while. A bit of female love-making with Cherry and me to take your mind off men altogether.'

Suzie was doubtful. 'Oh, I don't know, Hils. I . . . I don't think I could get into –'

'Rubbish, Suzie, of course you would. In a heartbeat,

if I know you. And it's just what you need; the perfect
. . . what's the word?'

'Therapy?' Suzie suggested.

'Yes, that. Listen, you asked my advice and now I'm
giving it to you – the best advice I ever have. If Michael
reappears in your life, then he does. And knowing how
you feel for him I really hope that he will. But meantime,
like I said, you mustn't put your life on hold while you
wait. You still have needs, love, Michael or no Michael.
And a three-in-a-bed with Cherry and me would do you
the world of good.'

Just as she said it Cherry re-emerged from the kitchen,
carrying an opened bottle of wine and three glasses.

'Oooh, are we going to play sexual sandwiches?' she
enthused as she set down the glasses and poured wine.
'Baggsie I be the filling first.'

She handed the glasses round, and found her seat
again on the arm of Hilary's chair.

Suzie sipped at her wine. 'No, I, er . . .'

'*Yes,*' Hilary interjected, firmly, 'that's just what we're
going to do. Or something like it, anyway. Though I
don't know why you're looking so cheerful about it,
young lady; I don't remember saying anything had
changed.'

Suzie thought she saw Cherry flinch at that, and a
look of what might have been sharp disappointment,
even mild horror, appeared in the girl's eyes. She turned
to Hilary, puzzled, wondering what her comment had
meant to have caused the reaction it had: what hadn't
changed?

Hilary chuckled. 'You see, Cherry and me have been
playing this little game,' she explained. 'Haven't we,
Cherry? It's called "No orgasms for the naughty slave".
She's being punished, you see, for a little infidelity of
her own: I caught her smiling at this girl at the gym. At
least' – she covered her mouth with her hand as if to
keep Cherry from hearing – 'that's my excuse.

'So, she hasn't been allowed to come since yesterday
morning. I've kept her stimulated, of course, pretty well

250

constantly, and she's been very close. But' – she patted Cherry's thigh as if in genuine sympathy – 'you poor thing, there've been no orgasms have there?'

'Not for me, no,' Cherry muttered pointedly.

'Well, what?' said Hilary with an air of innocence. 'You don't expect me to deny myself, do you? It's not me who's being punished, is it? And a slavegirl's first and foremost duty is to see to her mistress's needs; to see she's kept properly satisfied.'

My God, thought Suzie, feeling for the girl. Kept aroused, deliberately stimulated for all that time, and not permitted to come. While at the same time having to satisfy Hilary (who, knowing her, would no doubt have enjoyed many a climax too, just to add to the poor girl's suffering; to heighten her sense of her own deprivation). She must by now be cruelly aching, climbing the walls with frustration. And Suzie's own loins tingled, as if aching in sympathy.

'And I'll bet,' Hilary was saying, still chuckling at the dismay on Cherry's face, 'that right now the thought of a threesome – all the excitement of that, the stimulation of three naked bodies writhing together, when you're still not allowed to come – is just about driving you crazy, isn't it?'

Cherry only groaned in reply, and shifted her hips as if uncomfortably aware of her longing.

'Well,' said Hilary, 'I had said you weren't going to come until tomorrow night, hadn't I? But if Suzie's going to join in with us, well, I'm not that cruel: I might just relent and let you off early.'

At that, Cherry's eyes flashed imploringly to Suzie's, as if begging her to agree.

And Hilary said, 'Come on, Suzie, you wouldn't want to disappoint my little minx here, now would you? Keep her waiting until tomorrow night before she gets to come. And besides . . .' She reached out a hand to the blonde girl's pubis; stroked the flaxen hair for a moment. Then she pushed open her thighs, and her finger went between them.

'Oooh,' said Cherry, which seemed to be her favouite utterance.

'You can't deny, Suzie, that you'd like a bit of this.'

Suzie's eyes were riveted on Cherry's glistening sex as Hilary's finger slid along it. The lips were swollen with need, she could now see, and were purplish in colour; evidence of her prolonged arousal. And she herself began to feel hot as the girl was aroused even further. It was tempting.

'Or ...' Hilary went on, stopping and turning to Cherry. 'Put your tongue out, Cherry.' The girl dutifully obeyed, pointing her pink tongue between her parted lips and wiggling it suggestively. 'A bit of that,' said Hilary.

Suzie swigged at her wine, in a daze of indecision.

Hilary was still looking at Cherry. 'Hold yourself open for Suzie,' she commanded, abruptly.

There was a moment's hesitation, during which Suzie could almost feel Cherry's sudden tension, saw the blush that reddened her neck. But then the girl reached slowly down between her widely spread thighs and parted the outer lips of her sex; held them open with trembling fingers to reveal the pink inner core that was slick with her juices.

Something wrenched in Suzie's belly, sensing the girl's humilation at what she was having to do. Cherry might have a certain brazenness, she thought, remembering the casualness with which she had first come into the room, unperturbed by how little her shirt concealed; that her bush was partly on show. But her brazenness had its limits it seemed, and now as she sat there having to display herself in so indecent a fashion, it was clearly getting to her; her blush went all the way down to the swelling mounds of her breasts, which were rising and falling in time with her quickened breathing.

But Suzie didn't look away. She knew she was adding to it by openly staring into the gaping slit, and only thrilled in the reflection of the poor girl's shame.

'An invitingly proffered pussy and a willing tongue,' said Hilary. 'Yes or no?'

252

Suzie's eyes flicked from Cherry's obscenely exposed sex up to her tongue and back again; thrilled once more in empathy, knowing the worms of perverse excitement that even now would be snaking through the teenager's belly at having to remain as she was, at being so coolly offered for the sexual use of a stranger.

It was enough, the final straw, and she grinned salaciously, 'Well, why the hell not.'

'Oooh,' said Cherry, clearly relieved. 'Two lady bosses.'

Hilary shook her head, 'No, Suzie might be a boss at work. In bed she's just as submissive as you are.'

'Not always,' Suzie protested quickly. 'Sometimes I like to dominate.'

Hilary looked at her, her eyes questioning. 'And today?'

Suzie looked back to Cherry. The girl looked so deliciously submissive and yielding, sitting as she was. It would be very nice, she mused, to have that sweet young body at her command; that glistening pussy to tease or to punish at will; that tongue to direct where she would. But then her eyes found Cherry's eyes; read in them the rapture of the shame she was suffering, that special excitement she knew only too well, and she grinned a sheepish grin.

'Submissive,' she said quietly, lowering her eyes from the knowing smile that spread on Hilary's face.

The afternoon seemed to fly by, time lost in a molten lava of hot, naked flesh as the three women pleasured each other via a host of sexual games: naughty schoolgirl having to be spanked (Cherry); blue movie star (Suzie) being directed for the cameras; harem-mistress (Hilary, of course) putting the new wives through their paces, teaching innocent virgins the carnal pleasures and how to give those pleasures to others; other games, each flowing smoothly into the next as though it were a carefully orchestrated sexual symphony.

It was nothing short of fantastic. Cherry was everything

Hilary had claimed her to be, and more. And Hilary, in full-blown dominant mood, was more exciting than ever. And Suzie lost herself in an erotic dream-world, where emotional pain was a thing unknown and problems something other people had.

But later, back home in her flat, when the effects of the wine and the heady sex had begun to wear off, misery returned like a long-forgotten foe come to do battle anew.

Michael was gone.

And she sobbed once more.

Chapter Twenty-Three

*T*hat month took a year to pass. Or so it felt to Suzie. She had taken the first three days of it off – the three days folowing Michael's leaving – claiming a dose of the flu. Being the start of the new month, it hadn't much mattered. Not that her attendance for the rest of the month had mattered much either; she had spent most of it in an apathetic daze, feeling miserable and pining for Michael, and the magazine had been left largely to produce itself. Fortunately there had been, for once, some usable stuff in the slush-pile. And Keith Blundell had come up with an interesting angle on the indiscretions of the Catholic clergy, which had taken an entire page, and which had gelled nicely with that month's headline-making scandal. He had coined, as part of his piece, the name of a new Irish cocktail: the Bishop Casey – a large paddy with a Murphy on the side. And in the event, the issue had come together. Though it wasn't a great one, she knew.

She had coped with Bob Adams – whose evil had led to her heartbreak – by mostly ignoring him; forced to accept his presence professionally, but in personal terms no longer afraid to openly spurn him, less wary, now, of his influence with the Tauntons. Having bedded Clive – ironically, at Adams's instigation – she was confident of having some sway there herself, now; the balance of power somewhat evened. Though, in truth, she was less concerned about anything since Michael had gone: in the shadow of that, nothing much else seemed to have any meaning.

It was a month that had taken some struggling through. But she had survived. And had, at least, made the deadline.

'The courier's here, Susan. Are the paste-ups ready for them?'

Suzie looked up from her desk. 'As ready as they'll ever be, Sally,' she said wearily.

She fingered the large buff folder for a moment, feeling slightly guilty over its contents and almost reluctant to let it go to the printers; this public proof of her apathy, of her rare unprofessionalism. Though perhaps her concern was in itself a good sign, she mused: things were beginning to matter again.

She shrugged, and handed the folder to Sally.

'I'll tell you what, Sally,' she said with a sigh, 'give that to the courier, then I'll take you out for a drink. The month's all done and I could certainly use one.'

'Er, yes. All right,' said Sally, looking oddly nervous.

Suzie chose the wine bar on Fitton Street, and as the two walked in, even at four-thirty on a wet and wintry Tuesday afternoon the place was milling with people. She bought the drinks, a stiff Martini for herself and a spritzer for Sally, and they sat down at one of the few vacant tables.

Suzie sipped her Martini and looked around.

A cleric sat at a nearby table, his dog-collar gleaming as he nursed a coffee (*probably laced*, thought Suzie irreverently, Blundell's article still on her mind), in deep conversation with a mumsy, middle-aged woman who probably did the flowers for his church. She looked the type. And a group of yuppies stood at the bar, their portable phones spoiling the cut of their Herbie Frogg suits while they guffawed and snorted between mouthfuls of lager. A young couple held hands, staring doe-eyed at each other and sharing a shandy. And a large table of giggling girls celebrated one of their birthdays. A typical wine bar scene.

She turned her eyes to Sally, who was sipping her drink reflectively, evidently troubled. And Suzie was reminded of her odd nervousness earlier, when she'd asked her out for a drink; an agitation that, it now occurred to her, had been present in the girl for the past two or three weeks. Though she had been too engrossed in her own misery to have recognised it.

What was it? Was Sally planning to leave; to resign? Suzie hoped not: the girl could be dizzy at times, true, but she was willing and hard-working – at least, when her problematical periods were not playing her up – and she would be genuinely sorry to lose her.

'Come on, Sally, spit it out,' she said at last.

'Sorry?' said Sally.

'Whatever it is on your mind. Time to say it.'

'Oh.' The girl took a swig of her drink, apparently to give herself courage. Took a deep breath, and finally said: 'I'm . . . I'm a bit worried, Susan, to tell you the truth.'

'Oh? About what?'

'Well, is . . . is everything all right?'

Suzie cocked her head to one side. 'All right? All right in what way?'

'I mean, with the magazine and all.'

'Of course. Why wouldn't it be?'

Sally took another swig of her drink. 'Well, I, er, I don't really like saying, Susan. But it's just that all month you've seemed sort of different. As if you're worried, like. Like the magazine's in trouble or something, you know? Or I am?'

Suzie chuckled, suddenly glad that the problem was no more serious than that. 'Not at all,' she said. 'I'm happy enough with your work, Sally. Though you could try being a bit less scatter-brained, you know?'

Sally blushed, and grinned sheepishly. 'Yes, I know I'm a bit of a featherhead at times. I will try, I promise. And the magazine –'

'Is also fine. In great shape, in fact. Oh, I'll admit the present issue isn't the most brilliant we've ever done. But it's certainly OK – it'll do us no harm, let's put it that way. No, the only thing that could possibly harm *Woman Now* is if ever we missed the deadline. And we never do, do we?'

'No, but you've been so –'

'I know, I know,' Suzie cut in. 'I've been a bit out of it, haven't I? Almost as dizzy as you.' She winked kindly. 'But no, I've had a few personal problems, that's all. Nothing to do with the magazine. And I'm getting over them now. Really, everything's fine.'

Sally seemed to relax visibly, as if an enormous weight had come off her shoulders. 'Oh, thank goodness,' she said. 'I thought I was up for the high-jump, one way or the other. And my Dad'd kill me if I lost my job, whatever the reason. Besides, I love working for *Woman Now*.' She swigged her drink and added shyly: 'And, Susan, working for you.'

Suzie reached across the table and patted her hand tenderly. It was a friendly touch, but no more than that; certainly not a caress. It was funny, she reflected, how she never thought about Sally in any sexual sense. The girl was the same age as Cherry, and no less attractive, yet she couldn't think of her in sexual terms. Not like she thought about Cherry. Since that first afternoon at Hilary's flat, the three had had several such sessions. And Cherry, depraved little minx that she was, was as exciting in bed as Hilary was. By comparison, despite her voluptuous chest, Sally seemed so very young and innocent. Not like Cherry at all.

'Well, that's nice of you to say, Sally,' she said, withdrawing her hand, her thoughts making her suddenly self-conscious. 'And I'm sure we'll be working together for a long time to come.'

Sally looked pleased and Suzie sat back, wondering if

what she had said were really true; was she getting over her problems?

True, the pain of losing Michael was beginning to diminish – a little. The first week or so it had been almost unbearable. She had lived on the hope that he would come back to her. And that had been the really painful part: every time the phone would ring, her heart would stop: *was it him?* It never was. She had run downstairs every morning at the sound of the postman: *had he written?* Morning after morning she would cry when he hadn't.

But, gradually, hope had faded, and had finally gone. And, when it had, completely, she had begun slowly to get over it. After all, life did have to go on. As Hilary had said, there was no sense in her putting herself on hold while she waited – waited for something that almost certainly would never happen – and slowly she had come to accept it: Michael was gone and life went on.

But that still left her with other problems, like needing a man now and then.

And that thought spun her off into an entirely different world.

Suddenly the wine bar was a speakeasy in thirties America, the days of the prohibition. A honkytonk played in the corner, and the waiters wore shiny paisley waistcoats as they buzzed from table to table hustling illegal booze: yeasty beer, or vicious potato spirit that took the skin off your throat if it didn't make you go blind.

Just then there is a knock at the door, and a bouncer with wide lapels and Gatsby trousers slides back a panel. Recognises *Who? Al Capone? No, he was ugly. Bugsy Segal, then? No, wait, Frank Nitty. Yes, the one they called The Enforcer: the strong, masterful type. He was perfect.* Recognises Frank Nitty and welcomes him into the club. The big man enters surrounded by hoods and bimbos, and the entourage makes for the bar.

'I ain't seen that blonde with you lately, Frank,' says the barman, polishing a glass.

'She died,' says Nitty. 'Gonorrhoea.'

God, not that old joke? Yes, why not?

'But you don't die of gonorrhoea, Frank,' says the barman.

'You do if you give it me.' *Jesus, that's corny. And he'd better add:* 'But I'm clean now.'

Nitty turns from the bar, his eyes scanning the room. By and by they settle on Suzie's table and she gives him an encouraging smile. He has a strong, ruggedly handsome face, with a deep cleft in his square chin. *At least, he did in the TV series.* His pin-striped suit is cut to accentuate the width of his shoulders, trimming down to a narrow waist, and he looks huge and powerful as he saunters over. She catches her breath as he draws near.

But he doesn't stop. He passes her by, and instead goes to stand beside Sally.

Sally's eyes widen in terror as the big man towers above her, exuding menace. He reaches down and, wordlessly – this is a man who does as he pleases, who expects to be offered no challenge – he pops open the buttons of Sally's blouse. Her large breasts spill free with a jiggle, and Nitty takes one in an enormous hand, squeezing its nipple between finger and thumb.

'No, not her,' Suzie cries. 'She's so young and innocent. Take me instead.' She would gladly have added, 'Please'.

For this wasn't fair. She had conjured Nitty for herself, not for Sally. Nevertheless, the fantasy went on.

Nitty freezes her with an ice-cold look, and she is forced to watch in silence.

And a *frisson* of dark excitement tugs at the pit of her stomach at the sight of what Nitty is doing; lifting Sally's heavy breast by its nipple, now, making her writhe in a subtle blend of pleasure and pain. But just then there is a scream from somewhere across the room, a scream of real pain, and she looks for its source.

One of Nitty's hoods has dragged a blonde woman up to her feet. He is holding her wrist in an iron grip and is brandishing what looks like a flick-knife. The woman cringes before him as he draws the flat of its flashing blade lightly across her cheek, his thin lips twisting in a sadistic grin at her terror. Then, deftly, he slips the blade under the single strap of her dress, and in a quick upward jerk he slices the material through. The top of the dress begins to fall away, and the woman clutches it to her; her free hand desperately gripping it to her chest in a frantic attempt to protect her modesty.

But the gangster has other ideas; he pushes her hand away and rips the dress to her waist, to leave her buxom breasts naked and heaving. He stands back to regard them with a lascivious eye, and Suzie can only think: *Why her? Why not me?* as he steps forward again and pushes her down to her knees. Already tugging at the belt of his trousers.

She looks back to Sally. Nitty is naked now; is standing before Sally and is pushing his penis into her mouth. His erection is huge, and her jaws are forced wide to accommodate it. But there is no longer fear in Sally's eyes. What is it? Ecstasy? Maybe she is not so innocent after all.

Nitty begins moving his hips back and forth, his long penis revelling in the warm haven of Sally's mouth and seeming to thicken further as she expertly sucks him.

Suzie's loins ache in response, and she forces her eyes away to save herself the torment of further arousal. But there is nowhere to look: the entire room, now, is the scene of a wild orgy.

The group of yuppies who had stood at the bar were still there. But now are naked. And they are masturbating themselves as they chat, their erect penises extensions of their egos just as their mobile phones had been before. The hand-holding couple have gone well beyond holding hands: the girl is lying full length on a craps table, her skirt rucked up to her waist, and the lad is lying atop her pumping for all he is worth. And the cleric's dog-collar is clamped between the flower lady's naked thighs, his tongue snaking into her and making her squirm with previously unknown delight.

261

Nitty's bimbos have joined the party of giggling secretaries, now a writhing tumult of salacious, naked or near-naked flesh. And the gangster with the flick-knife is groaning in the throes of climax, his buttocks clenching and unclenching in spasm as he pumps his seed into the kneeling woman's throat; his tight grip on her hair holding her still to force her to swallow.

Everyone is engaged in sexual activity. Everyone, that is, but her.

But this wasn't fair: this was her fantasy, for God's sake! What the hell sort of a fantasy was it, to allow everyone else to have all the fun, but not her? But it seemed to have a life of its own, to exist beyond her conscious control. And still it went on ...

Sally too, now, is naked. She is still sucking on Nitty's organ, and Nitty is squeezing her swelling breast in return of the favour, filling her eyes with rapture. The gangster's heavy balls are tight in their sac, attesting to his arousal, but as Suzie watches they suddenly contract even tighter. His buttocks clench for control and he quickly pushes himself back, pulling his straining member free of Sally's mouth. It bucks and twitches erratically, and a dribble of clear fluid runs from the eye at its tip: he has clearly withdrawn not a moment too soon.

Bringing himself back from the brink, his cock beginning to calm, Nitty's hand leaves Sally's breast and travels lower; down over her ribs, her belly, until it reaches the chestnut bush at her crutch. Sally spreads her thighs for him, and his fingers part their way through the tangle of damp hair they find there.

'Oooh!' says Sally.

No, that would have been Cherry: even if she couldn't control the fantasy, Suzie told herself angrily, she could at least keep the characters true to themselves.

'Aaah,' says Sally. *Yes, more like it* as Nitty's fingers delve into the liquid heat of her sex. And she bears herself down against them the better to savour their probing, wanting them deeper.

There is a sudden howl of pain from the lad on the dice table, now bucking frantically between his girl-friend's thighs and squealing in agony. For one of Nitty's hoods has reached between his legs and taken a grip on his testicles; a grip so tight around their base as to prevent the poor lad's coming while at the same time spurring him to greater efforts to try. The gangster is laughing and taunting him, urging him on further with a tirade of mocking obscenities, and the lad is close to tears.

But his tortured testicles are not his only concern: a second gangster is straddling his girlfriend's chest, his cock at her mouth. Forcing the lad to watch, helpless, while his lover is orally violated; to suffer the humili-ation of it as her mouth is fucked by another man just inches in front of his eyes – that man's buttocks practi-cally shoved in his face to add vile insult to the injury of all else.

And, watching, the sheer cruelty of it sends a perverse and shameful thrill to throb between Suzie's legs; a des-perate need that longs to be satisfied.

And that has to be satisfied now.

As if in response to her thought, one of the women disentangles herself from the Sapphic Gordian knot in which she has writhed, and comes to her. She kneels before Suzie and puts her hands up her skirt in search of her panties. And then her panties are off and her skirt is up round her waist; her legs are spread wide and the girl is leaning in parting her lips, her tongue extending.

But this is not what she wants. Not what she really wants.

Nitty is now sitting in Sally's seat and Sally is sitting on Nitty; riding him with long, even strokes that have made his iron penis slick with her juices.

Suzie watches in envy. *That's what she wants. What she needs. A man.*

She tried to conjure it, but couldn't: the image just wouldn't come. The gangster remained with Sally. *But this is my fantasy, for God's sake,* thought Suzie in utter frustration: *why can't I have what I want in it?*

The girl's tongue is serving her well enough but it's not what she wants. She pushes the girl's face from her lap, irritated, looks longingly at Nitty's penis, burying deep into Sally, filling her with his maleness; reappearing on its outward stroke, glistening and hard and exciting. And she aches for it.

She looks around her at all the other men in the room: the waiters, the gangsters, the men at the bar with their erect penises swaying before them. So many men. So many cocks. But none available to her.

Not even in fantasy.

And then she sees him. He is wearing a pin-striped suit – one of Nitty's hoods now – but it is unmistakably him. That handsome face. That long blonde hair. Her Viking.

Her heart surges. If Nitty won't have her, if no other man in the world will have her, she can always count on her Viking.

Excitedly she beckons him over, spreading her legs for him in eager anticipation of his glorious cock. But though he sees her – yes, he definitely sees her – he ignores her completely; turning his back on her as he makes for the bar.

She groans, loud and long: Oh God, *et tu, Brute*.

It was the final straw, deserted by even her Viking; by her capacity to make her fantasies do as she wished. And, suddenly furious, she made it all go away; forced the wine bar to come back feeling tense and frustrated.

She lit up a More and blew out smoke in an irate huff.

'You looked as if you were miles away then,' said Sally. 'But I didn't like to interrupt in case you were thinking about those problems you mentioned?'

'No, I, er . . . no, I wasn't. I, er, was thinking about something else.' The image of her secretary, naked, impaled on rampant maleness, momentarily flashed back to her, and she felt suddenly empty. 'Though in a way, perhaps I was,' she muttered, reflecting that the most pressing problem right then in her life was the desperate need of a man: what Sally had had and she had not.

Sally nudged her arm and winked, nodding towards the bar. 'Me, I was thinking about *him*.'

Suzie's eyes followed Sally's to where a man had come in, evidently while she'd been off in her dream. It wasn't Frank Nitty, but he was a hunk all the same.

'Yes, he is a bit of a dish, isn't he?' she agreed.

The man was clearly out on the prowl – everything about him confirmed it – and as his scanning eyes came to Suzie she gave him an encouraging smile. But he ignored her no less completely than her Viking had done, as if she were not even there, and his eyes moved on – to Sally. He sipped his drink and winked at her over the rim of his glass.

'I think he fancies me,' Sally whispered excitedly.

Suzie smiled wanly. 'I think you're right, love,' she said. 'Him and Frank Nitty both.'

'Pardon me?'

'Nothing, Sally. Just thinking aloud, that's all. Listen, I have to pop back to the office: there's something I have to do.' Her change was on the table and she pushed it towards Sally as she got to her feet. 'You stay and have another on me.' She tapped her nose conspiratorially. 'And good luck with the hunk.'

Back in her office, Suzie sat at her desk and stared at the phone, thinking.

An idea had been brewing at the back of her mind for a day or two now. It was a risky idea, she knew. But the result, if it came off, easily warranted such a risk. And feeling frustrated and angry as a result of her fantasy, she was in just the right mood to chance it. It was now or never.

Her mind made up, she took a deep breath and reached for the phone.

'Clive Taunton, please,' she said, when it was finally answered.

'Speaking.'

'Ah, Clive. Susan Carlton here.'

'Susan, hello. Er ...' Suzie could almost see him

265

glance at his watch. 'We haven't a problem with the deadline, have we?'

'Not at all, Clive, no. The paste-ups went off with the courier dead on time as usual. No, that's not why I'm ringing. I, er, do you remember the night of the party?'

'How could I ever forget, Susan? What, oh yes.'

'Well, you know how much I enjoyed it that night. With you especially. And I was just wondering if you and I might, ah, you know, from time to time.'

'Are you serious, Susan? Nothing would give me greater pleasure. But, ah, what about your boyfriend? I mean, I thought –'

'It . . . it didn't work out.'

'Oh, I'm sorry.' He sounded almost sincere.

'But there is another problem, Clive.'

'Oh?'

This was the crunch: how would Taunton react to what she was about say?

'Yes, it's Bob Adams.'

'Bob?' He sounded surprised. 'But how's he a problem?'

'Well, you know he and I were, er, seeing each other.' *God, how lies, once told, had to be perpetuated.* 'Well, we're not any more. And ever since we stopped he's become a real pest. He won't seem to understand that I'm no longer interested, you know?'

'Yes, he can be a bit persistent, old Bob, can't he? He was always the same, about everything.'

Good. This couldn't have been going more sweetly. So far.

'Well, as I said, Clive, I'd love for you and I to . . . I mean, I'm not looking for a relationship, you understand. But just now and again.'

'Yes, yes, I understand. Go on.'

'But I just couldn't, you see, not while Bob's around. He'd be sure to find out. And if he knew I was seeing you, he'd be so jealous and vindictive. Well, Clive, you know yourself what he's like; he'd be impossible to work with.'

'Mmm. Yes, I see.' There was silence for a while, during which Suzie could almost hear the cogs turning in Taunton's brain as he considered the problem.

She held her breath, waiting and listening to dead static.

At last he went on: 'W-e-e-ell, he has been with *Woman Now* for an awfully long time. And people do get stale in jobs: company policy to move staff around from time to time . . .'

Brand new company policy, thought Suzie with a silent chuckle. This was going to work.

'I suppose it is time we found Bob a different position. A new challenge for him, what. Oh, yes, quite; a new challenge.'

Suzie crossed her fingers: *it was time for the big one.*

'Clive,' she said slowly, 'could this new challenge for him carry a lower salary, by any chance?'

There was a moment's pause, then Clive chuckled. 'Am I hearing the wrath of a woman scorned, here?'

'He's the reason it didn't work out with my boy-friend,' Suzie told him truthfully. 'Why Michael left.'

'Ah,' said Clive knowingly. 'I see.' There was a second short pause, then he said hesitantly: 'Susan, erm, how frequently were you thinking of, ah, you and me . . .?'

'Seeing each other? Oh, I don't know: I thought it would be nice if we could get together perhaps once a month, something like that?'

Clive suddenly chuckled again. 'Would a much lower salary for Bob be in order?'

Suzie could hardly believe it. 'Yes, Clive, it would,' she said, punching the air in triumph.

'Then, leave it to me.'

Suzie's heart soared. *She had done it*. Not only would she be rid of bastard Bob Adams for good, but she had her revenge on him too. Sweet, sweet revenge. Not quite total ruination, perhaps, as the heroine of a Fay Weldon novel might have exacted, but it was good enough. And a monthly romp with Clive Taunton was a small price to pay. Who knew, it might even be fun.

They said their goodbyes and she broke the connection.

But kept the phone to her ear. That was business taken care of, now it was time for pleasure.

She dialled a second number, feeling her sexual juices already beginning to flow as she waited for the phone to be answered.

'Grace,' she said, at the sound of the familiar voice. 'Suzie Carlton.'

'Oh, hello, Miss Carlton. And how are you?'

'I'm fine, thanks. Couldn't be better. You?'

'Brisk, as usual. Now, what can I do for you?'

Suzie smiled. 'Meat on the hoof for Friday, eh?'

'Certainly, Miss Carlton. The next on the list?'

'Why not?'

There was a guttural chuckle.

'Got a cock like a rock, love.'

BLACK
lace

NO LADY
Saskia Hope
30-year-old Kate dumps her boyfriend, walks out of her job and sets off in search of sexual adventure. Set against the rugged terrain of the Pyrenees, the love-making is as rough as the landscape.

ISBN 0 352 32857 6

WEB OF DESIRE
Sophie Danson
High-flying executive Marcie is gradually drawn away from the normality of her married life. Strange messages begin to appear on her computer, summoning her to sinister and fetishistic sexual liaisons.

ISBN 0 352 32856 8

BLUE HOTEL
Cherri Pickford
Hotelier Ramon can't understand why best-selling author Floy Pennington has come to stay at his quiet hotel. Her exhibitionist tendencies are driving him crazy, as are her increasingly wanton encounters with the hotel's other guests.

ISBN 0 352 32858 4

CASSANDRA'S CONFLICT
Fredrica Alleyn
Behind the respectable facade of a house in present-day Hampstead lies a world of decadent indulgence and darkly bizarre eroticism. A sternly attractive Baron and his beautiful but cruel wife are playing games with the young Cassandra.

ISBN 0 352 32859 2

THE CAPTIVE FLESH
Cleo Cordell
Marietta and Claudine, French aristocrats saved from pirates, learn their invitation to stay at the opulent Algerian mansion of their rescuer, Kasim, requires something in return; their complete surrender to the ecstasy of pleasure in pain.

ISBN 0 352 32872 X

PLEASURE HUNT
Sophie Danson

Sexual adventurer Olympia Deschamps is determined to become a
member of the Légion D'Amour – the most exclusive society of French
libertines.

ISBN 0 352 32880 0

BLACK ORCHID
Roxanne Carr

The Black Orchid is a women's health club which provides a special-
ised service for its high-powered clients; women who don't have the
time to spend building complex relationships, but who enjoy the
pleasures of the flesh.

ISBN 0 352 32888 6

ODALISQUE
Fleur Reynolds

A tale of family intrigue and depravity set against the glittering
backdrop of the designer set. This facade of respectability conceals a
reality of bitter rivalry and unnatural love.

ISBN 0 352 32887 8

OUTLAW LOVER
Saskia Hope

Fee Cambridge lives in an upper level deluxe pleasuredome of
technologically advanced comfort. Bored with her predictable husband and pampered lifestyle, Fee ventures into the wild side of town,
finding an an outlaw who becomes her lover.

ISBN 0 352 32909 2

THE SENSES BEJEWELLED
Cleo Cordell

Willing captives Marietta and Claudine are settling into life at Kasim's
harem. But 18th century Algeria can be a hostile place. When the
women are kidnapped by Kasim's sworn enemy, they face indignities
that will test the boundaries of erotic experience. This is the sequel to
The Captive Flesh.

ISBN 0 352 32904 1

GEMINI HEAT
Portia Da Costa

As the metropolis sizzles in freak early summer temperatures, twin sisters Deana and Delia find themselves cooking up a heatwave of their own. Jackson de Guile, master of power dynamics and wealthy connoisseur of fine things, draws them both into a web of luxuriously decadent debauchery.

ISBN 0 352 32912 2

VIRTUOSO
Katrina Vincenzi

Mika and Serena, darlings of classical music's jet-set, inhabit a world of secluded passion. The reason? Since Mika's tragic accident which put a stop to his meteoric rise to fame as a solo violinist, he cannot face the world, and together they lead a decadent, reclusive existence.

ISBN 0 352 32907 6

MOON OF DESIRE
Sophie Danson

When Soraya Chilton is posted to the ancient and mysterious city of Ragzburg on a mission for the Foreign Office, strange things begin to happen to her. Wild, sexual urges overwhelm her at the coming of each full moon.

ISBN 0 352 32911 4

FIONA'S FATE
Fredrica Alleyn

When Fiona Sheldon is kidnapped by the infamous Trimarchi brothers, along with her friend Bethany, she finds herself acting in ways her husband Duncan would be shocked by. Alessandro Trimarchi makes full use of this opportunity to discover the true extent of Fiona's suppressed, but powerful, sexuality.

ISBN 0 352 32913 0

HANDMAIDEN OF PALMYRA
Fleur Reynolds

3rd century Palmyra: a lush oasis in the Syrian desert. The beautiful and fiercely independent Samoya takes her place in the temple of Antioch as an apprentice priestess. Decadent bachelor Prince Alif has other plans for her and sends his scheming sister to bring her to his Bacchanalian wedding feast.

ISBN 0 352 32919 X

OUTLAW FANTASY
Saskia Hope

On the outer reaches of the 21st century metropolis the Amazenes are on the prowl; fierce warrior women who have some unfinished business with Fee Cambridge's pirate lover. This is the sequel to *Outlaw Lover*.

ISBN 0 352 32920 3

THE SILKEN CAGE
Sophie Danson

When University lecturer Maria Treharne inherits her aunt's mansion in Cornwall, she finds herself the subject of strange and unexpected attention. Using the craft of goddess worship and sexual magnetism, Maria finds allies and foes in this savage and beautiful landscape.

ISBN 0 352 32928 9

RIVER OF SECRETS
Saskia Hope & Georgia Angelis

Intrepid female reporter Sydney Johnson takes over someone else's assignment up the Amazon river. Sydney soon realises this mission to find a lost Inca city has a hidden agenda. Everyone is behaving so strangely, so sexually, and the tropical humidity is reaching fever pitch.

ISBN 0 352 32925 4

VELVET CLAWS
Cleo Cordell

It's the 19th century; a time of exploration and discovery and young, spirited Gwendoline Farnshawe is determined not to be left behind in the parlour when the handsome and celebrated anthropologist, Jonathan Kimberton, is planning his latest expedition to Africa.

ISBN 0 352 32926 2

THE GIFT OF SHAME
Sarah Hope-Walker

Helen is a woman with extreme fantasies. When she meets Jeffrey – a cultured wealthy stranger – at a party, they soon become partners in obsession. Now nothing is impossible for her, no fantasy beyond his imagination or their mutual exploration.

ISBN 0 352 32935 1

SUMMER OF ENLIGHTENMENT
Cheryl Mildenhall

Karin's new-found freedom is getting her into all sorts of trouble. The enigmatic Nicolai has been showing interest in her since their chance meeting in a cafe. But he's the husband of a valued friend and is trying to embroil her in the sexual tension he thrives on.

ISBN 0 352 32937 8

A BOUQUET OF BLACK ORCHIDS
Roxanne Carr

The exclusive Black Orchid health spa has provided Maggie with a new social life and a new career, where giving and receiving pleasure of the most sophisticated nature takes top priority. But her loyalty to the club is being tested by the presence of Tourell; a powerful man who makes her an offer she finds difficult to refuse.

ISBN 0 352 32939 4

JULIET RISING
Cleo Cordell

At Madame Nicol's exclusive but strict 18th-century academy for young ladies, the bright and wilful Juliet is learning the art of courting the affections of young noblemen.

ISBN 0 352 32938 6

DEBORAH'S DISCOVERY
Fredrica Alleyn

Deborah Woods is trying to change her life. Having just ended her long-term relationship and handed in her notice at work, she is ready for a little adventure. Meeting American oil magnate John Pavin III throws her world into even more confusion as he invites her to stay at his luxurious renovated castle in Scotland. But what looked like being a romantic holiday soon turns into a test of sexual bravery.

ISBN 0 352 32945 9

THE TUTOR
Portia Da Costa

Like minded libertines reap the rewards of their desire in this story of the sexual initiation of a beautiful young man. Rosalind Howard takes a post as personal librarian to a husband and wife, both unashamed sensualists keen to engage her into their decadent scenarios.

ISBN 0 352 32946 7

THE HOUSE IN NEW ORLEANS
Fleur Reynolds

When she inherits her family home in the fashionable Garden district of New Orleans, Ottilie Duvier discovers it has been leased to the notorious Helmut von Straffen; a debauched German Count famous for his decadent Mardi Gras parties. Determined to oust him from the property, she soon realises that not all dangerous animals live in the swamp!

ISBN 0 352 32951 3

ELENA'S CONQUEST
Lisette Allen

It's summer – 1070AD – and the gentle Elena is gathering herbs in the garden of the convent where she leads a peaceful, but uneventful, life. When Norman soldiers besiege the convent, they take Elena captive and present her to the dark and masterful Lord Aimery to satisfy his savage desire for Saxon women.

ISBN 0 352 32950 5

CASSANDRA'S CHATEAU
Fredrica Alleyn

Cassandra has been living with the dominant and perverse Baron von Ritter for eighteen months when their already bizarre relationship takes an unexpected turn. The arrival of a naive female visitor at the chateau provides the Baron with a new opportunity to indulge his fancy for playing darkly erotic games with strangers.

ISBN 0 352 32955 6

WICKED WORK
Pamela Kyle

At twenty-eight, Suzie Carlton is at the height of her journalistic career. She has status, money and power. What she doesn't have is a masterful partner who will allow her to realise the true extent of her fantasies. How will she reconcile the demands of her job with her sexual needs?

ISBN 0 352 32958 0

To be published in December . . .

DREAM LOVER
Katrina Vincenzi

Icily controlled Gemma is a dedicated film producer, immersed in her latest production – a darkly Gothic vampire movie. But after a visit to Brittany, where she encounters a mystery lover, a disquieting feeling continues to haunt her. Compelled to discover the identity of the man who ravished her, she becomes entangled in a mystifying erotic odyssey.

ISBN 0 352 32956 4

PATH OF THE TIGER
Cleo Cordell

India, in the early days of the Raj. Amy Spencer is looking for an excuse to rebel against the stuffy mores of the British army wives. Luckily, a new friend introduces her to places where other women dare not venture – where Tantric mysteries and the Kama Sutra come alive. Soon she becomes besotted by Ravinder, the exquisitely handsome son of the Maharaja, and finds the pathway to absolute pleasure.

ISBN 0 352 32959 9

WE NEED YOUR HELP . . .
to plan the future of women's erotic fiction –

– and no stamp required!

Yours are the only opinions that matter.

Black Lace is the first series of books devoted to erotic fiction by women for women.

We intend to keep providing the best-written, sexiest books you can buy. And we'd appreciate your help and valued opinion of the books so far. Tell us what you want to read.

THE BLACK LACE QUESTIONNAIRE

SECTION ONE: ABOUT YOU

1.1 Sex (*we presume you are female, but so as not to discriminate*)
Are you?

Male	☐
Female	☐

1.2 Age

under 21	☐	21–30	☐
31–40	☐	41–50	☐
51–60	☐	over 60	☐

1.3 At what age did you leave full-time education?

still in education	☐	16 or younger	☐
17–19	☐	20 or older	☐

1.4 Occupation _____

1.5 Annual household income

under £10,000	☐	£10–£20,000	☐
£20–£30,000	☐	£30–£40,000	☐
over £40,000	☐		

1.6 We are perfectly happy for you to remain anonymous; but if you would like to receive information on other publications available, please insert your name and address

_____

_____

_____

_____

SECTION TWO: ABOUT BUYING BLACK LACE BOOKS

2.1 How did you acquire this copy of *Wicked Work*?
    I bought it myself ☐   My partner bought it ☐
    I borrowed/found it ☐

2.2 How did you find out about Black Lace books?
    I saw them in a shop ☐
    I saw them advertised in a magazine ☐
    I saw the London Underground posters ☐
    I read about them in _____
    Other _____

2.3 Please tick the following statements you agree with:
    I would be less embarrassed about buying Black
    Lace books if the cover pictures were less explicit ☐
    I think that in general the pictures on Black
    Lace books are about right ☐
    I think Black Lace cover pictures should be as
    explicit as possible ☐

2.4 Would you read a Black Lace book in a public place – on a train for instance?
    Yes ☐   No ☐

SECTION THREE: ABOUT THIS BLACK LACE BOOK

3.1 Do you think the sex content in this book is:
    Too much   ☐   About right   ☐
    Not enough   ☐

3.2 Do you think the writing style in this book is:
    Too unreal/escapist   ☐   About right   ☐
    Too down to earth   ☐

3.3 Do you think the story in this book is:
    Too complicated   ☐   About right   ☐
    Too boring/simple   ☐

3.4 Do you think the cover of this book is:
    Too explicit   ☐   About right   ☐
    Not explicit enough   ☐

Here's a space for any other comments:

SECTION FOUR: ABOUT OTHER BLACK LACE BOOKS

4.1 How many Black Lace books have you read?   ☐

4.2 If more than one, which one did you prefer?

4.3 Why?

SECTION FIVE: ABOUT YOUR IDEAL EROTIC NOVEL

We want to publish the books you want to read – so this is your chance to tell us exactly what your ideal erotic novel would be like.

5.1 Using a scale of 1 to 5 (1 = no interest at all, 5 = your ideal), please rate the following possible settings for an erotic novel:

Medieval/barbarian/sword 'n' sorcery ☐
Renaissance/Elizabethan/Restoration ☐
Victorian/Edwardian ☐
1920s & 1930s – the Jazz Age ☐
Present day ☐
Future/Science Fiction ☐

5.2 Using the same scale of 1 to 5, please rate the following themes you may find in an erotic novel:

Submissive male/dominant female ☐
Submissive female/dominant male ☐
Lesbianism ☐
Bondage/fetishism ☐
Romantic love ☐
Experimental sex e.g. anal/watersports/sex toys ☐
Gay male sex ☐
Group sex ☐

Using the same scale of 1 to 5, please rate the following styles in which an erotic novel could be written:

Realistic, down to earth, set in real life ☐
Escapist fantasy, but just about believable ☐
Completely unreal, impressionistic, dreamlike ☐

5.3 Would you prefer your ideal erotic novel to be written from the viewpoint of the main male characters or the main female characters?

Male ☐ Female ☐
Both ☐

5.4 What would your ideal Black Lace heroine be like? Tick as many as you like:

Dominant	☐	Glamorous	☐
Extroverted	☐	Contemporary	☐
Independent	☐	Bisexual	☐
Adventurous	☐	Naive	☐
Intellectual	☐	Introverted	☐
Professional	☐	Kinky	☐
Submissive	☐	Anything else?	☐
Ordinary	☐	_____	

5.5 What would your ideal male lead character be like? Again, tick as many as you like:

Rugged	☐		
Athletic	☐	Caring	☐
Sophisticated	☐	Cruel	☐
Retiring	☐	Debonair	☐
Outdoor-type	☐	Naive	☐
Executive-type	☐	Intellectual	☐
Ordinary	☐	Professional	☐
Kinky	☐	Romantic	☐
Hunky	☐		
Sexually dominant	☐	Anything else?	☐
Sexually submissive	☐	_____	

5.6 Is there one particular setting or subject matter that your ideal erotic novel would contain?

_____

SECTION SIX: LAST WORDS

6.1 What do you like best about Black Lace books?

_____

6.2 What do you most dislike about Black Lace books?

_____

6.3 In what way, if any, would you like to change Black Lace covers?

_____

6.4   Here's a space for any other comments:

_____

_____

_____

_____

_____

Thank you for completing this questionnaire. Now tear it out of the book – carefully! – put it in an envelope and send it to:

Black Lace
FREEPOST
London
W10 5BR

No stamp is required if you are resident in the U.K.